Dee Williams was born and brought up in Rotherhithe in East London where her father worked as a stevedore in Surrey Docks. Dee left school at fourteen, met her husband at sixteen and was married at twenty. After living abroad for some years, Dee and her husband moved to Hampshire, close to the rest of her family. She is the author of nine hugely popular sagas set in Rotherhithe.

Also by Dee Williams

SORROWS AND SMILES

Dee Williams

headline

First published in 2000
by HEADLINE BOOK PUBLISHING

First published in paperback in 2000
by HEADLINE BOOK PUBLISHING

1

ISBN 978 0 7472 6109 4

Typeset by
Letterpart Limited, Reigate, Surrey

Printed and bound in the UK by
CPI Mackays, Chatham ME5 8TD

HEADLINE BOOK PUBLISHING
A division of the Hodder Headline Group
338 Euston Road
London NW1 3BH

www.headline.co.uk
www.hodderheadline.com

This is for my son-in-law Gez, who gave me the information regarding the sailors who were interned in Holland during the First World War.

Also for Carol, Emma and Samantha
Love you lots.

Chapter 1

Pam King was walking hand in hand over the lush grass with Robbie Bennetti, steadily climbing the hill towards the Greenwich observatory. She knew what they were doing was wrong. Her grandmother would be very angry if she ever found out she was with Robbie, but when Pam smiled up at him her heart missed a beat. However, she couldn't help remembering the scene a few weeks ago when she had first innocently told her gran and her mother who she was going to the pictures with. Ivy King, her grandmother, had pulled herself up to her full five feet four. She was a slim and very upright woman who, despite her age, still had a full head of dark hair only lightly sprinkled with grey. Her dark eyes were bright and had blazed with anger. She had shouted in a way she had never shouted before, saying she didn't want Pam to get involved with that family. Pam had laughed nervously and asked why, but her grandmother had simply said it was something that happened long ago, the Bennettis were no good and she mustn't have anything to do with them. Pam couldn't believe she was being forbidden to see Robbie, and that made her more determined than ever to go out with him.

How dare her gran tell her who she could and couldn't go

1

out with, she'd fumed. She was eighteen and quite capable of making up her own mind. She'd turned to her mother. 'Mum. Why can't I go to the pictures with Robbie?'

Rose King had looked from one to the other, still shocked at her mother-in-law's uncharacteristic outburst. She couldn't understand why Ivy King had objected so vehemently to her daughter's request. She herself couldn't see any harm in it. After all, everybody knew that the Bennettis were well off, a respected family. 'Gran must have a good reason,' was all she could think of to say, aware she should support Ivy's stand. They'd always agreed to back each other in matters of discipline: the two of them had brought Pam up alone, for Pam's dad had died before she was born.

Finally Pam stormed out of the kitchen and Rose put to Ivy the question she'd been dying to ask.

'I don't understand, Ivy. Why are you so against Pam seeing this boy?'

'I can't tell you, but it's for the best.'

Rose looked shocked.

'And don't you go looking down your nose at me. She mustn't have anything to do with that family.'

'But why?'

'I have my reasons.'

'But what harm will it do?'

'They are no good.'

'She might be over him in a few weeks,' Rose protested, 'so is it that important?'

'Yes. So let that be the end of it.'

Rose sighed and carried on with her knitting. She knew it wasn't any good arguing with her mother-in-law once she had made up her mind.

When it went quiet Pam, who had been listening outside the door, crept up to bed.

As she lay thinking about Robbie she smiled to herself when remembering their first date. She couldn't help it, despite her gran's disapproval. She gave a little giggle when she thought about how she and her friend Jill had been eager to try out the new false nails that were all the rage. They were both always ready to have a go at anything new as soon as it came on the market. That evening in the cinema with Robbie, when the lights went up, Pam had been horrified to find that when she took off her gloves, the nails came with them and the glue had left her own nails black and hairy from the fleece lining inside her gloves. She felt so embarrassed she'd kept her gloves on all evening. She blamed Jill for not trying them out first.

Jill was a true friend and had proved it that night by offering to give Pam an alibi when she went out with Robbie and also on the few occasions since. She was doing the same, today, for the Greenwich trip.

'Penny for them?' Robbie's voice interrupted her thoughts.

'Sorry. I . . .' Pam's voice trailed off, but she knew she had to tell him what was bothering her.

'Pam, what's up? You've been in a dream all day. I thought coming up here to Greenwich was a great idea.'

Still hand in hand, they carried on walking for a moment before Pam replied.

'It was. And I'm ever so pleased we did. Let's sit down for a bit.'

'Well then, what's the trouble? I don't get many days off, especially at this time of the year, and when I do you seem to be in a different world.'

Pam looked at him and smiled. Robbie was tall with dark curly hair and deep brown eyes that, when he winked at her, made her melt. He was so good-looking and always kind and thoughtful: in fact everything a girl could wish for. In her wildest dreams she never thought he would ask her out, and when he did, he never tried to paw her like Luigi Cappa was always trying to whenever she got near him or his father's ice-cream van. But she couldn't help worrying about her relationship with Robbie. No matter how fond of him she was, it could only lead to trouble if her gran ever found out about it.

Pam didn't know why Gran was so against his family. It wasn't as if they were true Italians: the Bennettis had lived in this area for generations. Anyway, the war had been over for years and Mr Bennetti had even served in the British Army. The family was not only well to do – had an ice-cream factory that supplied the shops – but well thought of too. One son, Ricky, was a singer who had made records. Robbie had been to grammar school. Even as a small child Pam had worshipped him – though whenever she smiled at him he would blush and walk away. When their business really began to grow, his family had moved to Southwark, and it was only in a chance meeting in a cinema queue that they met again. They had seen each other a few times before Robbie told her how he had dearly wanted to take her out for ages but he'd never had the courage. And now they were together, her gran disapproved!

On the occasions Pam had been out with him she had had to lie to them and it was beginning to get to her. She hated being deceitful.

Pam smiled at Robbie and hugged her knees. 'I have to

tell you that my gran don't approve of you.'

He fell back on the grass laughing. 'Is that it? Is that what you're down in the mouth about?'

She nodded.

'You are daft.'

'S'pose I am.'

'It's not as though I'm coming to your place to tea and spilling it all down myself, now is it?'

'No.' But she secretly did want to take him home, just to show them what a smashing bloke he was.

'Anyway, don't worry about it. I promise I won't ask your gran out.'

Pam giggled. 'You'd better not. Robbie, has your family got a dark secret?'

He laughed again. 'What sort of dark secret?'

'I don't know.'

'Can't think of anything. Tell you what, I'll ask my dad.'

'Will he tell you?'

'It depends on what it is . . . Race you to the top of the hill,' he added, instantly dismissing the subject.

For the rest of that lovely summer day they laughed and enjoyed themselves, but once again she had to tell her mother and grandmother she had been out with Jill.

The next day, while they were walking home from work, Jill asked Pam: 'So where did you go?'

'To Greenwich.'

'That's all right then, 'cos I've been there. If your gran asks I can tell her all about it.'

The girls always made sure they got their stories right.

'I wonder why your gran's so against Robbie.'

'It's not just Robbie, it's all the Bennettis.'

Jill giggled. 'Here, you don't think your grandad was playing around, do you?'

Pam laughed back. 'Shouldn't think so, Grandad was in the navy for years. He was a prisoner in Holland for a while so I don't think he had much of a chance to get up to any naughties. 'Sides, if he had wanted to do anything like that he would have done it in another country.'

Jill nudged Pam. 'Here, can you imagine our grandparents doing things like that?'

'Well, they must have done at some time otherwise we wouldn't be here. But really, thanks, Jill, for saying I've been out with you. You're a real mate.'

Jill's deep blue eyes sparkled and she flicked back her blonde hair. Over the past few months she had been experimenting with peroxide and now with the sun bleaching it, it was getting fairer than ever. 'It'll cost yer.'

'What and how much?'

They turned the corner into Newbury Street with its row of terraced houses. Apart from a few empty spaces where before the war houses had been, it looked the same as most streets in Rotherhithe. Small concrete fronts lay behind low walls with the almost obligatory lace-curtained front-room bay window. Front doors opened up into long narrow passages with a kitchen at the end, leading through into the scullery and then out into the back yard. The yard was another small concrete area, often with a brick air-raid shelter outside the back door. Most of the landlords were beginning to put bathrooms in their properties, so they now only had two bedrooms instead of three, but the majority of tenants still liked to keep the old outside lav. The street was gradually being transformed with fresh paint and new decorative ideas, some of the houses even had cars parked outside as they were bought up by young couples.

Jill pointed to an ice-cream van. 'A cornet from your secret admirer?'

Pam could feel herself tensing. 'He ain't no admirer of mine.'

'You've gone ever so red. Come on, let's get a wafer from him.'

Pam tried to smile but she felt very embarrassed, for there serving ice cream from his father's van was Luigi Cappa. 'No, I'd better not. Gran will have my dinner ready.'

'P'raps you're right. But you are daft. He fancies you like mad. I wish it was me. 'Sides, I reckon he's got more go in him than Robbie.'

'How do you know?'

Jill grinned. 'Can see it in those wicked big brown eyes. They make me go all weak.'

'Well, you ask him out then.'

'I might do that. Say, we could go out in a foursome.'

'Can't see that. You know how Robbie and Lu used to fight at school.'

'That's when they were little. They've grown up since then.'

'Have they?'

'Well, we certainly have,' Jill preened.

Pam and Jill were more like sisters than friends. There was only four months' difference in their ages and for all of their eighteen years they had lived in Newbury Street. Jill's gran, Lil, lived next door to Pam and her family. Both Lil Hunter and Ivy King moved there when they were young brides before the First World War and, like their grand-daughters, had grown up together.

Since they had left school at fifteen the girls had both worked for Worth's; the company supplied bathroom and kitchen fittings to the plumbing trade. Pam was in the accounts office while Jill was on the customer counter, which probably was the reason she was the more outgoing of the two. She had to be cheeky, the way some of the men spoke to her.

Jill grabbed Pam's arm and tucked it through hers. 'Come on, let's give him the glad eye.'

Pam giggled. 'I bet that's not all you'd like to give him?'

'Chance would be a fine thing when all he does is gaze at you with those wonderful eyes.'

'Hark at you.'

'Well, I ain't got anybody in tow at the moment and I'm desperate for a bit of loving.'

Pam laughed. 'Give it time.'

Together they tottered along on their high heels. Jill had long shapely legs and her mini skirt just about covered her bum. They knew when their grandmothers saw them they would shake their heads and, tutting, announce that they were in moral danger and young women didn't behave like that in their young days. But this was the swinging sixties and the girls were determined to enjoy every moment of it.

'Hello, Lu,' shouted Jill as they passed the ice-cream van.

He gave them a wave and smiled showing his white even teeth. 'Hi, girls. And how are the two best lookers round here then?'

Jill giggled. 'Fine.' She crossed the road and called to Pam. 'I'll be over later, then we can try out that new varnish.'

'OK.' Out of the corner of her eye Pam watched Lu bend down and, looking at his reflection in the window, confidently run his fingers through his thick dark hair. He certainly thought a lot of himself; he was so different to Robbie.

Pam let herself into the house that she and her widowed mother shared with her gran. If only her grandmother would tell her what dark secret she knew about the Bennettis. It couldn't be *that* bad, surely. Pam knew that many years ago both the Bennetti and the Cappa families had lived in the same road near Deptford. Mr Bennetti and Mr Cappa's fathers had had an ice-cream business together. She had been told that it was when the old Mr Bennetti opened the factory and Mr Cappa took over selling the ice cream that the rivalry had begun and the partnership broke up. The rumours were that Luigi's mother left home and ran off with an American, leaving her husband to bring up their three boys, who were very young at the time. Could that have had anything to do with her gran? She couldn't see how.

'Hello, Mum,' said Pam, pushing open the kitchen door.

Rose King ran her hands down the front of her floral pinny and, pushing a strand of her fair hair from her face, held her cheek up for her daughter's kiss. 'Been busy?' she asked.

'Yes, what about you?' Pam's colouring was the opposite from her mother's. With her dark hair and eyes Pam had been told so many times that she was the image of the father she had never known.

Her mother continued to lay the table. 'Not too bad. There was a funeral so we had to get the wreaths out before they wilted in this heat.' Rose had worked in the local florist for as long as Pam could remember.

Pam looked round the kitchen. It was warm and cosy in the winter but hot and stuffy today, as it was throughout the summer. The room was functional but not over furnished; a square table stood against the wall with four chairs that had green leatherette seats pushed under it. Two armchairs with wooden arms stood one each side of the fireplace; there was a sideboard in one of the recesses. A wooden shelf with a beige cotton runner on it filled the other recess and that held their precious radio. Like most people in the road they rarely used the front room and it always felt damp and smelt musty. Pam had wanted them to rent a television like Lil next door, but so far Ivy had resisted, saying she could always keep Lil company if there was something she wanted to see.

'Where's Gran?'

'Next door. Dinner's ready so you'd better give her a call.'

Pam went into the back yard and looked over the fence at her and Jill's grans sitting in the tiny yard on the hard wooden kitchen chairs. They appeared to be catching the last rays of June's warm sunshine before it disappeared behind the chimneys. They were deep in conversation. 'Mum said to tell you dinner's ready.'

'OK, love, just coming.' Ivy gave Pam a smile.

'All right then, gel?' shouted Lil, turning to face Pam. Somehow Lil, who had her eyes permanently squinted against the cigarette smoke that curled ever upwards, managed to keep the cigarette between her lips whenever she spoke.

'Yes thanks.' Pam couldn't remember ever seeing Lil without a cigarette in her mouth. The front of her grey hair, which she wore pulled back into an untidy bun, was yellow and her teeth stained. All the kids affectionately called her Fag Ash Lil, but she didn't mind. She was a kind, friendly person, a widow like Ivy King, but she lived alone even though her son Bob and his wife Doreen, Jill's parents, only lived across the road. Her other son, Sid, had moved to Australia not long after he married. Ivy King had had only one child: Pam's dad.

Ivy pushed open the rickety piece of wood that served as a gate between the two houses and took hold of Pam's arm. 'I do wish you wouldn't wear such short skirts. Lil was just saying that if young Jill's get any shorter she might just as well not bother wearing them at all. Every time she bends down you can see all her knickers. It ain't right. Lil reckons that all the blokes at work must keep making her go up and down the ladder to get things off the top shelf just so they can have a good look.'

Pam laughed. 'It's the fashion. 'Sides, mine ain't as short as Jill's.'

'Might be the fashion but it can lead to all sorts of troubles. You mark my words, young lady.'

Pam grinned. 'Yes, Gran.'

That night, as Pam lay in bed, her thoughts went back to Robbie. She propped herself up on her elbow and looked across at her mother who, with her head resting against the wooden bed-head, was reading. They had shared the same bedroom since the landlord had the bathroom fitted in Pam's room – and, much to Ivy's disgust, had put up the rent.

11

'Mum, don't you really know why Gran is so against Robbie Bennetti?'

Her mother put her book down. 'No, I don't. Have you been seeing him?'

Pam nodded. 'A couple of times.'

'Well, don't let Ivy find out.'

'I get so angry with her telling me what to do and who to see.'

'She's only got your best interests at heart.'

Pam pouted. 'But, Mum, I'm old enough to do what I want.'

'Not in Ivy's eyes.'

'Do you think my dad knew anything about the Bennettis?'

Rose King's face clouded over. 'I don't think so.'

Pam watched her mother look over at their wedding photograph on the dressing table. Pam knew her mother, who in the picture was glowing with happiness, was wearing a wedding dress that belonged to a friend. During the war nobody could afford to waste their precious clothing coupons on such frivolous things as that. Her father, in his army uniform, was very good-looking, upright with a lovely smile.

'I wish I'd known him,' whispered Pam.

'So do I. He was a kind man.'

Dan King had been killed almost at the end of the war. He had managed to survive the fighting abroad only to be caught in a fire after a doodle bug had fallen and set light to what used to be the newsagent's on the corner of Newbury Street. There was only an ugly empty space there now. Pam had been told he had run through the flames to rescue the owner when the gas main exploded. Pam often wondered

12

how her gran and mother could pass the space and not get upset. She also knew that it was while he was on that last leave that she was conceived. In the spring, the site was full of wild flowers, as though a testimony to his bravery. When she was alone she would walk past very slowly and imagine that he was watching her.

'If I get a chance I'll ask Lil,' said her mother, interrupting her musing. 'She might know. After all, they've been friends for years and I shouldn't think they've got any secrets from each other.'

'Thanks, Mum.' Pam smiled at her mother. Although Rose was thin she was still good-looking. Life had been hard for her. Her parents had moved from London during the war after they had been bombed out along with the factory Grandad Mallory worked in. They went with the factory when it was relocated up North and over these past few years Pam had been aware they weren't in good health. Rose had stayed in London to marry Dan King and after he was killed she'd thought it was her duty to stay with Ivy as her mother-in-law had no one else.

Pam had only seen her grandparents a few times. Granny Mallory was a short white-haired lady and Grandad was thin and frail-looking with lovely twinkling eyes. Pam remembered that on the few times she'd seen them, her gran seemed always to be smiling.

Pam reflected on her mother's life. Over the years Rose had been out with one or two gentlemen friends, but they'd never lasted long. She always said she wouldn't marry again. In many ways that pleased Pam; she didn't want to share her mother with anybody. It must have been a struggle for her to bring up a daughter, but she had never let Pam really want for anything. When she had been little there had been times when she got upset if Jill had something and she didn't, but only rarely. As she got older she realised that her mother was the sole breadwinner, and how hard that was for her. Kennett's the florist was always busy; thankfully Rose loved her job.

Pam suddenly asked, 'Mum, do you like Robbie?'

'Don't really know him.'

'He is nice.'

'Well, just be careful.'

Pam smiled as she settled down. At least she had her mother's approval. Somehow she would prove to her gran just what a smashing bloke Robbie was, even if the family did have a dark secret.

Chapter 2

One evening, a week after Pam had been to Greenwich with Robbie, the girls were walking home from work when he pulled up beside them in his father's van.

'Here's lover boy come to whisk you away,' said Jill.

Pam's face lit up. 'Hello.'

'Pam, can I have a word?' He looked anxiously at Jill as he jumped down from the van.

'Don't mind me. I'll walk on,' said Jill, not attempting to hide the fact that she was a bit miffed.

'Pam. You know my brother, Ricky?' said Robbie, taking her arm and moving her away from the van.

She nodded.

'Well, he's getting married.'

'That's nice. Who's the lucky girl?'

'Esta. She's a dancer in his show.'

'Where's he now?'

'Jersey.'

'He's got a smashing voice. Have you been over there to see him?'

'No. His season's the same as ours and we're much too busy to get away.'

'He's so good-looking. When's he coming back?'

'He's not getting married here.'

'So where then?'

'Italy.'

'Italy! But why?'

'She's Italian and she wants to go back home to get married. My mum and dad are over the moon about it and we'll be going there for a couple of weeks.'

'When's that?'

'At the end of the season. October.'

'Lucky old you. So why are you telling me all this?'

'I was wondering if you'd like to come to Italy with me?'

Pam's mouth dropped open. 'What? Me go to Italy?' she whispered. 'With you?'

'Not really with me, but I thought you could stay in the same village. I'll find out all about it as soon as I've had a word with Ricky. He's making all the arrangements.'

'I'd like that, but I'm not sure.'

'Well, give it some thought. I've got to get off. Can I see you at the weekend?'

She nodded and he hurried back to his van.

'So what was all that about?' asked Jill as they stood and watched him drive away.

'He wants me to go to his brother's wedding.'

'Wow. Ricky's getting married. I bet that'll be a big posh affair. Who's he marrying?'

'A dancer in his show.'

'When is it?'

'October.'

'Will you be able to go?'

'I hope so. Guess what? It's in Italy.'

'What? Why Italy?'

'She's Italian.'

Jill laughed. 'And I suppose Robbie's got the mad idea to take you with him?'

Pam nodded excitedly.

'No.' Jill couldn't believe her ears.

'I'll have to get a passport.'

'You're going to go?'

'If I can. I can't let an opportunity like this slip away, can I?'

'Will he pay?'

'Don't think so.'

'Can you get the money?'

'I don't know, but I'm gonner try. Just think – Italy!'

'Lucky old you. What about your gran?'

'It ain't up to her.'

'Don't forget you've got to get your mum to sign for your passport as you're under age. Will your mum let you go off with the Bennettis?'

'Shouldn't think so for one minute – unless . . .' She looked at Jill and grinned. 'What if you come with me?'

'Cor, I'd like that. But lover boy won't pay for me as well.'

'He didn't say he was going to pay for me.'

'I wonder how much it'll cost?'

'Don't keep asking questions I can't answer. I'll have to ask Robbie. It would be great though. Fancy, we could be going to Italy.'

'Just think of all those wonderful Italian blokes! I've come over all funny just thinking about it. But will he mind me going with you?'

'Why should he if you're paying? Mind you, we might palm you off with one of the bride's family if we want to be on our own.'

17

'Now that sounds a good idea. I wouldn't mind that. As soon as you can let me know. I'll get some books from the library so we can gen up on it. Where does she live?'

Pam shrugged her shoulders. 'Pity we ain't got time to go to evening classes to learn the lingo.'

Jill giggled. 'And meet the teacher. I wonder if he's Italian? Here, I know how to say *volare*. Dean Martin sings about it. I think it means love.'

'I thought it was goodbye. *Amore* is love.'

'All right, clever clogs. I can soon learn to say that. *Amore*. How's that?'

'Said with feeling.' Pam giggled. 'Well, that's all you'll need to know.'

As they walked home their excitement at the prospect grew and grew.

'We've got to find out if the boss will let us both have time off together,' said Pam, beginning to get practical.

'Will we go for one week or two?'

'Dunno. Just a week I should think, but let's find out how much it'll cost before we ask for time off.'

'Good idea.'

All through dinner Pam's mind was full of going to Italy and being with Robbie. She dearly wanted to tell her mum and gran but decided to approach Rose alone – and tentatively – first.

While she was in the scullery helping her mother with the washing up, Pam said casually, 'Me and Jill are thinking of going on holiday together in October.'

'That's nice. Anywhere exciting?'

'Italy.'

The plate Rose was holding fell back into the water with a splash. 'Italy? Why Italy?'

Pam could feel her face flush. 'We just thought it would be different, that's all.'

'But, Pam! Italy! That's a long way away. How will you get there?'

'Fly.'

'Fly? What, in a plane?'

Pam laughed. 'Course. I ain't flapping me arms all the way.'

'You don't have to be funny. You wouldn't catch me going up in no airplane. Is it safe? And what about the food?'

'We'll be all right.'

'Those sorts of places are full of foreigners and they eat all sorts of funny stuff. What made you think about going to a place like that?'

'We just thought we'd like to have a bit of an adventure, that's all,' said Pam, putting the clean plates into the green and cream kitchen cabinet. She glanced out of the window that looked out on to the back yard; she couldn't face her mother while telling lies.

Her mother eyed her suspiciously. 'What sort of adventure?'

'Mum, don't be so old-fashioned. A lot of girls go abroad for their holidays now.'

'So how much is this going to cost you?'

'We don't know yet, we only started talking about it today.'

'Well, I don't think you should go.'

Pam didn't answer. If her mother was against even the

idea of her going to Italy, Pam knew she would have a fit at the thought that her daughter would be with Robbie all week.

Later that evening Pam went over to see Jill.

'Hello, love,' said Jill's mother. 'She's upstairs.' She raised her eyes and tutted. 'Doing her hair as usual.'

Pam pushed open the bedroom door. Since Jill's elder sister Helen had married and moved out Jill had had a room to herself, which was something Pam would dearly like. At times she certainly envied Jill. Her dad had a good job and they didn't seem to lack for anything. Jill always had new clothes, while Pam had to make do; Jill kept most of her wages while Pam had to help with the housekeeping. But she wouldn't change anything, not really, she loved her mum and gran so much.

Jill's parents were one of the first in the street to have a television. They had recently bought a new radiogram and it stood proudly in the front room. They didn't mind the girls trying out the new dance steps so long as they took their shoes off and didn't damage the Cyril Lord carpet. They had just had it fitted, and it went with their new contemporary–style three-piece suite. The room looked very modern.

Jill was sitting at the dressing table brushing her hair. 'What d'yer think?' she asked as she curled her hair round her finger.

'Looks great, but you ain't no Marilyn Monroe.'

'I hope not, she's dead and these ain't as big as hers.' She cupped her breasts with both hands.

Pam laughed. 'Have you told your mum about Italy yet?'

'They think we're mad.'

'Will they let you go?'

'Don't see why not. What about your mum and gran?'

'I didn't tell Gran, but Mum thinks we're mad as well. As soon as we can we'll see about getting a passport and then I'll ask Robbie what we have to do next.'

'It'll be great,' said Jill. 'Will it be hot?'

'Should think so.'

'I'll have to get meself some new clothes and a new bikini. Just think about those wonderful Italian shoes and handbags. I hope they don't cost too much.'

For the rest of the evening they sat talking and planning this holiday of a lifetime.

After Robbie had told them what the air fare was, he said he would try and get them digs in a house near to the bride's home; that should be a lot cheaper than staying in a hotel. When they worked out the cost they decided a week was all they could afford, although Robbie was going for a fortnight.

The girls had been to get a passport form and then on to have their photos taken.

As soon as they sat down on the bus Jill began reading the leaflet. 'It says here we've got to get a doctor or priest or somebody in authority to sign, and our parents have to as well, as we're under twenty-one.'

'That shouldn't be difficult,' said Pam.

'When are you seeing Robbie?'

'Hopefully at the weekend.'

'Will your mum sign this?' Jill waved the leaflet.

'I don't see why not if she knows I'm going with you.' Pam gazed out of the window. What if her mum and gran found out that she was going to spend the week with Robbie? She knew Jill would never tell. She smiled to herself. Any photos she had taken with Robbie would have to be kept a secret, but it was all still going to be so wonderful.

Although Ivy King wasn't happy about it, Rose signed the papers and the girls sent off for their passports.

When Robbie saw Pam at the weekend he told them where to get their airline tickets. Everything was going smoothly.

'I can't wait for October,' said Pam as she and Robbie walked home from the pictures. 'What's Italy like?'

'Don't know. I've never been there.'

'Your family came from there.'

'That was years ago.'

'But you and Ricky have got Italian names. Roberto and Ricardo.'

He laughed. 'You make us sound like a double act. Dad was always worried that he might lose his roots so he gave us those names.'

'Haven't you anyone left over there?'

'No one close, as far as we know, although Dad thinks he's got some distant relation still alive, and as Esta comes from near to where Dad's family lived, they're going to try and find out.'

'That'll be nice for him. Did you mind Jill coming as well?'

'Course not.' He put his arm round her waist. 'As you said, your mum and gran might not have let you come otherwise.'

Pam giggled. 'I feel ever so guilty.'

'Well, don't. We'll have a great time. I only wish you could have stayed for more than a week.'

'I don't mind.' She smiled up at him and he held her close, kissing her eager lips.

'We're going to have a great time with all that sun and warm nights.'

Pam trembled at the thought of it. 'I'm sure we can get Jill off with someone.'

'From what I've heard about Italian men, they'll be falling over themselves to go out with Jill, especially as she's blonde. But don't you go off with anyone else. Remember, you're mine.'

She felt so happy: he wanted her to be his alone and she was going to be with him for a whole week! She was already eagerly ticking off the days; four months seemed to be a lifetime away.

It was when the girls had less than a week to go before their holiday that Pam said goodbye to Robbie, who was leaving the following day.

'I'll be at Milan airport waiting for you.'

'You'd better be.'

'I'm really looking forward to it.'

'So am I. I get goosebumps every time I think about it.'

Robbie gently kissed her lips. 'See you on Saturday, in Italy,' he whispered.

She giggled. Her heart felt as if it would burst as she watched him walk away.

On Monday evening Pam was going over to Jill's. They were almost beside themselves with excitement. All week they had been comparing their new clothes and carefully packing them in their suitcases. Rose had even given Pam a few pounds to help her out. Earlier the girls had fallen about laughing at their glum expression in their passport photographs.

Jill was still hugging her passport to her and laughing at her photograph when Pam walked in. 'I can't believe I look such an idiot.'

'We were told not to laugh and that was very hard.'

'We're going. We really are going.'

'I hope I'm not sick,' said Pam.

'Why should you be?'

'Dunno. Excitement.'

'Daft 'ap'orth.'

'Only four more days to go then I shall be in romantic Italy with my Robbie.'

Jill grinned. 'I wonder who I'll find over there?'

'You might find your Mr Right.'

'I don't want to get married. Well, not just yet. Do you?'

'Ain't really thought about it. But Mrs Bennetti does sound rather nice.'

'Couldn't see your gran being pleased about that.'

'You didn't happen to ask *your* gran what her problem is?' Pam wondered.

'No, I forgot,' Jill said sheepishly. 'I didn't think anything more about it.'

'Thanks, friend.'

'Don't worry, you'll find out about it one day.'

'I'm not so sure about that.'

Across the road in number 28 the radio was playing softly. Ivy was sitting reading the evening newspaper while Rose was getting on with her knitting.

Suddenly Ivy looked up from the paper. 'Here, you seen this?'

'I only had a quick glance. Why, is it something interesting?' asked Rose.

'It says here that "that popular singer Ricky Bennetti is getting married." '

'That's nice. When?'

'Monday the twenty-first of October.'

'Next week. I bet that's gonner be a big wedding. It's a pity Pam and Jill won't be able to see it. Who's he marrying?' Rose asked.

'Some Italian.'

'That's nice for the family.'

'The crafty little mare,' shouted Ivy.

Rose looked up. 'Who? What?'

'Young Pam.'

'What you talking about?'

'This.' Ivy hit the newspaper with the back of her hand.

'What's Pam doing in the newspaper?'

'She's not in the paper. It's Italy. He's getting married in Italy. All the family will be there.'

Rose jumped up. 'Let me look.' She snatched the paper from her mother-in-law.

'She's going to be with that boy. Did you know that?' Ivy's face was filled with anger.

'No, I didn't.'

'Has she been seeing him?'

'I think so.'

'And you let her?' Ivy shouted.

'I didn't see the harm in it.'

'Well you can see now.'

'What is it that you've got against them?' Rose defended herself, puzzled.

'They're wicked. They're no good.'

'What makes you so sure? You don't even know the lad.'

'I don't have to.' Ivy snapped, getting to her feet. 'I'm so angry. I'm going to see if Lil knows anything about this. You know what'll happen, don't you? She'll be coming back up the spout.'

'How can you be sure?'

'Why else would she follow that lad halfway round the world if it wasn't to get up to some hanky panky?'

'No, not my Pam. Besides, she don't have to go all that way for hanky panky.'

'You mark my words. She's only going for one thing!' yelled Ivy as she disappeared out of the back door.

Rose sat and reread the paper. Why had Pam deceived them? Rose looked into space. She didn't have to tell them lies. Tears filled her eyes. It was at times like this she wished she had someone to share her problems with. 'Why did you have to leave me, Dan?' she whispered, choking back a sob. Why hadn't Pam told her the truth? She always thought they were close. Was she losing her daughter? And why was Ivy so against her seeing Robbie?

Chapter 3

Pam was quietly singing to herself when she walked into the kitchen, but when she saw the look on her mother's and gran's face, she stopped.

Silently, her gran, who was sitting in her armchair, leaned over to the shelf at the side of the fireplace and turned off the radio.

'Have you got anything to tell us?' asked her mother, her voice even and flat.

'What d'you mean?'

'This here holiday,' said Ivy. 'Who's going to be there?'

Pam held on to the table; she felt the colour drain from her face and her knees go weak. They knew. But how did they find out? She was trying to think fast.

'Jill, of course.'

'Who else?' asked Ivy.

'What d'you mean?' Pam repeated.

'You know full well what Gran means. Now tell us the truth!'

'I don't know what you're talking about!'

'It's in the paper,' said Ivy with a smug look on her face.

'What is?' Pam was desperately trying to brazen this out.

'The Bennetti wedding.' Ivy picked up the newspaper

that was at her feet and thrust it at her granddaughter. 'See for yourself.'

Pam's knees buckled and she slumped into a chair. 'Who's getting married?'

'The son, Ricky, and all the family's going to the wedding.'

'That's nice. It should be a big affair if it's in the papers, but then Ricky is very popular, he's even got a record on the radio.' Pam knew she was babbling on.

'They're going to Italy for the wedding,' said Ivy.

'Italy? Why's that?'

'He's marrying an Italian.'

'That's nice,' repeated Pam.

'You're going to Italy.'

'Yes. That's a coincidence. When is it?' Pam tried to sound lighthearted.

'Monday,' said Ivy.

'Is that why you're going there? Are you going to the wedding?' asked her mother outright.

Pam knew she couldn't lie, not to their faces. 'Yes,' she whispered.

'Well, you're not going,' said Ivy.

Pam grinned. 'It's too late now. You'll just have to let me go.'

'Is it? We'll see.'

Pam watched her grandmother take some papers from her overall pocket and after, tearing them into little pieces, throw them on to the fire.

'What are you doing?' shouted Rose.

'No. Stop it!' screamed Pam when she finally realised what the papers were – her airline ticket and passport!

'Mum, stop her.' Springing to her feet, Pam grabbed the poker from the companion set and frantically began trying to rake the bits from the flames. 'Where did you get them from? You've been through my things.' Pam, her voice rising again with panic, was glancing from one to the other: 'And you let her?'

'Honestly, Pam, I didn't know,' said Rose. She looked at her mother-in-law in amazement. 'I don't believe you've just done that,' she said softly.

'She ain't going.'

Tears began to stream down Pam's face as she watched her passport photograph contort as it melted. 'They've gone. They've gone. You're a wicked old woman. You just want to stop me from enjoying myself. What am I going to tell Jill?' She buried her head in her hands and cried as though her heart were breaking.

Rose gasped. 'I think that was a bit extreme,' she said to her mother-in-law. Going over to her daughter she put an arm round Pam's heaving shoulders and held her close. 'She was really looking forward to that holiday.'

'What about Jill? What about all the money we've spent?' cried Pam.

'Shouldn't tell lies, should you?'

'Does it matter if the Bennettis are going to be there?' sobbed Pam.

'I don't want you to have anything to do with them.' Ivy fidgeted uneasily in her chair.

'Why? Why do you hate them so much? What have they ever done to you?' Pam brushed away her tears with the back of her hand, smearing her mascara all over her cheeks.

'It's for your own good.'

'My own good?' repeated Pam. 'Who says so?'

'I love you and don't want you to get hurt.'

'Well if you ask me your so-called love for me is – is a sham!' Pam's tear-stained face was full of fury. 'I don't believe you. You're just a selfish old woman that don't like to see people enjoy themselves. I'm never going to speak to you ever again.' She wanted to hit her grandmother, she was so angry.

Ivy was visibly shocked. 'I only did what I think is right.'

Rose sat down. 'I just don't understand.'

Pam burst into tears again. 'What can I do? I'll never get another passport in time to go now.'

'You have got to trust me,' Ivy insisted.

'Don't talk to me. I'll never be able to trust you again.' Pam fled from the kitchen, slamming the door behind her. She ran up the stairs and threw herself on the bed.

Why had her gran done it? How could she? She loved her gran and mum dearly, and thought they loved her. How could they do such a thing?

'I can't believe you did that. Why? What's she going to tell Jill?' asked Rose looking at the closed door. 'What on earth happened to make you hate the Bennettis that much?'

'Forget it.'

Rose gave a silly laugh. 'Forget it? Just like that? I don't think Pam's going to forget it. Is it that bad?'

Ivy poked at the ashes. 'It's something that happened years ago and I'm not particularly proud of it.'

'All sounds a bit sinister to me.'

'I'm not going to talk about it.'

'Does Lil know about this secret?'

Ivy shook her head.

'Did you tell Lil what you suspected and that you wasn't going to let the girls go to Italy?' Rose was trembling with anger.

'Yes.'

'And what did she have to say?'

'Not a lot.'

'I would have thought she would have punched you on the nose, stopping her granddaughter from going on a trip of a lifetime.'

'They're young. They've got plenty of time to do things.'

'I can't make you out at times. Is Lil against the family as well?'

'No,' Ivy said, stony-faced.

'Sometimes I wonder what gets into you.'

'I have my reasons.'

'Well, whatever they are they had better be more than just good, because believe me, it's going to take Pam a long while to get over this. That's of course if she ever does.'

'I've got a bit put by so I'll refund the money they've spent. Perhaps they can go somewhere else.'

'Not without a passport, Pam can't.' Rose sighed. She knew she couldn't argue with Ivy. Ivy was the dominant one. Like her daughter, Rose knew when she had lost. 'I'm going up.'

Ivy sat and looked at the pieces of burnt paper flapping in the grate. She knew she had done the right thing. Her granddaughter must be kept away from the Bennettis at all costs, before it got too serious.

Pam pretended to be asleep when her mother came to bed.

She sensed her mother still hadn't been told the reason why Ivy had acted the way she had. She heard her mother give a deep sigh and knew she was upset, but Pam didn't want to talk any more. She was too upset herself.

Both had had a restless night. The next morning Pam knew she had to tell Jill as soon as possible.

'Christ, you're early,' said Jill when she opened the front door. 'I'll just get me bag. You don't half look rough.'

'Not had a lot of sleep,' said Pam as they walked along to catch the bus for work.

'Why's that? Still thinking about the good time you're gonner have with Robbie?'

Pam stopped. 'No. Jill, I've got something to tell you.'

'What's wrong?' Jill who had also stopped, looked at her, her face full of worry.

'I can't go on holiday.'

'Why not? Is your mum ill?'

Pam shook her head.

'Well then.' Jill's eyes were searching Pam's sad face. 'Why can't you go?'

Tears filled Pam's eyes. 'Me gran tore up me tickets and passport.'

'What?' Jill's eyes opened wide with disbelief. 'What did you just say?'

Pam repeated the sentence.

'Why?' screamed Jill. 'What she do that for?'

'She read about Ricky's wedding. It was in the paper.'

Jill stamped her foot in rage. 'And you, you silly bugger, told her you were going, I suppose?'

'She got it out of me.' Pam sat on the small wall fronting Dolly Windsor's house. She looked up at Mrs Windsor who was sitting on the window sill cleaning the outside of her bedroom windows. She was always cleaning.

Jill waved her arms. 'You should have used your loaf and made up something, said it wasn't anywhere near there! Italy's a bloody big place.'

'I couldn't think quick enough.'

'Obviously. What am I going to do now? D'you know, Pam King, I could thump you. I really could. I'm so bloody angry.' Jill was standing over Pam. 'I was really looking forward to going away. Going abroad for the first time ever.'

'So was I.'

'And what about all the money I've spent? Me new clothes? Remember it was your idea in the first place, now all me money's gone.' Jill's eyes were filled with tears and anger.

'What's going on down there? What's all this 'ere shouting about?' Doll Windsor had turned herself round. 'Reckon all the street can hear you two!'

'Sorry,' said Pam.

'Everything all right?'

Pam nodded.

'It ain't yer gran, is it, Jill?' Mrs Windsor leaned further out. She was a thin wiry woman, always on the go, who relished any bit of scandal she was able to pass on.

'No, it's personal,' said Jill. 'Come on, we'll miss our bus then we'll be late for work and if I get stopped any money for being late, that will really be the end of a perfect day.'

Pam was too upset to talk and walked on with her head down.

Jill was striding out angrily. 'Don't want her to hear all our business, it'll be up and down the street before we've

33

got on the bus. Christ, she must have the cleanest windows in London.'

Pam looked behind her at Doll Windsor. She was watching them walk away. Pam knew her bright eyes had been searching her and Jill's faces for a hint of what they had been arguing about. Pam had always been intrigued with Mrs Windsor. No matter what time of day it was, she was always made up. With blonde frizzy hair and bright pink rouged spots on her cheeks she looked like a doll – perhaps that was how she got her name. Nobody knew how old she was. Mr Windsor was a quiet little man who always appeared to walk two steps behind his wife.

For the rest of the day Pam avoided Jill and they were even silent all the way home.

'Hi, girls,' shouted Lu from his ice-cream van parked at the top of Newbury Street. 'Getting yourselves all tarted up for the big holiday?'

'Don't talk about it,' said Jill.

Pam hurried past.

'Why? What's happened?' asked Lu.

'We ain't going?'

'I thought it was all sorted.'

'It was.'

Pam looked over her shoulder at Jill who was standing near the van, glaring at her. She knew Jill was about to tell Luigi Cappa everything. Well, she'd just leave her to it.

'Hello, love. Everything all right?' asked Rose when Pam walked in.

'No. She's lost me my best friend now.' Pam stared angrily at her gran.

'There's no need to be rude,' said Rose.

'Ain't there? Jill ain't talking to me. I'm going upstairs.' Tears began to sting her eyes all over again.

In the bedroom she sat on her bed and let the tears fall. What about Robbie? What would he think when she didn't get off the plane? There was no way she could get in touch with him. All her plans and dreams had been quashed. She couldn't believe it was possible to be so unhappy.

Why had her gran done it? Throughout her life Ivy had been firm but always kind. Her gran had looked after her when she was young and her mother had had to go to work. They used to sit and listen to the radio together; they would do puzzles, drawing and painting. In the summer they would have picnics in the park with Jill. Life was always filled with laughter. As she grew older and went to school it was Gran who met her and bought her ice cream. She was always there when Pam needed a shoulder to cry on if she was unwell, or fell over.

What had brought this sudden change? Pam knew she couldn't stay in this house any longer. She had to get away. But where could she go? She pulled her new suitcase out from under the bed and, taking her clothes out, gently fondled the bright pink bikini. She had wanted Robbie to see her in it and know what a smashing figure she had.

'Dinner's on the table,' Pam's mother shouted up the stairs.

Pam didn't want to go down and face them but knew she had to. She pushed her suitcase back under her bed.

'Why don't you and Jill go to Cornwall?' said Rose as she put a plate in front of Pam.

'It's not very warm there, is it?' Pam prodded a potato. She wasn't hungry.

'It's supposed to be very pretty though.'

'So's Italy,' Pam growled.

'How long are you going to keep this nonsense up?' said Ivy.

Pam threw her knife and fork on to the table. 'Nonsense? Is that what you think it is?'

'Now come on, eat your dinner,' said Rose.

'I don't want any. I'm going out.' Pam quickly left the room.

'You know, this is going to take a long while to heal,' said Rose sadly looking at the closed door.

'She'll come round,' said Ivy confidently.

Pam walked to the park. The nights were drawing in and the air felt damp. She had to get away, but where could she go?

A motor bike drew up beside her.

'Thought it was you. What you doing out here on your own?'

'Hello, Lu.' Pam couldn't ignore him; besides, she needed someone to talk to.

'That's a bit rough you not going away now. Jill told me all about it. She's very upset.'

'I know. So am I.'

'Where're you off to now?'

'I don't know. Just walking. I can't face staying in all evening. And I certainly won't be welcome over at Jill's. What are you doing here anyway?'

Sitting astride his motor bike Luigi took a packet of cigarettes from his leather jacket and offered her one.

Pam shook her head. 'No thanks.'

'I've just finished for the day. Business tends to drop at

this time of year once the school kids have gone home. I'd ask you out, but I've got to get home. Dad starts raving a bit if I'm late home for me tea. I can give you a lift back to your house if you like.'

She gave him a light smile. 'No, ta. That's all right. I'll be going back home a bit later. Want a bit of breathing space. How are all your brothers?'

'Not bad. We all tend to do our own thing now. Marc takes the other van out when he's not in any trouble, and as you know Al's married and lives not too far from here.'

Over the years there had been a lot of gossip about the Cappas. They lived the other side of Rotherhithe, almost into New Cross. Talk was that the old grandfather had come to England before the first World War, and when it was over he'd become part of the ice-cream business with old Mr Bennetti. He was supposed to have got them into a lot of debt and Mr Bennetti took over the factory while he finished up with a horse and cart. Before the old boy died, his son, Lu's father, took over the horse and cart. Now he had two vans which Lu and his brother Marco took out, while the Bennettis had the factory and sold to the shops. Mr Cappa drank a lot and he was often seen staggering down the road singing. It was also said that he used to beat his wife before she left him. Nobody really knew if any of this was true, but whatever, the boys had grown up very tough and streetwise.

'So what you gonner do about this 'ere holiday then?' asked Lu, taking a long drag on his cigarette and blowing the smoke high into the air.

'Can't do anything, can I?' Me gran went and burned me passport.'

'So Jill said. That's really tough.' He glanced at his watch. 'I'll have to go. You sure I can't give you a lift?'

'No, thanks all the same.'

'Look, if you want anyone to talk to, I'm always around.'

'Thanks, Lu.'

'Must go. See you then.'

Pam watched him roar off, the studs on his black leather jacket glinting in the streetlights. She suddenly realized that that was the first time she'd really talked to him on his own. Usually they met when he was serving ice cream or with others and then he was full of bravado. Perhaps he wasn't as bad or as conceited as she'd always imagined. He was certainly very good-looking. She smiled at the thought of him being frightened of his father. He must be a bully, but then he had had three boys to keep in order.

Did her gran have any big secret about the Cappas? And would she approve of her talking to Luigi?

As Pam passed the Odeon cinema she stopped. They were showing *Escape by Night*. On the spur of the moment she decided to go and see it. Although it was a war film, who knows, it might give her some ideas on how to escape from her grandmother . . .

Chapter 4

It was late when Pam opened the front door. The light was still on in the passage. She stood at the foot of the stairs and listened for the radio; she couldn't hear any sound so guessed her gran and mother were in bed and, hopefully, asleep. Taking off her shoes, she began to make her way upstairs when the kitchen door was suddenly pulled open.

'Pam! Where on earth have you been? We've been worried sick.'

'Why?'

'Come in here.'

'I'd rather go to bed.'

'Come here.' Her mother's low whisper was forceful.

Slowly, with her shoes in her hand, Pam went into the kitchen. 'Well? Where is she?'

'Sit down. If you mean your grandmother, she's gone to bed.'

Pam slumped into the chair. 'Why's that? Couldn't she face me?'

'Where have you been?'

'The pictures.'

'We've been very worried. It's not like you to go off like that.'

'Well, things have changed.'

'Your grandmother is very upset.'

Pam nearly leaped out of the chair. '*She's* upset? What about me and Jill? If you ask me I think she's gone round the twist.'

'I think she regrets what she did.'

'Thanks. It's a fine time to have regrets. Me and Jill aren't speaking. Robbie is expecting me to get off a plane on Saturday, and I'm fed up.' Pam pulled at a thread on her cardigan.

'Don't do that, you'll make a hole.'

Pam had a frown on her face. 'I'll never forgive her, you know.'

'You will in time.'

'I don't think so. Have you finished?'

'Bob is taking you and Jill to Brighton on Saturday. Somebody he knows went there so he's going to find out about the hotel for you.'

'That's very exciting, I don't think.'

'Oh come on. It'll be for the whole of the week.'

'I don't want to go. Besides, I ain't got any money.'

'Gran's paying.'

'Big deal. What about Jill?'

'Gran's been over and tried to sort things out. I wish I was going.'

'Well, you go then.'

'Don't be silly. This is your treat.'

'Some treat.' Pam continued to pull the thread. 'Jill won't speak to me.'

'I'm sure she'll understand.'

Pam laughed, but she was fighting back the tears. 'Of course. Sorry you ain't going to Italy, but we'll take you to

40

Brighton, that should be nice.'

'Pam, you're making it very difficult.'

'Good. What did Jill's mum and dad have to say about all this?'

'I don't know. Gran went on her own to see them.'

'I bet she gave them a real sorry tale. I'm going to bed.'

'Don't you want a cup of cocoa?'

'No.' Pam made her way upstairs. She felt pangs of guilt at being rude to her mother: she knew it wasn't her mother's fault, Rose was trying to heal the situation as much as she could. But Pam couldn't help it. She wanted to be alone. She wanted to cry. She wanted Robbie to comfort her. Panic filled her. What would he think when she didn't turn up? Would he think she had been pretending about coming? Would he think she'd had a terrible accident? If only she could get in touch with him. She was so very angry and unhappy and it was all her gran's fault.

For the first time in their lives things were strained between Jill and Pam. As children they had had their ups and downs, but their disagreements had never lasted that long. This was different. For the rest of the week they went to and from work together with hardly a word passing between them.

On Thursday evening Pam was desperate to talk to someone, so, as soon as she finished her tea and without telling her mother, she went next door to Lil's.

'Hello, love. Come in,' said Lil on opening the door. 'What brings you round here?'

Pam quickly looked across the road hoping Jill hadn't seen her. 'I want to talk to someone,' she said, following Lil down the passage.

'Cuppa?' asked Lil when they went into the kitchen.

'No thanks.'

'I suppose it's about this business with your gran?'

Pam nodded and sat in the armchair. Slowly tears began to trickle down her cheeks.

'Come on, now. It ain't the end of the world.'

'It is to me.'

'Well, tears ain't gonner help.'

Pam sniffed. 'Why is she so against the Bennettis? Do you know?'

Lil sat opposite her and lit a cigarette with a piece of rolled-up paper that was sitting in the hearth. 'No, I don't, and that's the honest truth,' she said, blowing smoke high into the air. 'We both knew the old man when we worked at the factory but we was only there a short while as it wasn't long before we found we was both expecting.' Lil gave a little laugh. 'Both our old men were home at the same time. Funny that. Your grandad was in the navy and my old man was in the army.' Lil looked thoughtful. 'Mind you, she didn't like Bennetti all that much.'

'Did he ever give her any trouble?'

'Not that I knew of. We wasn't always on the same shift so he could have done when I wasn't there. That's all I can tell you. But it musta been something she can't forget or forgive otherwise she wouldn't be carrying on like this. It ain't yer gran's way. She loves you and wouldn't let any harm come to you, you know that, don't you?'

Pam nodded.

'Now, how about that cuppa, I'm parched.'

'OK.'

'I think you and Jill should go off and enjoy yourselves. I

know it won't be the same, but you're young and there's gonner be plenty of other times for you to go abroad.'

When Pam left Lil's she felt just a little bit better. But her gran's secret wasn't going to stop her being miserable.

Pam and Jill couldn't be angry with each other for long. The next day as they were walking home Jill asked, 'What time will you be ready to go to Brighton tomorrow?'

'Don't know. Don't really know if I want to go.'

'Can't say I'm looking forward to it. After all our plans.'

'At least you've still got a passport,' Pam said.

'I suppose we could try and go another time?'

'S'pose so. I'll make gran pay.'

'My gran reckons she's going round the bend to do what she did.'

Pam looked at Jill in astonishment. 'Did she say that?'

Jill nodded. 'Well, she ain't ever stopped you doing what you like before, has she?'

'No. But this was because I was going to see Robbie.'

'I know. When I asked my gran about that she said she didn't know what all the fuss was about. Did you know they both once worked with old man Bennetti?'

Pam nodded. She wasn't going to tell Jill she had spent some time with Lil asking her questions.

'It was in a munitions factory at the beginning of the First World War. They were both newly married and my grandad was in the army and yours was in the navy.'

'I know that.'

'Gran said Bennetti was in charge and they didn't have a lot to do with him.'

'That's all I was told.' Pam was pleased Jill had tried to

find out what the problem was. 'If this is over some silly row they had, what, fifty years ago, then I'll, I'll . . .'

'What?' asked Jill.

'I don't know. But there's going to be some changes in our house after this.' Pam strode purposefully home and slammed the door when she walked into the kitchen.

Ivy was sitting in her chair reading the paper. 'How long is this going to go on for, young lady?' she asked, peering at Pam over her glasses.

Pam went over to stand in front of her. 'Till I know the truth.'

'What about?'

'This business and the Bennettis.'

Ivy looked sad, but realized from Pam's stance that this time she was not going to give up. She took a quick breath and folded the newspaper. Taking off her glasses she waved at the armchair opposite her. 'You'd better sit down and listen. In many ways I'm really sorry, but I couldn't let you go. I don't want you to get too serious about him.'

'Why? What's the harm in it? He's a nice person.'

'I suppose you are entitled to some sort of explanation.'

Pam quickly sat down. At last she was going to hear what was causing all the fuss.

'I want you to know I'm truly sorry for what I did, but I was only trying to protect you.'

'Protect me from what? I'm eighteen and I think I'm old enough to look after myself.'

'That's as maybe, but till you're twenty-one you'll have to obey our rules.'

'Hummph,' sighed Pam, turning to face the fire.

'What I'm going to tell you mustn't go beyond these four walls.'

Pam sat up and leaned forward. 'Is it that bad?'

'Let's say it's something I wouldn't want everybody to know about.' Ivy leaned back in the chair and closed her eyes for a moment or two.

The frantic banging on the wall made Pam and Ivy jump.

'What's that bloody silly cow up to now?' shouted Ivy, jumping to her feet.

Lil always banged on the wall if she had a problem. This evening it sent Ivy hurrying through the scullery and out to the back of the house.

'What's wrong with Lil?' asked Rose as they hastily followed Ivy.

'Don't know,' said Pam, shrugging her shoulders.

They could hear Lil screaming out for help as they rushed into the yard.

Ivy threw the gate to one side and pushed open the back door. Smoke billowed out and Lil came staggering out to meet them.

'It's on fire,' she spluttered.

'What is?' screamed Ivy.

'Me and the scullery.' Lil was visibly shaking as she leaned against the small brick coal shed. Her face and apron had black streaks across them, the front of her hair was singed and she looked very dishevelled and harassed.

'Quick, Pam, grab that bucket and fill it with water,' yelled her mother as she moved inside.

Pam did as she was told. She picked up the galvanized bucket that stood under the big wooden mangle and ran into the scullery where her mother was stamping on a tea towel that must have been hanging over the cooker. Pam filled the bucket from the sink and promptly threw the water over the towel. Most of it went over the cooker and great clouds of steam rose in the air.

'I'm terrified of fire,' said her mother, looking very distressed.

'You did a grand job,' said Pam, putting her arm round her mother's shoulders.

'I suppose it's because of losing your dad in a fire and having to help put out all those horrible incendiaries in the war that upsets me so. Fire is such a dreadful thing.'

'Look at this silly cow,' said Ivy as they went back out into the yard. 'She'll end up having us all killed. Tried to light her fag with the gas.'

Lil was looking very sheepish. 'I only bent down to light me fag and then all of a sudden, whoosh, the gas flared up and burnt me nose. I grabbed the tea towel and the next thing I knew it was alight. I panicked and couldn't think, so I banged on the wall.'

'That's all right. There's not a lot of damage, but you might have a job lighting the cooker till it's dried out,' said Rose. 'Pam, why don't you go and get Bob to come over and have a look at it?'

Pam was grinning as she crossed the road and thought about Lil trying to light her cigarette. She lifted the shiny brass door knocker and rapped twice.

'Jill's upstairs,' said Doreen, Jill's mother, on opening the front door.

'It ain't Jill I've come to see, it's Uncle Bob,' Pam said breathlessly.

'Come in, love, he's in the kitchen. Bob, young Pam's here,' she called out.

'OK, love?' asked Bob, smiling.

'Yes thanks. It's your mum.'

'What she been up to now?'

'It ain't too bad, but she's had a bit of an accident.'

Bob was on his feet. 'Accident? What kind of accident?'

'She was lighting her fag and she caught the tea towel alight . . .'

Bob was already hurrying down the narrow passage. 'She's a bloody menace with those fags of hers, they'll be the death of her one of these days, you mark my words.'

'What's all the racket going on down there?' asked Jill from the top of the stairs.

'It's your gran,' said Doreen over her shoulder as she followed Bob and Pam out of the door. 'Seems she's been trying to set the house on fire.'

'What? Is she all right?' Jill quickly came across the road after them.

'Come through Gran's,' said Pam, pushing the front door open.

In the back yard Ivy was laughing. 'Look at the state of her face. She ain't got any eyebrows.'

'Those bloody fags,' said Bob. 'I swear they'll be the death of you.'

'Oh, shut your noise. It was just a bit of a slip-up.' Lil dragged hard on the cigarette that dangled between her lips. 'Can't do without me fags.'

'So what's the damage in there then?' Bob nodded towards the house.

'Only the cooker, and the tea towel of course,' said Rose.

'Better go and have a look.' Bob went inside his mother's house.

'The dinner!' Rose suddenly yelled and left the gathering.

'If you've spoilt my dinner I'll throttle you,' said Ivy to Lil who was still leaning against the coal shed, looking very shamefaced.

Pam followed her mother. 'Is it OK?'

'Yes, I must have turned the gas down before the pantomime started.' She laughed. 'Well, one thing you can say is that there's never a dull moment living in this street.'

Bob came into their scullery.

'Everything all right in there?' Rose asked Bob.

Pam looked for Jill but she must have stayed with her gran.

'Yes, thanks,' said Bob. 'I've managed to light all the gas rings. I don't know what's getting into those two lately. First there's Ivy carrying on like that and tearing up young Pam's passport and now Lil's trying to set herself alight.' He propped himself against the sink. 'D'you think they're going, you know, a bit bonkers? After all, they are getting on.'

Rose laughed. 'No, not those two, they've got all their marbles. Besides, it's not the first time Lil's had a bit of a fire.'

'No. Thank God it's never got out of hand. You'd think that after all the incendiaries and the fires she helped put out when she was fire-watching, she'd be a bit more careful.'

Rose nodded. 'She was very brave when my Dan got caught trying to rescue Mr James. She tried so hard to help us save him.'

Pam was standing next to her mother listening. She didn't know that Lil had been involved when her dad had been killed. These old ladies certainly had plenty of secrets.

When they finished their dinner Ivy announced that she

was going to Lil's to watch TV.

'That *Steptoe and Son*'s on tonight. I like that,' said Ivy.

'Why don't we have a telly?' asked Pam. 'I have to go over to Jill's to watch *Ready, Steady, Go.*'

'Lil reckons that's a load of rubbish.'

'She would.' Pam knew her gran would be at Lil's all evening. They'd have their bottle of stout and sit and watch TV till the end. She also knew that her gran's secret wouldn't be revealed tonight. What had she been going to tell her? Had she had an affair with Mr Bennetti? Pam laughed to herself. No, her gran was too straitlaced for anything like that. But then again, you never knew . . .

The following morning Bob drove Pam and Jill to Brighton. The girls were very quiet although Bob was trying hard to cheer them up. Pam looked at her watch. They should have been on the plane about now. She looked out of the car's window at the scenery rushing by; she wanted to cry again. She should have been looking at sun-scorched fields, olive trees and mountains, not green muddy fields with dirty-looking cows in them. Even the trees looked stark and bare with their falling leaves.

'You're booked into a nice place right on the front. There's plenty to do down here and some great shops and shows.' Bob was cruising slowly along the sea front looking for the hotel.

Jill sighed. 'Better make the most of it, I suppose.'

'Ivy's been very generous,' said Bob. 'What with paying for the hotel and giving you both pocket money.'

'So she should be,' said Pam angrily.

'I'm sure you two will enjoy yourselves.'

'Don't know about that,' said Jill looking at Pam. 'But we'll try.'

Pam wasn't so sure. She knew it was going to be a long week. But she had to cheer up for her friend's sake; after all, it wasn't Jill's fault and she must be just as disappointed as Pam was.

Chapter 5

For Pam, even though she had tried hard to have a good time, the week in Brighton seemed to drag. They had spent their days shopping with Ivy King's money and every night they were out dancing or at the cinema.

As the days had passed so the atmosphere between the girls had melted a little. Now they were sitting in the foyer of the hotel waiting for Jill's father to collect them and take them home.

'This turned out to be a lot better than I thought it would,' said Jill, kneeling on the chair and looking out of the window.

'That's 'cos you met that Billy.'

'He was ever so nice. I wish you'd been a bit more friendly with his mate Dean.'

They had met the two on their very first night in Brighton.

'He wasn't my type,' said Pam.

'Don't think anybody's your type.'

'I'm surprised you didn't get fed up with Billy, seeing him every night.'

'He's nice. You're getting to be such a misery.'

Pam didn't have an answer as she knew Jill was right.

'What if Robbie don't want to see you when he gets back?'

'I'll just have to wait and see, won't I?'

'He might have met some fiery Italian.'

Pam smiled sarcastically. 'Is Billy gonner write?'

'Course. And I'm meeting him up West next Saturday. So I'll need you to give me an alibi.'

'I can't do that.'

'Why not?'

'I don't know what we'll be doing.'

'Thanks. What about all the times I gave you one while you was out with Robbie?'

'Why can't you tell your mum and dad about him?' Pam didn't know why she was being unkind, but she was just so down.

'What if he don't turn up – then I'll look a right fool. Besides, they might think I've been up to no good.'

'Well, have you?'

Jill grinned. 'I ain't telling you. I really do like him, so go on, Pam, just this once. If he does turn up and we make another date, then I'll tell them.'

'Where can I go?'

'I dunno. Get lover boy to take you out.'

'What . . . what if he don't forgive me for not going to Italy?' Hesitantly Pam voiced her greatest fear.

'He will when he finds out why. I bet he'll be on your doorstep tomorrow on bended knees.'

'I don't think so.'

'But I thought he was coming home Sunday.'

'He is, but it won't be till late, and I can't see him on bended knees.' Pam refused to be cheered up.

'Here's Dad. Don't mention Billy.'

'Course not.'

★ ★ ★

Did you have a nice time, love?' asked her mother as Pam put her case on the floor and kissed her cheek.

'Not really. Where's gran?'

'She's gone up the shops.'

'I see. Didn't want to see me then?' Pam snapped. Her mood had not improved at all on the journey home.

'We didn't think you'd be home just yet. And Pam, don't start all that nonsense again,' sighed Rose.

'Is that what you think it is, nonsense? You know things will never be the same between Gran and me, don't you? I'm never going to forgive her.'

Rose sat in the chair. 'Please, Pam, try to see it from my point of view. We've got to live here. I can't afford to move anywhere else and if there's going to be all this animosity between you and Gran, well . . .' Rose put her head in her hands. 'I don't know what to say.'

Pam was filled with guilt. All her life her mum had been out to work to look after her and this was all the thanks she was getting. 'I'm sorry, Mum. I promise I'll behave.'

Rose smiled wearily. 'Thanks, love.'

Pam suddenly realized how tired her mother looked. 'Look, why don't you and me go to the pictures or something one night?'

'That would be nice. There's that *Taste of Honey* on at the Ritz, perhaps we could go next Saturday?'

'I don't know about Saturday,' said Pam, knowing she had to be out for Jill's alibi.

Her mother looked at her. 'Will that Bennetti boy be home by then?'

Pam looked down and nodded.

'When's he coming home?'

'Tomorrow evening.'

'Well, in that case we'd better make it another night, just in case.'

'Thanks, Mum. Oh, I've bought you and Gran a stick of rock.'

'That's nice. But I thought you were still angry with Ivy?'

'Well, yes – I mean no. Well, I couldn't leave her out, now could I?'

Rose smiled. 'Course not. Mind you, I don't know if Gran's teeth will stand it.'

'Mum wanted me to go to the pictures with her next Saturday,' said Pam on Monday evening as she and Jill dawdled home from work. Pam kept stopping and looking round hoping Robbie would come along; she was desperate to see him.

'What? How did you get out of that?'

'I told her Robbie will be home and I might be going out with him.'

'You didn't? And what did your mum have to say about that?'

'Not a lot really.'

'Didn't she mind?'

'No.'

'What about your gran?'

'She wasn't there.'

'What if he don't ask you out?'

'Then I'll go on my own.'

Jill smiled. 'Thanks.'

'Well, it's the least I can do.' Pam was sorry she had been so grudging about covering for Jill when Jill had first asked her.

'I think it is!' Jill's eyes twinkled mischievously.

Luigi was reading a paper when the girls reached his van.

'All right, Lu?' called Jill.

'Yer. What about you two, had a good holiday?'

'Not bad,' Jill grinned.

'Found yerselves a couple of good-looking blokes then?'

'Wouldn't tell if we had,' said Jill, tossing her hair back as she crossed the road. Today she was wearing it in a pony-tail.

'Are you all right, Pam?' Lu asked, his voice softening.

'Yes thanks. But Brighton's not like Italy.'

'Don't reckon it is. Brighton's not bad though. Me and Marc go down there on our bikes sometimes. Mind you, it can get a bit hairy when we meet up with the Mods, but it's a bit of a laugh.'

Pam had read all about the clashes between the Mods and Rockers. 'Ain't you afraid of getting hurt?'

'Na, me and Marc can stick up for ourselves and sometimes we like a good fight. Just as long we don't get our gear too roughed up. The Mods are more worried about getting their whistles mucked up.' He grinned, his white teeth in stark contrast to his tanned skin.

Pam smiled. With a name like Luigi it was strange him being a cockney.

'Pam, if you ain't seeing Robbie – is there any chance I might get a look in?'

She walked away. 'I shouldn't think so for one moment,' she said over her shoulder.

'Thanks a bunch.' He was leaning out of the van. 'You never know, you might be glad of my company one of these days.'

Pam couldn't think of anything to say. She knew that he was the last person she wanted to go out with.

All week Pam kept a lookout for Robbie but by Saturday she still hadn't seen him.

'I'm going to the pictures with Jill,' she said while they were having their tea.

Her mother gave her a knowing smile.

'If you like me and you could go next week, Mum.'

'That'll be nice.'

That evening as she sat alone in the darkened cinema, tears filled her eyes. She wasn't a bit interested in the film. Where was Robbie? He should be here next to her, holding her hand and telling her he loved her. Why hadn't he been to see her? Was he angry with her? All the hate she had felt for her gran returned.

'Well?' Pam asked Jill on Sunday morning as she walked into the front room. Jill had put a Connie Francis record on the turntable and was singing along with it. 'Did he turn up?'

Jill smiled. 'Course.' She hugged herself. 'He's really smashing. He's coming up here again next Sat'day.'

'Are you going to tell your mum and dad?'

She nodded. 'He's coming to pick me up at home.'

'Wow! Are we talking wedding bells here?'

'Don't be daft.'

'Well, he is the first one you've ever took home.'

'I know. And he's the first one that I've really liked.'

Pam laughed. 'We've been out with some right old dogs at times, ain't we?'

Jill grinned. 'D'you remember that couple of blokes who took us out for the day and we had to sit in the park and watch them fly their model planes?'

'God, that was so boring. And what about those sandwiches?'

'Smelly egg and a flask of tea.'

'After they told us they were taking us out and giving us a real treat!' Jill laughed.

'Some treat. Even the ducks swam away from those sandwiches.'

'I do like Billy, Pam.'

'I know how you feel.'

'Still not seen anything of Robbie then?'

'No, worse luck.' All week Pam had been tentatively asking anyone she thought might know where Robbie lived. He had never given her his address and all she knew was that when years ago they moved from Rotherhithe it was to a big house somewhere in Southwark.

'Don't worry about it, he'll turn up,' said Jill lightheartedly.

But Pam was worried. 'I wish I could find out where he lives then I could tell him what happened.'

'Have a look in the phone book. They must have a phone and there can't be that many Bennettis.'

'Jill you're a genius. Why on earth didn't I think of that.' Pam squealed. 'Let's go now.'

'Take a pencil then you can write it down,' said Jill.

They ran round the corner to the nearest phone box and

Pam excitedly began searching the directory for Robbie's number.

'Here it is. They live in Southwark Park Road.' She put her money in the box and began dialling. Putting her hand over the receiver she announced, 'It's ringing.'

After a while she replaced the receiver and pressed button B to get her money back.

'P'raps they've gone to church, after all they could be Catholics.'

Sadly Pam nodded. 'I'll try again tomorrow.'

'Cheer up. At least you've got his address.'

Pam looked at the piece of paper. 'But what if he don't want to see me?'

'Well, now you've got the chance to find out. Come on.' Jill put her arm through Pam's.

'Jill, could we go this afternoon? Just to see if he's home.'

'I can't. I promised Mum I'd help her cut out a new frock she wants to wear at Christmas. Why don't you come over and give us a hand?'

'OK. I ain't got anything else to do.'

The following evening Pam went to the phone box and once again dialled Robbie's number. Her heart was beating fast when a woman answered. She quickly pressed button A.

'Hello. Is that Mrs Bennetti?'

'Yes.'

'Could I speak to Robbie please?'

'I'm afraid Roberto isn't here.'

'Oh. When will he be home?'

'I don't know.'

'I'll give him a call some other time. Would you tell him Pam phoned?'

'Pam? Are you the young lady who was supposed to have come to Italy?'

'Yes.'

'Well, let me tell you he was very upset at being let down. Do you know, he spent most of the day hanging around the airport. Thought he had been made to look the laughing stock of the village and it upset him. He was very angry.'

'Tell him I was very sorry about that, and when I see him I'll explain.' There was no way Pam was going to tell his mother what had happened.

'I don't think he will be that pleased to see you, not now.'

'Well, if you could just tell him . . .' Pam put the phone down as the pips went. She leaned against the glass and wanted to cry. 'Please, Robbie, just give me a chance to explain,' she said out loud. The banging on the door made her look up.

'You gonner spend all night in there talking to yerself?'

'No.' Pam picked up her handbag and walked out.

'Silly cow,' said the man as he pushed past her.

'Well?' said Jill opening the front door before Pam had a chance to knock.

'Was you looking out of the window?'

'Course. By the look on your face you didn't get to talk to him.'

'No, he wasn't home and his mum said he might not want to see me again.'

'How would she know?'

Pam repeated the conversation she had had.

'What would she know? Write to him. You've got his address now.'

'I could do.'

'That way you can tell him all what happened.'

Pam brightened up. 'And I could tell him how I feel about him.'

'Shouldn't make it too lovey dovey, it might put him off.'

'I hope not. Jill, I do like him.'

Jill grinned. 'Who knows, we might even have a double wedding.'

Pam giggled. 'That would be really great.'

'Don't let's count our chickens just yet. They've got to ask us first.'

'I know. But it would be nice though.'

'Yer,' said Jill dreamily.

Once she got home Pam sat and wrote to Robbie. She didn't open her heart completely, but explained about her grandmother and what she had done. She also said that if his father knew what the problem had been all those years ago, she would dearly love to know.

As she wrote she knew the time when her gran would tell her secret had passed. As far as Ivy King was concerned Pam had had nothing more to do with young Bennetti so, the incident was over and done with.

At the end of the letter she signed 'with love'. In her heart Pam wanted to tell him that she loved him dearly, but decided to wait to see what kind of reply she received.

Chapter 6

Weeks went by and every day Pam slowly walked home from work hoping Robbie would come up to them. She hadn't seen or heard from him at all and was worried.

'I wonder why he hasn't answered my letter?'

'Dunno. He must have a good reason. Why don't you phone him again?' suggested Jill.

'I don't like to. I don't want him to think I'm running after him.'

'Well, ain't you?'

'I'd like to.'

'Well then, bury your pride and give him another ring.'

'I might do that. Will you come with me?'

'You don't need me in a phone box. You could go and see him at home.'

'I wouldn't know what to say.'

'Course you would. What about something like: Hello, lover boy.'

Pam couldn't help giggling. 'He'd run a mile.' Then she changed the subject; it was too painful. 'Looks like you and Billy are really making a go of it then. Comes up here every weekend now. His car is becoming a permanent fixture outside your house.'

Jill smiled. 'I'm going to let you into a little secret – but you mustn't tell anyone.'

Pam's eyes opened wide. 'You're not having a baby, are you?'

'No, daft 'ead. Billy's gonner ask me mum and dad if we can get engaged at Christmas.'

Pam threw her arms round her friend. 'Oh, Jill. I'm so thrilled for you.'

Jill was glowing with happiness. 'It's a good job we didn't go to Italy. Got a lot to thank your old gran for.'

Pam nodded sadly. 'I'm glad something good came out of it. So, when are you hoping to get married then?'

'Don't know yet. Got to do a bit of saving first.'

'I'm really pleased for you.'

'Now you've got to tell Robbie about that. I'll send him an invite to our engagement party.'

'You gonner have a party then?'

'Why not. 'Sides, if we get some presents it'll be a start to me bottom drawer.' Jill laughed. 'But don't say nothing yet, not till mum and dad know.'

Pam was happy for Jill, but she couldn't help feeling very sorry for herself. When would things begin to go right for her?

On November 22 the papers were full of President Kennedy's assassination. Everybody was glued to a television set and all their own little problems seemed insignificant in comparison as they saw the anguish on Jackie Kennedy's face as she cradled her husband after he had been shot. For days the incident was on everybody's lips. Every evening Pam would go over to Jill's and they watched in amazement when Lee Harvey Oswald was shot by Jack Ruby.

'That sort of thing could only happen in America,' said Ivy later that evening when they were sitting discussing the latest development.

By the end of the month it began to calm down and Pam's worries, never far from her mind, preoccupied her once more.

Why hadn't Robbie got in touch? He knew where she worked and what time she finished. Once again Pam wrote to him; this time she had an excuse. She told him about Jill and Billy and as Christmas was fast approaching, she sent him a Christmas card. She couldn't pluck up the courage to phone just in case he wasn't home: she didn't want his mother to think she was always pestering him.

With two weeks to go to Christmas, Jill was on tenterhooks. She was going to Brighton to spend the weekend at Billy's house. Her parents had agreed to the engagement and she was going to meet her in-laws-to-be for the first time.

'I wish it was me getting engaged and meeting my future in-laws,' said Pam as she watched Jill pack her case.

'I'm surprised Robbie ain't answered our invite to the party. Thought he might come and bring some exotic ice cream with him.'

'He seems to have disappeared. You don't think something awful has happened to him, do you?'

'Don't talk daft. You never know, you might get a really lovely Christmas card from him.'

'We shall see.' Pam thought there was little hope of that.

'Well, p'raps Billy will bring a nice bloke to our party for you.'

'Hmm, chance could be a fine thing.'

Jill sat on the bed. 'Pam, you'll have to try and forget Robbie. It's pretty obvious he don't want anything to do with you. How long is it now since you've seen him?'

'Eight weeks.'

'Eight weeks, and in that time you've written to him twice and phoned him, so I think that says it all, don't you?'

Pam nodded sadly.

'I'll tell you what, I'll invite Luigi Cappa.'

'What? What for?'

'You. He's a bit of a laugh. 'Sides, I've got to get the ice cream from somewhere.'

'Thanks a bunch.'

'No, I reckon it'll be good and I bet he can dance.'

Pam wasn't impressed one little bit with that idea.

Christmas had come and gone and tonight everybody was enjoying themselves. Ivy King and Lil were sitting at the far end of the church hall watching the young ones dancing and laughing.

'This bloody music will damage these kids' eardrums,' said Lil, shouting to make herself heard above the Beatles record.

'You're only jealous 'cos you can't get up there and have a dance,' said Ivy, tapping her foot in time to the music.

'Don't call that dancing, do you? Mind you, I wouldn't mind learning to do that there hand jiving though.' Lil started to wave her hands about. 'Seen 'em do it on the telly.'

Ivy shrieked with laughter. 'You, hand jive?'

'Well it's a lot easier than being on yer feet, ain't it?'

'That's a nice ring that Billy got Jill.'

'I know. I've had it shoved under me nose all over Christmas.'

'He's certainly a good-looking boy.' Ivy nodded towards Jill and Billy who were dancing energetically.

'Yer, he is.'

'Pam said he's a builder. That's a nice car he's got. Must earn a few bob these days with all the work that's going on.'

'D'yer know, he bought me a lighter for Christmas.'

Ivy tutted. 'It won't stop you from trying to set yourself alight though, will it?'

Lil grinned. 'Don't suppose so. I expect I'll keep forgetting to fill the bloody thing up.'

'Knowing you you'll probably blow yourself up with the petrol. Just make sure you don't take my house with you.'

'All right, Mum?' asked Doreen, coming over with another drink for her mother-in-law and Ivy.

'Food looks good,' said Ivy.

'Thanks. Jill and Pam have been working hard bringing it all over here. It's nice they've kept the Christmas decorations up,' said Doreen, looking up at the ceiling.

'Well, it ain't Twelfth Night yet,' Lil pointed out.

'Pam said they ain't getting married yet,' Ivy said.

'No, they've got to do a bit of saving first. I think they'll be moving to Brighton when they do. I'll really miss her.' Doreen stood and watched her daughter laughing with Billy. 'His parents are enjoying themselves. They seem like nice people.'

'Bob said they gave you a few quid towards this party?'

Doreen nodded at Ivy. 'Yes. Still wish she wasn't going to move away though.'

'All got to leave the nest at some time,' said Ivy.

'Young Pam not got anybody then?' asked Doreen.

'No, not that I know of.'

'And she'd soon put a stop to it if she did,' said Lil, pointing her thumb at Ivy.

'No I wouldn't.'

'Look, she's talking to that Cappa boy. You gonner go over there and stop that?'

'No I ain't,' Ivy snapped.

'Well, he's an Italian.'

'I know that, don't I?'

'I must go,' said Doreen, giving them a weak smile. She didn't want to get drawn into any of their arguments – which could go on for a long while.

'Good do this,' said Luigi to Pam as he downed his beer.

'Yes.'

'Cheer up, gel, she ain't getting married – well, not for a while yet.'

'I know.'

'Fancy a jive?'

'In a bit.'

'Is it all over with you and Bennetti then?'

'Looks like it.'

'So now's the time to let your hair down and start to have a bit of fun. He was always a bit of a bore. Look, if you like, we could go out for a spin on me bike one day.'

'No thanks, it's too cold.'

'I know how to keep you warm.' He moved closer and tried to kiss her ear.

'Don't.'

'I'll show you how to have a good time.'

'I don't want it with you.'

He backed away. 'You never know, you might be glad of my company one of these days.'

'You two enjoying yourselves?' asked Jill, coming over to Luigi and Pam. Her eyes were shining as she looked up at Billy. He was tall and broad with a blond quiff gently falling over his forehead. He had his arm round Jill's tiny waist.

'This is a great party,' said Luigi. 'I was just asking Pam here for a dance.'

'Good. Well, go on then,' said Jill pushing Pam into Luigi's arms.

Pam cursed to herself; it would have to be a slow one.

Luigi held her close, but as she danced her thoughts were on Robbie. It was his arms she wanted round her; his lips she wanted kissing her neck. Why hadn't he bothered to answer Jill's invite? She would phone him on New Year's Day and use that as an excuse to wish him all the best for 1964.

'I like you, Pam,' said Luigi. 'Don't keep pining for something you can't have.'

'What you talking about?'

'Bennetti.'

'Oh, him,' said Pam nonchalantly. 'I'd forgotten all about him.'

Luigi looked at her and grinned. 'I can see that. Just remember I'm always here for you.'

But it wasn't him she wanted.

★ ★ ★

On Wednesday morning Jill came racing over to Pam. She rushed into the kitchen waving an envelope.

'Guess what? I've got a letter from Robbie.'

Pam, who was standing looking in the mirror that hung over the fireplace, stopped putting on her lipstick and stared at Jill. 'You? Why you?'

'Hello, Jill, you're early,' said Ivy, walking into the kitchen.

Jill hastily stuffed the letter in her coat pocket.

'Did you say you had a letter—'

'It can wait,' said Jill quickly interrupting Ivy. 'It's only an answer to my invitation.'

'You invited the Bennetti boy?' Ivy must have been outside the open door and heard Jill.

'Yes, but he didn't come. Are you ready, Pam? We don't want to be late for work, do we?'

'No,' said Pam as if she was in a dream. As soon as they were outside she asked, 'What did he say?'

'He's still in Italy.'

'What? Did he ask after me?'

'It seems he was very disappointed when you didn't turn up. He said he answered your letter which his mother had sent on to him, but you've never bothered to write back.'

'Let me see.' Pam snatched the letter from Jill. 'I ain't had a letter from him. And what about the second letter?'

'He might not have got that just yet. Not with the post over Christmas.'

'But he got your invite.'

'I know, but don't ask me how.'

'Why didn't I get his letter? Unless . . .' Pam stopped dead in her tracks. 'Gran. You don't think Gran . . .'

'She wouldn't do a thing like that . . . Would she?'

'I wouldn't put anything past her.' Pam's face was full of anger.

'But why?'

'Don't ask me.'

'It can't be all Italians. She didn't seem to mind you talking to Lu.'

'Was that just because she couldn't make a fuss in front of everybody?'

'Could be, I suppose. It seems Rob's staying over there for a while.'

'That's nice for him. But I see he didn't give you his address.'

'No, he didn't.'

Pam choked back a sob. 'I wonder why?'

'He must have a reason. Perhaps he's coming back?'

'Could be.'

'Look, why don't you go and see his parents and find out more? I'm sure they'll explain everything.'

'You could be right. And if that old cow is stealing my letters I'll get him to send them to you.'

'Now that sounds like a good idea.' Jill linked her arm through Pam's. 'Here's our bus. Thank Gawd. Standing around in this cold will give me chilblains again.'

Pam smiled. 'Or, as your gran always says, "In that bloody short skirt yer'll catch yer death." '

They were both laughing as they got on the bus, but Pam wasn't thinking about Lil. Her mind was full of Robbie and all that lovely sunshine.

★ ★ ★

That evening when Pam got home she marched into the kitchen and, throwing her handbag on the chair, yelled, 'Have you been keeping my letters from me?'

Ivy King was sitting in her armchair with her eyes closed. 'Are you talking to me young lady?'

'What's all the noise about?' asked Rose, wiping her hands on the bottom of her pinny as she came in from the scullery.

'Did you know she's pinched my letters?' Pam shouted, pointing at her grandmother.

'What on earth are you talking about, Pam?'

Tears gathered in Pam's eyes. 'Robbie wrote to me but I never got the letter.'

'And you think I took it? Now what would I do a thing like that for?'

'Because you don't want me to see Robbie, that's why. What's he done that's so terrible?'

Ivy King sat up. 'I can assure you that no letter has come here for you, young lady.'

'Where is he?' asked Rose.

'Still in Italy.'

'But I thought . . . Who did you go to the pictures with that night?'

'Myself. It was to give Jill an alibi when she first went out with Billy.'

'You thought she was out with him?' Ivy looked very indignant.

'I wasn't certain and I didn't ask,' said Rose. 'Are you sure he's written?' she asked her daughter.

'He told Jill he had.'

'Did he give you his address?' Rose was anxiously trying to ease the situation.

'No he didn't.' Pam let her tears fall.

'Come on now,' said her mother as she put an arm round Pam's shoulder. 'He must have a good reason.'

'He must have written to me. Why would he say he had if it wasn't true?'

'I expect the post is funny from all that way away.'

Ivy stood up. 'Can't trust some people. And what upsets me is that you take his word against mine. He could tell Jill anything. And he didn't give her his address. Sounds fishy to me.'

Pam couldn't answer that.

'I'll just lay the table,' said Ivy going to the sideboard drawer and taking out the cutlery, began to set it out.

Pam went to her bedroom. She sat on the bed. Who was telling the truth? She had to speak to Robbie.

On Saturday, Pam, after a lot of walking, found the Bennettis' house. The front garden was paved with neat shrubs edging the path. The house had three floors and was built of red brick. The windows were draped with expensive-looking lace curtains; everything about it looked rich and lavish. Nervously she rang the bell.

'Yes?' asked the grey-haired woman who answered.

'Excuse me. I'm Pam King. I'm a friend of Roberto's.'

'I'm afraid the Bennettis aren't here.'

'Oh, when will they be back?'

'Not till late tomorrow. They went to their son's in Italy for Christmas.'

'Thank you.' Pam began to walk away.

'Did you want to leave a message or anything?' the woman called after her.

'No. No, thank you. I'll phone him later.'

'Roberto won't be coming home. Didn't you know? He's staying in Italy.'

Pam turned round. 'He is? Do you know for how long?'

'No. He's very happy over there. It seems they found members of Mr Bennetti's family when they went over for the wedding. I think young Roberto's staying for good. He's been working over there with the family.'

Pam held on to the gate post. 'Thank you,' she whispered before gathering herself together.

'What's your name?'

'Pam.'

'I'll tell them you called,' said the grey-haired woman.

'Thanks,' said Pam, giving her a slight smile before walking away.

Pam was so shaken she went straight round to Jill's to tell her what she had found out.

'And you should see his house, it's huge.'

'If you ask me you ought to forget him. You can't spend your life mooning about after him.' Jill was painting her nails. She flapped her hands in the air to dry them.

'It's all right for you, you've found your Mr Right.'

'You'll never find anyone if you wait around for Robbie. More so now he might be working in Italy.'

'If only I knew why he never got in touch. He had plenty of opportunities.'

'Oh for goodness sake, Pam, just forget about him, there's plenty more fish in the sea. Here, try this, it ain't a bad colour when you put two coats on.'

'Thanks.' Pam took the nail varnish but she was still thinking about Robbie. Italy was a long way away and she couldn't keep running after him, but somehow she had to find out if he still cared for her or not.

Chapter 7

Winter had given way to spring and Pam was feeling the urge to go out. She was desperate for some excitement in her life.

'Please, Jill, just come to the pictures with me?' begged Pam. 'I'm fed up with going with me mum.'

'I can't. I'm saving.'

'D'you know, you're getting to be a real bore with all this saving lark. We don't go anywhere now, no dancing and only the pictures now and again. It's times like this I wish I had a sister.'

'I'm always surprised your mum never got married again.'

'She's had a few men friends, but I think she's resigned herself to being a widow.'

'That must be awful – knowing you not going to have –' Jill grinned and nudged Pam – 'you know, any . . . for the rest of your life. It's like being a nun.'

They both laughed, but deep down Pam was sorry for her mother and sorry for herself. 'Please come out somewhere, *anywhere*, just for a change.'

'If I'm getting married in October I'll need all the money I can get. Besides, I see Billy most weekends so dancing's out. It's only another seven months to our wedding and I've still got to get my dress and yours, that's without all the clothes I need for my honeymoon.'

Pam sighed. 'So you keep saying. At least you'll be getting to use your passport.'

'I know. Paris sounds so romantic. Oh, I was so lucky to meet Billy! I am sorry about not being able to go out with you though.'

'Don't worry about it, I'll ask me mum to come with me. As usual.'

'I'm sorry, Pam, but you know how it is?'

'No, I don't. I ain't been married or had to save for a wedding.'

'You wait till you do. Tell you what, Billy's not coming up here this weekend so why don't we go up West next Saturday afternoon after work and look at some frocks. We might get some good ideas. I still think blue's the best colour for you.'

'Couldn't we go dancing after?'

'I don't like to. It don't seem right somehow – not without Billy.'

'Please yourself. But what about my birthday at the end of the month? It's on a Sunday this year.'

Jill stopped. 'I forgot about that.'

'Thanks.'

'No, I really am. We'll go out on that night, not that there's that much to do, but we could go to the pictures.'

'I'll ask Mum if you can come over to tea.'

'That'll be nice.'

Pam tossed back her hair as they continued to walk home. Although she was getting fed up with Jill keeping on about her wedding and felt mean about it, she really was looking forward to being her bridesmaid.

'Hello, gels. All right then?' Luigi was leaning out of his ice-cream van.

'It is for me,' said Jill.

'Looks like you can't wait to tie the knot then, gel.'

'It can't come soon enough.'

'You look a bit down in the mouth, Pam.'

'She wants to go to the pictures, but she ain't got nobody to go with, only her mum.'

'What about some of your mates from school?'

'They've all got their own friends.'

'Or boyfriends,' interrupted Jill, 'so she's a poor little wallflower.'

'Shut up, Jill.'

'That true?'

'No, it ain't.'

'As I keep telling you, I'll always take you.'

'Don't start on that again.' Lu had asked her out many times since Christmas, but she had always refused.

'I mean it.'

'Go on, why don't you take up his offer?'

Pam glared at Jill. 'I'll make up my own mind who I go out with, thank you.' She walked off in a huff.

Jill shrugged her shoulders and crossed the road.

'Thanks for trying, Jill.'

'Only sorry it didn't work,' Jill called back.

'Give it time,' yelled Luigi.

Pam stood at her door for a moment or two before going in. She wanted to go over to them and tell them both to mind their own business and stop discussing her as if she wasn't there. But then again, what Jill had said was true, she didn't have anyone to go out with and she was very lonely and getting to be a misery.

She waited till Jill went indoors before going back to Luigi.

He was smiling. 'So, what d'yer fancy?'

'Did you mean it when you said about us going to the pictures together?'

'Course. What night?'

'Would Friday be all right?'

'I should think so. I'll pick you up about seven.'

'OK.'

Pam was grinning when she walked in the kitchen.

'You look like you've lost a tanner and found a shilling,' said Ivy.

'I've just been asked to the pictures.'

'Oh yes, and who with?'

Pam was smiling. This was going to be one in the eye for her gran. 'Luigi Cappa,' she said defiantly and waited for the fireworks.

'That's nice.'

Pam sat on the chair deflated. 'He's an Italian.'

'I know who he is. He was at Jill's party and I've seen the van stuck in the road enough times.' Ivy gathered up her cardigan. 'I'm just popping next door to find out what's on the telly tonight.' With that she left Pam sitting staring at the open door.

'Hello, love, thought I heard you come in.'

Pam didn't answer her mother.

'Are you all right?'

Pam nodded. 'I've just told Gran I'm going to the pictures with Luigi Cappa and all she said was, "That's nice." '

Rose smiled. 'Well, it is. What you going to see?'

'I don't know. Is that all you can say?'

'What should I say?'

'Well, after all the fuss about Robbie, why has Gran changed her mind? Luigi's as Italian as Robbie is.'

Rose shrugged. 'Don't ask me.'

'I only said I'd go with him just to see what Gran would say. I expected her to go mad and start shouting again, but she didn't.'

'Perhaps she's seen the error of her ways.'

'Well it's too bloody late for me and Robbie, then.'

'Pam, don't swear, there's a good girl.'

A good girl was the last thing Pam wanted to be at this moment.

'When are you going with Luigi then?'

'Friday.' But now her gran seemed to approve, the idea didn't look so interesting. 'By the way, can Jill come over to tea on my birthday?'

'Yes. Why not?'

Despite her apprehension, on Friday evening Pam was in the front room looking out of the window waiting for Luigi to come roaring up on his motor bike.

'Bye,' she called out as she went out to meet him.

'Hop on,' he yelled.

She pulled up her skirt, cocked her leg over the pillion seat and, putting her arms round his waist, held on to him very tight. She had never been on the back of a motor bike before. The wind was making her eyes water and she was concerned it would make her mascara run. It was very exhilarating and with her head-scarf flapping behind her they raced along and were at the Ritz in no time.

She was pleased when they found the back row full, and when Luigi tried to put his arm round her, she quickly moved it away.

'Can't blame a bloke for trying,' he whispered.

'Just keep your hands to yourself.'

He didn't answer, but even in the dark she could sense he was smiling.

At the end, 'That wasn't a bad film,' said Luigi as they walked towards his motor bike. 'Fancy a drink?'

'No thanks.'

'OK, fair enough. I'm really glad you came out with me tonight.'

'Why's that?'

'It's always nice to have a girl on the back.'

'It is a smashing bike.'

'Yer, it is,' he said, proudly running his hands over the shiny chrome fuel tank. 'As soon as I've paid for it I'll go up to a bigger one.'

'Thought you might have got a car.'

'Na, it ain't got the same thrill.'

When they stopped outside Pam's house Luigi asked, 'Could we do this again one night?'

'Don't see why not.'

'By the way, did you ever find out what happened to Bennetti?'

'As far as I know he's still in Italy.'

'Why didn't he come back?' Luigi took a packet of cigarettes from the top pocket of his leather jacket and offered Pam one. She shook her head. 'Has he done a runner?'

'Why should he?'

'That family's bloody devious. I'm surprised his old man let him stay over there, not with the business expanding all the time, so it must be something pretty bad.'

Pam suddenly realized what Luigi meant. Was Robbie in trouble? 'I don't think he's done a runner. He only went to Italy because of his brother's wedding.'

'Yer, but what did he get up to over there?'

Pam began to think. 'Surely he would have told his mum to let me know?'

'Dunno about that. They might want to keep it a secret.' Luigi blew smoke high into the air.

'He must be over there with the family's blessing,' she said quickly.

'But is he? My grandad was working with the old Bennetti at the very beginning when they first came to England and started up in the ice-cream business. He soon found out that everyone could be set up, trampled on and bought off.'

'Is that what happened?'

'Yer. Poor old Grandad. He had the brains but not the clout. He finished up with the poxy horse and cart while Bennetti kept the factory. Even the bloody horse was only fit for the knackers yard. My dad's had to work hard all his life to keep our family together and to get what we've got. It don't take an Einstein to work out that two ice-cream vans have to take quite a few bob to keep us lot.' He ground his cigarette butt aggressively into the pavement.

Pam could see there was a lot of bad feeling towards the Bennettis. Did the Cappas know why her gran also hated them? There were so many things she wanted to ask him, about his mother leaving them and his grandfather, but knew she shouldn't dig too deeply: it might give him the wrong impression. 'I really must go in. Thanks for taking me out.'

'Pam, can we do it again?'

'I don't see why not,' she said pleasantly then quickly turned and walked away. She didn't want him to kiss her goodnight.

When she was in bed she thought about what Luigi had said. Were the Bennettis as black as his family and her gran seemed to think? Was Robbie in trouble? If Robbie were here he could defend his name. She turned over and smiled to herself. Luigi wasn't bad company and he was certainly good-looking. She'd noticed a lot of girls were giving him the glad eye and she guessed many would have loved to have been in her position tonight. Was she wasting her life pining over Robbie?

Pam was ready for work when Jill called earlier than usual.

'Well, how did it go?'

'OK.'

'Is that it? Just OK? Did he kiss you goodnight?'

'No.'

'Are you seeing him again?'

'Course. We see him every day, remember, he has the ice-cream van.'

'Stop trying to be so bloody funny. You know what I mean.'

'We didn't make any firm arrangements, if that's what you're on about.'

'Oh,' said Jill, deflated.

Pam laughed. 'But I will be going out with him again.'

'Great. That's really great. When?'

'Next week, I shouldn't wonder. Jill: Lu thinks Robbie has got himself into some sort of trouble in Italy.'

'No! Why does he think that?'

'Because the family hasn't told me where he is and he hasn't come home or written.'

'But he wrote to me.'

'Perhaps that was before and now he's in prison and can only send one letter out.'

Jill burst into a fit of laughter. 'What? Robbie in prison?'

'He might have done something to upset the Mafia.'

Jill had to sit on the wall, she was laughing so hard. 'Pam King, you are the biggest idiot I have ever met,' she screamed out. 'Robbie Bennetti in trouble with the Mafia? I think you're letting your imagination run away with you. You've been seeing too many films.'

Pam looked at the ground. She felt very stupid and uncomfortable. 'I didn't think it was that funny.'

'Didn't that woman at Christmas say he was working over there?' Slowly Jill was regaining her composure.

'Yes, but perhaps that's what they told her to say.'

'So, the plot thickens. You are daft. Come on, our bus will be along soon.'

As they walked along the road to catch the bus everything that Lu had said was going round and round in Pam's mind. She had to go and see Robbie's mother. She had to know the truth. Meanwhile Pam knew she was going to be bombarded with questions about her date with Lu. Jill wasn't going to let this rest, but Pam didn't mind. At least she had something to talk and smile about.

★ ★ ★

The following Friday Pam went to the pictures with Luigi again.

'D'you fancy a run out on Sunday?'

'Where to?'

'Don't mind.'

'But what about the van? Shouldn't you be working?'

'I'll get old Bertie to take it out. He don't mind working the odd Sunday.'

Lu had told Pam that Bertie, their mechanic, worked on the vans and sometimes took over if anyone was ill.

'I don't want to get involved with the Mods,' Pam insisted.

Luigi laughed. 'I wouldn't take you anywhere near to where there was going to be a rumble. No, I was thinking of somewhere in the country.'

'That would be nice.'

'I'll pick you up about eleven.'

'Shall I bring some sandwiches?'

'Why not.'

On Sunday morning Ivy watched Pam preparing the food and a flask.

'Don't like to see you young girls in trousers.'

'It's a bit warmer than a skirt.'

'And I don't really like you going out on that motor bike. Noisy thing.'

Pam threw the knife on the table. 'Is there anything I do that you *do* approve of?'

'Don't you start getting saucy with me, my girl.'

Pam sighed. 'I don't seem to be able to do anything right just lately.'

'Why couldn't you find yourself a nice boy like young Jill's got? He's got a car.'

''Cos there ain't that many about, and if I did, you'd find something about him you didn't like.' She grabbed up her bag and went into the front room to wait for Luigi.

The sun was warm on her face and it made the road ahead of them shimmer as they went roaring along. Pam was definitely enjoying every moment of it and gradually became confident enough to release her tight hold on Luigi.

After a while they stopped.

'This is a lovely spot. You can see for miles. Where are we?'

'Surrey. Box Hill.'

After wandering around and taking in the sights and the smells Pam sat on the grass. 'This is really nice. D'you fancy a sandwich?'

Luigi nodded. 'I'll get them.' He took the bag from his pannier.

Pam began to pour out the tea.

'Thanks for coming out with me,' said Luigi.

'Thanks for asking me.' For the first time in ages her eyes were shining. She was so enjoying her day out.

'Pam, you know I really like you.'

She suddenly became apprehensive. 'I like you too, but I'm not ready for any romance yet.'

He laughed. 'Romance. Blimey, that's an old-fashioned word.'

'I'm an old-fashioned girl.'

'What does that mean?'

She looked away. 'I think you know.'

'This is the swinging sixties.'

'That's as maybe. But I'll be saving meself.'

'You could always go on the pill.'

The look she gave him said it all.

He laughed again. 'OK.' He raised his hands. 'So me bringing you here to try and have me wicked way was a waste of time then?'

'Yes it was, and if that's all you brought me up here for, then hard luck.'

'No, honest, Pam. I didn't – well I thought I might try it on, just in case you wanted to. But don't worry. I won't try anything.'

She smiled. 'That's good. I don't fancy walking all the way home on me own.'

'I'd never do that to you.'

When they'd finished their lunch they wandered over the hill admiring the view. Pam found him easy to talk to and as they both sat and relaxed in the warm sunshine, she began to ask him about his family.

'Is your mother still alive?'

'Don't know. She left Dad not long after I was born. He said she went off with a Yank.'

'That's sad, not having a mum. My dad was dead before I was born. He was killed when a flying bomb hit what used to be a shop on the corner of our street.'

'Yer, I know.'

She looked up. 'You do?'

'Me dad told me.'

'It seems to me that everybody knows everybody else's business.'

'I think that was because it was such a terrible thing and it happened in the war.'

'I s'pose so.'

'You don't mind people knowing, do you?'

She shook her head.

'I think not having a mum around is why our Marc went off the rails when he left school. He can remember Mum. I can't,' he said sadly. 'Marco finished up in Borstal for a while. When he came out me dad gave him the biggest hiding of his life. It was after that Dad made him learn to drive and Dad bought another van. When I learned to drive Dad gave up working. Up to a point Marco's tried to toe the line ever since.'

'Don't see him about much.'

'No, he's got a different round to me. And he takes more money than me, and that keeps him in good favour with Dad. Mind you, he's always been the blue-eyed boy even though he's been trouble.'

Pam laughed.

'What's so funny about that?'

'You, calling Marc a blue-eyed boy when I expect he's got lovely dark eyes like you.'

Lu's face broke into a grin. 'So you think I've got lovely eyes, do you?'

'Yes,' she said, quickly trying to hide the fact that she'd noticed his eyes. 'Now, what was you saying about Marco and your dad?'

'Not a lot to say really. Just that at times he seems to hang around with the wrong sort of company and it would upset Dad if he found out.'

'It must have been hard for your dad to bring up three boys.'

'Yer. D'you know, when me and Marc was little, me dad

used to take us with him in his van. The fights me and Marc used to have while Dad was trying to serve! We must have been a right handful at times. What with running the van and doing the cooking and like, he should be sitting back taking it easy now. He thought that when Al married Jean they would live at our house, but she wanted a place of her own.'

'Can't blame her.'

'But she should have lived with us and helped Dad. She sometimes comes round and does a bit of cleaning, but I don't like her, she's a hard cow, always wants her own way. I think even Al's frightened of her.'

Pam laughed. Although she was older and they had never spoken to her, Pam knew all about Jean. She lived a few streets away and was always shouting at the kids playing in the street. She was always well dressed and walked about with her nose in the air. Most people felt sorry for Al, who was the oldest of the three boys. 'I wouldn't have thought that the Cappa boys would be frightened of anyone.'

'Don't you believe it.'

Although Pam would have dearly loved to ask more questions she didn't want to appear too nosy. She was warming to Lu and this family that carried on despite all odds.

After a while it was time for them to leave. When she sat on the bike behind Lu and held on to him she put her head against his back. Despite all her previous thoughts about him being a show-off, she was beginning to understand that he was a caring person.

'Thanks for a smashing day,' said Pam as she got off the bike outside her house. 'I've really enjoyed myself.'

'So have I. P'raps we can do it again?'

'I'd like that.'

'Would you? I'll tell you something, Bennetti must be in trouble, either that or a bloody idiot. Fancy not coming back to take a smashing girl like you out.'

Pam grinned, embarrassed. 'Best be going.' She didn't want him to kiss her goodbye as she could see Jill in her pyjamas at her window, and she didn't want her friend to get the wrong idea.

Pam knew Jill would be over early for work tomorrow to hear all about her day out.

She closed the front door and stood for a while. He was good company, but no, she'd done the right thing, she didn't want him to get any ideas.

Chapter 8

'You were so lucky today, the weather's been really lovely. Did you have a nice time?' asked Rose King when her daughter walked in.

'Yes I did.'

Her mother laughed. 'Just look at your face, you've really caught the sun.'

Pam glanced in the mirror over the fireplace and grinned. 'So I have. Me nose looks a bit red though, but look at me arms? That's gonner be something to show off at work tomorrow.'

'You'd better put some calamine on 'em, they look a bit sore to me,' said her gran.

'They'll be all right.' Pam moved her watch strap to admire the different colours on her arms.

'Well, where did you go?' asked Ivy.

'Surrey. To a place called Box Hill. It was ever so high up, you could see for miles. Any tea left?'

'There's some in the pot if you fancy it. It's not been there that long. Did you want something to eat?' asked her mother.

'No thanks. Me and Lu stopped at a café and had egg and chips. I'll have a wash, then I'll go on up. It's been a long day.' Pam didn't want to spend too much time with them as

91

she knew they would soon get round to discussing Luigi and she didn't want that.

As expected Jill was over promptly the following morning full of questions about Pam's trip with Luigi.

'Hello, girls,' called Doll Windsor as they walked past her house. She was on her hands and knees busy scrubbing her front doorstep. She straightened up and, sitting back on her haunches, brushed a stray blonde strand back from her forehead. Her bright yellow rubber gloves matched her hair. 'See you've caught the sun, Pam. I saw you go out on young Luigi's bike yesterday. Nice boy. He can be a bit of a cheeky sod at times, but he's a nice boy. Don't care for that sister-in-law of his round the corner though. She's got a mouth on her, that one has.'

The girls began giggling as they carried on past her house.

'She'll want to know the ins and out of all you got up to if we stop,' said Jill.

'So would Gran, I shouldn't wonder.'

'Well, what did you get up to?'

'Nothing. We're just friends.'

'So where did you go?'

Pam went into great detail of where they went.

'I've never heard of Box Hill,' she exclaimed when Pam finished telling her where they'd been. 'So you didn't have a roll in the hay then?'

'No we didn't.'

After talking about most things including the fact that Jill noted that Luigi hadn't kissed her good-night, Jill asked, 'Did he say any more about Robbie and the Mafia?'

'No.' Pam wasn't going to go into that again, not with Jill, but she was determined to find out more.

That evening after they had finished dinner, Pam went out. She was hoping Jill hadn't seen her as she made her way to the phone box.

As soon as the phone was picked up she pushed button A and said, 'Hello, is that Mrs Bennetti?'

'Yes. Who wants to know?'

'This is Pam. Pam King.' She gave a nervous little cough; the phone was beginning to get hot and sticky in her hand. 'I'm a friend of Roberto's. Could I speak to him please?'

She heard Mrs Bennetti take in a quick breath. 'I'm afraid not. He doesn't live in this country any more.'

It was Pam's turn to take a deep breath. 'Why?'

'I think that is his business, don't you?'

'Perhaps I could have his address then?'

'No. He doesn't want you to write to him. He doesn't want anything to do with you.'

Pam was stunned. She felt the tears stinging her eyes. 'But . . . But why?'

'He's very happy in Italy. So please stop calling this number.' The phone was replaced.

The buzzing on the line filled Pam's ears. Carefully she replaced the receiver and left the phone box. As she walked slowly home she went over and over the brief conversation she'd just had. None of it made sense. He had told his mother he didn't want anything to do with her, but why? If he was so angry at her not going to Italy, why didn't he tell her? She had written and explained it all to him, so why didn't he acknowledge that? Or was

Luigi right, and his mother was trying to hide something more sinister? Could she find out where he was? Could she go to Italy to find him?

'If you ask me you shouldn't be wasting your life waiting for him,' said Jill when she heard what had happened when Pam had phoned Mrs Bennetti. 'He's got your and my addresses, so if he really cared for you he'd find a way of getting in touch. You might even get a card on your birthday.'

'I shouldn't think so. I know you're right, but I can't help hoping. I was even trying to work out a way of getting to Italy.'

Jill threw her head back and laughed. 'How're you gonner do that? Hitch your way? I can just see you, you who ain't been anywhere on your own. You wouldn't even know where to start.'

'It was just a thought.'

'If I was you I'd be a bit kinder to Lu. He's good-looking, got a smashing motor bike and he fancies you like mad.'

'So what?'

'I think you should try a bit harder, that's all. Even your gran approves of him.'

'I know. That's funny, ain't it? I must admit that even if he can be a bit loud, he is good fun.'

'Well then. Don't go wasting your life waiting for something you can't have.'

Pam giggled. 'Hark at you.'

'Honestly, Pam. I want to see you happy and even you must admit that Lu brings a smile to your face.'

She nodded. 'OK. I'll give it a go.' She had to admit to herself that he was fun to be with. He did take her out and he was good-looking. Perhaps she should try a little harder now that Robbie had made it very clear that he didn't care for her after all.

Pam's birthday tea was very boring and she was pleased when Jill suggested they went to her house to watch the television.

The Sunday outings with Luigi had stopped as he had to work, but every Friday evening throughout April, Pam was able to go to the pictures with him.

'I wish we could go to the Palais one Saturday,' said Pam when Lu dropped her off outside her door.

'You know I can't go through the summer – well, not just yet, not at this time of the year. Me and Marc have to take our vans out otherwise Dad will go mad.'

'That's a shame. What about Bertie?'

'Dad ain't all that keen on letting him take the van out. He's frightened he's gonner fiddle him. No, you'll just have to wait till winter, when the trade drops off.'

Pam nodded. She was pleased in many ways that Luigi was at least considering taking her out in the future. She also knew he wouldn't be involved with the Mods and Rockers if he was working. That thought surprised her. Why was she suddenly concerned at what he did?

Time sped by that summer and Pam found she was enjoying being with Luigi more and more. She let him kiss her and put his arm round her in the pictures although she wasn't ready for any real romance just yet. In many ways she was beginning to get fond of him, but when things began to get a bit heavy she pushed him away. Still, he made her laugh, despite her worries that he might pick a fight and show her up.

'Can you give this invite to Lu?' asked Jill handing Pam an envelope. Jill was getting so excited about her wedding.

'Course. Are you going to ask Robbie?' Pam tentatively asked as they made their way to work.

'No, don't see the point.'

'I can't believe so much has happened in the past year.'

Jill smiled. 'Nor can I. This time last year we were getting ready to go off to Italy and I hadn't even met Billy.'

'I know, and I thought everything was going so well with Robbie and me.'

'Just goes to prove you never know what's round the corner. You ain't still carrying a torch for Robbie, are you?'

'No,' Pam said rather abruptly. 'But I would love to find out why he ditched me so quick.'

Jill tucked her arm through Pam's. 'I shouldn't worry about it. I reckon you're better off without him.'

'I think you're right.'

A few nights later, when Pam and Luigi were outside the cinema, Pam handed him an invitation. 'Jill asked me to give you this as she don't know your address and didn't want to give it to you when you was in the van.'

'I reckon you're gonner look really smashing at this 'ere wedding,' said Luigi, opening the envelope and looking at the printed card.

'I hope so.'

'I really appreciate Jill and Billy inviting me.'

'Will you be able to get the afternoon off?'

'Yer.'

'That's good.'

Luigi looked at Pam. 'D'you really mean that? D'you really want me there?'

'Course.'

'Won't I cramp your style with all the other blokes buzzing round you?'

'No.'

'Pam . . .' Luigi bent his head and whispered as they shuffled along in the queue towards the box office. 'I know you've kept me at arms' length, but I really do like you.'

'And I like you, you're a good friend.'

'I'd like to be more.'

Pam glanced round, embarrassed. She knew people were listening.

'Do you really want to see this film?' asked Luigi.

'Not fussed.'

'Look, why don't we go to the coffee bar round the corner for a change?'

'OK.' Pam was pleased he didn't suggest anywhere more private and it would be nice just to sit and talk. She really did enjoy his company, she realized.

Jill was beaming. She peeped out of the bedroom window. 'Looks like the whole of Newbury Street is out there.'

'They've all come out to wish you good luck, girl,' said Lil. 'Helen, come and look after young David, he's being a right little bugger.'

'I said he was too young to be a page boy,' said Jill's

sister Helen as she fussed round her four-year-old son.

'Don't wonner wear this sissy thing.' He pulled at the frills on his shirt.

'Well, I like being a bridesmaid and I'm going to behave myself,' said Jill's five-year-old niece Carol, as once again she looked at herself and preened in front of the mirror.

'Of course you are, darling,' said her grandmother. 'We ain't had a wedding in this street for years.'

Jill's mother adjusted her hat yet again. 'Are you sure this is all right?' She too peered in the mirror.

Bob tutted and looked at his wife. 'I've told you, Doreen, you look smashing. Now you and Mum, young Pam and the kids get down and into the car. Mustn't keep Billy waiting, and we can't go till you do.' Bob looked at his daughter standing in the doorway and said proudly, 'You look lovely.'

'Thanks, Dad.'

Pam swallowed hard as she kissed her friend goodbye. Then to the sound of the neighbours shouting out compliments and their good wishes – among other things – she manoeuvred herself into the car with Lil, Doreen and the children. 'She does look lovely,' said Pam.

'All brides have that certain glow. You wait till it's your turn, young Pam,' said Lil grinning. 'I must say you look really smashing in that frock, blue suits you.'

'It was Jill's choice. The colour *is* nice, and the neck's not too low.'

'We're so lucky with the weather,' said Doreen looking out of the car window. 'I was a bit worried about it when I woke up this morning, but it's turned out all right.' She smiled at Pam. 'It makes all the difference to the photos, don't it? Her flowers are lovely, I must remember to thank your mum.'

Pam knew it was her mother's present to Jill. That way they didn't have to spend too much on a gift.

Everything went off perfectly, even young David behaved himself in the car and in the church. Later, after the meal and speeches, everyone began to dance and enjoy themselves. When it was time for Jill and Billy to go on their honeymoon Pam found it hard not to cry.

'I'm gonner miss you,' said Pam, holding her friend close.

'And I'm gonner miss you. You must get Lu to bring you down to Brighton to see us when we get back.'

'I will. I will. I'm gonner be so miserable without you.'

'Come on, Jill, we must go.' Billy was standing behind waiting for his bride.

Throwing confetti, Pam ran with the crowd to the car and watched it till it was out of sight.

'Come on, love. Dry your eyes,' said Lu, taking her arm.

'I'm really gonner miss her. We're more like sisters than friends.'

'I know. I promised her I'd look after you.'

Pam looked up at him through her tears and smiled. 'You did? Thanks.' She put her arm through his and wandered back into the hall.

As the evening wore on the drink flowed, the music got louder and everybody was up dancing.

Luigi and Pam did the twist and jived together; when a slow song came on, Luigi held Pam very close. 'Pam, I think I'm in love with you.'

She giggled. 'You're drunk.'

He nuzzled his head into her neck. 'No I ain't. I do love you, Pam King, and I want to marry you.'

Pam stopped suddenly and he nearly fell over. 'What did you just say?'

'I asked you to marry me.'

'I can't.'

'Why not?'

Pam didn't reply.

'It's that bloody Bennetti, ain't it?'

'Shh, Lu, keep your voice down.'

'No I won't. D'you want me to get down on me bended knees?'

Pam quickly glanced around. She was embarrassed. People were looking. 'Don't be so daft. It's the drink talking.'

'It ain't the drink. I really love you, Pam.' He took her by the arms and kissed her lips hard.

Whoops and catcalls went up. 'Atta boy,' someone yelled. 'Go on, give her one,' shouted another.

Pam struggled to get away from him and ran from the hall. Luigi followed close behind.

She turned her back on him. 'How dare you make me look such a fool.'

'I didn't mean to. It's just that you look so lovely. I just couldn't resist you. And if you want I will get down on my knees and ask you to marry me.'

Pam began to giggle. 'You wouldn't, would you? What about your suit?'

'I don't care.' With that Luigi was on his knees and holding her hand. 'Christ, I never thought I'd be doing this.

Will you, Pam King, marry me? Please? And hurry up, this concrete's bloody hard on me knees.'

Pam was laughing. 'Why are you asking me all of a sudden? We're good friends and that's the way . . .'

He sat back on the floor and started to laugh with her. 'Me dad needs a cleaner.'

'What?'

'I'm only kidding.' He patted the floor. 'Come and sit down here with me.'

'Is it cold?'

'No, not when you've got my love to keep you warm.'

She hitched up the long skirt of her bridesmaid's dress and, with great difficulty, sat on the floor next to him.

'I really do love you, Pam, and, yes, perhaps a few pints have given me enough Dutch courage to ask you. I thought this was a good time. So, what's your answer?'

'I don't know. I'm very fond of you, but marriage – that's a very big step and I can't give you an answer, not straight away.'

'Why not?'

'I just don't know. Give me time.'

'Your gran likes me.'

'I know, but only because I told her we're friends.'

'I know you could learn to love me. Unless . . .' He stopped and became serious.

'Unless what?'

'The Bennetti curse.' He spat the words out.

Pam laughed. 'What are you talking about?'

'Our family has been cursed by them for generations. It's him, ain't it? Have you heard from him?'

'No. No, I haven't.'

'So what's stopping you then?'

'I don't know. My gran might not approve.' How could she tell him that she still clung to the faint hope that one day Robbie might come back into her life?

'Well then, if it ain't Bennetti, let's go and find out what your gran will say about it.' He stood up.

'No. No, don't.' Pam grabbed his arm. 'I'll tell her.'

'You will?'

Pam nodded. She knew what Ivy King thought about the Italians and as she was under age she had to get her mother's consent. Pam was also aware it was her grandmother who ruled the house, so felt sure she was on a safe thing.

Luigi pulled her to her feet. 'Come on, let's go and ask her.'

'I'd rather wait till I get her on her own.'

'Well, I'd rather hear what she's got to say now.'

'What if she makes a fuss? We can't spoil Jill's wedding day.'

'Jill's gone, besides she wouldn't dare. Not in front of everybody.'

'You don't know my gran.'

But, ignoring her protests, Lu grabbed her hand and pushed open the door to the hall.

The sound of music and laughter and the smoke assaulted Pam's senses. What if her gran said yes? She knew she was trapped. Everybody would say she would be a fool to turn him down.

'And where have you two been?' Ivy King didn't miss a thing.

'Outside.'

'I know that. So what have you been up to then?'

Pam tutted and turned away.

'I've been asking Pam here to marry me.'

'What?'

Ivy screamed it out so loud everybody stopped talking and looked over at them.

Lil came bustling over. 'You all right, gel?'

Ivy nodded. 'Yes thanks, Lil.'

Rose, who had been dancing, came hurrying to her mother-in-law's side. 'You've gone a funny colour, you're ever so pasty-faced. What's wrong?'

Ivy smiled. 'It's just that I've had a bit of a shock.'

'Shock, what sort of shock?'

Pam stood watching all these people standing round Ivy. She felt like she was in a dream. Luigi had his mouth open in total surprise at Ivy's outburst.

Ivy stood up. 'Your daughter's gonner get married.'

'What?' It was Rose King's turn to scream it out. 'Who to?'

Ivy pointed to Luigi. 'Him.'

All at once the noise started again. People were coming up to Pam, kissing her and shaking Luigi's hand. She was swept along into the middle of the room. She could see her mother was looking confused and bewildered, but she wasn't as confused and bewildered as Pam was feeling at that moment.

Chapter 9

Much later that night, as Pam lay in bed, she found her head wouldn't stop reeling through drink and the events that had led up to her drinking too much.

Everybody had seemed to ply her and Luigi with alcohol to celebrate their engagement. She turned over. Her engagement. She didn't even remember saying yes to him. Her mother and gran had been pleased when he asked them and her mother had hugged her and cried a little. She said it was through happiness and only wished her father were there to give them his congratulations. Though she knew it was selfish, Pam had always been pleased her mother had never found another man to love, as she couldn't bear the thought of having to share her with someone else. Now she was going to be married and move away and her father wouldn't be here to comfort her mother. A tear slowly trickled down her cheek. If only Granny and Grandad Mallory lived near. Would they be well enough to come to the wedding? Her wedding! Was she doing the right thing? Panic filled her. Tomorrow Luigi was taking her to meet his father to ask him if they could live there after they were married. As she became caught up in the euphoria, she remembered telling him she wanted to wait till they found a small flat somewhere, but Luigi said they didn't have to wait if they lived with his dad and Marco. Did she want that? She knew Marco had been in trouble in the past, but what sort of man was Mr Cappa? There was talk that he liked a drink.

The light was boring through Pam's eyelids even before she tried to open her eyes. She put up her hand to shut out the sun's rays as she heard her name being called. Her head was throbbing and when she did manage to get them open she saw her mother standing over her with a cup of tea in her hand.

'Good morning. Well, you certainly sprung a surprise on everybody last night. I wonder what Jill's gonner say about all this? Did she know?'

Pam tried to shake her head but it hurt too much. 'No,' she croaked. 'I didn't even know meself.'

'Oh.' Her mother sat on the bed. 'You two hadn't discussed this before then?'

'No. He just asked me out of the blue, and when I said I didn't think Gran would approve he said he'd ask her, and that was it really.' Pam sat up. 'Do you think I'm doing the right thing?'

'Well, that's up to you. Do you love him?'

'I don't know.'

'You should be sure before you make such a huge commitment. Remember it's for the rest of your life.'

'I know.' Pam drank her tea. 'This is good.'

'You're very young to make such a big decision,' Rose smiled. 'But then I can't shout – I wasn't much older than you when I got married. But that was because of the war and we didn't want to wait, in case . . .' Rose left the sentence unsaid.

'I expect it'll be a few years before we . . .' Pam couldn't bring herself to say 'get married'. It was a big step – was she ready for that yet? She was fond of Lu, but marriage? If only Jill were here, she needed to talk this over with someone. Jill had known almost right away that she wanted to marry Billy and couldn't wait. She was head over heels in love with him and never stopped talking about him. Perhaps if she could persuade Lu to have a long engagement then she would love him enough to be eager to get married too.

'Come down when you're ready,' said her mother, interrupting her thoughts. 'What time is Luigi picking you up?'

'Not till this evening after he finishes. He has to take the unsold stock back to the warehouse first, then he's coming over on his motor bike. Mum, do you like him?'

'I don't know him. All I know is that his family are a bit . . . well, loud, but that's only what I've heard. I don't really know that much about them.'

'What about Gran?'

'She seems pleased enough.'

'His grandfather was Italian.'

'I know.'

'So why does she approve of Luigi and she didn't like Robbie?'

'I don't know. Are you still pining for that boy?'

'No. It's been a year since I heard from him. He's probably got a girl be now.'

'Just as long as you're sure and this isn't because of Jill getting married and you're frightened of being left on the shelf.'

'What, at nineteen?' said Pam, trying to make it sound convincing.

'That's all right then. I must go.'

Her mother left. Was she sure? Pam didn't know the answer to that.

Lil was sitting at the kitchen table talking to her gran when Pam walked in. She looked up. 'Hello, young Pam. All right then?'

Pam nodded.

'Fancy you and that Luigi gonner get wed! That was a right turn-up for the book.'

Pam glanced at her grandmother who was beaming. 'He seems a nice enough young lad.'

Rose King pushed an ashtray towards Lil. 'Looks like we've got a bit of saving to do.'

'Don't like to worry you, gel, but our Jill's wedding cost a packet.' Lil squinted at them through a haze of blue smoke. 'Good job my Bob's got a few quid.'

Rose King pulled at threads in the brown chenille table-cloth. 'I don't suppose we'll have as many as Jill did. We ain't got that many on our side. But I'll be able to make all the buttonholes and bouquets, so that'll help.'

'What about your mum and dad, Rose – will they be coming?'

Rose shook her head. 'They live too far away. Besides, they ain't in all that good health. They're getting on a bit now.'

'That's a shame. There's a few of his lot, ain't there?' Lil asked Pam.

Pam pulled the spare chair from under the table and plonked herself down. She couldn't believe this conversation. They were planning her wedding. She didn't even know if she was doing the right thing. 'Just his dad, two brothers – they're both older than Lu – and Al's wife, as far as I know.'

'So when's the great day gonner be?' asked Lil.

'I don't know. Not for a while.'

'June's nice. That'll give us a few months to get some bits in,' said Ivy.

Pam could see her gran certainly approved and was enjoying her moment of glory.

'Where're you gonner live?' asked Lil.

'Don't know. We haven't discussed it. It all came as a surprise to me.'

'You mean you didn't know?' Lil flicked the dangling ash that was hanging precariously from the end of her cigarette into an ash tray. Pam had been watching it mesmerized, waiting for it to defy gravity and drop. But Lil was an expert.

'No.'

'You must have had some idea,' said Ivy.

'No, I didn't. When he asked me outside I laughed and said me gran wouldn't approve and with that he went straight into the hall and asked you.'

'I reckon that's real romantic,' said Lil. 'Did he go down on one knee?'

Pam blushed and looked down.

'He must have,' said Ivy enthusiastically. 'I bet he did.'

'And you obviously approved,' said Pam.

'Well, don't sound so upset.'

'You wouldn't even let me go out with Robbie and yet you don't mind me marrying Lu. What's the difference?

They both had Italian ancestors.'

Ivy began to look uncomfortable. 'Those Bennettis are a devious lot. They're no good and I didn't want you mixed up with them.'

'It doesn't matter now,' said Rose nervously. 'He doesn't live in this country any more.'

'Don't he?' said Lil. 'Why's that?'

'Don't know,' said Rose, looking at Pam.

'Well, it's all water under the bridge now,' said Ivy.

'I'll make some more tea,' Rose stood up quickly.

''Bout time too,' said Lil. 'Me throat's that parched. It feels like a sewer. Must have been all that singing last night. It was a lovely do. I wish I had more granddaughters.'

'I'll see to the tea,' said Pam. She didn't want to listen to them planning her wedding and she could see her gran wasn't going to say anything more about the Bennettis.

'Mind you, I think you're a bit young,' said Ivy.

Lil began to laugh. 'Christ, hark who's talking! You was only what – eighteen?'

'Things was different then, there was a war on.'

Lil gave her friend a knowing look. 'Yer, I know. I was there, remember?'

'I told me dad,' said Luigi when Pam opened the front door for him. 'He said he's looking forward to meeting you. Are you ready?'

'Yes. Bye,' she yelled out and, without waiting for an answer, followed Lu to his motor bike.

Pam knew the Cappas didn't live that far away, but was surprised to see it wasn't after all in the run-down part of Rotherhithe, near New Cross. Some of the houses seemed to be very nice but Lu pulled up outside one that was quite large, if a bit shabby-looking. The two ice-cream vans she knew so well, with 'CAPPA ICES' in capital letters on the front, were parked on the bomb site next door. Pam thought their business was better than the house showed. So different to the Bennettis. She got off the bike and followed Lu down the side of the house and into the back yard.

'It's only me,' he shouted as they made their way through the back door into the kitchen.

Pam looked at the pile of dirty dishes still on the table. The whole place smelt of smoke and cooking.

Pam could hear the sound of the television before Lu pushed open a door to another room.

In one armchair next to the fireplace sat Mr Cappa.

'This is Pam,' said Lu proudly.

Mr Cappa, a small man with a shock of grey hair, turned; his deep-set brown eyes quickly ran over Pam. He gave her a quick nod. 'Hello. Sit yourself down. I like this *Beat the Clock*.' Pam couldn't take her eyes off his baggy brown cardigan. There were burn holes dotted all over it.

Slouching in the other armchair opposite his father, with his legs dangling over the arm, was Marco. Although she hadn't seen him for years she was taken back by his dark smouldering good looks. He reminded her of James Dean. When he jumped up she could see he was head and shoulders taller than his brother.

'So, what have we here? Young Pam King. I hear you're gonner become part of the family.'

Pam could only give him a weak smile.

'Can I give the bride-to-be a kiss, young bruv?'

He didn't wait for an answer and taking hold of Pam

kissed her hard on the lips. He tried to force his tongue in her mouth but she kept her lips tightly closed. She wanted to push him away, but didn't want to make a fuss.

She looked pleadingly at Lu but he said nothing.

'If you ask me he's too bloody young to know his own mind, let alone get married.' Mr Cappa's eyes didn't leave the television screen all the while he was talking. 'You ain't up the spout, are you?'

'No, I am not,' said Pam rather more loudly than she intended.

'Take no notice of him. Here, give me your coat.' Lu helped her take off her coat and directed her to the sofa on the opposite side of the room. He sat next to her and put his arm round her.

It was cold away from the fire and she was glad of his warmth and snuggled close to him, then she began to look around.

The sofa felt sticky and the fireplace with its tiled surround looked as if it hadn't been cleaned for years. The mantelpiece was a jumble of cigarette cartons and odds and ends including a pretty vase that was stuffed full of papers. Above her in the centre of the ceiling the glass lampshade was broken. The dresser at the side of the fireplace had a mish mash of crocks, newspapers and magazines papers piled on it. She knew then she didn't want to live here. The very thought of it made her cringe.

As soon as *Sunday Night at the London Palladium* was over Mr Cappa filled his pint glass with beer from the bottle he had at the side of his chair, then he turned to face his son and Pam.

'Don't know why they have to keep bringing these

bloody Yanks over here. Who was that bloke anyway?'

'Roy Orbison,' said Pam, wide-eyed. She had been sitting watching, fascinated.

'Never heard of him. Bloody Yanks. Well, young lady, when are you and him thinking of getting hitched?'

'I don't know.'

'Well, I don't like the idea of you taking me son away from me. Don't like the idea of him sharing his lolly with a stranger.'

Pam went to speak but Lu pulled her closer. 'I expect Pam will stay on at work, won't you?'

Pam nodded.

'That won't be so bad, then.'

'I reckon it'll be rather nice to have a smashing-looking girl in the house. We could do with someone to liven up our lonely dark nights.' Marco gave her a wink.

'And since when have your dark nights ever been lonely?' asked Lu.

Marco grinned.

'Now don't start, you two. Perhaps it could be a good thing.'

Pam felt like running away. What had they been discussing? She wanted to shout out, I don't want to live here, but thought better of it. She felt very vulnerable.

'Make the girl a cup of tea,' said Mr Cappa to Marco.

'Her name's Pam, Dad.'

'I ain't very good on names.'

'So will this mean goodbye to a new bike then?' asked Marco, bringing in the tea.

'Shouldn't think so. As soon as I've done paying for this one I'll part exchange it and use the Triumph as the deposit.'

'I'll tell yer, mate, there ain't nothing like the thrill of having a Vincent throbbing between yer legs.' Marco gave Pam a wink and a grin. She cringed. And if they were going to save to get married surely Lu would change his mind about getting a bigger bike, she thought.

As soon as they finished having their tea Pam said she had to be off.

'So soon?' said Marco.

'I have to be up early.'

'That's the best thing about taking out the van, we don't start work till later when the streets are well and truly aired.'

'Yer, but we have to go to the factory to pick up the goods and we have to work in the evening and weekends, don't we.' Lu helped Pam on with her coat.

'Only in the summer,' said Mr Cappa. ''Sides, it keeps you out of trouble.'

Marco grinned. 'I used to quite enjoy a bundle down at Brighton duffing up those silly ponces on their glorified lawnmowers.'

'Just you keep out of trouble, my boy. Remember, all the time you live under this roof you'll do as I say. You're still not too big to feel my strap,' said Mr Cappa.

'Ready, Pam?' Lu took her arm and propelled her through the doorway into the kitchen. 'Take no notice of those two, they're always at each other's throats.'

Pam was very quiet as she sat behind Lu. She didn't like his father or his brother, but knew she couldn't tell him so.

At her door he held her tight. 'I do love you, Pam.'

She lifted her face for him to kiss her goodnight. She held him close.

'I'll see you as soon as I can,' he said. He didn't bring the van into Newbury Street in the winter as not many children lived there.

'OK.' She stood and watched him go off. Tears filled her eyes. What was she letting herself in for? But she wasn't going to marry his father or brother. One thing she was certain of was that no way would she live in that house.

'You're back early,' said her mother when she pushed open the kitchen door.

Pam gave a little laugh. 'Didn't want to wear out me welcome.'

'What they like?'

'All right. Where's Gran?'

'Next door.'

'I saw a bit of that *Sunday Night at the London Palladium*. It's very good.'

'They've got a telly?'

'We'll have to get one. It'll be nice before the winter.'

'Yes it would, but it'll be a while before we can afford the rent every week, especially now we've got a wedding to save for.'

'That'll be a few years yet. We've got to do a bit of saving ourselves first.'

'I hope you're going to have a white wedding,' said Rose.

'I haven't given it any thought.'

'Well, just think how the neighbours will talk if you don't.'

'I wouldn't be doing it for the neighbours.'

'No, I know. But it would please your gran and me.'

'We'll have to wait and see, and as I said it'll be a few years yet before . . .'

Rose King put her hand on her daughter's. 'Pam, I want you to be happy. So if you're not sure . . .'

Pam smiled. 'I will be sure when the time comes.'

'I do worry about you. You're all I've got.'

'I know.'

Rose brushed a tear from her eyes. 'Sorry about that. But I can't help thinking how proud your dad would be of you. You've grown into a lovely young lady.'

'Don't, Mum. You'll have me in tears. I wish Dad was still here too.'

'So do I.'

'Do you mind if I go on up? I think I've had a bit of a full weekend.'

'You can certainly say that.'

Pam kissed her mother goodnight and left her with her own thoughts.

Chapter 10

On Monday morning Pam sat on the bus feeling very sad and lonely without Jill to talk to.

When she arrived at Worth's Plumbers, the men inquired how Jill's wedding had gone, and made a few ribald remarks. She wasn't going to tell them that she was now engaged. She sat at her typewriter and engrossed herself in the stack of invoices before her.

As the week went on so Pam withdrew more and more into her shell.

'I don't know what's the matter with you,' said Ivy. 'You've been like a bear with a sore head all week.'

'I miss Jill,' Pam said as she stood in front of the mirror doing her hair. It was Friday night and she and Lu were going to the pictures as usual. 'I wish she was going to live round here.'

'Don't talk so bloody daft, she's married and she's had to go where her husband's work is. She's gonner be leading a different life from now on,' said Ivy. 'Instead of mooning about you should be doing something useful like a bit of sewing for your bottom drawer.'

Pam wanted to laugh. What did she know about sewing?

'You off out tonight?'

'Yes. Tell Mum when she gets in that I've had my dinner.'

'Let's hope that bloke of yours can bring a smile to your face.'

'His name is Lu. I wonder if Jill will come up and see her mum on Sunday?'

'Dunno. They might want to spend their first weekend at home in their own place.'

'Jill can't cook.'

'Well, she'll soon have to learn. If you want to keep a man happy, keep him well fed. Look, why don't you ask your young man to tea on Sunday? It'll give us a chance to meet him properly and find out a bit more about him.'

'I suppose I could.'

'That's settled then. I'll ask your mum to get a few extra bits in and I'll show you how to make a cake.'

Her gran was certainly making sure she was going to be a good wife, thought Pam as she made her way into the front room to look out for Lu.

'Pam, d'you mind if we don't go to the flicks tonight? We could go to a coffee bar. There's something I want to talk about.'

'OK.' She cocked her leg over the pillion seat of his bike and they roared off up the road.

In the coffee bar Pam asked Lu if he'd like to come to tea on Sunday.

'Yer, why not. I'll be round as soon as I've finished. Now the clocks have gone back it gets darker earlier so I'm not out so late. Pam, about us getting married.'

Pam looked up from stirring her coffee. He had a very serious expression on his face. Had he changed his mind?

'Yes,' she said timidly.

He touched her hand. 'Have you any idea when you'd like to tie the knot?'

'No. Can't say I've given it that much thought, it all happened so quickly.'

He sat back. 'Oh. I thought you was dead keen.' A look of rejection filled his face.

'I do want to get married, but let's wait a while, shall we? We've got to save up and we are a bit young.'

'I'll soon be twenty-three and you're, what . . .'

'I'll be twenty next March. As I was saying, let's wait a while and save a bit. After all I ain't got a dad that can pay for a big slap-up do. Not that I mind if we don't have one, but I think me mum wants me to get married in a church and that still costs quite a lot. What do you want?' She knew she was blabbing on.

He looked so deflated. 'Well, at least let me buy you an engagement ring, just to make it all official like.'

Pam smiled. 'I'd like that.'

'Well, you go and pick one out and then—'

'How much should I go up to?'

'Dunno, really. I can't say I've ever looked at the price of things like that.' He smiled. 'Only been interested in bikes.'

'Lu, would you sell the bike if we needed the money?'

'Dunno about that. It would have to be for a bloody good reason.'

'What about to buy a house?'

He leaned across the table and held her hand. 'I'd have to think about it. Wouldn't like to be without me own transport, but honestly, Pam, I'd do anything to make you happy.'

She felt very flattered. 'You are very sweet.'

'Well, at least with a ring everybody will know you belong

to me. But we could get married real soon if we live with me dad and Marc.'

'I would rather we wait till we can afford a flat or something.'

'Please yerself.'

Pam noticed a couple of blokes at the next table; one of them was grinning at her.

'Ah, hark at love's young dream,' he said to his mate. 'Will you buy me a ring?'

'The only one you'll get is through yer nose,' said his friend.

'In that case you ain't my friend any more.'

Lu turned. 'Just shut it, mate.'

'I ain't your mate. If you won't buy me a ring, can I come to the wedding then?'

Lu turned away.

'If yer like I could take the little lady to bed just to show her the ropes and let her see what a real man's made of.'

Pam couldn't believe the speed at which Lu jumped up and dragged the loud mouth up by his coat collar.

The cups on the table crashed to the floor and everything went quiet except the jukebox, where Connie Francis was belting out 'Stupid Cupid'. Then a couple of girls started screaming and the owner came racing round from behind the counter. He pushed the girls to one side and grabbed Lu who was on the floor battling with the troublemaker. He pulled Lu off and marched him towards the door.

'Get out. Get out the pair of you – and you,' he said to Pam. 'Or else I'll call the law.'

The other bloke brushed himself down. 'I'll get even with you, Cappa,' he said, walking towards the door. He stopped, turned, and pointing a finger at Lu, added menacingly, 'You mark my words. You ain't heard the last of this.'

'He started it!' Pam screamed at the owner, pointing to the bloke as he left.

'Leave it out, Pam,' said Lu.

'I don't care who started it. Out,' said the owner, pushing them through the door.

Outside it was pouring with rain. Pam anxiously looked up and down the road, afraid those blokes would be waiting for them. They hurried to shelter in a shop doorway.

'We should have gone to the pictures,' said Pam.

Lu put his arm round her shoulder. 'Thanks for sticking up for me.'

'I was frightened for you. I thought you might have got hurt. Did you know him?'

'Seen him around.'

'He knew your name.'

'A lot of people know us, don't they? See us on the van. I think him and Marc had a bit of a go at one time over some money, but I don't know that much about it. Nobody is gonner talk about you like that. But let's forget about him. Come here.'

She turned her face up towards his and he kissed her; she kissed him back. She snuggled up to him. She was happy. She knew he would be able to look after her.

On Sunday morning Pam raced down the stairs when she heard Jill shout out her name. As soon as she was in the hall Pam threw her arms round her best friend. 'It's so good to see you. I saw Billy's car and I knew you was here. I've got so much to tell you. What was Paris like?'

Jill stood back. 'Well, let me get me breath back first.'

'Let's go to my room. We can talk up there.'

'Hello, Jill,' shouted Rose who was standing with Ivy at the kitchen door. 'All right?'

'Yes thanks.'

'Married life suiting you then, gel?' asked Ivy.

Jill leaned over the banister as she climbed the stairs behind Pam and replied with a grin, 'I should say so. So. What's all this I've been hearing about you and Lu?' said Jill, sitting on the bed.

'I'm engaged.'

'So Mum said – and at my party as well. Is it for the right reasons?'

'What d'you mean?'

'You're not doing it in case you can't find anyone else, are you?'

'No, course not.'

'Do you love him?'

'I don't know. What is love?'

'Don't ask me. All I know is that as soon as I saw Billy I knew I wanted to spend the rest of my life with him. Do you feel that way about Lu?'

Pam shrugged.

'You've got to be sure.'

'What was Paris like?' asked Pam, deliberately changing the subject.

'Wonderful. We did so much, saw all the sights. Even been up the Eiffel Tower. I'm so lucky to have found Billy. And he don't mind that I'm not a very good cook. His mum's gonner teach me. As soon as we get our holiday photos I'll show you them. I can't wait to see the wedding photos. We were so lucky with the weather.'

'You did look lovely.'

'So did you. No wonder Lu proposed.'

'I miss you, Jill,' said Pam softly.

'I expect you do. But you wait till you're married. It's a lot different then. You won't have time to get lonely.'

'Lu wants me to live at his dad's house.'

'What's it like?'

'A slum.'

Jill's mouth dropped open. 'It's not that bad, is it?'

'Well, no, but with three men living there it does lack the womanly touch.'

'What's his dad like?'

Pam screwed up her nose. 'He likes a drink and I wouldn't trust Marco further than I could throw him.'

'Why's that?' said Jill, eagerly leaning forward.

'You should have seen the way he leered at me and he tried to kiss me – You know, french kiss!'

'No! Did you let him?'

'Course not.'

'You're not going to live there, are you?'

'Not if I can help it. I told Lu I want us to have our own place.'

'They're a bit hard to get, but believe me it will be for the best.'

Pam nodded. 'I know.'

'What did your gran say when Lu asked her? Fancy him doing it at the wedding.'

'I think it was just to make sure she couldn't show herself up by saying no. He's coming to tea tonight.'

'That should be interesting. Wish I was a fly on your wall.'

123

'So what's married life like?'

Jill giggled. 'All right.'

'Is that it? Just all right?'

'I ain't going into all the details but, take it from me, it's great.'

'Guess I'll just have to wait and find out for meself. But honestly, Jill, it is so good to see you. Will you be up here very often?'

'Don't know. It depends on Billy's job. I might even learn to drive.'

'No.' Pam laughed. 'I can't see me learning to ride a motor bike, can you?'

'Lu'll have to get a car when babies come.'

'I can't imagine me as a mum. What about you?'

'I'd love to have a baby, but we've decided to wait a few years.'

Pam sighed. 'You are lucky. Everything has fallen into place for you.'

Jill put her arm round her friend. 'And so it will for you. Why don't you get Lu to bring you down to see us. It's only a little flat, but we'll manage.'

'I'd really love that. I'll ask him tonight. Can I phone you at work?'

'Dunno. I'm a bit worried about starting a new job; Worth's Plumbers is all I've ever known.'

'You'll be all right.'

'Selling toiletries in a department store is a bit different to selling ballcocks to cheeky blokes. And it won't be as much fun.'

They laughed together, but both knew that their lives were changing. They were growing up.

★ ★ ★

Luigi was sitting at the table being interrogated by Ivy. She had asked after his father, saying she knew Lu's grandfather during the first war, when she was young and worked in a munitions factory. Lu was very surprised at that.

'You knew my grandad?'

'He was more on the management side. Didn't see that much of him. Me and Lil next door were on the production line. We both left when we was expecting.'

'Fancy that.' Lu looked at Pam before asking Ivy, 'Did you know the old man Bennetti?'

Pam felt her face turn scarlet. Why did he have to bring that name up?

'Yes, I knew him,' said Ivy. 'Never liked him. Nasty piece of work.'

'That's what my dad says. He can't stand to hear his name. They done us out of a lot of money, you know.'

'I did hear.'

'More tea, Lu?' asked Rose, who had been very quiet all through this conversation.

'Yes please. This cake is great.'

'Thank you, son,' said Ivy beaming.

'Don't get things like this at home. Dad ain't that good a cook. Jean, that's Al's wife, used to bring in our dinner when she lived round the corner, but then she moved. Dad reckons she did that on purpose.' He laughed.

'I'll have to give you a piece of my cake to take home,' said Ivy.

'Thanks. That'll be great.'

Pam knew then that he had won her gran over, and if she wanted to get out of this engagement she would have to battle with her gran as well as Lu. She smiled at Lu and he winked back. Her heart gave a little leap. Was this love? She did like him very much and suddenly she realized that she felt a bit odd, sort of incomplete, whenever he wasn't around. She missed him if she didn't see him every day. It was then she was sure she was doing the right thing. She wanted to spend the rest of her life with him. This *was* love. Whatever the Bennettis had done in the past, Robbie Bennetti was out of her life now.

Chapter 11

Two weeks after Jill's visit Lu took Pam down to Brighton. She was huddled close behind him, the wind stinging her eyes and making them water, but she didn't care: she was going to see Jill. It was times like this when she wished Lu had a car, but she knew he wouldn't swap his beloved motor bike.

It took them a while to find the address and when Jill opened the door the warmth swept over Pam.

'I'm frozen,' she complained as Jill hugged her.

'It is a bit nippy out there,' said Lu, taking off his goggles.

'Ought to get yourself a car,' said Billy to Lu as he took his leather jacket and gauntlets from him.

'This is very nice,' said Pam, looking round the room.

'Billy did it up before we moved in.' Jill was beaming proudly. 'It's not very big but it does us for now.'

Pam took off her glove and began waving her left hand about.

'Oh,' screamed Jill. 'You've got your ring. Let me see.'

Pam waggled her fingers in front of Jill.

'It's lovely. I like solitaires.'

'You get more for your money,' said Lu, putting his arm round Pam's waist.

'It ain't that big a diamond,' said Pam. 'But I like it.'

'So when's the wedding then?' asked Jill.

'We haven't got a date yet, but don't worry, you'll be the first to know.'

'I'd better be,' Jill laughed. 'Let me show you around.'

'That'll only take a few minutes,' said Billy. 'It ain't exactly a stately home.'

'It is to me,' said Jill as they moved from the main room into a small compact kitchen then into the bedroom.

Although it was small and sparsely furnished Pam did so envy Jill. It was her and Billy's own home. They had their own front door and didn't share it with anyone.

'This is just what I want,' said Pam.

Sitting on the small sofa Lu looked confident and, brushing back his hair with both hands, said, 'Well, me girl, if you play your cards right you might just get something like this.'

Pam kissed his cheek. 'It depends on what I have to do.'

'Marry me, that's what.'

All day they chatted and laughed; they even enjoyed Jill's cooking. Jill told them she was leaving her job as it was too boring; she had found another in the office of a builders' merchants. 'It's where Billy's boss gets his stuff from. It's more pay and I might be able to phone you from work. That'd be better than doing it in me lunchtime in a smelly phone box. And,' she said with great emphasis. 'We're saving up to buy a place of our own.'

'What, have a mortgage and all that?' asked Pam.

Jill nodded. 'It might be a bit difficult with Billy being in the building trade. He don't get paid when the weather's bad. But we're determined.'

'I'd like to find something a bit run down, then I'll be able to do it up,' said Billy.

'You are so lucky,' said Pam, smiling at them.

Later, in the kitchen, Jill hugged Pam. 'I'm really pleased about you and Lu. And Pam, don't get me wrong, I know a wedding is going to cost quite a few bob so, if you want, you can borrow my dress and veil.'

'Thanks.'

'We can do a few alterations on it, just to make it look a bit different, then nobody will be any the wiser.'

'I'll remember that.' Once again Pam felt the familiar envy seep into her. Jill had everything, even a new wedding dress.

The day sped by and all too soon it was time for Pam and Lu to go.

'I hope we can come again?' said Pam.

'Of course you can,' said Billy. 'You know you are always welcome.'

'Thanks.'

'I'll always be grateful to your gran mucking up your holiday,' Billy added, grinning. 'That was the best thing that ever happened to me.'

Jill quickly dug Billy in the ribs.

'I'm glad it turned out all right for you both.' Pam waved goodbye as they drove away, her thoughts on her future.

But they had only gone a little way from Jill's when Lu suddenly stopped.

'Is anything wrong?' asked Pam.

Lu turned off the engine but didn't get off the bike. 'I don't know. Pam, you have got over Bennetti, ain't you?'

She gave a little laugh. 'Of course. Why?'

'You turned pale and looked ever so sad when Billy mentioned that holiday business.'

'I still ain't forgiven me gran for doing me out of my trip to Italy.'

'Are you sure that's all it is?'

'Yes. Now come on, let's get home.' She put her arms round him and, nestling against him, held him very tight. She *was* sure she had got over Robbie, but there was always that sneaking worry at the back of her mind. If he ever came back into her life, would she run to him with open arms?

Two weeks before Christmas, Pam was taken back when Lu said out of the blue, 'Dad wants to know if you can come to dinner on Christmas Day? We're going round to Jean's.'

'I can't. I have to be with me mum and gran, but it was nice of them to ask me,' said Pam hurriedly. She knew she didn't want to go round there, she might end up doing all the washing up.

'Al and Jean are looking forward to meeting you. What about in the evening?'

'I'll ask me mum.'

'Good.'

'Can't say I like the idea of you not being here all evening. It's going to be boring and miserable with just me and Ivy,' said Rose when she heard what Lu had planned.

'Thanks,' said Ivy. 'So I'm boring and miserable, am I?'

'I didn't mean that. I suppose we've got to get used to the idea of sharing you.'

'You could always go over to Doreen and Uncle Bob's with Lil.'

'What's Jill doing this year?' asked her mother.

'Staying in Brighton with his people,' said Ivy before Pam could answer. 'And I can tell you Lil ain't all that pleased about it.'

'Christmas's supposed to be a happy time,' said Pam.

'And it's also a family time,' said Ivy in her matter-of-fact way. 'That's the trouble when today's youngsters move away.'

'Billy's parents are Jill's family as well now. It's very hard to please everybody,' said Pam, wishing she hadn't started this conversation.

'I know it is, love,' said Rose. 'But you can't tear yourself in two.'

Pam knew how hard it had been for her mother to stay here in London after her Dan had been killed. There must have been times when she wanted to be with her own parents but she'd always said it was her duty to look after Ivy who had no other family.

'I've been to see about getting a telly,' said Ivy. 'It'll be here for Christmas, so that might stop you being bored.'

'That's wonderful,' said Pam. 'But I really do have to go and show me face.'

'Course you do, love,' said her mother. 'It's always hard to make the break. Perhaps Lu can come to tea on Boxing Day.'

'That'll be nice. I'll ask him.'

Pam felt very guilty as she kissed her mother and gran goodbye on Christmas evening. She had told Lu not to bother to come and get her as she could easily walk the few streets. Although she didn't really know Al and Jean, Lu had told her about Jean's reputation for not making people welcome and she really didn't want to go to their house. But she didn't have a lot of choice if she wanted to show Lu how much she cared for him.

'Come in, Pam,' said Al when he opened the door. The hall was warm and had a lovely faint smell of cooking. Pam was surprised to see Christmas decorations in the hall, it made the place look very festive. 'We've really been looking forward to meeting you. Let me take your hat and coat.'

Pam smiled. Lu had told her about Al. She knew he was ten years older than Lu and that he was foreman at the furniture factory. He'd started work there when he left school at fourteen and went back again after he was demobbed. He had never worked for his father. Lu told Pam that when Mr Cappa came out of the army he bought an ice-cream van and when his wife left him he used to take Marco and Luigi out with him. Everybody felt sorry for him having to drag two youngsters about. There had been many rows when Al wouldn't leave his job to serve ice cream. When Marco was old enough to drive Mr Cappa'd got another van and when Lu could drive, the old man gave up working.

Jean was a secretary in the office where Al worked and that's where they had met. They had been married about five years. Lu had told Pam that Jean was a very forthright person who didn't suffer fools gladly. He wasn't that fond of her, but she was a good cook.

'Welcome to the family.' Al kissed her cheek.

'Thanks.'

Al had a shock of dark hair and with his brown eyes you

could see he was a Cappa. He was about as tall as Marco but not so broad.

'Thought it was you,' said Lu, coming up to her and kissing her lips.

Pam felt embarrassed, but neither of the men noticed.

'This way.'

Pam followed Al and Lu into the front room where a blazing fire was burning in the grate and a Christmas tree with lights and baubles glinted in the corner. The room had paper chains, bells and stars hanging from the ceiling. It looked warm and inviting.

Mr Cappa was sitting on the expensive-looking sofa with a glass of beer in his hand, watching the television. He was wearing a new cardigan. He looked over his shoulder and gave Pam a nod. 'All right, gel?'

'Yes thanks.'

Marco was sitting in one of the two matching armchairs; the furniture all looked very new. He jumped up when Pam walked in.

'That's a bit of luck, you're right under the mistletoe.' He took her into his arms and kissed her full on the mouth; once again he tried a french kiss but Pam was ready for him this time and quickly pulled away.

'So this is Pam King. I've seen you about.' Jean Cappa looked Pam over.

'Thank you for inviting me here tonight,' said Pam.

'It wasn't me.'

'Would you like a drink, Pam?' asked Al hastily.

'Yes please.'

'We've got Babychams.'

'That's fine.' Pam felt very uneasy, as if she were on show.

'Come and sit here,' said Lu, patting the sofa. 'Move up, Dad.'

Mr Cappa tutted, and his eyes never left the television.

'This is very nice,' said Pam, looking round.

'We both work hard for it,' said Jean abruptly.

Immediately Pam wished she was back at home. There she could at least relax. She knew she would be perching on the edge of her seat all evening; even though Lu had his arm round her, she sat stiff and upright. Please don't let me spill this drink, she thought to herself.

About nine o'clock Jean announced she was going to do the supper.

'I'll help,' said Pam, grateful for the excuse to stand up.

'Please yourself.'

In the kitchen Pam wanted to admire the decoration and fittings, but knew Jean would think she was being nosy. Instead she asked, 'What would you like me to do?'

Jean shut the kitchen door and turned on Pam. 'How well do you know the family?'

Pam was taken back. 'Not that well, I suppose.'

'I hope you ain't just trying to wheedle your way in 'cos you think the old man's worth a bob or two.'

'I . . .'

'Al's the oldest and when the old boy does pop his clogs it'll be up to him who gets what.'

Pam stared at Jean. She couldn't believe they were having this conversation. Suddenly, despite feeling intimidated and out of her depth, she knew she had to answer back. 'It's Lu I'm going to marry and I can assure you I'm not interested in anything Mr Cappa has.'

Jean went to the cupboard and taking out some jars

plonked them on the table. 'He might tell you that he rents that house and look as if he ain't got two ha'pennies to rub together, but *I* can tell you he's got a few bob stashed away and I ain't put up with his whingeing all these years to be done out of me dues.'

Pam was desperately hoping Lu would come in to rescue her.

'I don't know if you know but when we first married we lived near them.'

Pam nodded. 'Lu did tell me.'

'Did he. What did he say?'

'Just that you used to take them a dinner every night, and that you were, are, a good cook.'

Jean gave a slight smile at that. 'Every night I took them all in a meal. At weekends I did his cleaning and washing and he always told me that he'd leave me something in his will. He told me he had quite a bit, but he never paid me a brass farthing. He's a mean old sod. Every Christmas I have to have him here for Al's sake and he only takes his eyes off the telly to eat. Now you can see why I'm worried that you might get more than you deserve. You can take these pickles into the other room.'

Speechless, Pam picked up the jars and did as she was told.

'It's a bit cold.' Pam cuddled up to Lu as he walked her home.

'You was very quiet tonight.'

'I know. I was angry and frightened I might have said something I shouldn't.'

He stopped and Pam watched his breath forming clouds

in the clear chilly night air. 'Why? What happened? Was it Marc? I'll kill him if he tried to—'

'No, it wasn't Marc, it was something Jean said.'

'You don't wanner take no notice of her. Anyway, what did she say?'

'She reckoned I was only marrying you 'cos your dad has got a few bob and I wasn't to make up me mind that I'd get some of it.'

Lu burst out laughing and they moved on. 'Me dad got a few bob? Well, I'd like to know where he keeps it.'

'She seemed very sure about it.'

'I'll have to tell Marc this one.'

'No, don't, he might tell Jean.'

'I don't think so, he don't like her any more than I do.'

'But she did look after you all at one time.'

'Gave us a dinner, that's all.'

'What about the washing and cleaning?'

'I think she used to do a bit. It's Al I feel sorry for. He works all the hours God sends just to keep her in the luxuries she asks for.'

'She works as well,' said Pam, jumping to Jean's defence.

'I know, but she should be staying at home having babies.'

'Is that what you want me to do?'

'If you come from a good Italian family that's what you do.'

'But you ain't born Italian.'

'I know, but it's a good excuse to keep trying though, ain't it?'

'Lu, I'll be going on the pill when we're married 'cos I want to wait to have babies. I'd like a nice house with a garden first.'

He stopped again and, turning her head, he kissed her long and hard. 'You could go on the pill now.'

'No.' She pulled away from him. 'I want everything to be proper.'

'Why? This is supposed to be the swinging sixties. All the girls are on the pill.'

'Well, I ain't. I want my first time to be nice, not doing it in some grotty doorway. That's not what I want.'

He pulled her close. 'I love you very much, Pam King, and I promise I'll give you everything you want.'

She trembled and kissed him back.

'When shall we tie the knot?' he whispered as he kissed her ear.

'I don't know.'

'It would be great if we could do it next week.'

Pam laughed. 'Next week! My poor mum would have forty fits if I told her that.'

'I don't want to wait too long.'

'We'll talk it over. We'll have to find somewhere to live first and places ain't that easy to get.'

'We'll sort something out. I know a few blokes and I'll ask around.'

Pam kissed him. 'Thank you. Come on, it's cold.'

'I'll be able to keep you warm for the rest of your life.'

She smiled. That was a nice thought. And it was something she was looking forward to.

Chapter 12

The next evening they sat round the fire in Ivy's front room. The atmosphere was far friendlier than on Christmas night. The small tree wasn't as grand and the decorations not so plentiful but Pam was able to relax.

Ivy was full of stories about how she had looked after her granddaughter when she was young. Much to Pam's embarrassment Ivy brought out old photos, including one of her and Jill naked, running around on the beach when she was just two.

'That's when we went to Southend for the day with Lil and young Jill. We had a great time that day, couldn't keep the little devils out of the water. Soaked all their clothes, they did, and had to run about till they was dry.'

There was plenty of laughter and Pam could see Lu was enjoying himself, very much at home.

He was studying a photo of Pam. 'D'you know, I ain't got any pictures of me when I was little.'

Ivy took a breath. 'None at all, son?'

'No. I think Dad was too busy to worry about taking pictures.'

'That's sad,' said Ivy. 'Very sad.'

Pam's heart went out to him. What sort of childhood had he had? It must have been very hard.

DEE WILLIAMS

She looked at the blissful scene; she didn't want it to end. She was happy with the three people she loved.

Later that night Pam stood in the passage locked in Lu's arms.

'Did you mean what you said last night?' she asked.

'What, about getting married next week?'

'No, silly.' She laughed softly. 'About us looking for a place to live?'

'Course.'

'I'll be twenty in March and I was wondering ... it would be rather nice if we could have a June wedding.'

'Sounds great to me, but six months? Dunno if I can wait that long to ... you know.' He nuzzled his head in her neck.

She pushed away the hand that was cupping her breast and looked towards the stairs. Her mother and gran were in bed. 'You'll just have to. When shall we start looking?'

'Will your mum give you permission to get married?'

'I should think so. After all, they like you.'

He grinned. 'It's me winning ways.'

'Is that what it is?'

'If you like I'll start asking around in the new year.'

'Nineteen sixty-five. We're going to have a wonderful year.'

'I hope so.' He kissed her long and hard and even she wasn't sure if she could wait till June to prove how much she loved him. Six months was a long way away.

'June ...' said her mother the following morning.

'Can I?'

'I suppose so,' said Rose. 'Can't have you racing off to Gretna Green, can I?'

140

'Where you gonner live?' asked Ivy.

'Lu's going to ask around to get the feel of things and find out about rents and that. He knows a lot of people.'

'Don't you have to give these so-called money-grabbing landlords some sort of key money these days?' asked Ivy. 'Lil was telling me that Jill's bloke had to fork out fifty quid for their place.'

'I know, Jill told me.'

'So where're you gonner get that sort of money from?'

'I don't know.'

'P'raps he could sell that bike of his,' said Ivy. 'Noisy thing.'

'I don't think he would. We'll just have to save that bit harder, that's all.'

'Well, we'll have to start planning. We've got six busy months ahead of us.' Rose was trying to keep the disappointment from her voice. She didn't want her daughter to leave home.

'D'you think Grandad and Granny Mallory will come?'

'No, love. Grandad couldn't make the journey from Leeds. We'll try and get up to see them before and you can send them a bit of cake, they'd like that.'

'We can send them some photos as well.'

Rose smiled and nodded. 'P'raps you and Lu could go up and see them after you're married.'

Pam smiled back at her mother. 'Why not. That would be rather nice.' She hadn't seen her grandparents for many years. They lived so far away and her grandad wasn't very well. She knew her mother worried about them.

Time was flying past. It was Pam's twentieth birthday next

141

week. Jill, who was over the moon at the news of the wedding, was coming up for the weekend and they were going out. Pam had in the end decided to borrow her friend's wedding dress.

'I must admit I don't like the idea of it,' said her mother. 'It would have been nice if I'd had one to hand down.'

'There was a war on then, remember?'

'As if I could forget.'

'You still looked lovely.'

Rose gave her a weak smile. 'Thanks.'

'Look, Mum, if I'm going to have a white wedding it's pointless in me paying out that sort of money on a dress to wear just for a few hours when we might need it for furniture and things.'

'Suppose so. Has Lu had any luck with a flat yet?'

Pam shook her head. 'We've looked at some right old dumps and they want a fortune in rent. Just as well I didn't fancy any of them.'

'Well, time's getting on.'

'I know that, don't I,' said Pam agitated.

'Don't get shirty with me, young lady. I know you're under pressure, but it is your own making.'

'I'm sorry, Mum.'

'Are you sure you're doing the right thing?'

'Of course. Why did you ask?'

'You've been talking in your sleep.'

'Have I? What have I said?'

'I couldn't understand it, it was all a bit of a jumble.'

Pam smiled. 'That's all right then. I'm not giving any of me secrets away.'

'Have you got any then?'

'No, course not.'

Rose picked up the teapot and began pouring the tea into the cups. She pushed one towards Pam, grateful her hand was steady. She was worried and didn't like to tell her daughter that she had been calling out Robbie's name. Was she doing the right thing? Was she happy at marrying Lu? 'So, where are you all going on Saturday?'

'Only out for a meal, nothing expensive, but it'll be nice to go out with Jill and Billy. She's bringing her dress up, so if we need to alter it I've got plenty of time.'

'It should fit, you're about the same size.'

Pam sipped her tea. She would have liked her own wedding dress, but it wasn't to be and she was more concerned about getting a place to live. Some of them wanted such high rents. Should they wait a bit longer till they had more money?

'Penny for them.'

'I was just wondering who will be giving me away.'

'Why don't you ask Jill's father?'

'That's a great idea. Thanks, Mum. D'you think he'll do it?'

'I reckon he'll be more than pleased. After all he's known you since you were a baby. And Lil's like a second grandmother to you, isn't she?'

Spring had given way to summer. The nights were long and light and Pam didn't see that much of Lu, and she was beginning to get worried. It was only four weeks to the wedding and they still hadn't found anywhere to live. Every week she scoured the local paper looking for rented property.

'What we going to do?' she asked Lu after they'd looked at another place that was expensive, damp and filthy dirty.

'You know we could always stay at our place. I have got me own room, so it wouldn't be all that bad. Dad's really sorry we ain't moving in with him.'

Pam knew that was the last thing she wanted. She would rather cancel the wedding than move in with Mr Cappa. She had only been to the house a few times since Christmas and each time she'd felt uncomfortable. He hardly spoke to her and she couldn't understand why he wanted her to live there.

'Don't worry, I'm sure something will turn up.'

It was at the end of that week when Lu came round and told her he'd found something. They raced up to the High Street and he stopped outside the fish and chip shop.

'Here?' she said, getting off the bike.

'I was telling Frank last night and he said him and his missis was moving out of upstairs. He's bought a house over Blackheath way.'

'Will they let us have it?'

'Let's go and have a look first.'

Upstairs Elsie, Frank's wife, gave them a quick tour round.

'I know it ain't all that big, but me and Frank have managed all these years. You've got your own front door. By the way, we'll be taking most of the good stuff with us, but it will be partly furnished.'

'When are you moving?' asked Pam.

'The beginning of June. The light nights will give us a chance to settle in. When are you two getting married?'

'June the fifth.'

'That works out about right then.' Elsie went into a few dos and don'ts then finally said, 'Look, I must get back in the shop otherwise his nibs will start yelling for me. Come back next week and I'll get a rent book sorted out.'

'Thanks,' said Pam as they walked down the stairs. She knew they had found what she wanted. It was on the main road and above a fish shop, but she didn't mind.

'I can't believe it. Three pounds a week rent and she only wants twenty-five pounds key money.' Pam was almost beside herself with happiness and held on to Lu's arm as they walked out of the shop. 'Ain't you pleased?' she asked him.

'Of course I am, but there's a bit of work to do, and I don't fancy sleeping in that bed.'

'I must admit it does look a bit grotty, but she did say we could bring in some of our own bits and pieces. We could ask about bringing our own mattress.'

'That's not a bad idea. P'raps we could try it out first.'

She laughed and gave his arm a little punch. 'That's all you think about.'

He held her close and kissed her. 'I'm only marrying you so I can have me wicked way with you.'

'Well you've only got another four weeks to wait.' She laughed. 'I suggest you go and have a cold bath to cool your ardour.'

'You're a cruel woman and no mistake.' He kissed her forehead. 'That's why I love you.'

All the preparations were going as planned. They were having just a small buffet reception in the church hall and Rose, Ivy, Lil and Doreen had been doing the cooking. The day before the wedding Jean Cappa brought round some bits but she didn't stay.

'Fancy her bringing all this cheese,' said Ivy.

'And those biscuits,' added Lil. 'Mind you, I should think they could afford it.'

'She sent round all those lovely serviettes as well,' said Rose.

'I don't want anybody to think we can't give our Pam the best,' said Ivy.

'Nobody thinks that,' said Lil. 'What d'you want me to do now?'

'Sort out that salad stuff.'

Rose had been busy all day making the bouquets and buttonholes and they were outside with damp cloths draped over them so they didn't droop in the heat.

That night Pam lay in bed looking at Jill's wedding dress that was hanging behind the door, sheeted over. She couldn't believe that this time tomorrow she would be Mrs Cappa. Was she doing the right thing? Did she want to leave this comfortable home to live in a couple of rooms above a fish shop? Every night she would have to get her own dinner instead of walking in and just sitting at the table. They couldn't live on fish and chips. Every week she would have to do her and Lu's washing. She turned over. I don't remember Jill feeling like this the night before she got married, but then she really loved Billy and would do anything and go anywhere with him. Was that it? Did she really love Lu? Why did all these doubts creep into her mind?

The following morning the sun streamed through the window. Pam looked up above and said a silent thank you. That was every bride's wish, that the sun would be shining on their great day.

'You look lovely,' said Rose with tears in her eyes as Pam stood in front of the mirror and made the final adjustments to her dress. She didn't want her daughter to leave home. All these years she'd had her to cling to and work for; now Pam was going.

'Thanks, Mum.' Pam held her mother close, biting her lip to stop it trembling. 'The flowers are wonderful.'

'Well, if I can't give me own daughter the best bouquet I can make, where would we be?'

'You ready, Rose?' shouted Ivy up the stairs. 'The car's here.'

Ivy had been up earlier to wish Pam luck; she too had tears in her eyes. 'I only wish it was your dad that was giving you away,' she had sniffed and quickly left the room.

Jill was Pam's matron of honour and she had insisted on buying her own dress. As she stood in the doorway looking at her friend, she said, 'That frock didn't look nearly as good on me as it does on you.'

'Thanks. You didn't mind me doing the alterations, did you?'

'Don't be daft. Course not. I'm only glad it's being used again. It don't look the same now.'

Pam smiled.

Bob shouted up the stairs, 'Come on, you lot, it's time to go.'

'OK, Dad.' Jill kissed Pam's cheek. 'See you in church.'

Pam nodded. She was alone. After all the build-up these past months, now it was actually going to happen. She was going to marry Luigi Cappa. She put her veil back over her head and discreetly pulled back the net curtain and looked below at the neighbours gathered round the gate. Dolly Windsor was up the front as usual.

'You ready love?' She hadn't heard Jill's dad come up the stairs and although Bob's voice was soft it made her jump.

She nodded.

'Not got second thoughts, have you?'

She grinned. 'No, course not.'

'Well, if you have, now's the time to skip the country.'

'What, and miss my weekend down at Ramsgate?'

They laughed together. Everybody knew they could only go away for the weekend as Lu had to work. His father had told him he couldn't spare him for a whole week. So they'd settled for a weekend at Ramsgate. Not for her a trip abroad wearing a neat suit and hat like Jill. They were going to Ramsgate, on the motor bike.

When Pam walked down the aisle, Lu turned, smiled and gave her a wink. Her heart jumped. He was so good-looking and she loved him so much.

After the meal, during which, Pam noted, Jean wrinkled her nose at the wine, it was time for the dancing and drinking. Pam did worry that Mr Cappa might get drunk, but to her relief he behaved himself. That could have been because Ivy and Lil kept him talking a lot of the time. They said they were reminiscing.

Although Pam knew her wedding wasn't as grand as Jill's, everyone said they were enjoying themselves.

Pam felt both happy and sad when it was time for them to leave.

First Marc held her close and kissed her full on the lips.

'Welcome to the family,' he whispered when she pulled away.

'That looked interesting,' said Jill drily.

'Don't worry. I'll make sure he keeps his distance.'

'I hope so. You have a smashing time,' said Jill clutching her friend.

When Rose held her daughter tight, she croaked. 'God bless love.'

Pam was trying to fight back the tears.

Rose took Lu's hand and kissed his cheek. 'Take care of her,' she whispered. 'She's all I've got.'

Lu put his arm round his mother-in-law's shoulder. 'Don't worry. I'll look after her.'

There was plenty of shouting and laughter when Pam and Lu went to leave and everyone saw his motor bike had a 'just married' sign tied to the back.

'Are you going to take it off?' asked Pam smiling.

'No fear. I want the world to know what a lucky bloke I am,' he grinned. 'I've just married the prettiest girl around.'

Pam kissed his cheek and hopped on the bike behind him. She held him tight. She was so happy she couldn't speak.

After the Ramsgate weekend it was back to work for Luigi, but Pam had taken the week off and spent her time cleaning the flat. They had a little kitchen, a bedroom, a living room and a very compact bathroom. Downstairs their front door opened up on to the street below so they didn't have to go through the shop.

Every evening the smelly fat from the fish and chips wafted up the stairs. Would she ever get used to it?

After her first day back at work she felt miserable as she

walked home. She was nearer to Worth's now and didn't have to catch the bus. Why didn't she feel elated at having her own flat to go to? She was happy when Lu was around but as it was summer he seemed to spend all his time out with the van.

Her mother had popped in to see her and told her to come to dinner on Sunday.

'We can save a plate for when Lu gets in,' she said.

So on Sunday Pam went to her mother's.

'Everything all right then, love?' asked Ivy.

'Yes. Great,' she replied cheerfully.

'How are you managing?' asked her mother.

'All right.'

'If there's anything we can let you have, you only have to ask.'

'I know that, Mum. I'll just take a few more of my bits tonight.' She went up to what used to be her bedroom and sat on the bed. She loved Lu, so why did she feel so down? Why wasn't she bubbling over with joy, just as Jill was? She wandered over to wardrobe and took out a couple of skirts. They smelt clean and fresh. She buried her head in them and cried. What was wrong with her? She needed someone to talk to.

'Can't you have one Sunday off?' Pam asked Lu on Monday when he got home.

'You know I can't so don't keep on.'

Pam turned away and went into their tiny kitchen.

Lu came up behind her and put his arms round her waist and kissed the back of her neck. 'You know Dad depends on me and Marc,' he whispered.

'Why can't you leave Marc to get on with it? You don't live there now. Why can't you get another job somewhere else?'

'I couldn't let Dad down and I couldn't work for anyone. No, I've got to be me own boss. Besides, you knew all this when you married me.'

'I know, but I didn't think I'd be so lonely.'

He turned her to face him and kissed her long and passionately. 'I know what'll cheer you up,' he said, slipping his hand inside her blouse and steering her towards the bedroom.

'I'll make a cuppa,' said Lu, smoothing down his hair and lightly kissing her cheek. He walked naked across the room.

Pam watched him, admiring his lovely body. He was so good looking and he loved her. She was very lucky.

She lay on her back listening to the sounds from the street below. As it was early Monday evening it wasn't as noisy as the weekend when the pubs turned out and everybody wanted fish and chips to take home. Their first Friday night in the flat she'd thought she wouldn't be able to sleep at all, what with all the shouting and singing, but after making love she'd found she relaxed and, snuggling in Lu's arms, had soon dropped off.

Lu climbed back into bed. 'I've been thinking. As soon as I can I'll take a Sunday off and we could go and see Jill, how d'you fancy that?'

She quickly sat up. 'That sounds wonderful. Thanks.'

'I know a better way you can thank me.'

When Lu made love to her she knew she loved him and wanted to be with him for ever.

Chapter 13

Pam pulled her scarf tighter round her neck and thrust her hands deep into her coat pockets. She used to hate the winter but now, since being married to Lu, there was a good thing about the dark evenings: the fact her husband would be home when she walked in. The flat would be warm, the kettle singing softly on the gas stove and the dinner simmering. She smiled to herself. He loved her so much that sometimes they didn't even wait to have dinner first. She crossed the road and looked up. The flat was in darkness. Where was he?

As she mounted the stairs she called out his name. There was no reply. She turned on the light and looked around for a note, but there was nothing. Everything was just as she had left it that morning.

She shivered and quickly plugged in the electric fire, then made herself a cup of tea. As she sat in the armchair nursing the cup she reflected on the past five months of her married life. She was happy in many ways, but loneliness was her biggest problem. After always having her mother, gran and Jill around she felt very alone with no one to talk to. Suddenly she regretted the fact that she and Jill had been so close and not had other friends. Even at work there were only the young spotty apprentices who wandered round the yard waiting to load the vans for their bosses. The bosses were usually old men and they didn't often come into the office unless it was to argue and complain about a bill; you certainly couldn't have a decent conversation with any of them.

Pam loved Lu and was very happy when they were together, but in the summer she saw so little of him and the only thing she had to look forward to was spending Saturday afternoon shopping and Sunday at her mother's. Perhaps this Sunday they could go down and see Jill again.

She looked at the clock on the wall. It was nine o'clock. He should have been home hours ago. Where was he? Panic filled her. Had anything happened to him?

Perhaps he'd left a message with Elsie. Pam hurried down to the fish shop.

'Hello, love, you having a bit of fish tonight? Got some nice skate in,' said Elsie who, because it was Tuesday, their quiet day, only had Tom, the lad who helped her, in.

'I don't know. I'm a bit worried about Lu. Has he been in?'

'No, can't say I've seen him. Have you, Tom?'

Without looking up, Tom shook his head as he swished the fish around by its tail in the creamy batter, then placed it in the sizzling hot fat.

'You don't want to worry about your old man, you'd know soon enough if anything was wrong,' said Elsie. 'Blimey, half the time things round here ain't even happened before you hear about 'em.'

'Yes, I'm sure you're right.'

'I'm glad you've settled in OK.'

'Yes it's very nice. What about you now the winter's here?'

Elsie smiled a big wide smile to match her big wide frame. 'It's lovely. Was the best thing Frank and me's ever done. Mind you, I dunno what he'll be like come next summer, he loves that garden and I reckon I'll have hell's own job to get him here then.'

Pam smiled. 'It must be a nice change for you both to smell flowers and not fish.'

Elsie laughed. 'I should say so. Now don't you go worrying, that boy'll be home before long, just as soon as his stomach starts rumbling.' She turned to the customer who had just walked in. 'Yes, love. What can I get you?'

Pam moved out of the way. 'I guess you're right. Bye.' Slowly she walked up the stairs. Where was Lu? He always let her know where he went and if he was going to be late.

She sat listening to the radio, letting her thoughts drift. They hadn't had a chance to go and see Granny and Grandad Mallory before or after they were married; perhaps they could go now, before the bad weather came? Pam had written to them and sent them the wedding photos and a piece of cake. It was in the winter that she wished they had a car; she didn't really relish going all that way on the back of a motor bike.

Suddenly she began to get angry. 'If he and Marc have been looking at a new bike, I'll . . . I'll . . .' she said out loud.

For a while after they were married Lu had been talking about trading his bike in for a larger model but Pam had been against it. We need the money, you can't go wasting it, she had told him. That had made him angry and they had had their first row. He had said it was his money, and complained that all his life he'd had to look after his dad and help keep him, now *she* was telling him what to do with his money. She had cried and said she was working and wasn't a burden. He had been very sorry he had upset her, and had tried to see things her way. It was then they had decided to save enough to put a deposit on their own house one day, like Jill and Billy were planning to do. They knew they would never get a council house, not till they had hordes of kids and Pam didn't want that, not yet.

Had Marco made him change his mind? Marc was always edging him on, saying his bike was faster and challenging him to race whenever they could. At times they were like little boys. Or had something happened . . .? She couldn't even bear to think of it.

It was ten o'clock when the sound of feet on the linoed stairs woke her. After her anger had subsided she had sat listening to the radio and must have dozed off. The door opened and Lu walked in.

Pam jumped up and threw her arms round his neck. 'Where have you been? I've been so worried about you.'

He untangled her arms and pushed her away. It was then Pam realized he looked drawn and dishevelled. 'What is it? What's happened?'

'I've been at the police station for hours.'

'Oh my God,' she said putting her hand to her mouth. 'What's happened?'

'That bloody brother of mine. He had been causing, as they politely put it, an affray.'

'Who, Marc?'

Lu nodded.

'What's he done?'

'Been in a fight.'

'Is he all right?'

'He's got a few bruises, but the other fellow ain't so good.'

'Who was he? Did you know him?'

'I've seen him around. I think he's a bit of a fence, but I'm not sure.'

'You mean he buys stolen goods?'

Lu nodded again. 'Got any tea?'

'So what's Marc been up to?' asked Pam as she made a pot of tea.

'He didn't say much. Just that he reckons this bloke tried to do him out of some cash and when he couldn't get it, he went for him. Someone sent for the police and Marc finished up in the nick.'

'That's awful. D'you want something to eat?'

'No thanks. I'll pop down and get a few chips 'fore they close. It's a cuppa I'm dying for.'

Pam put a cup of tea on the table. 'Does your dad know about this?'

'It was him that told me when I took the van back this afternoon. I had to go to the nick and take him home. It seems the bloke ain't gonner press charges. I expect he's got too much to lose.'

'Has Marc been pinching things?'

'He's always done a bit of wheeling and dealing. And this isn't the first time he's been in trouble. He was in Borstal when he was young.'

'I know, you told me. I would have thought he'd learned his lesson then.'

'Not our Marc.'

'So what happens now?'

'Nothing. He makes me bloody sick. All our adult lives we've had to look after Dad and all he seems to do is upset him. Don't know why Dad thinks so much of him. I expect he likes the money he brings in.'

'Come on, sit down.'

Lu passed his hand wearily through his hair. 'Thanks. I'm so glad I've got you to come home to.'

'So am I.' She kissed him tenderly. 'I'll pop down and get you some chips before Elsie closes up.'

The next day things went back to normal. On Friday Lu took Pam to see his father and Marco was his usual charming self, except he was sporting a large bruise on his face.

'That looks painful,' said Pam as she took off her coat.

'It ain't so bad as the other bloke's.' Marc grinned and lightly touched his cheek.

'You mark my words, you'll be the death of me,' said his father.

'I told you, I was only trying to bring in a few extra bob. Since he got married,' Marc pointed his finger at Lu, 'and what with the winter an' all, things ain't so good round here. How was I to know the stuff I got from that bloke was hooky?'

'If you got it off a bloke in a pub it was sure to be suspicious, so don't start trying to put the blame on me,' said Lu.

'Well, if you still lived here we'd all be better off.' Marc looked angry.

'What's wrong with us wanting our own place?' asked Lu.

'First Al, then you,' said Mr Cappa, turning on Lu and Pam. 'Families are supposed to stick together. In the old days the kids looked after their parents, now it seems they can't wait to get away. You make me sick.' He banged his fist on the table making Pam jump. 'You and Al and that stuck-up wife of his and this one' – he pointed at Pam – 'ain't much better.' He turned his back on Pam. 'Go on, get out, get out the pair of you,' he shouted, glaring at Lu.

Terrified at such a show of temper, Pam picked up her handbag and hurried for the door.

'I'll call in tomorrow,' said Lu as they went out of the room.

'Don't bother,' yelled his father. 'I'll find someone else to take the van out.'

Outside Pam clung to Lu's arm. 'What we gonner do? You've just lost your job.'

Lu laughed. 'Don't you believe it. The old man always goes off like that when things don't go his way.'

'But . . . but this is all Marc's fault.'

Lu kissed her cheek. 'I know. We've been all through this before. Don't take any notice, it'll be all right in the morning.'

'I hope so.' Although jobs were relatively easy to come by, Lu didn't have a trade and had always said he wouldn't work for anyone and the last thing she wanted was for him to be moping about the place all day.

The next morning when Pam got to work she got straight on the phone to tell Jill about it. They often had a chat on Saturday mornings when their bosses weren't around.

'You should have seen Marc's face.'

'That's a shame, he's such a handsome bloke,' said Jill.

'Well, it was his fault.'

'So what about Lu? Will his dad stop him from taking the van out?'

'He says not, but their old man's got a rotten temper. Anyway, could we come down tomorrow?'

'We're coming up.'

'That's good. I need to talk to someone.'

'Why? You're not expecting, are you?'

Pam laughed. 'No, are you?'

'No. Look, I must go, see you tomorrow.'

'OK.' Pam put the phone down and looked at the clock. She rolled another sheet of paper into her typewriter. Only another hour till twelve then I'll be off, she said under her breath.

Lu had been right and over the weeks that followed there wasn't any change in their circumstances. Lu was still working for his father and they popped in once a week to see him. Nothing was ever said about the night he threw them out. Billy brought Jill to see her family and some Sundays Lu took Pam to Brighton. On other Sundays Pam and Lu would have tea with her mum and gran. They would exchange all the gossip but Pam never mentioned that Marco had been fighting, or that Mr Cappa had thrown them out.

Christmas was in three weeks' time and Pam had made up her mind she wasn't going to spend it with Lu's family.

'We'll have to go and see them some time over the holiday,' said Lu when they were discussing it.

'Not for a whole evening though.'

'What if Jean asks us?'

'I don't suppose she will, but if she does we'll just have to say we've made other arrangements. 'Sides, I'd rather be at Mum's.'

'So would I.'

'That's settled then. We could go and see your dad on Christmas morning.'

'OK. If that's what you want.'

Pam smiled. She'd been pretty sure she'd get her own way. 'Look, on Christmas Eve why don't we go dancing?'

'Now that's what I call a great idea.'

Pam knew that Lu loved to please her: she was so lucky.

On Christmas Eve Pam finished work early. She didn't hang around at the firm's party: she knew that as the men got drunk they would only want her around to kiss and to paw over. Lu was already home and they had dinner together, then she got dressed and made up her face. She felt like a teenager again. They hadn't been dancing for several weeks and then only in the church hall. This time they were going to a proper club.

It was cold as they pulled up round the back in the car park.

'Got some nice bikes here,' Lu said, wandering over to look at them.

'Don't get any ideas.'

'Thought I might be getting one for Christmas.' Lu took her arm to steer her towards the door.

'Now, how would I get a thing like that in your stocking?'

He gave her a quick kiss. 'I can always dream.'

They spent a wonderful evening dancing and talking. 'This is going to be the best Christmas I've ever had,' Pam exclaimed.

'Me too,' said Lu.

All too soon they were playing the last waltz.

'This has been a really smashing night. I don't want it to end,' said Pam.

Lu held her tight, kissed her and whispered, 'We can carry on when we get home.'

'That's the best bit.'

After queuing for ages to get her coat from the cloakroom, she tucked her arm in his and they wandered back to the car park stopping every few steps for more kisses.

'You Luigi Cappa?' A man dressed in black leather stepped out of the darkness.

'Yer. Who wants to know?'

'Me. I had a bit of a bust-up with the other wop a few weeks back. You know, your brother.'

Two more blokes materialized out of the night.

'So what? That's his problem,' said Lu as one of the bullies came right up to him.

'I've come to teach him a lesson,' said the talkative one. 'But as he ain't here, you two will have ter do.'

Pam caught her breath and looked round the dark car park. It was deserted. They were alone. Should she run and get help?

Lu pushed Pam to one side. 'Leave her out of it, mate. She ain't a Cappa.'

'I ain't your mate. And as she's married to one, in my eyes that makes her a Cappa,' he said menacingly.

'How do you know that?'

'I know a lot about you and yours. And I don't like any of yer, d'you hear?'

Pam was trembling; she began to cry. She was so frightened. What was going to happen to them?

'Shut it, gel.'

One of the two thugs sat on Lu's bike. 'Nice machine, this,' he said, stroking the petrol tank. 'Reckon it can go a fair lick.'

'Get off.' Lu went to lunge at the bloke, but as he did so the other one came up behind him and forced Lu's arms behind his back. The first bully punched him in the stomach. Lu went down like a sack of potatoes.

'Stop it. Stop it,' screamed Pam racing towards Lu.

'Ah, hark at love's young dream. It ain't no good you screaming, love, you ain't going nowhere – well, not just yet anyway. Hang on to her, Ron, while me and Steve here carry on with the business.'

Two arms held Pam in a vice-like grip. 'Let me go, you bully!' she shrieked.

He laughed. The smell of beer almost knocked her out. She closed her eyes; she couldn't bear to look at her dear Lu being savagely kicked and beaten. She tried to get away by squirming and wriggling and kicking her captor's shins, but seemed to be making no impression. She couldn't do anything to help Lu.

The thug who was holding her was still laughing. 'Right little eel, ain't yer? Watch it, gel, otherwise I'll have to take you round the corner and then who knows what might happen.'

Pam wanted to be sick. She was crying loudly and

uncontrollably. 'Let me go. Let me go.'

'Now, as if I would do that? And you'd better keep yer voice down unless you want me to shut you up.'

Lu was laying on the ground moaning.

'Stop it. Stop it. What has he ever done to you?' yelled Pam at the one who had been kicking her husband.

He stood back as though he was examining his handiwork. 'Fer Christ's sake, try to keep her quiet, Ron. She's drivin' me mad.'

Ron went to kiss her but she kept turning her head, shouting out Lu's name. She was so worried about him. He barely seemed to be moving.

Listen, gel,' said the one who appeared to be the leader. 'It ain't him I've got a beef with. It's that brother of his. Right sod he is, but he's a bit more streetwise than this one. Just tell our Marco that if he does any more deals like the last one, he'd better watch out, as then it'll be him lying here, and he might not be able to get up again.' He turned to walk away. 'And tell him that funerals cost a few bob these days. By the way, Merry Christmas. Come on, lads,' he said over his shoulder.

When her arms were released, Pam grabbed the thug's hand and bit into it hard. He yelled out and swore at her. Looking up, she saw his other hand as it came down on the side of her face. The pain made her cry out and her teeth rattled. As she hit the ground everything went black.

Chapter 14

Pam could hear muffled sounds. She tried to open her eyes. All she could see was a fuzzy white haze. Where was she? She went to move but couldn't. Why was she in so much pain? What had happened? She closed her eyes again. The air smelled like a pine forest. She felt warm and safe.

'Pam, Pam are you awake?' A soft voice was calling her. She turned her head. It hurt.

'Pam love, it's me, Mum.'

Once again she tried to open her eyes and get them focused. 'Mum!' She croaked. Her jaw hurt. 'What's happened? Where am I?' Her left eye refused to open to much more than a small slit. She put her hand up to it. It felt puffy and painful.

Her mother took hold of her hand. 'It's all right, love, you're in hospital.'

'Hospital? Why?' Pam couldn't think straight, her brain was in such a muddle. She made an attempt to get her mother's face clearly in view and to sit up, but her shoulder and arm hurt, so she sank back into the fresh, clean smell of the pillows, her eyes closed once more.

'Don't move,' said her mother.

Everything was flashing past Pam and she couldn't stop it. What was she doing here? Had she had an accident?

What was her mother doing here? She slowly reopened her eyes. This time she could see the drawn, worried look on her mother's face. Next to Rose sat her gran. 'Gran,' whispered Pam.

'Yes, love. I'm here.'

Slowly tears began to trickle down her cheeks. 'What's happened to me?'

'I'm sorry, Pam, but I'm afraid some blokes have given you a bit of a bashing,' said Ivy, struggling to keep her voice under control. 'And if I ever lay me eyes on the sods, I'll kill 'em.'

'Why did they hit me?'

'Don't you know?' asked her mother. 'Don't you remember?'

She went to move her head. 'No. Why me? Where was I?'

Pam watched as her mother's tears ran unchecked.

'I'll go and look for a doctor and tell him she's come to,' said Ivy. She stood up and placed a reassuring hand on Rose's shoulder. 'Don't worry, they said that she might suffer a loss of memory but that it probably would only be temporary.'

'Can't you remember anything?' pleaded her mother.

'No.' Pam closed her eyes again. Why would someone want to beat her up? What had she done? Her muddled mind was going round in circles. 'How did I get here?'

Pam felt a cold hand take hold of her wrist. She opened her eyes to see a young man in white coat was smiling and taking her pulse.

'Hello, Mrs Cappa.'

'Cappa?' repeated Pam slowly. 'My name's King, not Cappa!'

Her mother took in a sharp breath and the doctor gave her a worried look.

Suddenly Pam screamed out, 'Lu. Lu! Where's Lu? Where is he?' She tried to get off the bed, but two strong hands held her back. 'They kicked him and . . .' she stopped. 'Is he . . . Is he dead?'

'No,' said the doctor. 'He's been knocked about a bit but he's a strong lad and he'll be back on his feet before long.'

'Is he here?'

'Yes, in the men's ward.'

'I want to see him.'

'All in good time.'

'Please let me.'

'Just listen to the doctor, Pam.'

'Mum, go and see him. Tell me he's all right.'

'I've seen him.' Rose gave a very weak smile. 'He's not too bad.'

Pam forgot her own pain. She was feeling stronger. 'What does that mean?'

Ivy came to the rescue. 'He's got a broken arm and he's badly bruised.'

'We're waiting for the X-ray results to see if there are any internal injuries.' The doctor turned to Ivy and Rose. 'Unfortunately as it's Christmas Day things are taking a bit longer.'

'Christmas Day,' said Pam as the jigsaw in her mind began to make sense. 'This was supposed to be the best Christmas we've ever had.' She began to cry.

The doctor patted her hand, but didn't speak. He moved away.

'We'll make up for it when you get home,' sniffed Rose.

'Look, they've got some decorations up.'

Pam glanced around. She was in a small ward on her own. A few paper chains were wound round a picture and also the mirror over the sink.

'D'you know who did this to you?' asked Ivy.

'No.' Pam didn't want to say anything till she'd seen Lu.

'I see,' said Ivy knowingly.

Pam lay back and closed her eyes again.

'Do you want anything, love?' asked her mother.

'Only to see Lu.'

'As soon as it's possible I'm sure they'll let you.'

Pam didn't reply. She was far away dreaming of the Christmas they had been planning.

'Are you awake?' A familiar voice came into her dreams.

Pam opened her eyes. 'Jill.' Once again Pam's tears began to flow.

'Don't cry. My poor darling.' Jill blew her nose. 'Well, this is a bloody fine way to spend Christmas, I must say.'

'I'm sorry.'

'No, no. I didn't mean . . .' Jill took Pam's hand. 'I'm sorry.' She looked uncomfortable.

'I'll leave you two alone for a bit,' said Rose.

'Good job it's Christmas,' laughed Jill, 'otherwise we wouldn't be bringing you all this fruit.' Jill looked at her friend whose face was swollen and bruised. She wanted to cry with her. 'You know me – I'm only kidding. Is there anything I can get you?'

'Could you go and see Lu?'

'I did that when we first came in here. You was asleep

and your mum said she would be staying here in case you woke up.'

'How is he? Mum said he's all right, but you'll tell me the truth.'

'He don't look too good.'

'He ain't gonner die, is he?'

'No, course not. And when the bruises go down he'll be his old handsome self again. He's had to have a few stitches, but when they come out he'll be as good as new. He has got a broken arm, so that'll take a while to heal.'

'I want to see him.'

'I'm sure as soon as they know you're all right they'll let you. Your mum said they were keeping you in here under observation as you've got a large lump on the back of your head and because of the shock.'

'Is he awake? Did you talk to him?'

'Yes, for a little while.'

'Who's with him?'

'His dad.'

'What about Marco?'

'I didn't see him.'

Pam quickly glanced at the door. She could see her mother and gran talking behind the glass. 'This is all his fault.'

'It is? How do you know that?'

'The bloke told us.'

'Was it just one?'

'No, there were three of 'em.'

'Three! Poor Lu.'

'Oh Jill, it was awful. I'll kill Marco for letting this happen.'

'Come on now, don't get yourself in a state. It won't do you any good.'

'Don't tell anyone what I said, just in case Lu don't want anyone to know.'

'Course not. He sends his love and wants to see you as soon as he can.'

A slight smile lifted Pam's tear-stained face. 'And I want to see him. I don't know what I'd do without him now.'

'I know how you feel.'

'Thanks for coming – and on Christmas Day as well.'

'Don't worry about it. We're gonner be here till Monday so if you can come home then, Billy said he'll collect you.'

'Thanks.' Pam lay back; she felt exhausted.

'You take it easy.' Jill kissed her goodbye.

Pam could hear her mother and Jill talking in soft whispers at the door, but didn't understand what they were saying. Gradually everything was becoming clearer. 'His bike,' she suddenly called out. 'His bike. What's happened to his bike?'

'I think Marco has gone to get it,' said Rose, hurrying to her side.

'I hope those blokes didn't smash it up. Oh Mum, he'll be so upset.'

'Don't worry about it,' said Jill who had come back in when she heard Pam cry out. 'It was insured, wasn't it?'

'Yes.'

'It might be all right,' said her mother.

'I hope so. How did I get here?'

'One of the band from the club went into the car park and saw the two of you on the ground. He called an ambulance, then the police came and got me. Good job you had my name and address in your handbag.'

'And it's a bloody good job whoever it was didn't swipe it,' said Ivy.

'We don't think anything is missing,' said her mother.

'I didn't have a lot in it.'

Ivy gave a little cough. 'The doctor don't think they . . . they did anything to you . . . you know?'

'Know what?' asked Pam.

'Well, you still had your knickers on.'

Pam began to cry again.

'Ivy! What's the matter with you? Fancy telling her that,' said Rose, her voice rising.

'She might wonder!'

'Let her get over the shock of being in here before you start going into details like that.' Rose King was very angry.

'If they had done something like that I know Lu would kill them,' said Jill very quietly.

'That's if he knows who they are,' said Ivy.

Pam lay back. She was trying hard to remember what had happened, but the last thing she could recall was that thug hitting her and her falling to the ground. Had she been raped? How would she know?

The door banged open and Lu was there, sitting in a wheelchair that was being pushed in by his father.

'Lu,' Pam cried out.

'He won't give 'em any peace till he's seen her.'

'Pam, oh Pam, I'm so sorry.' His eyes filled with tears.

'I think we'd better leave 'em for a while,' said Ivy.

Lu's wheelchair was pushed as close to the bed as they could get it. He winced and with his good hand held his ribs.

171

The family filed out of the room.

'My darling,' said Lu trying to give her a kiss. 'I've been so worried about you.'

'I've been worried about you.' Once again her tears fell as she looked at his battered face.

'I'll never speak to Marco again after what he's put you through.'

'Have you told anyone who it was?'

'No. But I will when I get Marc alone.'

'Don't talk about him. What about you? I can see you've got a broken arm. Will that cut leave a scar?'

There was a deep red weal down the right side of his face that was held together with black stitches, it looked angry and inflamed.

'Won't know till the stitches come out.'

'Does it hurt?'

'Not too bad. I've got a couple of badly bruised ribs, but they ain't broke, so that's a good thing. They've just told me they've seen the X-rays and everything seems to be fine inside.'

'Thank God. Do they know how long we'll be in here?'

'Not long I hope, not once they know we're all right. Your face don't look so good.'

She gave a slight smile. 'And you ain't exactly the handsome bloke I married.' Pam gently touched his cheek, then her own. 'This was my own fault really. You see I bit his hand, really hard.'

'You didn't.'

'That's when he hit me.'

'Don't worry. When I'm back on my feet I'm gonner look these buggers up, then we'll see who's who.'

'No, Lu. Promise me you'll never have anything to do with them.'

'I can't promise you that, Pam. I can't let 'em think they can get away with this.'

The door was pushed open and this time it was a nurse who came in. 'Come on, Mr Cappa. You shouldn't be out of bed. You can see your wife later.' She expertly turned the wheelchair round in the small room and took him away.

As he was about to disappear out of the door he blew Pam a kiss. 'Love you,' he called out.

'Love you too,' she said, settling back down in the pillows. She thought about what her husband had said. She didn't want him to get involved with those blokes again. The next time he might not be so lucky.

On Monday Pam was allowed home, but Lu was going to have to stay in hospital for a few days longer. True to their word, Billy and Jill came to collect her.

'We're taking you to your mum's for now. She reckons you ought to stay with them till Lu can come home.'

Pam was in no mood to argue: in many ways she was pleased she was going to be looked after and have someone to talk to. But she didn't want to leave Lu in the hospital on his own.

'You can go every day to see him,' said her mother as she fussed around her.

On Saturday Lu was allowed home and Pam decided to get a taxi rather than let Marco bring them home in the van.

'What about the money?' asked her mother when she told them what she was going to do.

'I don't care. I don't want him getting on a bus.'

'I'm sure Marco would be only too pleased to bring him home.'

'No. I don't want him to.'

'Please yourself, but I still think it's a waste of money.'

That evening they wanted to be alone in their flat. They turned the lights out and sat by the glow of the electric fire, listening to the radio.

'Pam, how much money we got?' Lu asked.

'Why?'

'You do realize I can't take the van out with a broken arm.'

Pam sat upright. 'We've got enough to pay the rent for a few weeks. Anyway, I'll be back at work next week so that'll help.'

'But this'll take weeks.' Lu raised his plastered left arm.

'Won't your dad give you some money?'

'No. He always reckons we just about bring in enough to cover the outgoings.'

'Do you believe that ?'

'Don't see any books, do we? But I'll ask him for a bit of help.'

She kissed his cheek. 'Don't worry about it. You get better first.' She nuzzled against him. Lu had always left their savings to her. She didn't see the point in telling him they would only be able to manage for about a month without his wages. She would have a word with Elsie and see if they could pay a bit less rent till Lu was back at work. They would be able to pay back the arrears as soon as he started again.

Pam had never told Lu what her gran had said and when she asked the doctor, he told her she had nothing to worry about, she hadn't been touched by the gang. Would Lu have still wanted her if they had?

'Penny for them.'

Pam smiled. 'I was just thinking how nice it is to be home.'

'I certainly agree with that.'

Pam turned her head and let him kiss her.

Chapter 15

On Monday morning Lu said he was going to see his father while Pam was at work.

That evening, Pam arrived home before him and anxiously waited for him to return. He looked very angry when he walked in.

'Bloody buses. Been standing at the bus stop for hours, then got all the aggro of finding the fare with one hand. I tell you, Pam, this is gonner get me down.' He waved his plastered arm at her.

'Never mind, you're home now. Was Marco there?' asked Pam helping him off with his coat.

'I waited for him, that's why I'm a bit late.'

'Did you tell him who it was that—?'

'Course I did, and I described the blokes.'

'Well?'

'He said he didn't know them. He reckons they only said that.'

'Why should they?'

'I don't know, do I?'

'I thought you said Marco had done business with him.'

'Well, that's what the bloke said.'

'What about your father? What did he have to say about it?'

'He believed Marc of course, and said I was daft to get involved.'

'What did he think, that we let them beat you up?' Pam was angry, but she tried to hide her feelings. 'I've made some tea.'

Lu was looking in the mirror. He gently ran his fingers along the red weal down his left cheek. 'I've got to carry this with me for the rest of my life.'

Pam wanted to cry for him, he had always been so proud of his looks.

'And that sod of a brother of mine has got away scot-free.'

'Try not to be bitter about it.'

'Bitter?' Lu shouted. 'Of course I'm bitter. Bloody bitter. I'm not gonner let them get away with this.'

'Please, Lu, let it go.'

'How can you say that? I could kill them, and Marc, for what they've put us through.'

'Lu, think of me. What if they kill you? What would I do without you?'

'They ain't that daft. They wouldn't kill me.'

Pam knew there was little point in trying to console him when he had every right to be angry.

Although Pam was back at work, Lu wasn't and he was finding it more and more frustrating sitting at home. One evening when Pam came home she found him sitting at the table with a glum look on his face.

'What's wrong with you?' she asked, taking off her coat.

'I'm bloody fed up, that's what. Stuck in here day after

day. I can't ride me bike. I can't work . . .' He banged the table with his good fist.

'It's no good you getting upset.'

'It's all right for you. You can still go to work and meet people.'

'Oh yes. I see a lot of people where I work. Why don't you go and see your dad?'

'Saw him this afternoon, and all he could say is that it's a good job it's winter and not summer, otherwise he'd be losing a lot of money.'

'He ain't offered to help us out though, has he? How does he think we're managing?'

'He gave me a couple of quid.'

'Well then, why didn't you go to the pictures or something?'

'Didn't want to.'

'For goodness' sake, stop acting like a child.'

'I feel like a bloody child, having to be waited on hand and foot. I can't even cut me dinner up, or put me own socks on.'

'You will.'

'Yer, when?'

'Come on, Lu. Getting cross ain't gonner help.'

'It'll help me.'

'I'll make some tea.'

'And, Pam?' There was real anger in his tone now. 'Did you ask Elsie if you could pay her less rent for a while?'

'Yes. Why?'

'She wanted to know how long for, and if we was going to pay the arrears.'

'I told her that as soon as you was back at work she

would get all the money we owed. What's wrong with that?'

'I wish you'd told me. I felt a right twit when she was talking about it.'

'Didn't see the point. Besides, I think you was still in hospital. She ain't worried about it, is she?'

'Dunno.'

'Well, what did she say?'

'She just hoped it wouldn't go on for too long.'

'Well, it won't, will it?'

'Don't like living off me wife.'

Pam laughed. 'I seem to remember seven months ago saying something like: for better or worse, and in sickness and in health.'

'Well, it was all right to say it, but I didn't expect it to happen.'

'We never know what's round the corner.' She kissed his forehead. 'Now let's have some tea.'

As she stood in the kitchen watching the gas flame lick the sides of the kettle, she reflected on the past month. All this sitting around was beginning to affect Lu; he was definitely getting down in the dumps. They were having the odd quarrel now. But what could she do? Their savings were also going down. What would happen when they couldn't afford to pay the rent? Her wages just about covered other things like food, gas and electric. Why did it have to be winter? The fire had to be on, more so now Lu was home most of the time. She noted the pile of shillings she left beside the meter every day went down at an alarming rate. She hated Marco so much. He had made Lu so bitter. How dare he mess up their lives in this way? They didn't even have anything to sell, only Lu's beloved motor bike. But Pam knew she dare not even mention that. Nor would she ever ask her mother for help. Where was it all going to end? His plaster should be off soon; she prayed there wouldn't be any complications and then they could pick up their lives again. If there were . . . She looked down at her hands. There was always her engagement ring. Then the shrieking whistle on the kettle startled her and she got on with making the tea.

'So how are you two managing?' asked Ivy as they walked in in time for their usual Sunday dinner.

'Not too bad,' said Pam quickly.

'I expect your dad's giving you a few bob to help out,' Ivy said to Lu.

'He does a bit. But it's winter and he's only got one van on the road.'

'I thought he had a bloke to give him a hand.'

'He does sometimes, but Dad don't trust him.'

'What about your rent?' asked Rose. 'Don't let that slip otherwise you could be out.'

'I don't think Elsie's like that,' said Pam.

'Don't you believe it, girl,' said Ivy as she dished out the potatoes. 'All landlords are like that. No rent then you're out.'

Pam looked at Lu who said nothing.

Later, Pam was helping her mother wash up when Rose asked, 'Lu don't look very happy. You two had a row?'

'He's fed up with being at home all day on his own.'

'Why don't he go out with Marco?'

Pam took a breath. She had never told her mother or gran that it was because of Marco that they'd been beaten up;

only Jill knew that. 'I don't think Lu would do that. He couldn't really serve with only one hand, could he?'

'No, suppose not. Look, if you find it hard, let me know. I've got a bit put by for emergencies.'

'Thanks, Mum, but we'll be all right. Besides, his plaster's due off soon.' Pam knew her mother had her parents and Ivy insured, but was always worried it wouldn't be enough when the time came, so she had a little put by for when it was needed.

'Have you heard from Grandad lately?' asked Pam.

'Yes. Funnily enough I had a letter yesterday. He's not that well. I really would like to go and see them.'

'Can't you get time off?'

'I'm going to ask Mrs Kennett on Monday, but she does rely on me.'

'I know, but you hardly take any holiday.' As Pam slowly dried the plate she'd been holding her thoughts went to her grandparents. She and Lu really should make the effort to go and see them when Lu had his plaster off.

At the end of the week, when Pam took the rent down, Elsie asked, 'Look, love, I didn't wanner say anything, but we're a bit worried about the rent.'

'Don't worry, Elsie. Lu's having the plaster off in a few days and then he'll be back at work.'

'That's good. Frank's been worried you'll do a runner.'

Pam laughed. 'We wouldn't do a thing like that!'

'That's what I said. Frank said you might not, but there's a lot what would.' Elsie smiled relieved.

That upset Pam, but she didn't dwell on it. 'I'd like two small bits of cod and three pennyworth of chips for tonight,' she said, eager to get away from the subject of the rent.

Elsie set about filling the paper. 'I've put a few extra chips in.'

'Thanks.'

Pam slowly made her way back upstairs. Hopefully they would be able to pay off the debt soon.

Today was the day they had been waiting for. The day Lu was having his plaster off.

'Well,' said Pam when she burst into the flat and threw her handbag on the chair. 'Is it all right?'

This time Lu was smiling as he waved his arm at her. 'It feels a bit funny, all light like, but the doc said it will at first. It's gone a bit thin.'

She took his hand. 'It looks all right to me.'

'I'm taking the van out tomorrow.'

'Will you be all right?'

'Course. Dad said he'll come with me in case I have a job with the handbrake.'

'Why didn't your dad believe you when you told him it was Marco's fault?'

'He reckons it was me own fault for mixing it.'

'You didn't stand a lot of chance, did you? You told him there were three of them?'

'Course. Now let's drop it, shall we?'

Lu hadn't said a lot about that night at all. Several times she had broached the subject but each time he had quickly dismissed it. And, Pam thought, there wasn't really any point in dwelling on what had happened.

Spring was in the air when Lu next took Pam to Brighton to

see Jill and Billy. This was going to be the last Sunday Lu had off and she was determined to make the most of it.

Pam hugged Lu and nestled her head against his back. His leather jacket felt warm next to her cheek. She was happy. They were beginning to pay the back rent and she was sure that everything was going to turn out great for them.

'You both look good,' said Jill on opening the door.

Pam hugged and kissed her friend. 'And so do you.'

All day they talked about their hopes and dreams for the future.

'I would love to give up work and stay home with a baby,' said Jill.

'So would I. Fat chance of that all the while we live in a flat.'

'We're saving to buy a house one of these days.'

'I can't see that happening to us.'

'What are you doing about your twenty-first?' asked Jill.

'Not a lot really.' Pam didn't want to tell them they didn't have the money to do much. 'Gran's making a cake and we'll get a bottle in, nothing exciting.'

'That's a pity, thought you might be having a bit of a party.'

Pam half laughed. 'No, we ain't as lucky as you.' Pam was remembering Jill's twenty-first a few months back. She had the church hall and a lovely cake and all her relations came to help her celebrate.

'Don't forget to save us a bit of cake. And guess what?' said Jill excitedly. 'Me and Billy are going to Italy.'

'That's great,' said Lu. 'Whereabouts?'

'We were thinking of going to Rome. It looks a wonderful city.' Jill laughed. 'It would be a right turn-up for the books if we bumped into Robbie. By the way, Pam, did you ever find out why your gran got so upset about you going out with Robbie that time?'

Pam felt the colour drain from her face. 'No.'

'Thought she might have told you when you married Lu.'

Pam wanted to change the subject. 'That's all water under the bridge now. It'll be really nice for you to go abroad again, but I thought you was saving up to get your own house?'

'We are, but we both feel we need a holiday. And as I missed out on Italy before, Billy here thought I deserve it.' She grinned and kissed his cheek.

Although Pam loved Jill there were times when she could hit her, she was so self-satisfied.

'So when you going on this holiday?' asked Lu.

'We thought about October sometime,' said Billy. 'When the nights start to draw in the building trade drops off a bit. I can't not be here through the summer.'

'That's a bit like me. Have to work bloody hard through the summer. Pam, what say we go with 'em?'

'Don't know about that. It'll cost a few bob.'

'Who cares. Let us know what date you've got in mind and perhaps we could think about it.'

'That would be really smashing,' said Jill. 'Good job we ain't put on a lot of weight and can still get into our bikinis.'

'Now that's something that's got to be worth waiting for,' said Lu, looking smug.

'I don't want to go to Italy,' said Pam when they got home.

'Why?'

'I just don't, that's all. Besides, we can't really afford it.'

'I know.'

'So why did you say . . .'

'I just wanted to get your reaction.'

'Why?'

He threw his jacket on the chair. 'Thought you might like the chance of perhaps bumping into lover boy Bennetti again.'

Pam laughed, but she was angry. 'What? Italy's a big place. Is that all you said it for? Or was you being the big Luigi, trying to make out we can afford the same as Jill and Billy?'

Lu went into the kitchen.

'Don't you walk away from me while I'm talking,' she yelled, following him.

'It's Bennetti, ain't it? He'll always be around, lurking in the back of your mind.'

'Don't talk so daft. You're the one who brought it up.'

'But you've never really forgotten him, have you? What if he was to walk through that door right now? I bet you'd be all over him, more so now I've got this.' He pointed at the ugly red scar on his face.

Tears filled her eyes. 'I love you. No scar's gonner change that. You'll always be your handsome self as far as I'm concerned.' She went to touch his cheek but he pushed her hand away.

'Don't.'

'What is it? Why are you acting like this?'

'I dunno.' He hung his head. 'I suppose . . . I'm afraid I might lose you. After the fight, and me not working and looking like this . . .'

'You'll never lose me.'

'That's what you say now.'

He walked out of the kitchen and Pam leaned against the cupboard. How could she prove to him that she loved him, really loved him? Why did he distrust her love?

It was an unseasonably warm evening for May. The bright red sun was making attractive streaks in the sky as it began to go down behind the houses. Pam walked slowly home from work. There wasn't any point in hurrying as Lu wouldn't be home till at least nine o'clock. There had been a heavy sultry feel to the day. Pam looked at the clouds building up behind her; she hoped there wasn't going to be a thunderstorm, she didn't like being in the flat on her own during a storm.

In a week's time it would be their first wedding anniversary. Such a lot had happened to them in the past year. In many ways they were closer, but she knew Lu still wasn't convinced she loved him. Sometimes she wanted to ask her gran about the Bennettis but decided that perhaps, in the long run, the mystery was best left unexplored.

As she walked past the fish shop window Elsie beckoned for her to come in. Pam really didn't fancy a chat, she wanted a cup of tea, but she couldn't ignore her landlady.

'I'm glad I've caught you,' said Elsie.

Pam made an effort to smile. She felt at ease now all the rent arrears had been paid up. 'Tom not in?' she asked.

'Yer, he's out back cleaning some fish.'

'Been a bit close today,' said Pam, just to make conversation.

'I should say so. It's been like a sweat box in here.' Elsie pushed a strand of hair back from her damp forehead; the odour of smelly fat from the fryers hung about her. ''Ave you got a minute?'

'Yes, of course.'

'I don't really know how to say this.'

The serious expression on Elsie's face suddenly filled Pam with panic.

'You know how much Frank loves that garden of his?'

Pam nodded slowly.

'Well, we've decided to get out.'

'What, out of the house?'

'No, the shop.'

'You're giving up the shop?'

Elsie nodded.

'What about the flat?'

'It goes with the shop.'

'Does that mean we'll lose it?'

'I'm afraid so.'

'But when?'

'We didn't like to say anything before, not till we was really sure. We're leaving at the end of the month.'

'What, this month? May?'

'No, June.' Elsie smiled. 'It'll be nice to have the rest of the summer just pottering about in the garden.'

'But what about us? Can we keep the flat?'

'No. I'm sorry, but the new people want it.'

'Where will we go?'

'I'm afraid I can't help you there, love. In some ways I'll be sorry to go. You've been good tenants, but me and Frank feel we've had enough. We've worked hard all our lives and now we think it's time we moved on.'

Pam couldn't believe her ears. They were losing the flat.

They were losing their home. 'Are you sure the new people want to live here?'

'Oh yes. Nice couple. Only young.'

At first Pam didn't notice the customer who had walked in.

'Hello, young Pam. Doing all right, are you? Don't see much of you now you've moved away.'

Pam smiled at Doll Windsor. 'Yes, thanks.'

'Been ter see me sister, so I thought I'd get a bit of fish to take home. Mind you, I'd better get a move on. Don't like the look of the weather.'

Pam was still smiling but it was automatic. Why did she have to come in here right at this moment. Had she heard any of their conversation? She didn't want her mother and gran to hear about it from a neighbour, she and Lu had to talk about it first. 'I must go,' she said, moving away.

'Nice seeing you again. I'll have two small piece of rock and three pennyworth of chips,' Doll said, turning to Elsie.

As Pam walked up the stairs Elsie's words went round and round in her mind. They were going to be homeless. What could they do? Where would they live?

Lu wouldn't be home for at least another two hours. She kicked off her sandals and slumped in the chair. The distant sound of thunder broke the silence.

'A storm, that's all I need now,' she said out loud. She went over to the window and watched the people hurrying along. 'With my luck at the moment, if I went outside, I'd probably be struck by lightning.'

Chapter 16

Pam clasped her second cup of tea with both hands and looked out of the window. The rain was coming down in stair rods. She watched mesmerized as it bounced up from the road and rushed along the gutters. The dirty water bubbled and swirled, fighting to get into drains that couldn't take it away quickly enough. She knew Lu wouldn't attempt to come home in this. She felt so miserable. She desperately wanted to tell him about their plight. What were they going to do? Next week was their first wedding anniversary. They had planned to have a meal out and spend a lovely evening together. Now, after that, they would be homeless. Her silent tears fell. How would they be able to find such a nice flat as this? And with such reasonable rent as well, that's without having to find key money.

She couldn't concentrate on anything; even the radio didn't seem to have anything on worth listening to. Gradually the sound of the thunder rolled away and the rain eased down to a drizzle. Again Pam stood at the window and waited for Lu. There wasn't a lot of traffic below and when the headlight of his bike came into view it brought tears to her eyes. What would he say? This was another huge hurdle that they would have to get over. Why did they always have so many problems?

★ ★ ★

Pam ran down the stairs and opened the door.

'This is a nice surprise,' Lu said, kissing her cheek.

She helped him off with his jacket. 'You must be very wet.'

'Not too bad. I waited till it calmed down a bit. You don't look very happy. Was you frightened?' He sat on the stairs and took off his boots.

'A bit.'

'Well, I'm here now. Is the kettle on?' He put his arm round her and they climbed the stairs.

Pam nodded.

When the tea was made she said, 'We've got a problem.'

'What's that? You're not up the spout, are you?'

'No. We said we'd wait till we got our own house, remember?'

'What is it then?'

'The flat. We've got to move.'

'What?'

Pam explained to him what Elsie had told her earlier.

'And all this is at the end of the month.'

Pam nodded.

'She ain't given us much warning. She could have dropped a few hints.'

'Perhaps they wasn't sure if the deal would go through?'

'Could be. But that don't help us any, does it?'

'What are we going to do?' Pam twisted her fingers together nervously.

'Don't know. I'll ask around tomorrow.'

'I'll go to the council.'

'That won't do much good,' said Lu.

'I know, but I'll put our name down anyway.'

They looked at one another, both trying to hide their apprehension behind brave smiles.

That night Pam found it difficult to sleep. Where would they live? As her mind turned the problem over and over Robbie and his big house kept intruding into her thoughts. But why? She knew she was over him, but that didn't stop her thinking about him and his parents' lovely home.

The following evening Lu was smiling when he walked in. He gave Pam a quick peck on the cheek. 'Not to worry about a place, it's all sorted.'

'That's great. Where?'

'We're gonner stay at Dad's till we find something.'

Pam felt she had just been kicked. 'What?' she whispered.

'Dad said I can have my old bedroom back. Don't look so down in the mouth. I'll tart it up a bit. It'll give us a bit of breathing space till something turns up.'

'I don't want to live at your dad's.'

'Can't say I'm over the moon about it, but what other option have we got if we don't find a place real soon?'

'I don't know.'

'We can't go to your mum's, she ain't got a spare bedroom, and I don't reckon they'll let us kip in the front room.'

'We could ask.'

'No we couldn't. It wouldn't be fair, not when there's a spare room at me dad's.'

Pam wanted to cry. She didn't want to live there.

'Anyway, it's all been settled. Just think how much we can save if we stay with him. I reckon we could even go to Italy with Jill and Billy now.'

Pam didn't know what to think. Even the thought of going to Italy paled into insignificance now. All she knew was that she wasn't going to live with the Cappas, not if she could help it.

'We've got to get out of our flat,' said Pam when she was at her mother's on Sunday. They were in the scullery preparing the dinner.

'Why? Ain't you been paying the rent?'

'Of course we have. Elsie and Frank are getting out of the fish shop and the new people want the flat.'

'Oh Pam, what are you going to do?'

'Look for something else.'

'But that ain't easy.'

'I know. Lu wants us to go and live at his dad's place.'

'That's nice of him, has he got the room?'

Pam nodded.

'I know you're not keen on them, but at least it's getting you out of a hole.'

'We couldn't stay here, could we?'

'I don't think that would work. Lu in a house full of nagging women?'

'What about me in a house full of men?'

'That's different. Men like to be in men's company; besides, I don't think Gran would like it – where would you sleep?'

'In the front room.'

'That wouldn't be very practical, now would it?'

Pam couldn't believe her mother was being so heartless. 'I thought you would be a bit more helpful.'

'Pam, it's not my name on the rent book.'

Pam felt desperate. 'What about Lil next door, would she take us in?'

'Wouldn't like to say.'

'Could you ask her?'

'I suppose it wouldn't do any harm, she can always say no.'

Pam kissed her mother. 'Thanks. Anything's got to be better than living with the Cappas.'

'They can't be that bad.'

Pam laughed. 'You don't know them.'

'Pam, I wouldn't bank on Lil, she's been on her own for a good many years now, and these old ladies don't like changes.'

'But you said, there's no harm in asking.' Pam went into the kitchen. She felt a lot happier as she took the cutlery from the dresser drawer and began putting it on the table. She was singing when Ivy, who had been at Lil's all morning, walked in.

'Well, you look a bit chirpier than when you first came in. What's cheered you up?'

'Mum's gonner ask Lil if me and Lu can live with her.'

'What?'

'We've got to get out of our flat as Elsie's gonner retire and the people who are taking the fish shop over want to live there.'

'No,' said Ivy. 'When you got to get out?'

'The end of June.'

'Christ, that ain't given you much time to find another place, has it?'

Pam shook her head. 'That's why we was wondering if Lil would give us a room, just for the time being, till we found something.'

'Wouldn't like to say. She can be a funny bugger at times, but I'll pop in after dinner and ask her.'

Pam threw her arms round her gran. 'Thanks.' All things that had been said in the past had long since been forgotten.

That evening when Lu arrived at Pam's mother's he found Pam very excited. She hurriedly told him that Lil had agreed to them staying there. 'She's really looking forward to having us there. She even wants to cook for us.'

Lu looked from his mother-in-law to Ivy. 'That's nice of her.'

'You don't look exactly over the moon about it, son,' said Ivy.

'Well, I'd made up me mind that we would be staying with Dad.'

'But this'll be much better,' said Pam. At least, she wanted to add, living with Lil meant she wouldn't be waiting on the old man and Marco.

'But we wouldn't have to pay Dad much rent, that way we could save really hard and then put a deposit down on a place that much quicker.'

'Don't worry,' said Ivy. 'Lil won't charge you much. Reckon a packet of fags will keep her happy.'

'No,' said Pam looking very serious. 'It's got to be done all proper like. With a rent book an' all.'

Ivy laughed. 'Please yourself.'

'Wait till Jill hears about this,' said Pam with a smug look on her face.

Lu was quiet for the rest of the evening and when they arrived home he said, 'That was bloody sneaky of you.'

'What?'

'Asking Lil if we could stay there. What you got against my family?'

'Nothing.'

'Dad won't be very happy to know you've changed your mind.'

'You knew I didn't want to live there, so why say I changed my mind? Why are you so keen to go and stay with them?'

'It's convenient.'

'Who for? Them or me? Besides, I don't want to have to look after them.'

He ignored that and said, 'I wouldn't have to go and get the van every day, would I, not if I lived there.'

'You've got your bike.'

'Yer.'

'Anyway, it's all settled.'

'It certainly is.'

Pam was a little worried at his tone. What had he had in mind?

Jill was pleased they were going to live with her grandmother and said if she and Billy had been living in London she would have done the same thing.

Everybody fussed round them when they arrived at Lil's with the van. The small amount of furniture they had easily fitted into Lil's sparsely furnished house.

'I'm so pleased to be back in Newbury Street,' said Pam.

'Will you still be going into yer mum's for Sunday dinner?' asked Lil.

Pam looked at her mother. 'I don't know.'

'I'd like 'em to, that's if that's all right with you, Lil,' said Rose.

'Course, that way I can still go over to Doreen. She does a nice dinner.'

Pam was smiling so hard she thought her face would crack right in half. She couldn't believe their luck. One minute they were down in the dumps, then the next everything was going their way. Even Lu was beginning to come round.

Now, when Pam came home from work in the evenings, she didn't have to face a lonely flat while Lu was out on the ice-cream van. Lil was such good company as they sat and had their meals together; they'd laugh as Lil told Pam about the things she and her grandmother got up to when they first moved to Newbury Street. They were both young brides at the beginning of the first war. Although Pam knew they had both worked in a factory, she was surprised to learn that before the war her grandmother had been a suffragette.

'I didn't know that,' said Pam.

Lil lit another of her endless cigarettes. 'Don't think it lasted long. She didn't mind throwing the odd stone, but the thought of being caught and sent to prison put her off. Think it might have been the prison overalls. She was a very smart young woman in her day.' Lil laughed. 'You should have seen some of the hats she used to wear, bloody great things full of dead birds and feathers. Your grandad always said that's what made him look at her, her hats.'

'What was me grandad like?'

'A nice man. He had lots of dark hair and lovely brown eyes. He was very quiet even though he was a sailor. Ivy loved him very much. She used to jump up and down when she saw him coming down the street; she always knew right away 'cos he had a real sailor's roll. She thought it was the end of the world when he got interned in Holland. When she found out they were letting 'em home on leave she couldn't believe it.' Lil stopped for a moment and flicked her ash into the fireplace. 'D'you know, now I come to think of it that musta been the time she had a bit of a run-in with Bennetti.'

Pam sat up. 'Why? What happened?'

'I'd forgot all about that. Your grandad was coming home on leave and she asked Bennetti if she could have some time off. He was our foreman, you know?'

Pam nodded enthusiastically.

'Well . . .' Lil looked thoughtful. 'She was a long while in his office and when she came out I could see she was a bit ruffled and she'd been crying. She never did say what happened, just snapped me head off.'

'Did she get the time off?'

'Only two days, but then it didn't matter after that 'cos on that leave she fell for your dad.' Lil gave Pam a huge smile. 'Dan was a lovely boy, masses of dark hair like Harry. Your gran has had it bad. First her husband and then her only son. Wars are bloody awful things.'

'But Grandad didn't get killed in the war. Mum said he died at the start of the last one.'

'Yer, heart attack.'

'Did your husband get killed in the first war?'

'No, poor sod died in the flu epidemic that was just after. Mind you, getting gassed didn't help him none. A lot of men died then – right, that's enough of being morbid.' Lil narrowed her eyes as the trail of smoke drifted up from the cigarette dangling between her lips. 'Let's get this lot cleared away before your old man comes in and wants his tea.'

Pam kissed Lil's cheek.

'What's that for?' Lil asked, grinning and touching her cheek.

'Taking us in and making me happy. I think I can understand why Gran was so against Robbie now. If only she had told me.'

'Your gran can be a funny cow at times, Pam. You ain't got any regrets about marrying Lu, have you?'

Pam smiled and shook her head. 'No. None at all. Now how about we do the washing up and then we can watch the telly?'

'Good idea.' Lil put the cigarette out with her nicotined-stained fingers. 'And Pam.'

'Yes?' said Pam as she gathered the plates ready to take into the scullery.

'I'm really enjoying having you two here.'

'And I can't begin to tell you how much I'm liking it. The thought of living with the Cappas . . .' She shuddered. 'Life's great now!'

The following day on her way home from work, Pam bought two bunches of flowers and a box of chocolates. First she went into her mother.

'Didn't see the point in buying you flowers as you work with them all day, so I got you these.'

Rose took the chocolates. 'Thanks, but why? It ain't me birthday.'

Pam grinned and handed her gran one of the bunches of

flowers. 'I know. I just feel so happy that I thought I'd treat all the people I love.'

Ivy looked amazed. 'What's she putting in your tea?' She inclined her head towards the wall.

Pam just laughed.

'Well, I'm glad to see you're happy anyway,' said Rose. 'I'll put these in water.' She took the flowers from a bewildered Ivy.

Lil too looked so bemused at her gift that Pam started laughing all over again. 'Don't normally get a present for nothing.'

'It's my way of saying thank you,' Pam insisted.

'But you give me rent money each week.'

'This is because I enjoy your company.'

'Ta, Pam. You're a good girl.'

The weeks sped by. One evening Rose called in on Pam as soon as she got home.

'What is it, Mum, you look as if you've been crying.'

Rose sat at the table. 'It's your grandad. He's taken a turn for the worse. I've got to go up and see him.'

'Of course you have. How did you find out?'

Rose handed Pam a letter. It was just a single page in Granny Mallory's spidery writing.

'When are you going?'

'Tomorrow. I've asked Mrs Kennett and she said she could manage for a couple of days, we ain't got that many orders and her son will help her out if need be.'

'Did you want me to come with you?'

'No. I'll be all right. I can telephone you at work and let you know when I'll be back.'

'Phone me anyway. Give my love to Granny Mallory.'

'I will.' Rose held her daughter tight. What would she find when she got to Leeds?

For days Pam worried about her mother and was pleased Rose managed to find time during the day to phone her at work and tell her about her grandfather's progress. He seemed to recover and Rose decided she could come home at the end of the week.

Pam always felt guilty that she hadn't been to see her grandparents since she and Lu got married, but they seemed so distant, in years as well as miles. She'd resolved to go in the winter once Lu's broken arm had healed, but even though Lu had had the time then, it'd been too cold to go all that way on a motor bike and he'd said they couldn't afford the fare by train. There always seemed to be some obstacle in the way to use as an excuse, and so it was always put to one side as something to do 'one day'.

It was now the middle of September and Lu had been very quiet when he came in from work. Pam could tell something was wrong. She wanted to talk to him on his own, but it was difficult with Lil always around and she didn't like to suggest they went upstairs as it looked as if they were going up for other reasons. Pam wanted to discuss this holiday they were supposed to be having. Since they'd been living with Lil and able to save up, Italy was becoming more than just a dream. But whenever she brought it up he quickly dismissed the subject. She wanted to get it settled. Finally Lil announced she was off up to bed.

As soon as the door closed Pam asked, 'What's the

trouble? Have you and Marco been having words again?'

'No.'

'You been down in the mouth all evening.'

'It's all right for you. You and Lil can chat away. I feel like a spare part.'

'Is that it? This is better than me being stuck in a couple of rooms all on me own.'

'But we don't get any time to talk.'

'Well, we can talk now, so what's bothering you?'

'Nothing. I'm going up.'

Pam wasn't sure he was telling her the truth. They did need to get away – she knew they ought to have some time on their own, but this had been his busiest time. She was looking forward to the winter Sundays when they could just go off for the day. She was worried about him being home earlier when the evenings started closing in. Would he want to be here on his own with Lil? Perhaps while Pam was at work he could spend more time with his father.

'We're certainly able to save a lot more now,' Pam whispered that night as they lay in bed. 'Do you think we could go on that holiday? We need to know as we've got to get a passport and . . . I've got to get time off.'

The streetlamp flickered through the curtains, making moving patterns round the room. Pam looked at Lu who was lying on his back gazing up at the ceiling.

'I don't want to go with Jill and Billy.'

Pam was taken aback. 'Why? A while ago you was all for it.'

'Things have changed.'

'What things?'

'We ain't ever on our own, and if we go away with them,

well, you know what I mean?'

Pam raised herself up on her elbow. 'No, I don't.'

'We can't get away from this family.'

'Jill's different.'

'No, I'm sorry, Pam. If we go away it's got to be on our own.'

Pam lay back down. 'OK, if you say so. Where were you thinking of going?'

'What about going back to Ramsgate?'

'Ramsgate? Why Ramsgate?'

'We had a good time there, and besides, we can go on me bike.'

'Oh great. I want to go somewhere where I can dress up, somewhere exciting.'

'Well, we can't afford it.'

'Yes, we can.'

'I've bought a new bike.'

Pam was stunned.

'Did you hear what I said?'

'Yes.' Pam whispered.

'Haven't you got anything to say?'

'If you've bought it then there's not a lot left for me to say.'

'It was a bargain. And I'm getting a good price for mine.'

'So when're you getting it?'

'As soon as the paperwork's done. It ain't much a week.'

Pam didn't ask how much, she was too upset. 'I wish you'd talked it over with me.'

'Why?'

'Well, it is my money as well.'

'No it ain't, it's what I earn.'

'So.' Pam sat up and plonked her hands on the eider-down. 'What you earn is your own, and what I get is ours. You've got some funny ideas about sharing.' She was trying very hard to keep her temper and not shout as Lil was in the next room.

'It ain't like that.'

'So what's it like then? Go on, tell me.'

'I've been doing a few deals on the side.'

'Who with?'

'Well, Marc had this—'

Pam was so angry she wanted to hit him. She'd never felt like this before. She turned to Lu and raised her fist. Tears ran down her face; slowly she lowered her arm. 'Marc? I didn't think you'd have anything more to do with him.'

'He is me brother.'

'He's always been the one what gets you into trouble. I would have thought you'd have learned your lesson the last time. You're reminded of it every time you look in the mirror.'

'That ain't a nice thing to say.'

'I don't feel nice. I feel very angry. I never thought you'd get mixed up with the things Marc does.'

'It's all right. It's legit.'

'How can it be if Marc's involved?'

Lu tried to pull her to him but she moved to the edge of the bed.

'Pam, don't get upset. It's a smashing bike. You wait till you see it.'

'No, thank you. I'm not interested in the bike, it's the money and how you got it what worries me.'

'Oh come on, Pam, you ain' got nothing to worry about.

Let's make the most of it while we're young enough to enjoy it.'

'I wanted to go abroad.'

'We will. I promise.' He leaned over and kissed her arm. 'I do love you. I tell you what, when the time comes and if we need a bit extra to get a nice house, I'll sell it.'

'You will?'

'That's another promise.'

Pam knew she couldn't be mad at him for long. As she snuggled back down he hugged her close and all her niggles about him getting mixed up with Marco's deals soon disappeared.

Chapter 17

After their week at Ramsgate Pam felt relaxed and happy despite being disappointed at not going to Italy. They stayed at the same guest house and wandered round doing the things they had done on their honeymoon. They were having fun and laughing together and for the first time in months were alone. Pam didn't want it to end.

When they arrived back at Lil's, they found, wedged up against the clock on the wooden mantelpiece that had cigarette burn marks along the edge, a postcard with a picture of Rome on the front. It was addressed to Pam and Lu.

'Looks like they're having a good time,' said Lil, handing the postcard to Pam. 'I got one as well.'

Pam recalled how upset and angry Jill had been with Lu when Pam had told her they were going to Ramsgate instead.

'Seems you just ain't meant to go to Italy,' said Jill. 'D'you think he bought that bike on purpose?'

'Don't think so.' But the thought had crossed Pam's mind once or twice.

Lu was happy with his new bike, it was fast and had a lot of gleaming chrome. It attracted plenty of admiring glances from other bikers. Pam couldn't see him selling it to put a deposit on a house. At the moment she wasn't worried about that. In fact the only little niggle at the back of her mind was the time Lu spent – or so he said – with his father. He never seemed to be short of money these days and when she queried that he said his father had started to give them more.

'Why wasn't he a bit more generous when you had your broken arm?'

'It was winter then. You should just be grateful for the bit extra now.' And, as far as Lu was concerned, that was the end of the explanation.

With the autumn came rain and plenty of it. It was late one evening when Lu got home and Pam just had to comment on the amount of time he was spending at his father's.

'Don't sell much this weather so I decided to give him a hand with other things. That place needs a few jobs done on it, decorating and such.'

'Thought the landlord did those sorts of things.'

'Don't think he does much.'

'Is Marco helping?'

'Yer. Why?' Lu was very vague.

'Didn't think you two was into this decorating lark.'

'Gives us something to do.'

At the end of October everybody sat in silence watching the terrible tragedy at Aberfan unfold on their TV screens.

'I feel so sorry for those parents. It's bloody awful losing your child. Don't matter how old they are,' said Ivy quietly, shedding a few tears.

Rose only nodded as she too sat speechless.

A man was saying, through his tears, that all the local

people knew a stream ran under that tip.

'Why does the government let these things happen?' asked Pam.

'They call it politics,' said Ivy angrily.

Time went on and it wasn't long before the shops were putting up their Christmas decorations. Pam shuddered when she remembered how they had spent last Christmas.

'D'you fancy going out this Christmas Eve?' Lu asked her.

'No thanks. I don't want anything like that to happen again.'

'Don't worry about it. I think Marc has seen to those blokes.'

Pam didn't reply. Whatever Lu said in Marco's defence, she would never forgive him. And she didn't really understand why Lu had forgiven him so readily, as every time he looked in the mirror he must be reminded of that terrible night.

It had been many months since Pam had been to see Lu's father and she looked about her when they walked in on Christmas morning. 'So, what decorating have you been doing?' To her it all seemed just the same.

'Decorating? Oh, it's mostly upstairs,' Lu said hurriedly.

Pam looked at him suspiciously. Was he going to tell her it was for her? Was he still hoping they would move here one day? He didn't offer to take her up to see his handiwork.

'What's she on about?' asked Mr Cappa.

'Nothing. Don't worry about it, Dad.'

Mr Cappa didn't make any more comments; he just poured himself another drink from the bottle at the side of his chair.

Nothing had changed there, either, Pam thought to herself. But Christmas was everything Pam had hoped for, without any hitches. She knew she would have to spend one night round at Jean's; Lu said Al had insisted. They decided to go round on Boxing night. It was the same as the year before last, with Mr Cappa, after having a few drinks, sleeping in the armchair, and Marco trying to be the big 'I am'. As usual he was smartly dressed. Gone was his Teddy boy look; now he was sporting a frilly shirt. Al, quiet as always, was pleasant and Pam enjoyed talking to him. She tried to keep out of Jean's way, but when Jean suggested Pam help her with the supper, she had no choice. Pam followed Jean into the kitchen a little apprehensively. To Pam's surprise Jean did not mention the family's so-called wealth, but she did say she was pleased to see them, especially after what had happened last year. She also commented on Lu's scar, saying she wouldn't let anyone get away with it if it had been her Al.

As Jean had obviously never been in that situation Pam didn't really think she should make such rash statements, but she left the thought unsaid.

As the evening wore on, with Pam chatting politely to everyone, she felt she had done her duty for this year. She was glad when it was almost over.

She was leaving the bathroom when Marco came up the stairs.

'You ain't got a lot of time for me, have you, sis?' he said, blocking the top of the stairs.

'No,' said Pam. 'Not after what happened to me and Lu.'

'I've been making a few inquiries and when I find out who those blokes are, they'll have me to answer to. But I swear on my mother's life that at the moment I don't know who they were.'

Pam laughed. 'You are wicked. You don't even know where your mother is.' But another thought quickly dashed across her mind: didn't Lu tell her a while back that Marc had got it sorted?

'Honest, Pam. I was really worried about you and Lu.'

She knew it wasn't wise to mention what Lu had said just now. 'OK. I suppose I've got to believe you. Can I pass please?'

He smiled. 'Of course.' To Pam's surprise he bowed low and stepped aside.

Much to Pam's relief 1967 started uneventfully. She and Lu still went to the pictures every Friday evening and often stopped on the way home for fish and chips. The couple who were running the shop now looked contented. They had cleaned the place up and put in a few tables and chairs where you could sit and eat; it was all very pleasant, but Pam couldn't help but wish they still had the flat above.

It was a cold clear February night; reluctantly they left the warmth of the fish shop. As they made their way home, Pam got down and huddled as close as she could behind Lu. Her eyes were watering with the cold; how she longed to be in Lil's cosy kitchen and for him to get a car.

As much as she wanted a place of their own so they could start to think about a family, to go home from work to Lil's every day was still bliss. The fire ready roaring, the cups of tea put in her hands and her dinner on the table was like a little bit of heaven. Although she knew Lu wasn't that happy staying there, Pam was loving every minute of being looked after. She let her thoughts drift to how many times she and Lil had sat and talked of the things Lil and Ivy had done when they were young. How in the first war they had clung together and helped each other, always praying their husbands would come home safely. How when Sid died of the flu, Ivy and Harry had been there to help Lil with her two boys. How desperate they had been when the depression came and Harry was out of work. They'd shared what they could.

'Your grandad was a lovely man,' Lil had said one evening last week, as they'd drunk their tea. 'He never complained when I was in your gran's crying 'cos I didn't have anything left to pawn. He'd have given me his last shilling if he'd had one,' she'd sniffed.

When Lil'd managed to get a cleaning job Ivy had looked after her boys as well as taking in washing.

'You should have seen the water running down the walls in your scullery when she had the old copper alight. She worked bloody hard, but still always had some kind of hot meal ready for me when I got home. My hands used to be red raw in the winter with all the soda water. Didn't have nice hot water in those days, you had to scrub steps with cold. It was hard work. It upset Harry, he didn't like me and your gran working like that, felt he was letting her down. Your gran was in a terrible state when he died. It was so sudden.'

The tears had sparkled in Lil's eyes as she reminisced.

'When the second war came and our boys had to go off

we both cried for days. My oldest, Sid, was the first, then your dad and Bob went together. I was the lucky one, both mine came back.'

'It must have been awful when my dad was killed,' Pam had said.

'It was. And so near home as well.'

'I often look at the empty space and try to imagine me dad talking to me.'

'That's nice. Your poor mum. In some ways it was a good job she found out she was expecting you soon after, as it helped them both.'

'Gran has always been good to me, even if I have been a bit of a so and so at times.'

'You was only being a kid. Liked to feel your feet now and then.'

'I expect you miss Sid? Were you upset when he went to Australia?'

Lil smiled. 'Yer, but he seems happy enough, and settled. That's all you can want for your kid.'

'D'you think he'll ever come back?'

'Dunno. Shouldn't think so. I'd like to see the kids. P'raps one of these days I'll be able to go and visit him.' She laughed. 'Don't think I'd fancy being on a boat all those weeks, though.'

'You could always fly.'

'What, me? Na. Wouldn't like to go up in one of those things.'

'I would,' said Pam wistfully.

''Sides,' continued Lil, interrupting Pam's thoughts, 'just think of the cost. Sid went out on one of those assisted passages. Mind you, he can only come back if he pays his own fare and that'll cost him.'

If she'd been Lil, Pam would have moved heaven and earth to get to Australia. How exotic it sounded: She longed to travel more, to go abroad like Jill had. Perhaps one day they would have the money . . .

When Lu turned the bike into Newbury Street he jammed on the brake and Pam, who still had her eyes closed and was thinking of foreign holidays, almost lost her balance.

'What you do that for?'

'Look.'

Pam put her head above his shoulder. 'My God. What're they doing there?'

Lu didn't answer but moved as fast as he could along the crowded road, dodging the people who had come out of their houses to look at the scene.

They could see a fire engine was outside numbers 28 and 30. Panic filled Pam and when Lu stopped the bike, she almost fell off in her eagerness to see whose house it had been to.

'My mum and gran,' she yelled, pushing through the gathering and running up to a fireman who was rolling up the hose.

Lu was beside her holding her arm. 'What house you been to, mate?'

'Number thirty. It's a bit of a mess inside, mostly water.'

'Lil,' screamed Pam, looking up at the first-floor window, which was their room. 'Is she hurt?'

Dolly Windsor grabbed her hand. 'Yer gran and mum's all right, but poor old Lil didn't look so good when they brought her out. Took her off in an ambulance. Was her fault, by all accounts.'

Pam pushed Doll out of the way and ran into number 28. 'Mum. Gran,' she screamed out as she charged down the passage. She almost fell into the kitchen as her mother opened the door.

'Oh Pam.' Rose held out her arms and Pam ran into them. Rose's face was streaked with dirt and her hair at the front singed; her dress was dirty and damp.

'What happened?' called Lu breathlessly, right behind Pam.

Ivy was sitting in the chair holding a glass and crying, her tears making clean streaks down her dirty face.

'Thank Gawd both of you wasn't in there,' said Ivy.

'Was it her fags?' asked Lu.

Ivy nodded.

Lu paced the small kitchen and, making a fist, hit his hand. 'I'm always telling her to be more careful. Is she badly hurt?' he asked softly.

'She leaves her fags all over the place. That mantelpiece in there is full of burn marks.' Pam was angry.

Rose let go of Pam and sat at the table. 'Sit down.'

Quickly, they both did as they were told. Tears ran unchecked from Pam's eyes. She shuddered; she felt cold even though the room was warm. She didn't want to be told anything bad. She loved Lil; the old lady was almost part of the family. 'Is she badly hurt?'

'We don't know, but it seems she's had some kind of stroke.' Ivy dabbed at her eyes. 'We don't know much just yet. Whether it was that what made her drop the fag or she'd fallen asleep and the shock brought it on – we won't know . . .'

'Bob and Doreen have gone with her to the hospital,' said Rose.

'I'll phone Jill tomorrow,' said Pam quietly. 'Oh Mum, I don't want anything to happen to . . .' She began to cry and Lu put his arm round her shoulders.

'I always said those bloody fags would be the death of her one of these days, the silly cow.' Ivy's voice rose in anger.

'What's it like in there?' Lu inclined his head towards the wall.

'Not good,' sniffed Ivy.

'How did you know about it?' asked Pam.

'First we heard was the bloke over the back shouting and yelling. We rushed into the scullery and heard the crackling. Smoke was coming out of the back bedroom. We both tried to get up the stairs but the smoke . . .' Ivy stopped.

'It was awful. I rushed over to Bob,' said Rose. 'He's got his hands badly burned. Doreen ran up the road and phoned the fire brigade.'

'I tried to get back in. I was calling to Lil, but she didn't answer. I couldn't see. The smoke.' Ivy was staring into space. 'I couldn't help her.'

'It's terrible in there, and the water from the hose is running down the stairs.' It was Rose's turn to speak. 'I don't know what the bedrooms are like.'

'Who got her out?' asked Lu.

'Her son. Bob. I keep thinking of my Dan,' said Rose. 'How Lil tried to help him out when he got killed.' Tears spilled from her eyes. 'And we couldn't help her.'

Pam went to her mother and held her close. 'Did you see her?'

'Just the top of her head. They wrapped her in a blanket and put her in the ambulance.'

'Fire's a good servant, but a bloody bad master,' said Ivy.

'I'll put the kettle on,' said Lu. 'Try not to worry. She's a tough old bird.'

'There's a drop of whisky there,' said Ivy, pointing to a bottle on the dresser.

'No, ta all the same, I'll have tea. You have the whisky, it might help you sleep.'

'I won't go to bed till Bob gets back.'

'He might be at the hospital all night.'

'I'll still wait up. I wouldn't be able to sleep anyway till I find out how me old mate is.'

Pam thought her heart would break. What if it had been her gran? What would Jill say? Lu was quietly going about making tea and putting the cups on the table. Pam looked around at the three people she loved more than anyone else in the world. Please don't take any of them away from me, she prayed.

Each one was silent with their own thoughts as they sat drinking their tea. It was Ivy who spoke first.

'What are you two going to do tonight? Where are you going to sleep?'

'I don't think I could sleep,' said Pam.

'No, nor me,' said Lu. 'Would you mind if we stayed here the night?'

'Course not.'

'I don't suppose any of us will sleep, not till we hear how Lil is.' Rose began filling the teapot again. 'Good job I did the shopping yesterday and I got another quarter of tea.' She gave them a faint smile.

'What about all your stuff?' asked Ivy, beginning to get practical. 'It'll be in a bit of a state.'

'We'll worry about that tomorrow when it's light,' said Lu.

'Let's hope no bloody looters get in there first.'

'Surely no one would go in and steal things?' said Pam.

Ivy gave a hollow laugh. 'Don't you believe it. Saw some dreadful things in the war. While people were still buried alive in their shelters, there was thieving bastards pinching their clothes out of their wardrobes.'

'No,' said Pam truly shocked, not only at her gran's language, but at the thought that people could do such a thing.

'And I thought everybody helped one another,' said Lu.

'Some was too busy helping themselves,' Rose said wearily.

'Look, Pam, why don't you go and have a kip on my bed,' said Ivy. 'And you, Rose, you've both got to go to work tomorrow. I'll wake you if there's any news.'

Pam looked at Lu. She was suddenly feeling very tired. 'What about you, Lu?'

'I'll keep Gran company.'

'You don't have to, son.'

'No, I want to. Tomorrow I don't need to go out till the streets are aired, and anyway, we don't do a lot this time of year.'

'Please yourself,' said Ivy.

When Ivy didn't argue, Pam could see her gran would be pleased with a bit of company. She kissed her mother, Lu and her gran goodnight and went upstairs.

She only took off her trousers and jumper before she pulled back the sheet and snuggled between the blankets. She felt safe there in her gran's bed. It reminded her of how, when she was a little girl, she would creep in with her gran for a cuddle when her mother went to work. She always wanted to be told stories. Her thoughts went to Lil. If only they knew how she was. She closed her eyes. This was going to be a long night.

Chapter 18

'Pam. Pam.' An urgent voice was coming through her dreams. 'Pam, wake up.'

She blinked quickly then opened her eyes and sat up. Outside it was light. 'What is it? What's wrong?' She suddenly remembered all that had happened. 'Have you any news of Lil?'

Lu, who was standing over her holding a cup of tea, shook his head. 'No. But I thought I'd better wake you up to get ready for work. You was sparko.'

'I must have dropped off.'

He sat on the edge of the bed. 'You've been dead to the world all night. A couple of times I came up to see if you was all right, but you was well away.'

'There hasn't been any news of Lil then?'

'No, 'fraid not. I went over earlier but Bob and Doreen ain't back yet.'

'Have you been next door?'

He nodded. 'I just had a quick look. It's a right mess. A lot of stuff is black with smoke, that's without the water that's everywhere.'

'I ain't going to work today. I'm going in there and try to clear up.'

'You can't. How do we know if it's safe or not?'

'What d'you mean?'

'Well, I didn't go upstairs. We don't know if the floor-boards are still sound. What if the ceiling falls down?'

'Can't we try? I need some clean clothes.'

'Don't reckon they'll be very clean now.'

'Why? Was our room damaged?'

'Don't look like it, it was mostly Lil's room.'

'The stuff in the drawers should be all right then.'

'Well, come down and ask your mum what she thinks.'

'OK.' Pam slipped on her trousers and jumper and went down to the kitchen where her mother was busy making tea. She could see her gran hadn't been to bed.

'Not had any news then yet?' she asked her.

'No,' said Ivy.

'I ain't going to work today, I'm going in to try to clear up a bit,' said Pam.

'Is it safe?' asked her mother.

'That's what I asked,' said Lu.

'I can't sit here all day and not do something, 'sides it'll help the time to pass until we hear something about Lil. We should do soon. I couldn't bear to go to work, I'd be wondering about her all day.'

'Please yourself,' said Ivy. 'I'll stay in here and wait for Bob and Doreen.'

'I'll have to go off this afternoon,' said Lu, 'but I'll try and get back as soon as I can.'

Pam smiled at him. It was good to have someone to rely on in a crisis. 'Let's have this tea and a bit of toast then we'll go and see what needs to be done.'

'I don't want to go and leave you,' said Rose. 'But with only me there I don't have a lot of choice.'

'No, don't worry. We'll do what we can,' said Pam. She knew her mother's boss wasn't that well and when Mrs Kennett was off everything was down to her mother. She had the keys to open up and lock up again at the end of the day. Fortunately, Mrs Kennett's son always collected the flowers from the market for his mother's shop as well as his own.

'You'll let us know when you hear something, won't you, Gran?'

'Course I will.'

Pam pushed open the back door to number thirty very tentatively. The smell of smoke almost took her breath away.

'Let me go first,' said Lu as they made their way into the kitchen.

Pam looked up. 'Look at that.' The ceiling hung in great water bubbles. 'D'you think it's safe?'

'Wouldn't think so. I'll get a broom and release the water.'

'Better wait till we've cleared the table out of the way.'

Together they moved the table and chairs outside. Pam stood back when Lu took the broom handle and punched a hole in the ceiling.

'Ugh,' said Pam as, with a great rush, the water, laths and plaster came down. 'We'd better clear this lot up before we tread it everywhere.'

As soon as they had swept up the mess in the kitchen they began to work their way along the passage.

'This floor's all squelchy,' said Pam. 'I'll put these runners on the line then get a mop and broom and sweep it out.'

'If I was you I'd start at the top of the stairs.'

Pam looked up the stairs at Lil's bedroom. The paint on the door was blistered. 'Can we put the light on?'

'I wouldn't, not till we see if it's burned through the electrics, but I think it's safe to go up. Follow me.'

Very slowly they made their way up the stairs. The smell of smoke was getting stronger.

Pam put her hand on the banister. 'This is all grimy.' The smoke tickled her nose and she rubbed it with her grimy hand. 'Damn.'

'What's wrong?'

'Is my face dirty?'

He laughed. 'Your nose is, but don't worry about it, I expect it'll be a lot worse before the day's out.'

'We'll have to get these windows up here opened as soon as we can,' she said, trying to rub the smuts off her nose.

Lu pushed Lil's door open. 'It still feels warm.'

'It must have been awful,' Pam stopped and choked back a sob. 'I hope Lil's going to be all right.'

'Course she will.' Lu stood in the doorway with Pam looking over his shoulder.

'It looks a right mess in there,' she said.

'I'll go in first.' Lu trod very carefully as he made his way to the sash window and tried to push it up. 'It's stuck.'

Pam was right behind him. 'Look at her bed.'

Lil's bed was just a mass of soggy bedclothes, charred at the edges.

'It's a wonder she got out of that lot alive,' said Lu quietly. 'We'll need a bag to put all this in.'

Pam was still finding it hard not to cry. 'Poor Lil.'

She followed Lu across the tiny landing to their bedroom.

The smoke had blackened the wallpaper round the door and the soot appeared to have settled on every surface.

'It'll take ages to clean this lot up.'

Lu pushed up the window. 'Let's get some fresh air in here first.'

'Where shall we start?' asked Pam as she looked around.

'Get what clothes you want out, then take them over to your gran's. She might give 'em a wash if they need it. Then get some bags, or what about boxes? Have we got any of those we brought our bits over in?'

'They're downstairs in the front room.'

'I'll get them and start to clear Lil's bed.'

Pam began to take their clothes out of the drawer. 'These don't look too bad.' She sniffed them. 'They smell a bit. I'll put them on the line and give them an airing.'

'Right, I'll go and get the boxes.'

Pam was so pleased he would be here for a little while helping.

He called Pam after he'd stripped Lil's bed. 'I reckon she'll have to have a new bed. It don't look very safe. The wood round this spring's burnt.'

'We'll cross that bridge when she comes back,' Pam replied softly. 'I wish we knew how she is. This waiting is getting me down.'

Lu put his arm round her shoulders. 'Come on now. You're doing a grand job.'

She sniffed. 'It's going to take a long while to get everywhere clean.'

'Your gran's going to give us some clean bedclothes, so at least we'll be able to sleep here tonight. Do you want a hand getting those curtains down?'

She nodded, and they set to. There was so much to do.

'Pam! Pam! You there?'

Pam put her head over the banisters. 'Gran, what is it? Have you heard from Bob?'

'No, not yet, love. I've got a bit of dinner ready for you, so come on in before it gets cold.'

'What time is it?'

'Gone twelve.'

'Blimey,' said Lu. 'Is it that already?' They walked down the stairs together. 'Pam, will you be all right here on your own? I'll have to have a bit of a tidy-up before I go, but I'll try and get back as soon as I can.'

'You're gonner have a bit of dinner first, ain't yer, son?'

'Course.'

While Lu was washing, Pam told her gran what state the place was in. Then they sat quietly eating their dinner.

'That was smashing, Gran,' said Lu. 'I was starving.'

'I could see that.'

'Well, he's been working very hard,' said Pam. 'He's been up and down those stairs I don't know how many times.'

'I saw the pile of rubbish in the yard.'

'It wouldn't have been so bad if I could have got the window open, I could have chucked it out that way,' Lu said.

'You sure you two want to stay there tonight?'

'Ain't got a lot of choice,' said Lu.

'No, suppose not. There ain't any water in your room, is there? Only you can't sleep in a damp room.'

'No, Lil always shut the doors upstairs.'

'That's good. Glad to see she had a bit of common sense sometimes.'

'Now our window's wide open the smell is going off a bit,' said Pam.

'Look, I must go, otherwise the old man will be sitting stewing.' Lu quickly pecked Pam's upturned face and left.

'He's a nice lad,' said Ivy. 'I'm glad you married him.'

'So am I,' said Pam. 'I'll go back and do some more. I must clean those windows.'

'I'll give you some curtains for your bedroom. Good job I've got a spare pair.'

Pam was sitting on the window sill cleaning the bedroom window when she saw Bob and Doreen turn into Newbury Street. She almost fell off the sill. She hurried down the stairs, through the back and into her gran's. 'They're back,' she yelled as she rushed through the kitchen.

Ivy was right behind her and they reached their front door the same time as Bob and Doreen were at theirs.

'Ivy,' said Bob, catching sight of them hurrying across the road.

'Well?' asked Ivy breathlessly. 'How is she?'

Bob pushed open his front door. 'Come on in.'

They all went along the passage to the kitchen.

'I'll put the kettle on,' said Doreen.

Both Bob and Doreen looked tired and drawn. Their clothes were crumpled and they clearly hadn't had any sleep.

Ivy sat at the table. 'How is she, Bob?'

He too sat down and put his head in his hands and wept.

Pam didn't know what to say. She had never seen a man cry before. She stood staring at her gran and Bob, letting her own tears run unchecked down her dirty face.

'Oh my God,' whispered Ivy, putting her hand to her mouth. 'No, don't tell me. Don't tell me she's gone.'

Doreen came and put her hand on Ivy's shoulder. 'No, she ain't dead, but . . .' She stopped to catch her breath and wipe her eyes. 'She ain't that good.'

Pam felt this all had to be a dream. She wanted to wake up. It couldn't be real. This wasn't happening to the Lil she had known all her life.

Bob blew his nose. 'Sorry about that. She's had a stroke. She's lost the use of her right arm and her speech. Her burns are pretty bad, mostly her right arm and the side of her face. They think she had the stroke first and of course she was in bed having a fag.' He stopped and blew his nose again.

'Do they know what brought the stroke on?' asked Ivy. She looked up at Doreen who put a cup of tea in front of her. 'Thanks.'

Bob shook his head. 'I think it was just one of those things.'

'Lost her power of speech. Poor old Lil. That'll bloody well finish her off, not being able to answer back.' Ivy brushed the tears from her cheeks.

'She'll be in the hospital for quite a while. I phoned Jill and they're coming up tonight when Billy finishes. She can't get hold of him at work.'

'What about Helen?' asked Rose.

'I phoned Ted and he said they'll come as soon as they can get someone to look after the kids. Thank Gawd they've got a car.'

Pam sat quietly listening. She suddenly felt very sorry for Jill; Jill who had always had everything. Now she had a gran who was ill, very ill. It made Pam realize how lucky she was to have a gran who could walk and talk.

'Me and Lu have been clearing up over there. I think Lil will have to have a new bed when she comes home,' said Pam.

'Thanks, love. But don't worry about that. Let's get her well first,' said Bob.

'D'you know how long will she be kept in?' asked Ivy.

'They've no idea. Just got to wait and see.'

'Did she recognize you?'

He shook his head sadly. 'Don't think so.'

'It's a bloody shame,' said Ivy.

'Look, Gran, d'you want to stay here? I'll get back and carry on. Uncle Bob, is it still all right if me and Lu stay there?'

He gave her a weary smile. 'Is it safe?'

'Lu seems to think so. It's a bit of a mess, but we'll manage.'

'Well, if you're sure. We don't want any more trouble.'

Pam stood up. 'Are you staying, Gran?'

'No, I'll go home. You two look as if you could do with getting some shuteye.'

'Yer, we didn't get any sleep last night.'

'Look, I'll get you something to eat later on. Let me know when Jill gets here, they can have a bit of tea with us.'

'Thanks, Ivy.'

'Sit down. We'll see ourselves out.' She stopped at the kitchen door. 'She's more like a sister to me than just a friend and neighbour. Been through a lot together, we have.'

Nobody answered. They didn't have to. Everybody knew how close they were.

'Come on, Gran, you'd better make some cakes if they're all coming to tea.' Pam took Ivy's arm and led her across the road.

'Was that Bob and Doreen I saw?' said Dolly Windsor hastily coming up to them.

'Yes.'

'How is Lil?' she asked as she fell in step beside them.

Pam quickly answered. 'She's not too good at the moment.'

'Terrible thing, fires. All that smoke can ruin your lungs. Still, I expect Lil's lungs are like a coal mine already, the way she smokes.'

'We'll let you know when she's coming home,' said Pam, gently pushing her gran through the open door.

'Thanks.' Doll Windsor walked away, happy with the fact that she was first in Newbury Street to hear the news.

'That wasn't right what you just told her,' said Ivy.

'I know, but I didn't want to get in too deep. She would have kept us talking for hours if she knew Lil had had a stroke.'

'That's true.'

'D'you fancy another cup of tea?'

'Yer, then I think I'll have a bit of a lie down.'

'That's a good idea. You didn't get much sleep last night sitting in that chair, did you?'

'It was a bit uncomfortable, but I did doze off a couple of times.'

'I'll see to the tea.' Pam went into the kitchen and filled the kettle. She had seen her gran age overnight. How would she cope without Lil around? Please don't let anything else happen to Lil or my gran, she said under her breath.

Chapter 19

It was dark when Pam went back into her gran's. When she pushed open the door into the kitchen, she found the house was unusually quiet. She shuddered. It felt cold. She put on the light and stood for a moment, her thoughts flitting. In all her life she couldn't remember ever walking into this house without the lights on and the smell of cooking filling her nostrils. All she could smell now was smoke. It was clinging to her like an invisible blanket. The fire in the grate was very low; she went over and poked it, bringing it to life. Standing with the poker in her hand she stared at the flames. Her gran was right. Fire could be a good servant, but a terrible master.

She set about filling the kettle and getting the table ready for tea. Before she had left her clearing up next door she had looked out of the bedroom window and could see Bob's house was all in darkness. They too must be asleep; so far neither Jill nor Helen had arrived.

The kitchen door opened. 'Thought I heard someone,' said Ivy. 'I've had a lovely forty winks. Glad to see you've got the kettle on, love, I'm parched.'

'You didn't get any cakes made then?'

'No, they can have a bit of cheese on toast, and there's some biscuits as well.'

Pam had just poured out the tea when her mother and Lu walked in together.

'I see there's no light on in Bob's. Aren't they home yet?' asked Rose.

'Yes. They got home this afternoon.'

Between them Pam and Ivy related all they had been told about Lil's condition.

'A stroke,' said Rose. 'Poor Lil.'

'Will she get better?' asked Lu.

'It depends on how bad it is, she's an old lady, remember,' said Ivy softly.

'I don't look on her as old, she's got such a smashing sense of humour,' said Lu.

'We're all getting old, son,' sighed Ivy.

Pam looked at her gran. She wanted to shout out, You mustn't give up, but she knew Ivy was taking this very badly.

Late that evening, they were quietly listening to the radio when someone banged on the knocker, startling them. Lu went and answered the door. Pam jumped up and hugged Jill silently when she walked into the kitchen.

'I saw the light on so I knew you was still up. We've just got back from the hospital.' Jill stopped and wiped her eyes. 'Gran's on open order, that means we can go any time and visit her.'

'How did she seem?' said Ivy.

'It don't look like my gran laying there. Her face is all sagging down on one side and red with nasty blisters. With her good arm she keeps picking at the one that's bandaged. Some of her hair's burned and . . . Oh Pam, it's awful.' Her eyes were full of tears of pain and sorrow as she looked from one to the other.

'Did she know you?' asked Rose softly.

Jill shook her head. 'No. Will she ever get better?' Her voice was pleading for the right answer.

'What do the doctors think?' asked Ivy.

'They can't say just yet. If only she knew who we were and could talk to us. I just want my gran to talk to me.' Jill sat and cried pitifully, and there weren't any words of hope or comfort they could give her.

Pam went to her friend and held her close.

'Did Helen manage to get there?'

Jill nodded. 'Her and Ted couldn't stay too long as they've got the little ones to worry about.'

'If they want to bring them here I'll look after them for a bit.'

'Thanks, Granny Ivy, I'll tell Dad. He's gonner phone Ted's work tomorrow, just to let them know how she is.'

'Are you going home tonight?' asked Pam.

'No. I think Dad would like me around so I'm staying till the end of the week. Billy went home a while ago.'

They sat for only a little while before Jill left. Everybody had found conversation difficult. There was nothing to say that would make the situation better.

That night when they were in bed Pam held Lu's hand; she wanted reassurance that he was still there. Her mind was going over and over all that had happened in such a short time.

'You all right?' he asked.

'Yes, but I can't sleep.'

'D'you want to go downstairs?'

'No. That kitchen's in such a mess.'

'Good job we didn't wait for all that water to come down from the ceiling. At least we managed to save Lil's stuff from getting a soaking. Mind you, I don't know what the landlord's going to say about it all.'

'He will pay to get it repaired, won't he?'

'Dunno. It depends what sort of a bloke he is.'

'But Lil's been here for years.'

'I know. It has made a bit of a mess though.'

In the dark she grimaced as she remembered how Lu had punched a hole in the ceiling to release the water. Her mother had smiled as she picked out pieces of plaster from Pam's hair and said that it was like being in the war. But Rose hadn't said a lot about Lil. What was she thinking? Was she remembering how her husband had died and how Lil had tried to help rescue him? Pam knew she would never really find out exactly what had happened; perhaps it was too painful for her mother to recall.

Lu sat up. 'I'll go down and make us a cuppa.'

'OK.'

Although it was February and cold, they had left the window open as the smell of smoke still lingered. Pam lay listening to the sounds of people walking past. Sometimes the footsteps would stop and she would hear low voices; she guessed they would be looking at the house and talking about what had happened there. So many people knew Lil. She shuddered. Even with the extra blankets she couldn't get warm. Hurry up, Lu, she said to herself, I need a cuddle.

★ ★ ★

All week Jill had stayed with her parents. Every morning the Hunters went off to the hospital and, although it was late when they got home, they always came into Ivy's first with the day's news.

When they came in on the Friday evening Bob was looking a little brighter.

'So, how is she?' asked Ivy.

'We think she might be starting to remember who we are. When we got there this morning and started talking, she opened her eyes and for the first time took notice. She even tried to talk.'

'Oh, Bob, I'm so pleased.' Ivy put her handkerchief to her face. 'Think I'm getting a bit of a cold.'

'Every time one of us left the room her eyes followed us,' said Bob.

'She looks very frightened and confused,' said Doreen.

'I expect she's wondering what's happened to her,' said Ivy. She gave a little nervous laugh. 'Or she could be asking for a fag.'

'Over my dead bloody body,' said Bob. 'That's the last thing she'll get from me.'

'She will keep picking at her bad arm,' said Doreen.

'Poor Lil,' said Rose. 'It must be awful. Not knowing what's wrong with you and not being able to ask.'

'When I kissed her goodbye she didn't flinch and try to pull away like she's been doing,' said Jill with a catch in her voice. 'I don't know if that's a good sign or a bad one.'

Pam really felt for her friend.

On Sunday they were told that Lil was out of danger and now they could only go in at regular visiting times.

'That's good in some ways,' said Bob. 'But I don't like

the idea that she might think we've deserted her.'

'She won't think that,' said Ivy. 'Will they let friends in now?'

'I'll ask when we go in tomorrow.'

'That's good. I'd like to see her.'

'And I reckon she'll be pleased to see you.'

On Monday when Pam came home from work she went straight into her gran's as they were eating there at the moment. There was a note from Ivy and another from the rent man. Ivy had gone with Bob to see Lil. She got on and made the tea; it wasn't long before her mother and Lu arrived.

'I forgot the rent man came today,' said Pam, showing her mother the note, which just said he had called today.

'Don't worry about it, Ivy might have paid him.'

'But she ain't got Lil's rent book.'

'She's known him long enough to tell him what's happened.'

'I wonder if she showed him all the damage?' said Lu.

'I expect so.'

'I wish I'd seen him,' said Pam. 'Then I could find out when they'll be in to do the repairs.'

'Wait and see what Ivy knows. I'm sure she'll have it all sorted out.'

It was after eight when Ivy got home. She looked happy to have seen her friend but sad at the state she'd found her in.

'She's taking a little drink through a feeding cup and although she's very sleepy I think she recognized me.'

'Can she speak yet?' asked Rose.

'No, she just makes this funny noise. It's bloody heartbreaking to see her struggling to say something.' A tear ran slowly down Ivy's face.

'I'll make a pot of tea,' said Pam.

'It must be one of the worst things, to lose your power of speech.'

'I'm sure it will come back. Lil is a very determined lady,' said Rose.

'I hope so. When she gets home I'll be in there every day helping her.'

'I'm sure you will,' said Rose as she put the cups and saucers on the table.

'Can't she write things down?' asked Lu.

'Don't think she'll be able to, she's right-handed. 'Sides, there's plenty of time for that.'

'What about her burns?' asked Lu. 'Will they heal up?'

'The doctors hope so. But as one young whipper snapper said, "She is an old lady." I told him in no uncertain words that she might be old in body but she's got all her marbles and if we've got anything to do with it she'll be up and running before long.'

Pam smiled at her gran. Poor Lil wasn't going to get any peace when she got home; Ivy would soon get her on the road to recovery.

'Gran, did you see the rent man today?'

'Yes, love. I was going to tell you. I took him in and he just shook his head, but he's going to send a builder round to look at the damage.'

'Did he say when?'

'No, but don't worry, I'll be here to let him in.'

The following week the builder came to look at the damage in Lil's house.

'It's gonner cost a few bob,' said Ivy that evening when

they were sitting having their meal.

'That's not our worry though, is it?' Lu sat back and patted his stomach. 'That was delicious, as usual.'

Ivy smiled at him. 'Thanks, son. He did ask when Lil would be back. I told him I didn't know.'

'They won't throw us out, will they?' asked Pam, her voice full of alarm.

'Course not. Although the rent book's in Lil's name, they won't worry as long as she's around and the rent's paid.'

'But what if Lil don't . . .' Pam couldn't finish the sentence.

'Don't you go worrying your head about that. You two could always take it over. The rent ain't that much a week.' Ivy looked sad. 'I must admit after seeing her and the state she's in, I reckon it'll be a long while before she'll be able to look after herself again, if ever.'

'What happens when she comes out of hospital?' asked Rose.

'Don't know. I'll expect she'll have to go away to one of those places that teach you to walk and that.'

'Who will look after her when she's back on her feet?' asked Rose.

'I think Bob's already talking about their front room. Now both the girls have gone they'll have the space to look after her.'

'Will Doreen like that?' asked Rose.

'She won't have a lot of choice if that's what Bob wants, will she?'

'No, suppose not.'

Over the next month the builders came and gradually the house was put back in order.

'You wait till Lil sees this,' said Pam on Saturday afternoon when she was showing Bob and Doreen what a lovely job they had made of the house. They were standing in Lil's bedroom. 'It's a good job she never saw it when it was in a state.'

'It looks really nice,' said Doreen.

'If you like we'll take Mum's things out,' said Bob.

'But . . . But it's her house.'

'She won't ever be able to come back here,' said Bob.

'Why?'

'She can't walk at the moment as the stroke affected all of her right side and I don't think she ever will. I know she's always been independent, but this has beaten her.'

Pam slumped down on the springs of Lil's bed. 'What's me and Lu going to do?'

'Why don't you ask the landlord if you can take over the tenancy?'

'Could we?'

'Don't see why not. After all, you've been paying the rent.'

'You sure that's all right?'

'Course. They might put the rent up with a new agreement, but it shouldn't be much.'

'Are you sure you wouldn't mind?'

'I'd rather you be in here than a lot of strangers.'

Pam kissed Bob's cheek. 'Thanks. I can't wait to tell Lu.'

'About the furniture: if you fancy any of her bits let me know, and we'll get rid of anything you don't want,' said Bob.

'I'll have a word with Lu.'

'I'll come and collect the rest of her clothes,' said

Doreen. 'I've been meaning to come over and get them.'

'Don't worry. Any time will do.' Pam was finding it hard to keep the joy from her voice. She and Lu were going to have a house. A whole house to themselves. But it was Lil's house. Why did it have to come to them through such terrible circumstances?

They moved downstairs and out into the early March sunshine. 'Give my love to Lil when you see her tonight.'

'Will do,' said Bob as he and Doreen went across the road.

Pam hurried into her gran's. She just had to tell her the good news. She was so lucky. Her mind was racing. When Lu came home this evening they would sit and discuss all the plans they had for their future together. It might even include a baby at last.

Pam looked at her mother's sad face. 'I'm so very sorry, Mum.'

Rose looked up from the letter she was reading. 'He's not been well for a long time and he was getting on a bit, I suppose, but it's still a shock.'

'I wish I'd known him. We never did get the chance to see them.'

'You lead very busy lives.'

'Are you going up in the morning?'

Rose nodded.

'I'll come with you,' said Pam.

'No, it isn't worth it. Mum's managed to get the funeral arranged and I'm going to bring her back down here. Funny, I always thought she'd be the first to go as she's often been so poorly.'

'Where's she going to stay?'

'Here.'

'But where's she going to sleep?'

'Ivy's going to put a bed in the front room.'

'Oh,' said Pam.

'Ivy's been very good about it. I wish the shop had a flat over it then I could have gone there to live.'

'How's Mrs Kennett going to manage?'

'I told her son and he's letting one of his girls come and take over for the time I'm away.'

'She's no better then?'

Rose shook her head. 'This is all we seem to hear these days. People being ill. Let's hope that this being the third – they say everything comes in threes – that it'll be the last.'

'I hope so. I'm really sorry about Grandad.'

Rose managed a slight smile. 'Well, at least you'll be able to see your other gran.'

'I'm looking forward to that. I still think I should go with you.'

'I'd rather be on my own.'

'As long as you're sure.'

Rose nodded and reread the letter with the spidery writing again.

Chapter 20

For Pam, everything was wonderful. Now she had both her grans living next door. Granny Mallory was frail, kind and gentle. How Pam wished she had known her grandad. Every day she would go in from work for a while and sit and talk to the granny she'd never known before. She would hold her thin scraggy hand and listen to all she had to say about her mother when she was little girl. She learned how pretty she had been and how well she'd done at school. Granny Mallory hadn't really known Pam's father and was upset at not being able to attend either her daughter's or her granddaughter's weddings. She also said how heartbroken she was when Pam's father died.

Tonight Pam was singing when Lu walked in.

'You sound happy,' he said, kissing her cheek.

'I am. Aren't I lucky? I've got a smashing husband, a nice house and two grans living next door. I hope nothing happens to them. I don't know what I'd do.'

'You're got to remember they are both old,' said Lu.

'I know.'

'Well, as much as I like 'em, I'm glad we ain't living in there with all those old dears.'

'We don't have to, do we?'

'No. This is gonner be all ours.' He picked Pam up and twirled her round and round.

Jill was pleased about them living in Lil's house. 'It'll be great having you just across the road from Mum and Dad. Mind you, I don't know how they'll manage when Gran comes out of hospital. They reckon they're gonner turn the front room into a bedroom, but I don't think Mum's all that pleased about it.'

'That's what my gran's done. What else can they do when someone has a job getting up the stairs?' asked Pam.

Jill shrugged. 'Can't your granny go upstairs?'

'No, it's her hip, it's awful to see her struggling. Good job we've still got the old lav outside.'

'It's so dreadful, getting old,' said Jill. 'Still, it'll be nice for Dad to have Gran home. He's beginning to look exhausted with all this going up the hospital nearly every night.'

'As you won't be up next weekend, me and Mum are going in to see Ivy on Sunday.'

'That's nice. Thanks.'

Watching Jill's wistful expression, Pam felt almost guilty at having her family so near.

The following Sunday, as promised, Pam and Rose went to see Lil. Pam had been shocked to see how ill she was and had almost walked past her. It had been very distressing to sit and watch this frail, wizened old woman try to talk. The burns had scabbed over and they looked very painful.

'If she stopped scratching them it would help,' said Bob. It was tragic to see him pulling his mother's hand away, begging her not to do it, and slowly and painfully trying to help her with her words.

But it was even more tragic to see the sadness in Lil's pale watery eyes and the frustration as she picked at her dead arm. Pam couldn't see how she would ever get better.

'Well, she'll never be the same,' said Rose as they made their way home on the bus. 'But give it time.'

Over the following month everything Pam and Lu had hoped for was coming true. They were planning how they would furnish the house and had even bought some of Lil's bits to get them started, including paying the rental on her TV.

'I love this contemporary stuff,' said Pam when they were standing gazing at the furniture in a shop window. They wanted to get some idea of the latest and trendiest designs.

'You'll have to hang on for a few weeks till trade bucks up,' said Lu. 'Tell you what, let's wait till we go to the Ideal Home Exhibition.'

She squeezed his arm. 'That's a great idea. Thanks. I'll really look forward to that.'

Lil was still in hospital but according to Ivy she was very slowly making progress. She was able to sit in a chair for a short while and could scribble a few words on a pad.

'It's like a spider crawling over the paper, I can't really understand it, but it's a good sign,' said Ivy.

Jill came to see her gran most weekends and some Saturdays she and Billy came to tea with Pam and Lu. Pam did enjoy playing housewife. She was so happy that she and Lu had even talked about starting a family.

'I reckon we should wait till our name's on the rent book,' said Lu. 'Just in case.'

'But what can go wrong?'

'Let's just wait and see.'

It was after they had filled in all the forms from the landlord and were waiting for a new rent book with their name on it to show they had taken over the tenancy that the bombshell dropped. The rent man left a letter telling them the landlord wasn't going to let the house any more, but they could buy it if they wanted to.

'We can't afford this sort of money,' said Lu, reading the letter over and over again.

'I thought that if you sell your bike . . .' Pam said hesitantly.

'And how do I get to work?'

'On a bus like the rest of us.' Pam snapped, trying to hide the disappointment in her voice.

'Thanks a bunch.'

'You always said you'd sell it if it would help.'

'But it won't help, will it? Where are we gonner get one thousand six hundred and fifty-nine quid from?'

'We can get a mortgage. We *are* getting it cheaper as we're living here.'

'That's very kind of him, I must say. But he ain't doing it as a favour to us. Can't you see, this way he don't have to pay the agent's fee. No, I'm sorry. I ain't gonner have a millstone like that hanging round me neck.'

'But it's the chance of a lifetime.'

'And what sort of money will we have to pay back every week? That's if we can find the deposit. And don't forget I ain't exactly in what they would call a stable job, am I?'

'I'm sure we'll be able to manage.'

'And what about the surveyor, solicitor and every other

Tom, Dick and Harry that wants a bit of our hard-earned cash for doing bugger all?'

'You're just trying to make it sound hard.'

'I ain't trying, it is hard, bloody hard.'

'I thought this is what you wanted?'

'I do, one day, when we've got a few bob behind us.'

Pam began to pull a sulky face.

'It's no good looking like that. We'll just have to find somewhere else to live if we can't stop here.'

'And where do you hope to find this wonderful somewhere?' Pam was angry; she didn't want to leave the house.

'I dunno. But you can put the idea of buying this place right out of your mind.'

'I wanted a nice house so we could start a—'

'Bloody hell, you ain't stopped taking the pill, have you? We talked about this. Of all the daft things. We can't afford a kid. I would have thought you'd have more sense than to—'

'I ain't stopped taking the pill!'

'Thank Gawd. Don't give me frights like that. It's no good, Pam. You can't blackmail me into buying this place.'

'Gran always said she'd—'

He banged the table. 'I might have guessed you'd go running in there to tell them.'

'It's me mum and gran, for Christ's sake. 'Sides, I didn't tell 'em. I ain't been in there. I waited till you got home.'

'Now I suppose you'll go next door and tell them we ain't buying it, pouring out all your woes to 'em.'

'Well, yes. Lu, why are you being so nasty about this? Can't we sit and talk about it?'

'No. I ain't putting all my money—'

Pam quickly interrupted him. 'It's my money as well, don't forget.'

'But it's my bike you're thinking of selling.'

'You could get a smaller one.'

'I don't want a smaller one. I can just see Marc's face if I turn up on a little pop-pop.'

'I thought Marc would rear his ugly head sooner or later in this conversation.' Pam was near to tears. She desperately wanted this house. She was happy here. 'I'm going next door.'

'You do that. Go and tell them that your wicked husband won't let you buy a house.'

Pam went out and slammed the front door. She didn't really want to go in to her mother's. She didn't want to let them know they had been arguing.

She sat on the window sill, feeling utterly miserable, when Dolly Windsor walked past.

'Hello there, Pam. What you doing sitting outside, forgot your key?'

'No. It's just that I thought I'd pop out for . . .' She bit her lip trying hard to think of an excuse. 'A bit of butter.'

'Ain't your gran got any?'

'I don't like to worry them.' She gave a little smile. 'Don't want them to think I can't manage.'

'Course not. I think you'll find that little shop round the corner's still open.'

'Thanks, Doll.'

'It must be nice for you to have both your grans living next door.'

'Yes, it is.'

'Like to see families all together. You know, you should have your coat on, it's a bit chilly out here now.'

'Yes. I'll just go back in and get it.'

'I hear Lil's making a bit of a recovery, but a stroke!' Doll looked up and down the road making sure no one was listening. 'They don't often get over a thing like that. Not properly, you know.'

'Time will tell.'

'She'll need plenty of care when she comes out. Who's gonner look after her?'

'I expect Bob has got that sorted.'

'Yes, of course. What's gonner happen to the house? You taking over the tenancy?'

'Don't know. We've got to wait and see. I'd better get me coat.'

'Yes, run along then. Nice talking to you.'

Pam didn't have any option but to go back indoors.

Lu was sitting watching the TV. He looked up when she walked in but said nothing as she cleared the dirty crocks into the scullery.

'Do you want a cup of tea?' she asked, poking her head round the door.

'No, thanks. Well, what did they say?'

'I don't know. I didn't go in.'

'Why was that?'

'As you said, this is your decision.'

He laughed. 'Since when have you listened to me?'

'It's not a question of listening to you. I can't buy this on me own, so if you ain't prepared to go along, well, there ain't no point in talking about it, is there?' She went back into the scullery. She almost threw the plates into the washing-up water and proceeded to give them the wash of a lifetime.

That night in bed, although she wanted him to hold her, she moved as far as possible away from him. Every time she felt his warmth she sighed and shifted just that little bit further over till she was frightened of falling out of bed. Suddenly he turned over and pulled her close to him.

'Now come on, stop this nonsense.'

'Leave me be. I don't call it nonsense. Just because I want to have a nice house and be a proper family.'

'I know. But look at it from my point of view. What if we have a bad winter and we don't sell a lot?'

'Can't you go and try to sell to the cafés and that?'

'You know the Bennettis have got that all sewn up.' He turned over on his back. 'You should have married him. He could give you everything you ask for. They're loaded.'

She too turned and gazed up at the ceiling. 'Why is it that when anything ain't to your liking you always bring up Robbie?'

'S'pose he always seems to be lurking in the background.'

'Oh yes. I can just see him hiding round the corner, waiting to pounce on me and whisk me away to his house in Italy. Don't talk daft.'

He turned to face her and propped himself up on his elbow. 'I'll always worry that that might happen.'

She swallowed hard. 'You don't have to.'

He put his arm round her and she melted into his arms and let his kisses lift her disappointment. Tears were running down her face. She loved him so much. What if they couldn't afford the house, they were young and they had each other.

★ ★ ★

The following evening Pam knew she had to tell her mum about the letter.

'What d'you mean you've got to move?' asked Rose.

'The landlord's selling the house.'

'What? He can't do that,' said Ivy.

'Yes he can and he is.'

'What if Lil wants to come back?'

'He ain't daft. He knows she wouldn't be able to look after herself,' said Rose.

'How does he know?' asked Ivy. 'In fact I went to see her this afternoon and she's looking a lot better.'

'Well, someone must have told the rent man,' said Rose.

'I bet it was that nosy cow Doll Windsor. She's been asking a lot of questions.' Ivy stood up, clearly furious. 'I've a bloody good mind to go up there and give her a piece of my mind.'

'What good will that do?' asked Pam.

'It'll make me feel better for one thing. Fancy chucking an old lady out of her house.'

'It's no good, Gran. We can't afford to buy it, so we'll have to find somewhere else to live.'

'How you gonner do that?' asked her mother. 'Places round here are like gold dust.'

'I don't know.' Pam was trying hard to stop a sob welling up in her throat.

'It's such a shame for these youngsters,' said Granny Mallory. 'How long can you stay there?'

'He didn't say. But now it's all done up I don't think it'll be long.'

'I reckon he's been waiting for something like this to happen, crafty sod. I bet he was insured and got all the work

251

done on the insurance, then decided to get rid of it while he could.' Ivy really was very angry.

'He did give us the option to buy it.'

'I bet he did. You wait till I see that rent man on Monday. He's got a lot to answer for.'

Pam wanted to smile. 'It's not his fault.'

'He told the owner, didn't he? And I don't want him thinking I'm on hand to show people round. If he reckons that, then he's got another think coming.'

Rose was staring into space. 'Could that happen to me?'

'What you talking about?' asked Ivy.

'You know. If anything happened to . . .' She couldn't bring herself to put into words her thoughts.

'What, when I peg out, you mean? Will you lose this house?'

Rose slowly nodded.

'You're Mrs King, ain't you?'

Again Rose nodded.

'Well then. The rent book don't say which one, does it?'

Rose shook her head.

Pam looked from one to the other. She was pleased that at least her mother wouldn't be thrown out on the streets.

When Lu came home he grabbed Pam and, pulling her close to him, plonked a loud kiss on her cheek and announced he'd got an answer to their problems.

'Great. Is your dad going to lend us the money towards the . . .' Her voice trailed off when she saw the look of amazement on his face.

'No. He said we could live there if—' He too stopped in mid sentence when Pam jumped back.

'We ain't going through all this again, are we? You know how I feel about living with your dad.'

'I know,' he said wearily, 'but what else can we do? You try and come up with an answer that ain't gonner cost us an arm and a leg.'

'I don't know. But I ain't living at your dad's.'

Lu stormed out of the house and she heard the roar of his motor bike as he drove off. Tears filled her eyes. He had never done anything like this before.

She tried to settle and watch the television, but couldn't concentrate. What if Lu had an accident? It would be all her fault.

She woke up with a start when the high-pitched noise from the blank television screen invaded her dream. Lu wasn't home. Fear filled her mind. What would she do if he was lying in some hospital? That dreadful night when they were attacked came back to her and her tears fell. Please don't let anything happen to him.

She was making herself a cup of cocoa when she heard the front door close. She threw open the kitchen door.

'Where have you been? I've been worried sick about you.'

Lu was sitting on the bottom of the stairs unlacing his boots. He grinned. 'Been out with Marc. I'd forgotten what it's like to have a night out with the boys.'

'You've been drinking?'

'I had a few.'

'So you can afford to buy drinks and not—'

With one boot off he jumped up and grabbed her arm. 'Don't start on that again. And for your information me and Marc have been working out a little scheme to earn ourselves a bit extra.'

'And what dodgy business is he setting you up for?'

'It ain't dodgy.'

'If Marco's involved, it's got to be dodgy.'

Lu sat back down and removed his other boot. 'You ain't got a lot of love for my family, have you?'

Pam felt guilty at that and couldn't think of an answer. 'Well, we never did find out what Marc had been up to when we got . . .'

'Forget it,' he shouted. 'That's all water under the bridge.' He pointed his finger at her. 'Just remember they are still my family. And I'm proud of my dad bringing us three up on his own. We never had a gran or grandad giving us handouts, so don't start getting on your high horse.'

Pam caught her breath. Lu hadn't shouted at her like that before. Was she being too hard on his dad?

Lu stood up. 'I'm going to bed.' He threw his leather jacket over the banister and went up the stairs leaving his boots where he had taken them off.

Pam sat on the stairs and pulled his jacket towards her and cuddled it. How could he forget what had happened because of Marc? Every time he looked in the mirror he must be reminded of that night. Despite the smell of his jacket bringing back so many happy memories, she was so miserable. Lu meant everything to her yet now they seemed to be arguing every day and it was all her fault. What if he had had an accident tonight? She had to make her peace with him. What was this deal he and Marco had done? Could it mean more trouble?

Tomorrow she was going to ask her mother if they could move in with them for a while. It would be a bit crowded, but if her mother went into Ivy's room they could manage.

What other option did she have anyway?

She hung Lu's jacket on the peg in the passage, put his boots in the kitchen, then went upstairs.

The light was off so she undressed in the dark. The sound of his snoring told her he had had quite a few beers and she would have to wait till tomorrow to tell him her plan.

Chapter 21

Pam was so angry when she left for work the next morning that she slammed the front door with all the strength she could muster. She had tried to tell Lu her plan while she was getting dressed but he'd chosen to ignore her. She had left him still in bed, which wasn't unusual. Since she'd got up she had been banging about the kitchen getting ready for work, hoping the noise would bring him down. When she took a cup of tea up to him he turned his back on her, complaining about his bad head, she felt tempted to throw the tea over him, but common sense told her she would only have to wash the sheets.

Why wouldn't he sell his bike? He could always get a smaller one. Was she being so unreasonable?

She hurried down the road, her temper ready to burst. She only hoped she didn't bump into Dolly Windsor, otherwise her nosy neighbour would get the full force of her anger.

When it began to rain, in many ways Pam was pleased, at least she could cry and no one would notice her tears. Why couldn't Lu see she was unhappy? If he really loved her, he would do all he could to give her what she wanted.

She was pleased to be at work; at least she had plenty of other things to do to keep her mind off last night's row, but woe betide any customers that came in moaning.

At the end of the day, when she turned into Newbury Street, Pam could see Lu's bike wasn't in its usual parking place under the window. Perhaps he was working late. When she arrived at the front door, she saw there weren't any lights on, so she decided to go straight into number 28.

'Hello, love, fancy a cuppa? Your mum won't be in till a bit later, seems she's got an order to get ready for some poor bloke's funeral tomorrow. She had to stay as she's still on her own. Sit yourself down. You look a bit down in the mouth.'

'Me and Lu have had a row.'

Ivy laughed. 'Well, that ain't the end of the world. That's what married life is all about: all sorrows and smiles. What was it over?'

'I won't go and live at his dad's house.'

'Oh.'

'I was wondering, could we stay here? Just for a while, just till we get a chance to look for somewhere?'

'What? Where would you sleep?'

'I thought if Mum went in with you . . .'

Ivy went and closed the kitchen door. 'I don't want Alice to hear this.'

'Where is Granny Mallory?' asked Pam.

'Having a little lay down. I don't want her to think she's in the way.'

Pam sat at the table and played with her fingers.

Ivy sat next to her granddaughter. 'Look, Pam, I don't mind me front room being turned into a bedroom for Alice, but I ain't having your mum move in with me.'

Pam stood up and pushed her chair away. 'I thought you would have helped us out.'

'I would, love. But I'm too set in me ways to stand any more upheavals.'

'Thanks a bunch.' Pam marched out of the kitchen.

'Where're you going?' shouted Ivy after her.

'To find a garden shed to live in.' Pam slammed the front door. This seems to be my day for slamming doors, she said to herself.

It was about eight when her mother came in. 'See Lu's not home yet. Ivy said you wasn't very happy.'

'I'm not. Me and Lu had a row and when I asked Gran if we could move in with you she said no. So much for being a loving family.'

Rose sat at the table. 'It ain't like that. Pam, be reasonable. Granny Mallory's upset. She thinks it's her that's stopping you from moving in. Ivy would love to help out, but she reckons you ought to go and stay with his dad, he's got the room. Besides, Lu will soon get fed up in a house full of women.'

'Mum, I'll end up being a skivvy for 'em. You ain't been round there and seen it.'

'Well, I think you ought to give it a try.'

'What if I don't like it?'

'I'm sure something will turn up, it always does.'

'I would have thought you'd be on my side.'

'Oh Pam. Don't say things like that. Ever since my mum and dad went north I've had to live with Ivy and go to work, now I've got my mum here too.' She looked sad. 'I've never been on me own.'

Pam glanced at her mother. She suddenly seemed to have aged. There was a sprinkling of grey in her hair and her eyes looked tired. 'Been busy?'

Rose nodded. 'I don't know how long I can keep this shop running on me own. I don't know how long Mrs Kennett is going to be away.'

'Have you asked her son?'

She nodded. 'He ain't got any idea.'

'What's wrong with her?'

'It's her legs, they keep swelling up, and when you're on your feet all day, it don't help.'

'Why don't you ask her for help?'

'I'll have to. She should be able to afford it.'

'Is it a good business?'

'Not bad. Anyway, this ain't helping your problem, is it?'

Pam shook her head. 'I forgot to ask Gran how Lil is.'

'About the same. I'll have to go, Ivy's been keeping me dinner warm all this time.'

'You came straight in here?'

'Well, she was a bit worried about you.'

'But not prepared to help.'

'Don't say that. And Pam, you going like that upset my mum. She thinks she's in the way.'

'It's not her I'm angry with.'

'I'm sure Ivy thinks she's doing the right thing.'

'So you reckon I should go and stay with Lu's dad?'

'Why don't you give it a try and if it's that bad, then we'll see about getting something sorted. At least you'll have your own room there.'

'Yes,' said Pam quietly. She was beginning to feel guilty only worrying about herself; she knew she was going to have to give in, if only to make everybody else happy.

Pam was just dozing when she heard Lu's bike come up

the road. She looked at the alarm clock; it was nearly one. Where had he been till this time? She knew the answer, he had been with Marco. Why was he suddenly going out with him? What deals were they doing? Knowing Marco, Pam was worried that it wasn't always above the law.

When she heard the third stair creak under his weight she turned over and pretended to be asleep. She didn't want a scene so late. But the following morning Pam knew she had to get this problem sorted out. She hated this not speaking.

She stood at the bottom of the bed. 'I've decided that if we can't find anything when we have to get out of here, I'll stay at your dad's.'

Lu pushed the bedclothes down and peered over the top of the sheet. 'What's brought this on?'

'You.'

'Why? What have I done?'

'Been acting like a kid who can't get his own way, that's what.'

He grinned. 'You won't regret it.'

'Why are you so keen to get me to move in there?'

'It'll make life a lot easier.'

'Who for, me or you?' She didn't wait for an answer; she left for work.

Every evening Pam studied the newspaper and if there was a flat or rooms to let she would hurry to the phone box, or write if it gave a box number. She wasn't having any luck, however. They had either already gone, or the rents were too high. Sometimes she and Lu did manage to look over a place, but it was usually so awful they couldn't get out quick enough.

At the end of the month they had to move as a young couple had bought the house.

'What a way to spend me birthday,' said Pam as she carefully put the last of the glasses in a box.

'It'll be all right when you've settled in,' said her mother.

'I can't see how.'

'Now, Pam, if you're going to go with that attitude, it'll never be right.'

Pam pulled a face behind her mother's back. She wanted to run away. She had made up her mind she was going to be unhappy there.

The few bits they had bought from Lil had been loaded on to the ice-cream van. Tearfully, Pam hugged her mother. She didn't want even to kiss her gran goodbye as she still felt Ivy had let her down.

'Come to tea tomorrow,' said Ivy. 'We'll have a bit of a special one for your birthday.'

'OK,' said Lu. 'Come on, love, jump in.'

Pam did as she was told.

It only took a few weeks, but Pam soon knew that living with the Cappas was just as awful as she had imagined it would be. She didn't understand why Lu couldn't see that she was unhappy. Every evening after dinner she had to get through the pile of washing up that the old man had left all day. Sometimes it was well into the evening when Lu and Marc arrived home; they were working late now that the evenings were drawing out. But she wasn't always sure they *had* been working, and they seemed to be laughing a lot together, as if they were sharing a private joke. When Lu kissed her she could definitely smell beer. If she ever commented he told her it was just to settle the dust. She felt like an outsider.

Sometimes Marc would come into the kitchen to help her. But he was always finding an excuse to push past her and touch her, and if she complained to Lu he dismissed it as her imagination.

'He knows you belong to me. And he wouldn't try anything so daft. I'm sorry, Pam, but you'll just have to make the most of living here. It would help if you tried to be a bit friendlier towards Dad and Marc.'

She wanted to scream at him. Why did he assume it was her fault there was all this tension? She didn't understand why he was accepting this life for her. She loved him, but at times she wondered if that was enough. Did he love her, or was she just a possession to him?

Mr Cappa always seemed to be complaining about anything she did; he didn't approve of anything she liked. She only felt really happy when she was at work or when Lu was making love to her.

Weeks went by and, with Lu and Marc out most nights, she had to sit watching the television programmes her father-in-law liked. She felt trapped. This was all her gran's fault. Why wouldn't Ivy let her live in number 28?

'D'you like me new shirt?' Lu was standing holding a shirt that was neatly folded in a box.

'That looks expensive.'

'Na. Fell off the back of a lorry, didn't it.' He laughed.

'I thought we was saving up.'

'Got to have a bit to spend. 'Sides, it was a snip.'

The following week it was a new watch for himself, then it was one for Pam.

'Was this pinched?' she asked when he showed it to her.

'No. Would I give you something like that?'

'Yes, you would. I don't want it.'

'Why?'

'I've got a nice one me mum bought me.'

'Well, now you've got two.'

'Lu, what's happening to you? Why are you behaving like this? Why are you letting Marc lead you on?'

'He ain't leading me on. What I do is me own business.'

She knew he was mad with her, because when he got in a temper the scar down his cheek became red and angry-looking.

'Listen: I don't want you or anyone else telling me what to do.'

'Lu, what's happening to us?'

'Nothing. Just leave me be.'

Pam was so unhappy that many nights she went to bed early and cried herself to sleep. She knew she would end up making herself ill, but couldn't do anything about it.

Pam was very surprised when one evening she opened the door to see Jean standing on the doorstep.

'Is the old man in?' she asked.

'Yes. Come in. Is Al with you?'

'No. I thought I'd come round on me own, just to see how you're making out.' She looked round the passage. 'Blimey. This looks a lot cleaner.'

Pam gave her a weak smile and led the way down the passage. When she pushed open the kitchen door to let Jean in, Mr Cappa turned and snorted. 'What d'you want?'

'That's very nice, I must say.'

'Don't often see you round this way.'

'I thought I'd pop in just to see how you're doing.'

'I ain't dead yet, if that's all you're worried about.'

'Would you like a cup of tea?' asked Pam.

'Yes, please.'

Pam went into the scullery and put the kettle on the gas. What did Jean want? Was she checking up on her? Pam had never forgotten the conversation she'd had with Jean a few Christmases ago. Did the old man have any money and was Jean still worried she was going to take it? She certainly hadn't seen any signs of it. And if he did have any where did it come from? She didn't think the boys brought in that much. Lu never had a wage packet. It was always cash in his hand. She didn't know what his father paid him from week to week. It depended on sales, Lu said. The shrill whistle brought her back to the boiling kettle. She made the tea and took it into the kitchen on a tray. 'Would you like a biscuit?'

Jean looked surprised. 'Never had this sort of treatment round here before.'

'This one's a good girl. She ain't after everything I've got. Looks after me and me boys a treat, she does.'

Pam was taken back at such praise. Normally when he spoke, which wasn't very often as he was too busy watching the television, it was only to criticize.

Jean scowled at Pam. 'You must be going mad stuck in here with this lot.'

'It's kind of Mr Cappa to take us in.' Pam wanted to say she didn't have a lot of choice, but decided against it. After all, it wouldn't do to let Jean see she was very unhappy. But Jean laughed, and as she left she said to Pam at the front door, 'Don't let him fool you.'

★ ★ ★

'Jean came round here tonight,' said Pam as she cuddled up to Lu when they were in bed.

'So Dad said. D'you know what she was after?'

'No, she didn't say.'

'She's obsessed with the thought that Dad's got some money hidden away somewhere.'

'Why?'

'Dunno.'

'Has Al ever mentioned it?'

'No.'

'You must know how much you and Marc take, after all you're the only ones who work for him.'

'Yer. Anyway, don't worry about it. If there was any money Marc would have had it away before now.'

Pam lay thinking about what Lu had said. Why did Jean turn up out of the blue? She must have had a reason. If only the old man went out sometimes while she was at home, she could have a poke round and try to find out if what Jean had said was true. There must be a bank book, after all he did run a business. She grinned to herself. Unless he kept it all hidden under the bed. That's if, as Lu said, Marc hadn't got there first. She knew Mr Cappa went out when she was at work, as he did most of the shopping and always needed to get his beer and tobacco. Did he own this house? If not, where was the rent book? She'd never seen one. Perhaps he kept that hidden away too.

Why was Jean so concerned about money? Did she know more than she was letting on? And had she come round to see if Pam had been spending the Cappas' money?

Chapter 22

It was Friday that same week when Jill phoned Pam at work.

'Look, we're coming up to see Gran and me and Billy was wondering if we could all go out tomorrow night?'

'Jill, I'd love that, what time?'

'We'll only pop in to see Gran for a little while, we can spend more time with her on Sunday afternoon. So what about half-seven outside the hospital?'

'That sounds great. I'll really look forward to it. How is Lil?'

'About the same. She sits in the chair for a little while but then she starts pulling at the bedclothes to go back in. It's awful to see her. I don't reckon she'll ever be well enough to come home.'

'I'm so sorry to hear that. Give her my love when you see her.'

'I will. Bye.'

Pam put the receiver down and sat back. Poor Lil. She had been so busy with her own problems these past months that she had tended to forget about other people. She rolled a new sheet of paper into the typewriter. She and Lu hadn't been out very much, so now at least she had something to look forward to.

★ ★ ★

'So where shall we go tomorrow?' Pam asked Lu as they were getting ready for bed. She had told him earlier what Jill had said.

'It's a bit out of the blue. Not sure if I can get away.'

Pam plonked herself on the bed. 'We never go out. We never get a chance to talk on our own. I'm fed up with just your dad for company most nights and if you won't come with me I'll go on me own.'

'Now, now.'

'Don't you "now, now" me. I do everything everybody asks me. All I want is a night out with Jill and Billy.'

Lu grinned. 'I love you when you get angry.'

She started to cry.

'What's wrong?' He sat beside her and, putting his arm round her, drew her close.

'I hate living here.'

He immediately pushed her away. 'I thought that was coming. We can't find anything at the moment so try and be a bit more understanding.'

'We don't even go out looking together any more.'

'You know I have to work late in the summer.'

She sniffled into her pillow. 'You could have some time off.'

'We've been through this before. Now come on, dry your eyes. Dad and Marc will be wondering what's going on in here if they hear you crying.'

She sniffed louder. She knew they were in bed listening to what she and Lu did. Some mornings Marc would make comments, which was very embarrassing and wasn't helping their love life.

'Besides, your mum and grans will think I beat you if you go over there tomorrow afternoon with red eyes.'

Every Saturday afternoon after she finished work, she went to see her grans and waited till her mother came in at four before going back to get Mr Cappa's tea.

'Tell your dad you're going to take me out.'

'I'll see.'

She knew by his tone that he wasn't going to.

'It's so good to see you. Where's Lu?' asked Jill, hugging and kissing Pam.

'He can't get the evening off.'

'That's a shame. Still, never mind, we've got the car. Hop in.'

'Where're we going?' asked Pam.

'Thought we'd just go for a drink, if that's all right with you?' replied Jill.

'Sounds great.' Pam was so pleased to be out. Lu wasn't with her but that wasn't going to dampen her spirits.

The three of them laughed and joked and talked about the past and their plans for the future. But as the evening wore on Pam grew increasingly sad as at that moment she didn't think she had much of a future. She also knew she was drinking far more than was good for her, but she didn't care.

Billy was getting another round when Pam, hanging round Jill's neck, said 'It's lovely to be out with you again,' and suddenly burst into tears.

'What is it?' asked Jill anxiously.

'Everything,' wailed Pam. 'I'm so miserable.'

'I can see that. You know you shouldn't drink gin.'

'Why not? I can drink what I like,' she sobbed.

'Of course you can.'

Billy put the drinks on the table. He looked at Jill who quickly shook her head at him.

He raised his eyebrows, embarrassed. 'I'm just going for a pee,' he said, eager to get away.

'Now, what's the problem?' asked Jill, handing Pam a handkerchief.

'Living with his dad.'

'Why?'

'I want me own place.'

Jill sat back. 'I must admit we was all a bit disappointed when you didn't buy Gran's place.'

'Not nearly as disappointed as me. I tried to get Lu to sell his bike.'

'Pam, I'm sure he had a good reason not to.'

'He's changed since we've been there. He goes out a lot with Marco and Gawd only knows what they get up to.'

'What makes you say that?'

'Well, they always seem to find enough money for beer and new clothes. Mind you, he tells me that most of the stuff falls off the backs of lorries.'

'Don't you believe him?'

Pam shook her head. 'I don't know.'

'What about you? You buying lots of new things?'

'No.'

'Thought I'd seen that coat before.'

'I might be wearing me old coat, but you should see the posh watch he gave me.'

'I thought your mum bought you one for your twenty-first?'

'She did.'

'Why ain't you wearing this new one then?'

'I'm frightened to.'

'You don't think Lu . . .'

'He tells me so many lies now. Him and Marc seem to have so many secrets that I don't know what to believe any more. There's me saving 'cos I want me own house, but it seems that his lordship ain't all that keen.'

'I'm surprised he goes out with Marc after what happened to you two.'

'So am I. And I do worry at what they get up to,' sniffed Pam. 'If he ever got hurt or put in prison, I . . .' She began to cry.

'Do you think they go out pinching things?'

Pam nodded, but before she could say any more Billy reappeared. Then, to her friends' astonishment, Pam drank her gin down in one gulp.

'I think it's time we made a move,' said Jill to her husband.

'OK.'

Pam went to stand up.

'Good job we've got the car,' said Jill. 'Otherwise I could see you falling off the back of Lu's bike.'

Pam didn't answer; instead she slowly slid to the floor.

'What we gonner do with her?' asked Billy as they made their way out of the pub with Pam dangling between them.

'Get her into the car.'

'Where does she live now?'

'I don't know the address off hand. Look, we'll have to take her back to her mum, she'll tell us where she lives.'

'OK.'

Jill smiled at Billy. She was so lucky to have someone so

loving and thoughtful. Why was Lu treating Pam like this?

'Mrs King, we've got Pam here,' said Jill when Rose opened the front door.

'Pam? What's wrong, is she ill?'

Jill grinned. 'No, she's drunk.'

'What? Where's Lu?'

'He couldn't come out with us and I'm afraid Pam had one too many.'

Rose looked at Pam who was being held up by Billy. 'Looks like she had more than just the one. You'd better bring her in.'

'We couldn't take her back to Lu's house as I'm not sure where they live.'

'That's all right. She don't look in any fit state to go there. Bring her through, Billy. Can you manage?' Rose asked as he struggled along the passage with the unconscious Pam. Rose pushed open the kitchen door.

'What's going on?' asked Ivy.

'It's Pam, she's drunk,' said Rose.

Granny Mallory smiled. 'These young girls certainly know how to enjoy themselves.'

'Here, sit her in this chair,' tutted Ivy, standing up. 'I bet she won't think she enjoyed herself in the morning.'

'She'll have to stay here the night. Thanks for bringing her home,' said Rose to Jill and Billy.

'I'll pop over in the morning to see how she is. We'll see ourselves out,' said Jill.

Rose could hear Jill giggling as they went. 'Sounds as if she's had more than enough as well.'

★　★　★

Pam opened her eyes and blinked rapidly. Where was she? Her head was thumping. She propped herself up on to her elbow. She was still dressed. This was her mother's room. She lay back down. Jill and Billy must have brought her home. Her stomach churned and she almost fell out of bed in her hurry to get to the bathroom. She was sitting on the floor holding on to the pan when her mother walked in.

'So, you enjoyed yourself last night then?'

'It must have been something I had to eat.'

Rose sat on the edge of the bath. 'You was drunk. It was a good job Billy had his car. Where was Lu?'

'He had to work.'

'I bet he's been worried stiff all night wondering where you was.'

'I don't think he will.'

'You two had another row?'

Pam didn't answer.

'I don't know what gets into you. D'you want any breakfast?'

Pam shook her head. 'Where did you sleep last night?'

'In the chair, and bloody uncomfortable it was an' all. I hope you ain't going to make a habit of turning up on our doorstep every time something goes wrong between you.' Rose left her daughter sitting on the floor.

Pam leaned her head against the wall. Even her mother was angry with her. Still it would do Lu good to find she hadn't been home all night.

It was nine o'clock when Pam heard his motor bike.

'Looks like you might have some explaining to do, my girl,' said Ivy.

Pam opened the front door.

'Where the bloody hell have you been? I've been worried sick about you.'

'Have you finished shouting on the doorstep?'

Lu quickly looked about. 'Well?' he said as he stepped inside.

Pam closed the front door. 'You know I was out with Jill and Billy. I got drunk, so they brought me home here, in the car, 'cos they didn't know your dad's address. Satisfied?'

Lu stood in the passage staring at her in disbelief. 'You got drunk?'

'I was paralytic.'

'That ain't nothing to be proud of.'

'Maybe not. But it helped me drown my sorrows.'

'What sorrows have you got?'

'If you don't know, there ain't a lot of point talking about it, is there? D'you fancy a cup of tea. There's one on the go.' She walked into the kitchen where Rose and Ivy were sitting at the table.

'Hello, son,' said Ivy. 'You ought to keep your wife under control. In a right state, she was, last night.'

'So I hear.'

'And this morning,' said Rose.

'Thanks a lot,' said Pam. 'Right, have you two got any more to add to all that?'

'It's no good you getting stroppy, young lady,' said Ivy.

'Why shouldn't I get stroppy?'

'I think I'll take you home before you say too much.'

'It ain't my home, and I'll go when I'm good and ready.'

'Pam, don't upset everybody. Be a good girl and go with Lu,' said Rose.

Pam could feel her tears welling up. She picked up her handbag and reluctantly kissed her mother and gran. 'Say goodbye to Granny Mallory for me.'

Sitting behind Lu on the bike she waved to Jill who was at her window. She still felt terribly miserable.

'So, what happened to you?' asked Mr Cappa when she walked in. 'He's been that worried about you.'

'I stayed at me mum's.'

'I know it ain't none of my business, but I think you should have told him what you was gonner do.'

'I didn't know meself, did I?'

'He shouldn't be wasting his time racing round looking for you, he should have taken that van out ages ago.'

Pam didn't bother to answer; she went upstairs.

All day she sat and stared out of the bedroom window. She wanted to get away, but where could she go?

Later that evening she decided to go for a walk. She needed to get away from the blaring television.

'Tell Lu, if he gets home before me, I won't be long.'

'He won't like you being out again.'

'He'll jolly well have to put up with it, won't he?'

'Don't you talk to me like that, young lady.'

Pam picked up her handbag.

Mr Cappa stood up and, blocked the doorway. 'I don't think you should go out.'

'Don't you tell me what to do.'

'Your place is here.'

'Get out of my way.'

He grabbed her arm.

'Let go, you stupid old man.' She pushed him to one side and hurried out of the house.

'Well, girl. You've really done it this time,' she said out loud as she made her way along the road.

Chapter 23

Pam didn't know how long she'd been walking. Her mind was in a turmoil, all rational thoughts banished as she tried to make sense of the situation.

She shivered. She was hungry and all at once realized she hadn't eaten all day. She knew she had no option but to go back and face Lu. It wasn't any good her going to Newbury Street as even her mother wasn't very pleased with her. Why did her life have so many ups and downs? And where would it all end? All she wanted was to settle down in a nice house, give up work and have at least two children. Why didn't Lu want these things? Was she being silly? Jill had never had to cope with the traumas she'd had to face, but then again Jill had other worries . . .

As Pam put her key in the lock, the front door flew open.

'Been waiting for you. Where the bloody hell have you been again?' Lu roughly took hold of her arm.

'Walking.' She pushed his arm away.

'Get in here.' He shoved her along the passage.

Pam was trying hard to keep her temper.

'Have you been drinking?' he asked. All the while he was prodding her in the back.

She stopped and faced him. 'No, I ain't. And if I was, it ain't any of your business.'

'It bloody well is my business. I don't want my wife hanging around pubs, getting drunk and showing herself up.'

'In that case you should take me out more often.'

'Give it a rest. Don't start on that same old story, don't go blaming me again. You knew the hours I had to work when you married me.'

'What's going on out here?' asked Marc, opening the kitchen door. 'So, the wanderer returns.'

'Shut it, Marc,' said Lu.

When they moved into the kitchen Mr Cappa looked up from the telly. 'Oh, it's you. I dunno how you've got the bloody cheek to walk back in here after what happened.'

'What you talking about?' asked Marc.

Mr Cappa's eyes never left Pam's face. 'I ain't told 'em you pushed me over.'

'What?' all three shouted at once.

Mr Cappa looked pleadingly at Lu. 'When I tried to stop her going out again, she pushed me over.'

Pam's eyes were wide open. She couldn't believe what the old man was saying.

'You pushed my dad over . . .' said Lu slowly.

'No, I didn't.'

'Look, I've got a bruise on me arm to prove it.' He began pushing up the sleeve of his grubby brown cardigan.

'Well, it wasn't me what done it.'

'He's an old man,' said Lu.

'I didn't push him over, I just moved him away from the door. He tried to stop me going out. I ain't a bloody prisoner.'

'Your place is here,' said Mr Cappa.

'I'll go where and when I like.'

'You won't,' said Lu.

'And who's going to stop me?' Pam was seething with anger. How dare they treat her like a child?

'Me. You shouldn't have pushed me dad.'

'I didn't. He's telling lies and you believe him.' Pam turned on her father-in-law. 'You're wicked, you are. A mean wicked old man.'

When Lu's hand hit Pam's face her teeth rattled. Tears filled her eyes and quickly spilled down her cheeks.

'Don't you talk to my dad like that.'

Pam put her hand to the side of her face to ease the stinging. 'I don't believe you just did that. You'd take his word against mine?' she said softly.

'Why would he lie?'

Pam began to sob. 'And you think I am?'

'Shouldn't have done that, bruv,' said Marc, putting his arm round Pam's heaving shoulders.

'She's my wife and I can do what I like.'

'No, you can't,' screamed Pam.

'You should have stayed in. You said you'd obey me, remember?'

'That don't mean I have to be at your beck and call – or his!' She turned on Mr Cappa. 'Go on, tell him the truth. Go on.'

Ignoring her, her father-in-law went over to the television and turned the sound up louder.

Pam was sobbing. 'Since I've been part of this family I've been beaten up and now even me own husband has started to hit me.' She raised her voice. 'I ain't ever been beaten in me life before.'

'More's the pity,' said Mr Cappa. 'Might have taught you to have a bit of respect for your elders.'

Marc was still holding Pam and she let herself be comforted by him. She couldn't understand why Lu was so angry with her and, worse, took his father's word against hers.

'Don't like to see a bloke hit a woman,' said Marc, pulling her closer and stroking her hair.

'No, but you're quite happy to beat blokes up though ain't yer,' Lu snarled.

'Shut your mouth. That's different.' He gave a nervous laugh. ''Sides, what's that got to do with you hitting Pam?'

'What's all this about?' asked Mr Cappa.

'Ask him,' said Lu.

'Leave it out,' said Marc.

'No, I won't. D'you know, he beat a bloke almost senseless a few nights ago.'

'What's that got to do with all this? I told you, he was part of the gang what beat you two up a while back. I wanted to show them they can't go round doing things like that to the Cappas.'

'That's what you say. I didn't recognize him. I reckon you just wanted to pick a fight.'

'Was he on his own?' asked the old man.

'Yes,' said Lu.

'Well, in that case you ain't got no worries, it's his word against Marc's, and with you to give him a alibi. You worry too much, Lu.' Mr Cappa continued to look at the television.

Pam moved away and sat at the table, holding her bruised face. She had to get away from these men. She didn't feel safe any more.

Marc lit a cigarette. 'Anyway, from what I gathered it was dark and you was knocked senseless. I was only protecting me family. Which seems to be a bit more than you're doing now.'

'She can't go round hitting Dad.'

'I didn't ask for your help, with that bloke, did I?' Marc snapped.

'I wasn't gonner get involved.'

'He ain't ever come home with blood on him,' said his father.

'No, that's 'cos he used a lump of wood. I'm more than surprised we ain't had the police round here. We would have done if that bloke had died,' said Lu.

Pam looked at Lu. 'What if Marc had got hurt?'

'He didn't give the bloke a chance. I wasn't even sure if it was one of that gang.'

'You two will be the bloody death of me one of these days,' said Mr Cappa. 'Now shut it, I'm trying to watch this.'

Marc stubbed out his cigarette. 'What's the matter with you lot? I try to look after me family and that's all the thanks I get.'

'I'm going to bed,' said Pam.

'That's right, walk away,' said Mr Cappa. 'You started all this, now me two boys are rowing.'

'That's nothing to do with me.' She went upstairs. She didn't want to hear what they were arguing about. She was hurt and knew that tomorrow she was going back home. She was going to leave Lu.

As she got ready for bed she could hear Marc and Lu yelling downstairs. She put the pillow over her head. She wasn't interested in any of the Cappas, not now.

She must have dozed off by the time Lu came up. She felt him get in beside her. This was going to be the last night they would share a bed. She was surprised when he gently kissed her cheek and whispered, 'Sorry.'

Why did he do that? What did he want? She guessed what was on his mind and wasn't going to give in to him. She lay very still. There was no way she was going to let him know she was awake.

The following morning she got up and as usual left Lu in bed. She almost cried out when she looked in the mirror and saw she had a black eye. That was it. That was the last straw. What would her mother and grans say? Would it go by Saturday? She couldn't face Jill looking like this – she'd never had to put up with anything like this. The humiliation . . . and what about the men at work? She'd never forgive Lu. Never. She quietly put a few clothes into a bag and went downstairs. She made herself a cup of tea, had her breakfast and left for work. As she quietly closed the front door she looked up at the house. This was going to be the last time she would ever set foot in there.

All morning Pam had kept her head down. There had been a few remarks from the men, but most chose to ignore it.

It was four o'clock when the phone rang.

'Worth's Plumbers,' said Pam. Someone in a call box pushed button A.

'Pam, Pam, it's me, Lu.'

She froze. How could he know she'd left him? She quickly put the phone down. He never phoned her at work.

Why wasn't he out with the van?

The phone rang again.

'Pam!'

'Look, if you're phoning to say sorry, don't bother.' Again she put the phone down.

She smiled when it rang for the third time. He's certainly persistent, she thought.

'Pam, please don't ring off,' he said urgently. 'I've got something to tell you.'

'I don't want to hear it. I'm leaving you, Lu, so don't keep phoning.'

There was a silence. She felt tempted to cut him off again, but she wanted him to squirm. She wanted him to plead.

'Pam, I'm so sorry.'

'I bet you are. It's too late. I'm going back home.'

She heard him catch his breath. He sounded as though he were crying. 'I can't believe this. To lose the two people I love most in just a day.'

'Two? What are you talking about?'

'Dad . . .' There was a long pause. 'Dad had a heart attack last night. He's dead.'

She sat quite still. She was numb. 'How did you . . . When did you know?' she asked softly.

'Not till this morning. Marc went into him when he didn't get up.'

Although she was sorry, she felt trapped. She had to go back to him. 'Lu, I'm so sorry. I'll come home straight away. Is there anything I can do?'

'Just be here for me.'

'I'll tell my boss. I'm really sorry.' Pam put the phone

down and cried. Was this her fault? If only she hadn't gone out. If only she hadn't started the row. She shivered at the thought that all the time she was getting ready for work this morning, Mr Cappa had been lying upstairs, dead. She couldn't tell him she was sorry. She couldn't bring him back, not now. Poor Lu. She had to get to him as soon as possible. He needed her.

Pam was surprised to see Al and Jean's car outside the house when she arrived. They were sitting at the table in the kitchen drinking tea when Pam walked in.

'Lu. Marc. What can I say?' Tears were running down her face. 'I'm so very sorry.' She almost threw herself into Lu's arms. 'D'you know how it happened?'

'No. He went to bed when we did and he musta gone in the night.'

'D'you think all the arguing last . . .'

'I don't think it helped,' said Marc.

'Have you two been arguing again?' asked Al.

'So, what was it over this time?' asked Jean. 'And that's a lovely shiner you've got there, Pam, who did it?'

Pam touched her face. 'I walked into the door.'

'That's what they all say.' She turned to Lu. 'So, did the old man try to stop you from bashing your wife?'

'It wasn't like that,' said Pam. 'I told you, I walked into the door.'

'I bet. So what was this row over?'

'Nothing important,' said Lu quickly. 'We mustn't blame ourselves, all families row. I'll pour you out a cuppa.'

'Thanks. What happens now?' asked Pam.

'There's got to be an inquest.'

'Why?'

'They've got to make sure he wasn't done in,' said Jean.

'That's a terrible thing to say,' said Pam, who was really shocked at her remark.

'No, it's true,' said Al. 'The police have got to make sure it was natural causes.'

'Why would they think anything else?' asked Pam.

'It was a bit sudden, and as far as we know he didn't have any problem with his heart,' said Al.

'And with that eye, you'd better stay out of the way when the police come,' said Jean. 'Otherwise they'll put two and two together and make half a dozen.'

Pam chose to ignore Jean and, turning to Lu, asked, 'What happens after they know it was a heart attack?'

'We'll have to see about the funeral.' Lu was still absent-mindedly stirring Pam's tea.

'And that'll cost you. Did he leave a will?' asked Jean.

'Trust you to ask that,' said Marc.

'Well, we've got to know.'

'Why? D'you fancy owning half an ice-cream van?'

'What about the house?'

'What about it?'

Pam could see Marc was beginning to get very angry with Jean.

'You think he owned it, don't yer?' said Lu.

'Yes I do, and so does Al, don't you?' She looked at her husband.

'I always thought he did. But I may be wrong.'

'Shouldn't you look for a will? He might have insurance. I can't see why we have to fork out for—'

Lu jumped up from the chair.

'Lu!' yelled Pam. 'Jean, let it rest. Can't you see they've

had a shock and they're upset. If there is a will and an insurance policy, we'll let you know.' Pam surprised herself and everybody else at being so outspoken.

Al intervened. 'Look. We can't do any good here today. We'll go on home. I'll call in tomorrow to see what's happening. Come on, Jean, let's leave 'em.'

Pam went with Al and Jean to the front door. 'Thanks for coming. Don't worry, we'll let you know as soon as we hear something.'

'You'd better,' said Jean.

'Let it be, Jean.' Al took her arm and led her to the car.

'I can't believe she only came round to see if there was a will,' said Pam when she was back in the kitchen.

'Well, I ain't going through his things,' said Marc.

'We can leave it for now,' said Lu, 'but it will have to be done sometime.'

'Is it that important?' asked Pam

Lu, who was sitting at the table again, asked, 'Have we got enough for the funeral?'

'Don't know what they cost,' said Marc.

'Look, don't worry about that now,' said Pam. 'I'm sure we can all find enough to bury him.'

Lu gave her a faint smile and put his hand on hers. 'Thanks.' He turned to Marc. 'What are we gonner do about the business?'

'Dunno,' said Marc. 'After all, Dad didn't do much, we collected the stock and looked after everything.'

'But we never paid the bills. We didn't even know what the stock cost or what profit he made. Let's hope he wasn't in debt.'

'We'll soon find out,' said Marc. 'As soon as this gets out

we'll have all the vultures flocking and banging on the door. D'you want to carry on with this lark?'

'What d'you mean?' asked Lu.

'Well, selling ice cream ain't exactly the best job in the world, is it?'

'Don't know anything else.'

Pam sat listening. Her mind was racing ahead. 'I think you'd better go through your father's things. We need to know if this house is rented. The last thing we want is for us to be out on the street again.'

'Even if the place if rented, the landlord wouldn't do that, would he?' asked Marc.

'Don't you believe it. That's how come we finished up here, remember?' Pam squeezed her eyes tight. She wanted to cry. She wasn't sure if it was for the old man, his two sons, or herself. But what was worrying her most was, would they end up homeless again?

Chapter 24

They were standing in the front room looking out of the window waiting for the hearse carrying Mr Cappa's body to arrive.

Although many of Pam's family had passed on, she had never been to a funeral before. She was not looking forward to this one.

Every evening since Mr Cappa's death, Jean had been round to the house. She said it was to find out if they needed anything, but the conversation always got round to the will.

'What about his room? Have you cleaned it out yet?' she'd asked Pam.

'Leave it out, Jean,' said Marc. 'We'll do it when we're good and ready.'

'I'll always give you a hand if it's too much for you,' Jean had whined.

'Thanks, but I'll be able to manage. That's when the boys are ready, that is,' Pam insisted.

'Christ, the old man ain't even buried yet,' said Lu angrily, but it didn't stop Jean going on.

Now Al interrupted Pam's thoughts. 'The flowers look very nice,' he said.

'Thanks. I'll tell Mum. She always does a good job.'

'Waste of money, if you ask me,' said Jean.

That was the sort of remark Pam expected from her; she just ignored it.

Pam had been to see her mother the day after Mr Cappa had died. Rose had offered her condolences but was more interested in Pam's eye.

'How did that happen?' Rose had asked when she walked in.

'I walked into the door,' was all she could think of saying.

Her mother gave her a knowing look and, to Pam's relief, didn't press for an explanation.

Ivy and Granny Mallory were full of sympathy for Marc and Lu.

'You said the funeral's on Wednesday?' said Ivy.

'I can't come,' said Rose. 'I'm still on me own at work.'

'I know that, but I thought perhaps you'd do some flowers from me and Lu. Marc wants some as well.'

'Course.'

'How are the boys taking it?' asked Ivy. 'It must have been quite a shock.'

'They're not too bad.' Pam didn't tell them that she was worried that they were just lazing about the house. She wanted them to sort out their father's room, but they said they'd do it later. She even told them to strip his bed, but so far the door to his room had remained firmly shut. They hadn't taken the vans out and the stock they had had in them had perished and had to be thrown away.

At least by the day of the funeral Pam's bruise had almost gone, but it was very upsetting that only Mr Cappa's three sons, Jean and herself had attended the funeral.

Standing near the graveside was a white-haired old man leaning heavily on a stick. After the interment, he turned and walked away without making himself known.

Pam asked Lu if he knew who he was, but he said he didn't. So she whispered, 'Well, I think you ought to go and find out who he is. He might be an old friend who don't want to intrude.'

Lu quickly caught him up and Pam watched them talking together. The old man's only movement was to shake his head and continue to walk on.

'Who was he?' asked Marc when they were in the car going back to the house.

'He wouldn't say, just that he was an acquaintance from way back. I asked him if he wanted to come back with us, but he said no. D'you know, I'm sure there was something familiar about him.'

'I thought I'd seen him before,' said Pam.

'P'raps he's been to see the old man at some time,' said Marc.

Pam shook her head. 'No. I don't think so. Your dad never had visitors, at least not while I've been living here.'

'You're not there all day though, are you?' said Marc.

'That's true.'

'He might be a customer,' said Lu.

'Could be,' said Marc. 'I shouldn't worry about it.'

Returning home, they went to sit in the front room. Even though it was the beginning of June and outside the sun was shining, the room felt cold. Like most people's front room, it was unused and uninviting. With just a brown Rexine three-piece and a small Paisley rug in front of the fire, it was sparsely furnished. They were having a drink and a few sandwiches Pam had made when Jean asked, 'You ain't found it then?'

'Jean, don't start all that again,' said Al, leaning wearily against the mantelpiece.

'Haven't really looked,' said Marc.

'Well, I think you should.'

'Don't worry, we will.'

'We've got to try and find a rent book,' said Pam. 'Lu reckons the rent was paid on a Monday.'

'I can't understand why you two don't know that much. I did everything for my dad when my mum died. I certainly knew who to contact about the rent. That's of course if he did rent.'

'We didn't interfere,' said Lu.

'What about the vans? Have you been out since?'

'Jean, I think that's Marc and Lu's business, don't you?' said Pam.

Jean glared at Pam, and Al hurriedly spoke up. 'Look, Jean, whatever dad left, if there is anything, I reckon it belongs to these two, don't you? They're the ones that have been working for him all these years and if there is a nest egg, then I reckon it's theirs.'

Pam could see that Al wasn't very pleased with his wife's constant questions.

'No, I don't,' said Jean, looking very haughty. 'You forget how when we was first married I looked after him, did his bloody washing and cleaned this house from top to bottom; then till we moved right away I always brought him and the boys round a hot meal. So if there is anything I reckon I should get some.'

'I thought you did that out of the goodness of your heart,'

said Marc. 'After all, charity begins at home.'

'I wasn't doing it for charity. Your father promised me something. He was a dark horse, believe me. I know there were things he didn't talk about.'

'How? Did he catch you snooping about?' asked Marc.

'No. I just know, that's all. And if you had any savvy you'd be looking for a will. Come on, Al, let's go.' She picked up her handbag and cardigan and walked out.

'I don't understand,' said Pam after Jean and Al had left. 'Why is she so obsessed with money?'

'I think that when they lived round the corner and she used to come here, Dad promised her he'd look after her in his will,' said Marc.

Lu gave a little smirk. 'He knew what she was like and that was his way of getting her to do things for us.'

'That was a bit cruel,' said Pam.

'If you ask me, they was both as bad as each other,' said Marc.

Lu sat back and drew long and deep on his cigarette. 'So, what we gonner do?'

'What d'yer mean?' asked Marc.

'The vans. We'd better take them out tomorrow, I suppose, otherwise we'll lose our pitches.'

'I ain't taking that bloody ice-cream van out ever again.'

'What?' yelled Lu.

Pam, who was taking the dirty cups and saucers into the kitchen, sat down on the hard sofa with a jolt. 'What are you going to do then?' she asked.

'Dunno yet. But one thing is for sure. I ain't selling ice cream ever again. Been waiting for this day all me working life, now it's here. I've got a lot of contacts to look up.'

'What about you, Lu?' she asked tentatively.

'Ain't got a lot of choice, have I? Don't know anything else, do I?'

'Well, you'd better do something. I ain't going to be the only one working in this household,' Pam snapped.

'Come with me, bruv. I reckon we could get some real money.'

'I ain't gonner get involved with your dodgy dealings again.'

'You wasn't so proud a while back.'

'It didn't do me nerves any good though, did it? Damn nearly lost Pam over me nerves. I ain't cut out for all that.'

'All what?' asked Pam.

'Forget it,' said Lu.

'I won't. What haven't you told me?' She was shocked to think that Lu had been mixed up with something and he wasn't prepared to tell her about.

'It don't matter now.'

Marc laughed. 'You worry too much.' He picked up the newspaper.

Pam sat looking from one to the other, but she knew neither of them was going to tell her. The subject was closed. She picked up the crocks again and went into the kitchen.

When they were in bed that night Pam tackled Lu once more about his business with Marc.

He propped himself up on his elbow. 'At first I was green, even a bloody idiot. I did go out with Marc on a few jobs. He told me he was buying the stuff from these posh houses. I was the driver most times and I panicked when I found out what he was up to. I ain't cut out for

294

that kinda thing. I swear I'm not getting involved no more.'

Pam put her arm round Lu and held him tight. 'Why didn't you tell me?'

'Are you kidding? You would have gone mad if you knew, and so would Dad.'

'That's true. Thank God you didn't get caught.'

'I'm sorry, Pam, I shouldn't have kept it from you.'

'Well, it's over now.'

'Was you really going to leave me?'

'Yes.'

He clutched her hand. 'Promise me you'll never leave me. I couldn't live without you.'

'You promise me you'll never hit me.'

He moved close to her. His face was above hers. 'That's something I'll regret for the rest of my life.'

He kissed her gently. Pam stared into his eyes and saw real sorrow there. At that moment she knew that their love would stand the test of time.

Lu did take the van out the following week but he was home early every evening.

'Lu, it's our second wedding anniversary next week. Could we go somewhere?' Pam sat next to him on the sofa.

'Why not? We'll go for a posh meal, just the two of us.'

'That'd be nice. Lu, has the wholesaler asked for money for the ice cream you've had, yet?'

'I told them I'd pay at the end of the month. It's the way Dad worked. They're sending his outstanding bill as well.'

'You are making enough money these days to pay for it?' asked Pam.

'I hope so. I didn't know what profit Dad was making. He never told us what he paid for stock, only what we had to sell it at.'

'Do you think he has got any money put away?'

'Don't keep on Pam, you're beginning to sound like Jean.'

'Thanks.'

Things had certainly changed in the month since Mr Cappa died. Pam's life had taken a turn for the better. Lu didn't stay out so late in the evenings, so now they could go to the pictures and even went dancing again. He didn't take the van out on Sundays, so some days they went off on the bike. For the first time in months Pam was laughing and very happy.

Most Saturday afternoons she saw Jill when she came up to see her gran. Sometimes they went shopping together. It was like old times, as they laughed and tried on clothes they had no intention of buying. Lil wasn't getting any better, but there was talk of her leaving the hospital and moving in with Bob and Doreen.

The only thing really bothering her was that she still had not been allowed in to clean Mr Cappa's room. She brought the subject up one evening.

'Look, that bed should be stripped.'

'No, leave it,' said Marc quickly.

'But why?'

'I don't want the room disturbed.'

'It'll have to be done one day.'

'I said leave it.' Marc's voice was rising.

'Pam, just do what Marc says,' said Lu.

Marc stood up. 'What's wrong with you tarts? You're getting as bad as Jean.'

Pam was surprised at how upset he was. 'No, I'm not. I don't want to pry into your dad's things.'

'We'll do it when we're good and ready,' said Lu.

Marc left the room.

Pam decided to let it rest for now. One Saturday afternoon when they were out she'd take the bedding to the launderette. As they never went into their father's room, they wouldn't be any the wiser.

'Are you sure you can afford to take all this time off?' Pam asked Lu one Sunday when they were sitting on the grass at Box Hill. 'Ain't you frightened of losing your pitch?'

'Not now that Marc's not worrying about it. He seems to be managing OK. And don't forget, he's paid that last ice cream bill of Dad's.'

'I wonder how he does it?'

'I wouldn't like to guess.'

'He ain't told you then?'

'He did ask me if I'd like to join his band of merry men.'

'What?'

'He reckons what he's doing now is legit.'

'Can you trust him?'

'Dunno. But he is me brother. Is he paying you money towards the food?'

'Course. Mind you, I don't know where he gets it from. What do you think of his lovely new suit?'

Lu was lying back with his hands under his head and a long blade of grass stuck in his mouth. 'He said he's gonner get another bike.' He propped himself up and spat out the grass. 'Mind you, if what he says is true and it is legit . . .'

'Please, Lu, don't get involved.'

'I might go along with him, just to find out. It could be all right.'

Pam could feel her temper rising. 'Why is it when we've just got ourselves together, you're thinking of going with him again? It always finishes up in trouble.'

'No, it don't. I just said I'd find out. There ain't no harm in that, is there?'

'I don't know. Does he have some sort of hold over you?'

'Don't talk daft. If I think it's at all iffy then I'll run a mile. I'm a lot wiser to his goings on now. Satisfied?'

She nodded, but she wasn't really. 'You haven't even started to clear out your dad's room, just 'cos Marc don't want you to.'

'I'll have a word with him tonight.'

'What about looking for a rent book? You two aren't concerned one little bit about the house, are you?'

'Don't worry about it.'

'I *am* worried.'

'Why?'

'Well, we ain't had a rent man call, have we?'

'No. But they'll be calling soon enough. Come on, Pam. Calm down.'

He put his arm round Pam and she lay next to him. She let the warm sun flow over her but she couldn't relax. He should be more concerned about the house. She didn't want to be out on the street again.

The following Saturday afternoon Jill wasn't coming up and Pam decided not to go and see her grans. She told Lu she was going to spring clean their room.

'Why?'

'It hasn't been done since we moved in.'

'OK. I don't know what time I'll be back. I've got to meet Marc later.'

'Lu.' Pam touched his arm. 'Don't get involved with whatever he's doing. I'm sure it ain't right.'

She'd really hoped after their conversation at Box Hill that he wouldn't get involved with Marc. Lu looked worried. 'I've got to see him.'

Pam shook her head. 'Please be careful.'

He kissed her cheek. 'I know what I'm doing.'

She knew Marc had been on to Lu to come in with him. Since his father died, Lu had been his lovely old self again. So many times he told her how sorry he was he hit her. She didn't want him getting mixed up with Marc again. She knew he must be up to no good. Where did he get the money he was always flashing about? It couldn't be from anything legal.

After Lu had gone she pushed open the door to Mr Cappa's bedroom. It smelled damp and musty. She shuddered. Nobody had been in since his body had been taken away: the sheets hadn't even been taken off the bed. She couldn't understand Marc and Lu. It was almost as if they were afraid to go in. But it *had* to be cleaned.

Pam opened the floral curtains; they smelled of tobacco. She pushed up the window to let in some air. His bedroom was at the front of the house. The view was very different to the back; they only overlooked other back gardens. This looked out over a playing field, which had once been a bomb site. After the rubble was cleared the council had kept it and it had remained green ever since. Mr Cappa had told her, on one of the very few occasions they had conversed, that they would surely build on it some day. Pam looked round the room. She had never been in here before. There was very little furniture. The double bed was pushed against the wall and had a beside cabinet next to it. His tin of tobacco had his Rizla papers on top and the ash tray still had half a hand-rolled cigarette in it.

There was an old oak wardrobe and matching chest of drawers. A brown leatherette chair stood under the window and flung over the seat were his trousers, shirt and the old brown cardigan with burn holes that he always wore. His braces were dangling on the floor. That was all the room contained.

She felt a little sad that she hadn't known him better. But he wasn't a man who liked to talk to women.

Pam set to and removed all the bedding. After tying it into a bundle she tossed it down the stairs. 'That lot can all go to the launderette later,' she said out loud.

Stupidly she glanced all about her before opening the wardrobe door. It was as if she was expecting someone to jump out on her. She felt guilty as she looked inside. There were just a few shirts hanging haphazardly on hangers and two suits, although she had only seen him in the dark grey one which he had worn at their wedding and Christmas. Two pairs of brown brogue shoes were at the bottom and a couple of ties hung on the rack. If she stood on tiptoe she could see two trilby hats on the shelf at the top.

Pam closed the wardrobe door. A lifetime and that's all the clothes he had. She was sure now that he never went out.

She was just about to open the top drawer in the chest when a loud rat, tat, tat on the front door knocker made her jump almost out of her skin. She stepped back full of guilt. She quickly looked out of the window and took a sharp breath when she saw a police car parked in the road. Her hand flew to her mouth as she raced down the stairs. What were they going to tell her? Was it Lu? In the short space of time it took her to get to the front door, she had him injured and dead.

Chapter 25

Pam threw open the front door.

'Mrs Cappa?' asked the older and broader of the two policemen who were standing on the doorstep.

Pam held on to the door for support. She nodded and mumbled. 'Yes. Is it my husband?'

The policeman who had spoken looked about him. 'Can we come in?' he asked abruptly.

Trembling, again she nodded and opened the front door wider. 'Come into the kitchen,' she croaked.

When they stepped into the passage the policemen asked, 'What's this?' With the toe of his boot he kicked the bundle of washing that was at the bottom of the stairs.

'It's the bedding from my late father-in-law's bed. It's to go to the launderette,' she said softly.

'I might get you to undo it later.'

'Why?' she asked in disbelief.

He ignored her question and said, 'Shall we move on?'

The two men followed her along the passage. The sound of their boots loudly striking the linoed floor filled her ears.

'What is it?' she asked when they were in the kitchen.

'We have a warrant to search this house.'

'What? Why?'

'We have reason to believe there's stolen goods hidden here.'

Although she wanted to laugh, a note of fear filled her. 'Who told you that?'

'We're not at liberty to say.' The older policeman was doing all the talking. He undid the top button on the pocket of his tunic and produced a piece of paper. 'The warrant,' he said, offering it to Pam.

She took it and glanced at it, but didn't really read it. 'What is it you're looking for?'

'We'll tell you when we find it. We'll start in the yard.'

Pam followed them outside and stood watching them go systematically through the piles of wood they kept for the fire. The collection of damp empty cardboard boxes that the ice cream came in was next to be scrutinized and, when they got to the old coal bin, they even raked around amongst the coal.

'I'd like to know what you're looking for?' she asked nervously again.

The only answer she got was: 'We'll do the rooms downstairs first.'

Pam felt like a puppy dog as she followed them from room to room. They didn't take long to empty the contents of the cupboards in the scullery and there were only old papers and magazines in the dresser that was dragged out and examined. The front room, which had no cupboards and was almost devoid of furniture, took just a cursory glance.

'We'll go upstairs now,' said the older man, but they stopped at the cupboard under the stairs. 'We'll look in there first.'

It took them a while to search through the junk. Leaving

the old bits of motor bikes and the tins of oil and paint spilling out into the passage, they then asked Pam to undo the washing. They sorted through it then walked up the stairs.

'Whose is this room?' asked the policeman. He pushed open a door.

'Me and me husband's.'

'Which Cappa is that?'

'Lu.' Fear grabbed her. 'Luigi. Have you arrested him?'

'No. Why should we?' The wardrobe was opened and their clothes pushed to one side. The shoes at the bottom were pulled out and the contents of the top shelf tossed on to the bed.

'Then why are you searching this house?'

'We've been given a tip-off.'

'But why? I don't understand.' She tried to say it with conviction, but she was frightened. What had Marc done? Had he involved Lu?

'Don't worry about it, Mrs,' said the younger policeman, who was now emptying the contents from the dressing-table drawers.

'I am worried. Very worried,' she said, grabbing her underwear and pushing it under the bedspread. 'Why can't you wait till my husband gets home?'

'Sorry, but we have a job to do.'

They looked in and under the bed and even fished about under the mattress.

Pam was beginning to panic when they moved into Marc's room and went through the same procedure.

'Marc's not going to be very pleased about this,' she said, looking at the mess in the middle of his bed – and relieved they found nothing. She asked as they left the room, 'Who's going to clear all this up?'

'That's not our problem. Whose room is this?'

'My late father-in-law's,' said Pam, holding the door open as they made their way inside.

'Would that be old Alberto Cappa?'

'Yes,' said Pam. 'He died six weeks ago. I was just cleaning it out.'

'Six weeks! You've taken your time cleaning it out.'

Pam suddenly felt dirty. 'The boys didn't want me to. They're still grieving.'

'Or hiding something,' said the older man. 'Let's have a look, shall we?'

Pam followed them into the room. She looked round. What could anybody possibly hide in here?

They sorted through the wardrobe, then moved to the chest of drawers. The young policeman tipped the contents of the first drawer, which only contained a couple of pairs of socks and some off-white underpants, on to the bed. The next drawer was unceremoniously emptied and, to Pam's surprise, was full of papers.

The older policeman shuffled through them quickly and threw them back down.

'This one's empty,' said the younger one on opening the bottom drawer.'

'Better look under this.' The older man nodded towards the bed; the younger wrinkled his nose at the stained mattress.

As Pam had stripped the bed they only had to lift the corner.

'I told you there wasn't anything here,' said Pam, almost

letting out a sigh of relief as she looked at another mess they had created.

The older one stood in the room and slowly looked around. 'You said the boys didn't want you to clean in here?'

Pam nodded.

'Pull the dressing table out,' he said to his colleague.

'Why?' shouted Pam as the dressing table was manhandled away from the wall. She gasped at the amount of cobwebs that were left hanging like net curtains.

'Ain't no one cleaned behind here for a couple of years, I'd say,' said the young one.

'I don't clean this room.'

'Can see that.'

'Right, young man. Pull the wardrobe out.'

Pam could only guess how filthy it would be behind there, but she was shocked when it wasn't only cobwebs they found.

'This looks very interesting,' said the older man, pulling out three pictures that had been covered over with brown paper.

'I expect my father-in-law didn't want to hang them up,' said Pam plaintively.

'Don't think he did.' He ran his finger along the top and looked at it before running it down the side of his trousers. 'No dust. They ain't been here that long.' He stood them against the wall and began to study them. 'How long did you say the old boy's been dead?' He was studying the paintings of fields and thatched cottages.

'Six weeks.'

'That's very interesting. You see these were only stolen

about a month ago along with some other stuff. Could be they're having a job to get rid of these.'

Pam sat on the bed. 'Stolen? I don't know nothing about that.'

'Don't suppose you do, but I bet your old man and his brother do.'

Pam felt her stomach turn over. How could Lu get himself mixed up with Marc when he had promised her? 'What happens now?' she asked.

'Depends. If they tell us all about this robbery and where they fenced the rest of the stuff . . .' He tutted. 'But I can't make any promises, you understand?'

Pam nodded.

'Tell them I'd like to have a word with them down the station, when they come in.'

'Yes. Yes, I will. Are you taking those?' Pam pointed to the pictures.'

'Course. Evidence.'

'But what if they do belong to my father-in-law?'

The older man gave a smirk. 'I don't think he had such good taste, or the money for such expensive collectors' items like these. Take these two, P.C. Fox.' He held out two of the paintings.

P.C. Fox did as he was told and, frozen to the spot, Pam watched the other policeman pick up the third picture.

'I need to take fingerprints, so tell the Cappas, that if they don't match any we've got, then they've not got any worries.'

'But what if . . .?'

'Then, my dear girl, it's prison for them,' he said as he thumped his way down the stairs.

When Pam heard the front door slam, she sat down on the bed completely bewildered. Prison. The word vibrated round inside her head. What would Lu and Marc say when they got home? Her heart was beating like a hammer. Why hadn't she gone to her gran's this afternoon? They couldn't have got in if she'd been out. Was Lu involved in this robbery? And did he know about the paintings? Could she have stopped the police from coming in the house? Her fingers curled round the warrant in her pinafore's pocket. How could Lu go back on his promise and go with Marc? Tears began to run down her face. What was going to happen to them now?

She let her hand absentmindedly run over the papers that were strewn over the bed. One or two caught her interest and she began looking through them.

She was shocked to see there were a lot of recent invoices from Bennetti's. Were they the only wholesalers? Did they get the ice cream from them? 'I thought the Cappas hated them,' said Pam out loud. 'But then I suppose business is business.'

She began to sift through the papers and carefully began putting them into neat piles. She smiled to herself. Wouldn't Jean have a field day if she were here. Did she know about the contents of this drawer? Pam found old bank statements and gasped at the amount at the bottom. Her interest heightened. She began to search for more bank statements – and could there be a cheque book? Guiltily she began to open letters. There was one from a solicitor. It only thanked him for coming to the office. The date was August 1945. Was this after his wife left? And why did he need to see a solicitor?

Pam was intrigued. A brown paper packet held a bundle of sepia photographs. There were pictures of the boys when they were young. Lu had said there weren't any photos of them when they were little. Why had his father hidden them away? There was a photo of a young woman, good-looking, laughing. Was this Lu's mother? She sat staring at a faded wedding photograph, Mr Cappa the groom. He looked so young and so happy. Why had he kept it if he hated his wife so much? Had he still loved her? Did Lu know this picture existed?

She carried on slowly going through the papers and letters, seeking anything that might help her understand this man, utterly fascinated.

The roar of Marc's powerful motor bike startled her. What time was it? She looked round at the mess and remembered the state of all the other rooms. She quickly put the papers back in the drawer; she didn't want him to think she'd been prying into his father's papers.

'Pam. Pam! Lu! Are you home?' he was shouting as he walked through the kitchen and into the passage. 'Bloody hell. What's been going on here? What's all this lot doing?'

She was trembling as she stood at the top of the stairs.

'There you are.' He was standing next to the junk from the cupboard under the stairs. 'I saw the back door was open and . . .' His voice trailed off. 'You all right? You're white as a sheet.'

'Marc . . .' Her tears began to fall.

'What is it? What's wrong?' He ran up the stairs and was about to take her in his arms, but she pushed him away.

'What have you done?'

'What're you talking about?'

'I've had the police round here and—'

'The police?' he yelled. 'What did they want?'

'They searched the house and found some pictures behind your dad's wardrobe.'

'What? You let 'em in here?'

'I couldn't help it. They had a warrant. Look.' She thrust the piece of paper at him.

'You dozy cow. What else did they find?'

'Nothing. Is Lu involved?'

He looked away.

Pam grabbed his arm. 'Marc. I asked you, is Lu involved?'

He shrugged her arm away. 'Get out of my way.' He hurried into his father's bedroom where the dressing table and wardrobe were still well away from the wall. 'Bloody hell. Did you let them do this?'

Pam didn't answer.

He came out on to the landing. 'You let them do that?'

'I didn't have any choice.'

He rushed into his room. 'I'll kill them, and you,' he yelled.

Pam sat on the top of the stairs listening to him crashing about. 'Marc, please tell me if Lu is involved.'

He came slowly out of his bedroom. 'What was you doing here? You're normally out on a Saturday afternoon. And what's all that?' He pointed to the washing at the bottom of the stairs.

'It's the bedding from off your father's bed.'

'What was you doing in his room?' His voice was quiet and menacing.

'I just thought I'd clean it up. It had to be done – it was unhygienic. He *died* in there!' She stood up.

'And I told you to leave it. If you hadn't been here they wouldn't have got in, and I was going to get rid of those pictures tonight. Now thanks to you . . .' His face was full of anger as he stepped closer to Pam.

Fear filled her. 'I'm sorry,' she stammered.

'I bet you are.' He lifted his hand and she stepped back, her foot missing the stair.

She felt as if she hit every stair as she fell. Although dazed she lay very still. She didn't think anything was broken. She didn't want Marc to think she was unhurt. She wanted him to suffer.

'Oh my God,' he yelled, racing down the stairs. 'Pam. *Pam.* Are you all right?'

She didn't answer.

'I'm so sorry.' He cradled her in his arms. 'I wouldn't hurt you for the world.' To her surprise, he began smothering her face with kisses. 'Please talk to me. Say something.'

Chapter 26

Pam pushed Marc away and struggled to sit up. 'Don't. Stop it. Leave me alone.'

'I'm sorry, Pam. Are you all right?'

'Just a bit shook up, that's all. That pile of washing helped save me.'

'Pam. I can't tell you how sorry I am. It was an accident. Are you sure nothing's broken?'

'I don't think so.'

He put his hand under her arms and helped, with some difficulty, to move her to the foot of the stairs, where she sat rubbing her elbow. She was confused and upset.

Marc plonked himself next to her and put his arm round her shoulders. 'Can I get you a drink or something?'

She shook her head. 'I'll be all right. I might end up with a few bruises though.'

'What will you tell Lu?'

'Don't worry. I'll think of something. You've got enough on your plate at the moment. I can't believe you let Lu down like this.'

'I didn't let . . .' His face turned deathly white and he quickly pulled his arm away from Pam. 'Lu!'

Pam followed the look in Marc's eyes. Above her, Lu was standing over them. 'I didn't hear you come in,' she said.

'Obviously.'

'I didn't hear the van,' said Marc, nervously jumping to his feet.

'No, I had a blow-out and the spare was flat. The van's in the garage. Bert said it'll need a new tyre. I had to walk all the way home.' Lu was leaning against the banisters. 'I must say this looks very cosy. Can I ask what's going on here?'

'Nothing. Well . . . It's not what you think, bruv.'

With Marc's help Pam slowly struggled to her feet.

'I fell down the stairs and Marc—'

'You was upstairs, together?'

'Well, yes. No,' Pam stammered nervously.

'Make up your mind. What was you doing upstairs together? Or shouldn't I ask?' His scar was beginning to turn an angry red.

'Lu, such a lot has happened.' She wasn't nervous now, she was cross. He hadn't asked her if she was hurt – unless he didn't believe her.

'I bet it has. How long has this little tête-à-tête been going on?'

'What are you talking about?' asked Pam. Why was there always this mistrust?

'And what's all this mess everywhere?' Lu kicked the bundle of washing.

'Could we go into the kitchen? I could do with a cup of tea.'

'I bet you could,' said Lu sarcastically.

'I'll put the kettle on,' said Marc, making a hasty retreat.

Pam held on to the wall as she slowly made her way along the passage. 'Lu, don't be so stupid. Nothing is going on, as you put it. I'll tell you something, we've got enough problems without you being daft.'

'I don't understand. What's been happening here? What's all this mess? And what's this lot doing all over the place?' He moved some large oil cans so they could get past.

'We've had the police here.' She pushed open the kitchen door.

'What?'

Pam tried not to wince, as she sat at the table, she didn't want them to see how much she was hurting. 'They found some paintings behind your dad's wardrobe.'

Marc put the cups and saucers in front of them.

Lu's face turned grey as he looked from one to the other. 'Oh my God.' He sat at the table and put his head in his hands.

After a tense silence he looked up and angrily shouted at Marc. 'This is all your fault. I told you this would all end in trouble. I told you to get rid of them, get them out of the house.'

'They was going tonight.'

Lu turned on Pam. 'What was you doing home anyway?'

'That's not important. What do you know about the pictures?' asked Pam.

Lu ignored that. He said. 'You'd better tell me what's happened here.'

Pam went into great detail about the afternoon's events.

When she had finished, she asked, 'Lu: did you have anything to do with this robbery?'

He looked at Marc. 'No. But I knew all about it. That's why we didn't want you to clean Dad's room, just in case you found those paintings.'

'That's the truth, Pam,' said Marc quickly.

'Have they got your fingerprints on them?'

Lu nodded. 'They must have, when I had a look at them.'

Pam choked back a sob. 'You've both got to go to the police station to have your fingerprints checked and answer some questions.' She turned on Marc. 'What kind of mess have you got us into now? And you,' – she pointed at Lu – 'how could you be so stupid? He's got us in enough trouble in the past, now we've got this to worry about – and after you promised me as well.'

'I wasn't there, Pam, I swear to you I wasn't there.'

'But will the police believe you?'

'I'll have to make them.'

'What if we scarper?' said Marc. 'We could go away.'

'What with?' asked Lu.

Pam smacked the cup she was holding down on to the saucer. 'Sometimes, Marco Cappa, you talk a right load of rubbish. If you think I'm going to spend the rest of my life running around the country like a criminal, then you've got another think coming.'

'I don't want to be banged up in some prison,' said Marc.

'You should have thought of that when you was out pinching and flashing your money about in your nice new clothes,' Pam retorted. She was very angry now.

'If you tell them who the fence was, perhaps they'll go a bit lighter,' said Lu.

'You don't know what coppers are like.'

'No, and I don't want to.'

'Besides, if I grass, someone will be sent round to carve me up.'

Pam gasped. 'What have you got yourself mixed up with? Heavens, in some ways it's a good thing your dad's not here.'

'And it would have been a good thing if you hadn't been here. Those paintings was going tonight.'

Pam began to cry. 'I can't believe this. It's like a nightmare.'

Lu put his arm round her. 'I'm sure it'll be all right.'

'How can you say that,' she sobbed, brushing his arm away.

'Look, Marc, I think we should go down to the station and tell them everything they want to know.'

'I ain't going.'

'You must. Pam's right. We can't spend the rest of our lives running away.'

'And I can't spend years being banged up. You don't know what it's like.' Marc lit a cigarette, his hand shaking. He stood looking at the empty fireplace. 'It's bloody awful,' he said softly.

They sat in silence and watched Marc take a few puffs from his cigarette before throwing it into the grate.

'I ain't going to give meself up, Lu.' He walked out of the room.

'Lu. Stop him.'

'It ain't no use.'

'But . . . Oh, Lu, what're we going to do?' She turned to her husband and wept on his shoulder.

'I don't know,' he said, gently patting her back. 'I just don't know.'

They heard Marc come racing down the stairs. The front door slammed shut and the roar of his motor bike vibrated round the room.

She looked up through her tears. 'What happens now?'

'I think we'll have our tea then I'll go to the police

station before they come here and get me.'

'How come you got yourself in this mess?'

'When we first moved here it seemed as though Marc was making plenty of easy money and I thought, I'd like some of that. Honest, Pam, I was only thinking of us, getting some money to put down on a house. I was such a bloody fool. I told you I thought he was just buying from those houses. But it wasn't as easy as that, and before I knew it, I was caught up. First of all and most of the time I only got goods in exchange for the jobs I helped with, you know, like the watches and clothes. I know I did the driving and it was wrong,' he added quickly. 'I swear I never went into any of the houses. At first it was a laugh, you know, I was being out with the boys, but then I hated it. I found it was getting to me. I wanted out. Marc thought it was all a big joke. When I hit you . . .' His face was full of pain and guilt. 'I never thought I'd do anything like that to you. I was so angry with you, myself, Marc and everything.'

Pam took his hand.

'I would never hurt you.' He kissed her hand. 'When Dad died and I nearly lost you, I knew then I'd had enough. I told Marc to get someone else.'

'So how come your fingerprints are on those pictures?'

'I told you. Marc showed them to me. He told me they were worth a mint but he had to wait for the right bloke. I was so angry when he put them in Dad's room. I didn't want you to be involved so I never told you.'

'But you were going to go with him again.'

'No. I wanted to find out what he was up to and to make sure he saw the fence and got rid of them at any price.'

'And you believed him?'

'I had to be certain he was getting shot of those bloody things.'

'Why do people have so many secrets? Why didn't you trust me?'

He shrugged. 'I didn't want you to worry. You do believe me, don't you?'

'Yes,' she whispered. 'But what you did was wrong.'

'I know now it's all blown up in my face. Pam, what am I gonner do?'

'Tell the truth.'

'But will they believe me?'

'They must.'

'But what about Marc?'

'He's left you to sort it out. If he was any kind of man he'd come back and face the music.'

Lu threw his arms round Pam. 'I don't want to lose you. I love you so much.'

'And I love you. I'll stand by you whatever happens.'

'I don't deserve you. Mind you, I was a bit worried back there. I thought you and Marc – you know?'

'Lu.' She tried to smile. 'We've had a few ups and downs, but whatever happens, I promise you, I'll always love you and stand by you.'

He kissed her lips with such passion, she knew that tea wasn't all they were going to have before going to the police station. And whatever the outcome, she would always love him.

Much later that evening they walked hand in hand to the police station. There they interviewed Lu and took his fingerprints. Pam was then told he was being held for questioning. She began to cry.

'I'll ask you again, Mrs Cappa. D'you know where we can find Marco Cappa?' The man at the desk drummed a pencil on his teeth.

'We told you. We don't know where he is.'

'So he's left his brother to carry the can. That's very brave of him. Don't worry, we'll find him. We know about Marco Cappa and we've got the registration number of his bike. He won't get far.'

'Can I see my husband?'

'Not till he comes up before the magistrate on Monday.'

'My husband didn't do the robbery you know.'

'So you keep saying. Now please, madam, go home.' The policeman turned away from the counter.

Pam walked out in a dream. What was going to happen to them? Why didn't Marc stay and face the music? Why should Lu take the blame for something he didn't do? She was sure he wasn't involved. She got on the bus and made her way to her mother's.

'Hello love. I've just got in meself,' said Rose when Pam walked into the kitchen. 'My God, what's happened? You look awful.'

Pam sat at the table and cried.

'You two had another row?' asked Ivy.

Pam shook her head.

'What is it, love?' Her mother sat beside her and, after giving her a handkerchief, held her hand.

'Lu's been arrested,' she sniffed.

'What?' It was more like an explosion when all three women shouted it out at once.

'How? Why? What's he done?' asked Rose.

Pam wiped her eyes and blew her nose. 'It wasn't him, it was Marc.'

'And has he been arrested as well?'

Pam shook her head. 'He went off when he knew the police wanted them.'

Rose put her hand to her mouth. 'Oh my God.'

'You'd better tell us all about it, girl,' said Ivy.

'I'll make us all a nice cup of tea,' said Granny Mallory.

Pam told them everything that had happened that day.

'And that coward Marc has buggered off and left Lu to carry the can,' said Ivy.

Pam nodded.

'I've put a little drop of whisky in her cup,' said Granny Mallory. 'It's good for shock.'

'What happens now?' asked Rose.

'I've got to wait till Monday.'

'Will he get bail?'

'I don't know. I don't know anything about what happens.'

'Poor little bugger stuck in a prison cell.'

Ivy's words made Pam cry again.

'Can I stay here the night? I don't fancy being in that house on me own.'

'Course you can,' said Rose. 'You can have my bed.'

'No, I'll make do with the sofa in with Granny Mallory, if that's all right.'

'Course it is, love. We can have a nice little chat.'

Chat was the last thing Pam wanted, she had too much to worry about.

'Have you had anything to eat?' asked Rose.

'Yes, we had tea before we went to . . .' She didn't have to finish the sentence.

'You said you was cleaning the old man's room. Ain't it been done before?' Pam could see Ivy was beginning to get curious.

'No, I told you. They didn't want me in there 'cos that's where Marc had hidden the paintings.'

'What were they like?'

'Didn't take that much notice really. They didn't have any glass in, they must have broken that.'

'Unless they was oils. They don't have glass in and they're usually very expensive, so I've been told.'

Pam suddenly took a sharp breath.

'What's wrong?'

She looked at her gran. 'I told you about the mess they left. When they tipped out one of the drawers in the old man's chest there was a stack of papers – letters, invoices, old photos, all sorts of things. With all the hubbub going on I forgot to tell Lu or Marc. They don't know what was in that drawer. There was a picture of Mr Cappa's wedding. Lu's mum was very pretty.'

'He kept the photo?' said Ivy.

'Did you know her?' asked Rose.

'No,' Ivy said.

'There was pictures of Marc, Al and Lu when they were little. I don't think they even knew they existed. Mr Cappa also had a bank account at some time. And in 1948 he had a lot of money. There was a statement that showed he had over two hundred pounds.'

'Blimey,' said Ivy. 'That was a King's ransom in them days.'

'It still is as far as I'm concerned,' said Rose.

'Has he still got it?' asked Ivy.

'Don't know. I didn't get a chance to go through the rest as that was when Marc came home. I'll get it all sorted out tomorrow. I'll have more time then. I was hoping to find a rent book. I've got to know if the house is rented.' Once again Pam's tears began to fall. 'What if Marc don't come back? And Lu gets put in prison? I'll have to get out. I can't afford to live there on my own, not with just my wages.'

'I'm sure something will turn up,' said Rose. Her face was full of grief for her daughter. 'If you like I'll come back with you tomorrow to help you sort through the stuff.'

'No, that'll be all right. I suppose I'll have to let Al know what's happened.'

After a while Granny Mallory and Pam decided to go to bed. Pam gave a little smile as she lay listening to her granny's deep and heavy breathing. She was pleased she was getting to know her, Granny Mallory was such a sweet, gentle little old lady. She was almost like someone out of a story book.

Pam lay watching the moonlight filter through the curtains and make pictures on the wall. What future did she and Lu have? Why had he been so stupid? He should have known that Marc would get him into trouble.

She was just dozing off when she heard raised voices. It was her mother; she was very angry. Pam was puzzled. Her mother never shouted. She rarely lost her temper.

Pam turned on to her back and listened.

'Don't you start blaming me,' shouted Ivy.

'If you'd let them move in here for the time being, this wouldn't have happened.'

'You can't say that. I reckon that Marco has some kind of hold over Lu.'

'No more than you've had over Pam all these years. If you'd let her marry that Robbie Bennetti she would have a nice house by now and none of these worries.'

Pam couldn't believe what her mother was saying. Did she think that she was still carrying a torch for Robbie?

'Don't start on that again.'

'We never did find out what you had against that family.'

'No and you never will now. But I'll tell you something; it was for the best.'

'I don't know how you can say that, not now . . .'

Pam was straining her ears as the voices died down. This was Marc's fault too: now her mother and Gran were arguing. Her curiosity got the better of her. She had to find out what else they were saying. She quietly slid off the sofa. Perhaps now her gran would reveal her secret?

Pam stood for a while.

'Are you all right, dear?' asked Granny Mallory, sitting up.

'Yes thanks, just been up for a wee,' lied Pam, scrambling back under the blanket. ''Night.'

'Goodnight, dear.'

The voices in the kitchen had stopped and Pam heard her mother going up the stairs to bed. Pam was disappointed not to have learned what Gran's secret was, but she loved Lu; whatever Ivy was hiding, it would never change that fact. Not now.

Chapter 27

Pam opened her eyes and, through the thin curtains, saw that the day had begun. Slowly and painfully she straightened her legs, giving a quiet moan as every muscle in her body protested. Falling down the stairs and then sleeping on the sofa was a lethal combination.

She looked across at her granny who was still fast asleep. Quietly and carefully, Pam sat up and swung her feet to the floor. She needed a cup of tea.

Pam was surprised when she pushed open the kitchen door to see her mother bustling about.

'You're up early,' said Rose, giving her a warm smile. 'Couldn't you sleep?'

'Not too bad.' Pam tried to mask her stiffness: she hadn't told them about her fall.

'There's tea in the pot. What do you fancy for breakfast?'

'A bit of toast will be fine.'

Her mother sat beside her. 'I think you should have a good cooked breakfast. Besides, it'll be like old times. I'll enjoy looking after you.'

Pam ached to throw her arms round her mother and tell her how much she wanted to be looked after. At this moment she needed all the love and protection she could find. But she knew she had to face up to things herself. 'I'll be all right.'

'Are you sure you don't want me to come back with you?'

Pam shook her head. 'When's Lil coming home?' she asked, deliberately changing the subject.

'They reckon it could be quite soon. Bob's been busy getting everything ready for her. Is Jill coming up next weekend?'

Pam nodded. 'I think so. I'll phone her in the week and tell her what's happened.'

'You may have a bit more news after Monday.'

'I hope so. I'll be back later.'

After breakfast Pam made her way back to the house. She could never call it home.

First she looked round the back hoping that Marc had seen sense and had returned, but his bike wasn't there. She pushed open the front door. The house was empty and felt eerie.

She went from room to room getting more and more angry and upset at the mess the police had made. When she got to Mr Cappa's room she emptied the drawer, scooped up the papers and took them downstairs. Plonking them on the table, Pam decided to put the rooms straight before attempting to go through them.

She was still upstairs struggling with the old man's wardrobe when a knock on the front door interrupted her. She looked out of the window and was startled to see Al's car outside. Jean was standing at the gate looking up at the window. Pam quickly darted back. What did they want? Did they know? The knocker went again. Should she go and let them in? They didn't have a key hanging on a string like everyone else as the family came in round the back. Had they tried the back door? Pam hadn't unlocked it. I bet Jean has got a key, she thought. Did she bring it with her?

'Yoo hoo. Pam, are you there?' Jean was calling through the letter box.

Pam felt trapped. If she let them in they would see all the papers downstairs on the table. She had to think fast.

She went into the bathroom, took off her top clothes and, putting on her dressing gown, threw water over her face and hair.

She ran down the stairs and shouted, 'Just coming.'

In the kitchen she quickly grabbed up the papers and, hurrying into the scullery, pushed them into the oven. She then opened the front door. 'Sorry about that, I was in the bath.' She patted her wet hair.

'That's all right,' said Al.

'What's been going on? We've had the police round our house,' said Jean over her shoulder as she marched down the passage. 'They wanted to search our house, but I told them it would be over my dead body.'

'Didn't they have a warrant?' asked Pam.

'Didn't show us one.'

In the kitchen Jean's eyes immediately began wandering about. 'So you had better tell us what this is all about.'

'Sit down. I'll make a cup of tea,' said Pam.

'Pam, we know Lu's been arrested and that Marc has scarpered,' said Al softly. 'Has he come back?'

With both hands, Pam held onto the teapot and shook her head.

'But we're not really sure what's happened,' continued

327

Al. 'They didn't tell us a lot. From what I gathered they were really looking for Marc.'

Pam sat at the table. 'They came here and found some paintings that had been stolen and Lu had to go and have his fingerprints taken. Unfortunately they were the same as what was on the paintings. They already had Marc's as he's been in trouble before. They also matched. But Marc went off as soon as he knew the police had been here; he said he's not staying to finish up in jail.'

'Silly sod,' said Jean. 'Does he honestly reckon he's gonner get away with it?'

Pam only shrugged. 'Lu's very upset at being accused.'

'Well, he would be, wouldn't he? What else did they find?'

'Nothing.'

'Did they have a good look?' asked Jean.

'Course. They turned everything out, even the drawers.' As soon as she said that Pam wanted to bite off her tongue.

'What about all that stuff in the old man's drawer, or . . .' She looked at Pam. 'You do know what I'm talking about, don't you?'

Pam felt the blush creep up her neck and deepen when it reached her face. She pulled her dressing gown tighter round her.

'You do know. You've seen them. Where are they?'

'Jean's always known about those papers, so you had better let us take a look at them,' said Al kindly.

'I never got a chance to really go through them,' said Jean with a smug look on her face. 'He was always behind me when I was cleaning his room. Watched me like a bloody hawk he did, but I knew they were there. I caught a glimpse of them one day. Bank books and statements that said he had a few hundred quid. Everybody thought I was daft, but I *knew*. So what have you done with them?'

'I bundled them up and took them to my mother's.'

'What? When?'

'Last night.'

'Did you read them?' asked Jean.

Pam shook her head. 'I didn't get a chance.'

'I don't believe that.'

Al frowned at his wife. 'Look, Pam, we could drive over and get them,' he said. 'After all, it is on our way home.'

She shook her head, trying to think on her feet. She wanted to read them first. 'They're going to see Lil – you know, the lady in hospital?'

'You must have a key.'

Jean must know she was lying through her teeth. She couldn't keep up this pretence any longer.

She began to cry. 'I'm sorry. I'm so upset at Lu being kept at the police station.'

'Of course you are,' said Al. 'It's only natural. I don't suppose you got much sleep last night worrying about all this.'

'No. I'll pour out the tea. I'm going over to Mum's later. I'll bring the papers back then. I don't fancy going out just yet.' The teapot was shaking in Pam's hands and as she slopped the tea into the cups she left a brown dribble of liquid on the cloth.

Jean let out a sigh. 'If you hold anything back, I'll . . . Well, then you'll have me to answer to, young lady.'

'Why should I do that?'

'Pam, as the oldest I have the right to sort out my father's estate.'

Pam wanted to laugh. 'Estate?'

'That's what they call it,' said Jean. 'Besides, we should see if he had some kind of insurance. Good job *we* had him insured otherwise we couldn't have helped out with the funeral.'

'Well, if there is anything I would rather Marc and Lu be here.'

Jean laughed. 'Fat chance of that if they're both banged up.'

'Well, we'll see what there is,' said Al. 'We'll come round tomorrow evening.'

'Yes. I should be able to tell you more about Lu then, as he has to go before the magistrate in the morning.'

'Oh yes. Of course. He could get bail.'

'Could he? Do you have to put money up?'

'Couldn't say.'

'I hope I've got enough.'

'Can't help you there,' said Al. 'Not at such short notice.'

'I'll take my post office book.' How could they both be so insensitive. Pam was angry. They hadn't once asked how was Lu taking all this.

She leaned against the door after they left and gave a sigh of relief. So Jean knew all about the papers. After getting dressed she went back into the kitchen, smiling to herself. Good job they hadn't wanted something cooked to eat, otherwise they might have got more than they bargained for.

Pam spread all the papers out on the table. What was it with these old people and their secrets?

Some hours later she sat back, her eyes wide with amazement as she looked at the neat collection of papers she had divided into some sort of order. She couldn't believe what she had in front of her.

The bank statements showed he had at least five hundred pounds in the bank last Christmas. The house deeds showed he owned the house. But she couldn't find a will. There were some legal-looking documents that looked like insurance policies; she had only glanced at them and put them back in the envelopes.

Pam still couldn't understand why so many of the invoices came from Bennetti's when they hated them so. There must be other wholesalers they could have dealt with.

But more puzzlingly: where had all his money come from? Why did he count every penny the boys brought in and when they asked for a rise, hit the roof? And why, when he had all that money, didn't he let Lu borrow some to buy Lil's house? How come Lu and Marc didn't know what they were taking every day? And why didn't they know what their father had? There were so many questions to be answered.

She had to show these to Al. He had to know and she had to make sure that Lu and Marc got their share when it was all sorted out.

Would they want to sell this house? What would it be worth? If they did, could they have enough to put a deposit down on a house of their own?

'We're rich,' she shouted, throwing some old papers into the air. At last things were going well.

Suddenly she came back to earth with a bump. What if Lu had to go to prison? Her tears began to roll. It wasn't fair. Nothing ever went their way. What was it Gran Ivy always said? Sorrows and smiles go hand in hand.

★   ★   ★

'Well, what was in those papers?' asked Ivy as soon as Pam walked in.

Pam was going to be very cagey about what she told them, at least till she was sure she had got it right.

'Can't understand some of them so I'm taking them to Al tomorrow. He can sort it out.'

'Is that wise, knowing what Jean's like?' asked Rose.

'He is the eldest.'

'Suppose so.'

'At least I don't have to worry about rent. I think he owned the house.'

'That's a relief,' said Rose.

'That old man was a crafty bugger. Fancy not letting on to anybody about that,' said Ivy.

'He probably knew what Jean was like and was worried she might turn him out.'

'Could be,' said Ivy.

'Looks as if there was a bit of money years ago.'

'Oh.' Ivy sat forward. 'How much?'

'Don't know. There was a bank statement for way back in 1945, he might have taken it all out by now.'

All evening Pam wanted to let her mum and grans into everything she'd found and tell them that Al and Jean had already been round. She had told so many lies today, but hoped it was for all the best reasons. As much as she loved Ivy, Pam knew she would find it hard to keep the news that her granddaughter may have come into some money to herself, and if she blurted it out to someone like Dolly Windsor, well . . . Pam couldn't bear to think of the consequences if it got round, especially with Jean living so near.

★ ★ ★

The following morning Pam went to the magistrates court full of apprehension. What would happen to Lu? She sat waiting till his name was called. She could have cried when she saw him. She wanted to run to him and hold him close. He looked pale and needed a shave. He seemed to have lost his upright stance. The curls in his hair were out of control and the black circles under his eyes made them look dark and sad.

He was asked his name and address, then released on bail. The officer told him he would be informed at a later date, when to appear in court.

Outside Pam hugged him and smothered his face with kisses. 'What happened? Did they believe you?'

He untangled her arms from his neck. 'I don't want to talk about it here. Let's get home.' Lu looked so downcast.

They turned the corner and the Cappa's house came in view. The ice-cream vans looked dirty and lifeless. They usually had laughing children round them, but today even they looked sad. Pam sighed. Whatever did the future hold for them?

She closed the front door behind them.

'This is what I wanted,' he said holding her close.

'What happened? Have they let you off?'

He let Pam go. 'I had to answer a lot of questions at the police station and I've got to go to court again. I couldn't help it, but I had to tell them about the other jobs. I told them I didn't know anything about the paintings or where they came from?'

'Did they believe you?'

He shrugged. 'I don't know We've just got to wait and

see. They also said I'd be in a lot of trouble if I absconded.'

Pam threw her arms round him. He held her close and kissed her long and hard. 'Let's hope Marc comes back and gives himself up.'

'I don't think he will. You don't know what it's like in there.'

'We've got to try and find Marc. He's got to come back and face the music.'

Lu shook his head. 'I can't see him doing that.'

'He must. Al and Jean are coming round tonight,' said Pam.

'What, to gloat? I don't want to see them. I don't want to see anybody.'

'They're coming round to go through your dad's papers.'

'Papers? What papers?'

'When the police turned out all the drawers there was all sorts of things. Did you know your dad had a bank account?'

'No.'

Pam collected the papers from the dresser and put them on the table.

Lu began looking through the various documents. 'Well I'll be buggered. Does Al know about these?'

'They know they exist. It seems Jean knew of them, but she didn't know all of it. They haven't seen them, the police went to their house looking for Marc.'

He gave a hollow laugh. 'I bet that upset her, a police car outside her house. Not good for the neighbours to know what's going on.'

'That's why they're coming round. I told them I took the papers to Mum's. I didn't want them taking them till you'd seen them.'

Lu gave out a long whistle. 'Five hundred quid? Where's he got that from?'

Pam shrugged.

'And all these invoices from Bennetti's.' He threw them back on the table. 'What's he been playing at all these years?'

'That's something you're never gonner find out. Not now.'

'And he does, did, own the house?'

'Yes. I haven't seen a will. Al will have to sort all this out as he's the oldest. I expect he'll want this house sold so he can have a third of the money.'

'I bet Jean can't wait to get her greedy hands on this lot. Fancy her being right about the old man.'

'Perhaps we can put a deposit down on a house when . . .'

'Hold your horses. You seem to forget, I might end up in prison.'

'Not if Marc comes back. He'll tell them you wasn't involved with stealing the paintings. Won't he?'

'He's got to come back first. But I don't hold out much hope of that.'

Lu sat and held the photograph of his mother. 'She was very nice-looking, wasn't she?'

'Yes. You look just like her.'

'I wonder why she left Dad.'

'America must have sounded very exciting.'

'But to leave us . . .'

Pam touched his hand. 'She must have had a good reason.'

Lu threw the photo to one side. 'Dad said she was a trollop.'

'I wonder why he kept these photos,' said Pam.

'I don't know. Why didn't she take us with her?'

'I'm glad she didn't, otherwise I wouldn't have married you.'

He kissed her hand. 'There's always got to be a silver lining in everything, I suppose.'

Although they sat and laughed at the photographs, they both had heavy hearts.

At seven o'clock Pam opened the front door to Al and Jean.

In the kitchen Al gave Lu a hug. 'This is a bad state of affairs,' he said, patting his back.

'Lu,' said Jean, barely nodding her head to acknowledge him as she sat at the table. Her face was a picture as she feasted her eyes on the papers.

'I've put them in some sort of order,' said Pam. 'There's some we can't make head or tail of, they look a bit like policies.'

Jean quickly leafed through them. 'Is this all of them?'

'Yes.'

'You wouldn't keep any back, would you?'

'*Jean,*' said Al abruptly.

'You'd better watch your mouth,' said Lu, jumping angrily to his feet. 'Otherwise I might go down for assault as well as theft.'

'Sorry.' She gave him a silly grin. 'I only asked.'

'I think we should go through them together,' said Al, trying to defuse the situation.

'You don't need me. I'll make a cup of tea,' said Pam eager to get away.

By the time Pam returned with the tea the look of

amazement on all their faces was almost laughable.

'You're never going to believe this,' said Lu. 'We reckon our old man had shares in Bennetti's.'

'Why do you think that?' she asked, sitting at the table.

'Those official-looking papers that we didn't understand, well, according to Al here, they're shares.'

'All this will have to go to a solicitor,' said Al.

'Will that cost much?' asked Pam.

'A few bob, but it'll be worth it in the long run.'

'That's why the crafty old sod used to buy from Bennetti's, he was looking after his own interests,' said Lu.

'And you and Marc didn't know?' Pam was bewildered.

'No. We only picked up the stock from the wholesaler's in the mornings and returned the unsold stuff at night. It wasn't from the Bennetti factory, and there was never any brand name on – well, not Bennetti's.'

'So whose name is on it?' asked Pam.

'R and R's Quality Ice Cream.'

Pam laughed. 'That's Ricky and Robbie. Don't you see, he named the brand after his sons.'

'D'you know, I never thought of that.' Lu sat back. 'You wait till Marc hears about all this.'

'That's if he ever comes back,' said Jean.

'He's got to,' said Pam with fear in her voice. 'He's got to tell the court the truth.'

'Look, we can't do any more till tomorrow,' said Al. 'I'll find out about a solicitor to sort this lot out, and you might need one as well, Lu.'

Lu nodded. 'I'll see what happens.'

'Don't leave it too long.' Suddenly it seemed Al had taken charge of the situation.

'What will we do about this place?' asked Jean, looking round the room.

'When it's all finalized we'll have to work out who gets what.' Al looked at Lu. 'If you want to stay in this house we'll get it valued.'

'That might not be my worry,' said Lu.

'Whatever happens we'll make sure Pam is looked after.'

'Thanks.'

Pam sat glassy-eyed. They were talking about her being alone, being looked after.

'As Dad didn't leave a will all this is going to take months to sort out, so don't worry about living here.'

'At least you haven't got any rent to worry about,' said Jean.

Pam gave them a weak smile. No, she didn't have to worry about rent, just her husband's future.

Chapter 28

On Monday morning, as soon as she could, Pam phoned Jill.

'Bloody hell,' was Jill's first comment on the news. 'When does Lu have to go back to court?'

'We don't know, we have to wait to be told.'

'And what about the old man owning that house? You've certainly had an exciting weekend.'

'A weekend we could have done without.'

'So you don't know where Marc's gone, then?'

'No. Will you be up this Saturday?'

'Yes. Pam, we've got some great news. We've bought a house.'

'That's wonderful. Where is it? Do your mum and dad know?'

'It's near where we live now. And no, they don't know, not yet, so don't say anything till we've told them.'

'Course not. See you Saturday.'

Pam put the phone down and tried not to feel jealous as she looked at the pile of work in front of her. Once again everything was going well for Jill.

That evening Pam left work on the dot to hurry home. She wanted to find out if Lu had learned anything about R and R wholesalers.

Lu was home before her. She rushed in, gave him a kiss and asked, 'Well? What did you find out?'

'Nothing.'

'What do you mean, nothing?'

'No more than what we know, that R and R is owned by the Bennettis.'

'And everybody knew that?'

He nodded. 'It seems that way.'

'But they never told you?'

'Didn't have any cause to, did they?'

'Suppose not. But I would have thought somebody might have mentioned it.'

'Not now. They're mostly new blokes what work there and we never had any reason to talk about the so-called feud that's been going on for years.'

'Suppose not,' repeated Pam.

'I'm not taking the van out any more.'

'Why?'

'I'm not working for Bennetti.'

'But you're not, you're working for yourself now.'

'I'm going to see Al and find out about selling both the vans.'

'What if Marc comes back and wants to carry on selling . . .' She stopped. What was the point? Their lives had been turned upside down.

'I'd like to know what my dad has been up to all these years. All our lives he told us how the family had been done out of everything by them and there he was, sucking up to them.'

'You don't know that.'

'Why else would he buy shares in their business?'

'We'll have to wait and see what Al finds out.'

'Dad was a crafty sod.'

'What are you going to do if you don't take the van out?'

'Does it matter? You won't be chucked out of this place.'

'I know that, but we've still got to eat.'

'Don't worry about it.'

'I am worried about it and it's no good you getting angry.'

'Why not? All my life we've been living a lie. And now I've got a prison sentence hanging over me. I think I've got every right to be angry – bloody angry. I hate my family.'

It upset Pam to see his face so full of pain and fury. 'You mustn't say things like that.'

'Why not. I remember when you hated your gran.'

'That was only because I couldn't get my own way to go to Italy.'

'Things might have been a lot different if you had. You might even be married to Robbie.'

She jumped up. 'Why is it every time something comes up, or goes wrong, everybody brings up Robbie Bennetti. I'm sick of it. I married you because I love you and to hell with the Bennettis. They seem to cause more rows between our families than anything else. Whatever happened in the past should be dead and buried, and that goes for my gran's problems as well.' Pam's eyes were blazing with anger. She plonked herself in the chair and stared at the television screen; she didn't know what she was watching. She hadn't told Lu about the conversation her mother and gran had had on Saturday night, which had been along similar lines.

Lu sat quietly watching her. He could find nothing to say.

★ ★ ★

At the end of the week Al popped in to tell them that all the papers were with a solicitor and as soon as he heard anything he would let them know.

Jill came up to see her gran and she and Pam went out on Saturday afternoon. When they were sitting having a coffee Jill brought out the brochures and told Pam all about the house she and Billy were buying. It was a new one on a new estate that Billy was working on. 'You must come and see it as soon as we get in.'

'It looks lovely. I bet yours will have a few extras.'

Jill beamed. 'I should hope so. You should see the bathroom. We can pick out our own colours, I'm having a yellow suite.' She giggled. 'It's ever so exciting. It's going to have central heating an' all.'

'You're very lucky,' said Pam.

'Well, you wait till they've sold Mr Cappa's house, you might be able to buy something like it.'

'And how will we be able to pay off a mortgage if Lu's in prison?'

'You mustn't think like that.'

'It's all I *can* think of. Now he's sold the vans the only income we've got is my wages. I don't know what I'm gonner do without him.' Tears filled her eyes.

'I'm sorry.' Jill hurriedly put the brochures in her bag. 'I've been blabbing on about what I've got and . . .' She stopped, she couldn't think of any words of comfort.

'It's all right. I'm just feeling a bit sorry for myself, that's all.'

'You've not heard from Marc at all then?'

Pam shook her head.

'How can he be like that?'

'I don't know.'

'What do your mum and grans have to say about all this?'

'They're very angry at Marc letting Lu take all the blame, and they're angry with Lu for getting himself into this mess.'

'You can't blame them.'

'I know. I try not to talk about it when I'm there. I ain't even told them he's sold the ice-cream vans.'

'That's probably very wise. But what're you going to do for money? Will Lu get a job?'

Pam shrugged. 'I don't know anything any more. In fact I'm fed up with everything. I feel like running away from it all.'

Jill looked at Pam. 'I'm really sorry things have worked out this way.'

'It's all right. You didn't come here to listen to me moaning. How's Lil?'

'I think she's improving.'

'That's good.'

'Not a lot, mind. It'll be hard work for Mum when she comes out of hospital. I don't know how she's going to manage. She's such a job to get on to the commode.'

'That's really sad. It must be awful for her, she was so independent.'

'I think it's not having her fags that upset her most.'

Pam gave a slight smile. 'I can imagine that.'

'I hear your mum might be taking over the florist's shop?'

'Yes. Mrs Kennett's not getting any better and her son suggested Mum took it over.'

'Will it cost her?'

'Only the rent and of course the flowers. She's taken on a nice girl who drives so there's no trouble with the deliveries.'

'Who's gonner get up at the crack of dawn to go to the market?'

'Mrs Kennett's son said he'd do it the same as he's always done.'

'Ain't he in competition then?'

'No, his shop's further along the river, near Greenwich, I think. I'm really pleased for Mum, she's been working hard all her life and now, with a bit of luck, things will be great for her.'

'She is good at her job.'

'Yes. It's about time things looked up for her, now we've got all this trouble to contend with. Still, I suppose that's the story of our lives.'

'Don't be such a Jonah.'

'You have to admit, it don't go right for us for very long, does it?'

'S'pose not. Drink up and I'll buy you another cup of coffee.'

'Thanks.'

Pam felt sick as she picked up the letter from the doormat. It had the county court's address on the back. Slowly she made her way upstairs and handed it to Lu. She sat on the bed waiting for him to open it.

'Well?' she asked.

'I'm to appear in court on the third of August. A preliminary hearing.'

'Two weeks' time.'

'Looks like it.'

'Are you going to see that solicitor Al told you about?'

'Dunno.'

'I think you should.'

'I ain't got a lot of faith in him. He seems to be taking for ever to sort out Dad's stuff.'

'Al told you. That's a different department.'

'I know.'

'Look, I've got to go. See you this evening.' She kissed the top of his head and left for work.

It's a good thing I've got a job to go to, she thought as she went to Worth's. Otherwise we'd starve.

That evening they sat and discussed if they should tell Pam's mum and grans the date of the hearing.

'They'll be upset,' said Lu. 'They'll have to know sometime.'

'I know. But it's for the best. I don't want them coming to court.'

'Well, it's up to you.'

'Let's just see how things work out, shall we?'

'OK. Pam, if I get put away you will go back home, won't you?'

She nodded. 'They'll have to make room for me somehow.' Her tears began to fall. 'Why does everything go wrong for us?'

Lu was sitting in the armchair. 'Come here.'

She sat on his lap and he kissed her wet cheeks. 'Listen. When we're old and have loads of kids round us we'll laugh at all the things that have happened to us.'

'Do you really think so?' she sniffed, wiping her eyes with the flat of her hand.

'I know so. All this has been a test and we'll come through with flying colours. You wait and see.'

'I hope so,' she said softly. 'I really hope so.'

For two weeks it had been hard for Pam to keep the news from her mother and grans. She hadn't even told Jill when the hearing was going to be for fear her friend would tell Doreen.

It was Tuesday evening, Pam and Lu were sitting quietly watching the television when there was a loud knock on the door.

'Who's that?' asked Pam.

'I'll go,' said Lu.

Pam could hear voices and was about to go into the passage to see who it was when the kitchen door opened and a thin wiry man in his late twenties walked in.

He held out his hand. 'Hello, I'm Ron, Ron Parker. Me friends call me Nosy.'

Lu was right behind. 'This is a bloke from the *Echo*.'

'The newspaper?' said Pam in disbelief.

'That's the one,' said Ron, handing Pam a calling card.

'What does he want?' asked Pam, ignoring him and talking to Lu.

Ron sat himself down at the table. 'My paper gets to know of any cases that might be of human interest. A lot of people know of Cappa's ice cream and so I've been told to come and get your angle.'

'How do you know about it?' asked Pam.

'Coppers,' said Lu irritably. 'How much does your paper pay them to keep you informed?'

'That ain't up to me. I just do as I'm told and, you never

346

know, it might do you a bit of good.'

'Ain't a lot to tell really. I didn't do it and that's about it,' said Lu.

'You're one of the Cappa brothers, right?'

Lu nodded. 'You know that.'

'And your brother's gone missing? You ain't got any idea where he is?'

'No.'

'That's a bit hard on you.'

'How do you know all about this?'

'Was you involved with this robbery?' asked Ron, ignoring Lu's question.

'No, I wasn't.'

Ron grinned. 'I like that, forceful. Shows character. Who did the paintings, and what were they about?'

'I don't know.'

'Were they portraits or scenes?'

'Houses and fields. I didn't take that much notice of them, only saw them once. Should I be telling you all this?'

Ron tapped his teeth with his pencil. 'I just want to get the facts right, mate, the facts,' he said in a phony American accent.

Pam smiled. He was like a breath of fresh air breezing through. 'Would you like a cup of tea, Mr Parker?'

'Call me Ron, and a cuppa will go down a treat. Thanks.'

When Pam put the tea in front of him she pushed the sugar bowl towards him too and watched in amazement when he put in four heaped spoonfuls and stirred vigorously. How could he stay so slim with all that sugar?

'How long have you been working for the *Echo*?' asked Pam.

Ron looked embarrassed. 'Not too long. We move around in this profession.'

'I don't know if I want me name plastered all over the papers,' said Lu.

'I promise it'll be in a good light. Might even do you a bit of good. You know, hard-working local boy caught up with villains. That sort of thing.'

Pam wanted to laugh.

'Then again it might not be in till after the trial, and even then, my editor might throw it out for legal reasons. Or if another big story breaks and steals my thunder, it could disappear completely.' He stood up. 'Well, it's been nice meeting you people. I wish you all the best for Thursday.'

'Will you be there?' asked Lu.

'Don't know.' He was shaking Lu's hand when there was an almighty crash mixed with sound of broken glass.

'The window,' screamed Pam and, with Lu and Ron following close behind, rushed into the front room. There was a brick lying in the middle of the floor. It had a piece of paper tied round it.

Pam wasn't sure whether to cry at the mess or laugh at Ron who was beside himself with excitement.

'This is great. It's like something out of the movies.' Parker picked up the note.

THIS IS JUST A WARNING, CAPPA, TO TELL
YOU TO KEEP YOUR MOUTH SHUT – OR ELSE.

Ron read it out loud. 'It ain't signed. Any ideas who could have sent it?'

Lu shook his head. He looked very pale.

Pam held on to Lu's arm. 'Look at the mess. What are we going to do?' she cried.

'Nothing,' said Lu quickly.

'But, Lu—'

'Pity we ain't got a photographer here, this would make a super picture,' Parker said, licking the end of his pencil before continuing to write.

'Look, can you leave us now?' said Lu.

'Sure, mate. This is going to make a great story.' He was whistling as he walked down the path. At the gate he turned and waved.

'What do you know about this?' asked Pam as she stood looking at the note.

'I'll tell the police.'

'Who sent it?'

'I think it might be from the fence Marc used.'

'Why do you think that?'

'I gave them a name.'

'Lu! Was that wise?'

'I don't know. I just wanted to help my case. I've got to give them all the help I can. I want to save my own skin. Look, Pam, I think you ought to go back home till this thing is all over.'

'No. I'm not going to leave you on your own.'

'What if I get put away? It won't be safe here.'

'Let's take one day at a time. Now help me clear this mess up.'

Together they set about making the window good with some plywood they found out in the back yard.

'You didn't make the front page,' said Pam, handing Lu the newspaper when she got home from work the following evening. 'I must just go to the loo.' She ran upstairs while Lu eagerly opened the paper.

'Here, Pam, come and listen to this. "On Thursday 3 August, Luigi Cappa will appear in court." That's all there is. Not even a mention of the brick.' Lu laughed. 'And there was me thinking I was going to be in the headlines.'

Pam came into the kitchen. 'Let me see.'

'It's that little bit down there. So much for poor old Ron's moment of glory.

'His editor obviously didn't think it was worth that much space.'

On Thursday Lu looked very smart as they made their way to the court. Pam wanted to hold him and not let him go. She was frightened she wouldn't see him again.

Lu wasn't due to be called until later so Pam sat outside in the warm sunshine waiting. She let her thoughts drift. How would she manage without Lu? He was so much a part of her life now. She couldn't imagine living without him.

Chapter 29

'All right, love?' said a voice Pam knew.

She looked up, startled. 'Gran, what you doing here?'

'I saw about this in the paper and I thought, She ain't going to tell us, so I decided to come and see for meself what's happening. Your mum couldn't come as of course she's got the shop to look after and I thought it'd be too much for Alice.' She sat next to Pam. 'Why didn't you tell us the date?'

'I didn't want to worry you. I thought I'd wait till it was over before I said anything.'

'You are a silly girl.'

'I would have told you, you know.'

Ivy patted her hand. 'I know, but it don't hurt to have a bit of support, now does it?'

Pam shook her head.

'Where's Lu?'

'He's had to go in.'

'Do you know what's happening?'

'No. He was waiting to see someone and they told me they would let me know when it's his turn to be called in.'

'I see.'

'We're hoping that he's been of use to the police, but I don't really know.'

All morning Pam and Ivy sat waiting for Lu to come out. It was a warm day and Pam was feeling more and more hot and bothered. She wanted to get away. What was going to happen to Lu? Two or three times Pam went inside to see if she could find out what was going on. She was desperately hoping that everything was going his way. When it was time for the court to have its lunch break everybody made their way outside. Today there were plenty of people milling about and Pam looked above the crowds for Lu.

Ivy took a deep breath. 'I wonder what's going on in there? D'you think there's anywhere to get a cuppa?'

Pam didn't answer; she was staring at the back of a man who was standing talking to a lovely young woman who was holding on to the handles of a very expensive pram. Pam's hand went to her mouth when he turned to face her.

A huge grin spread across his tanned face when he caught sight of her.

'Robbie,' she whispered.

'What was that you said, love? You'll have to speak up,' said Ivy, looking round. 'Bloody lot of noise some people make.'

Robbie came towards Pam. She felt her knees go weak. What could she say to him? Why did her gran have to be here?

'Hello, Pam. How are you?'

'I'm all right,' was all she could think of to say.

Pam saw Ivy had moved away slightly and was gazing across the road. 'Pam, they sell tea over there, I'll go over and get us a table.'

'OK.'

When Ivy was out of earshot Robbie asked, 'Is that the formidable Gran?'

That statement immediately got Pam's hackles up. 'Yes, it is.'

'Sorry, I didn't mean to offend. So how are you after all these years?'

'I'm fine, thank you. What about yourself?'

'Doing really great.' He had a certain air about him. Pam couldn't put her finger on it. He was still very good-looking, but he seemed taller. He was well dressed and appeared self-assured somehow. He wasn't the shy young man she used to know.

'Do you still live in Italy?' she asked.

'Yes.'

'So what are you doing over here?'

'It was my parents' wedding anniversary and as Dad's not that great, we came over to help them celebrate. When I saw that piece in the paper about Lu being in court, I made a few inquiries and found out he was married to a Pamela. Well, I put two and two together and guessed it was you and I thought I'd like to look you up after all these years.'

'You didn't write,' she said quietly.

'I did, but as you didn't answer I thought that was it.'

'I *did* write – but it doesn't matter now,' she added hastily.

'I moved about a bit at first. That could be why I never got your letters. A lot happened very quickly and I knew you would never come out to Italy, so I decided to get on with my life.'

'That's nice.'

'Are you happy?' Robbie asked.

'Yes very. Or I was till this happened.'

'It was rotten of Marc to run off like that.'

'You know all about that?' Pam exclaimed.

'Yes.'

'How?'

'Some people we know told me. I was sorry to hear about Lu's dad,' he added quickly.

Pam's head shot up in amazement. 'You know about that as well?'

'My dad told me.'

Pam was angry. 'Has he been keeping his eye on this family?'

'No. No, it isn't like that. He went to his funeral.'

'Why? I didn't see . . .' She stopped. 'Has he got white hair and walks with a stick?'

'That's right. Did you manage to talk to him?'

She shook her head. 'No. Why would he go to Mr Cappa's funeral?'

'Don't know much about it, but I gather it was something to do with the business. Shares. Dad had kept it very quiet and only told me after Mr Cappa died. Lu must know all about it.'

Pam wasn't going to pursue that line of conversation; she had to tell Al first, unless he already knew.

'So you're happily married, that's good. Are there any little Cappas yet?'

'No. What about you? Are you married?'

'Yes. That's my wife over there. Isn't she beautiful?' He beckoned to her.

The young woman came over. People were turning to look at her as she pushed her pram towards them. She was very slim and wore a gorgeous pale blue suit, which made Pam feel scruffy. Her long dark hair glistened in the sunlight. She had a beaming smile and was a lot taller than Pam in her wonderful beige high heels.

Robbie said something to her in Italian; she looked at Pam and answered. He turned to Pam. 'This is Maria. She's a little shy about speaking in English. I just told her I probably would have married you if I'd stayed in England.'

Pam took a breath. 'And what did she say to that?'

'That it was a good job you didn't come to Italy then.' He laughed. 'Look, why don't we all go out for a meal one evening,' Robbie went on. 'We don't go back till the end of the month. August is a holiday for most of Europe.'

'I don't know,' Pam was faltering. 'What if . . .' She stopped.

'I reckon he'll get off,' said Robbie. 'I don't think they've got enough evidence.'

'How do you know?'

He touched the side of his nose. 'I'm not saying another word.'

A quick thought rushed through Pam's mind and she wanted to laugh. He sounded like someone out of a gangster film!

'I got fed up with waiting for you. I've had my tea and yours.' Ivy was standing behind her.

'I'm sorry, Gran.'

'So who's this then?' she asked.

'Gran, this is Robbie Bennetti.'

Ivy's face went visibly white. 'What's he doing here?'

'He came to see me and Lu.'

'Why? To gloat?'

'No.'

Robbie was looking from one to the other. 'I came here to help.'

'What can you do for the poor buggers?'

'There might be something.'

'Gran. Listen. This is Robbie's wife and baby.' Tears began to fill Pam's eyes. 'Why can't you see. I love Lu and if there's the slightest chance anyone can help then I'll take it. I don't care who it is. So don't go pushing Robbie away again.'

'I'm sorry, love.' Ivy put her arms round Pam and held her tight. 'You've been through such a lot these past few years.'

Pam sniffed and wiped her eyes. 'What's your baby's name?'

They all turned to look at the baby who was lying on his back in the beautiful pram smiling and kicking his brown legs in the air.

Robbie grinned proudly. 'His name is Ricardo, same as my brother's.'

'He's lovely,' said Pam.

'Is he good?' asked Ivy, bending over the pram. She couldn't resist looking at him, despite all her misgivings.

'A perfect Bennetti,' said Robbie proudly.

Pam was holding the baby's tiny foot. Suddenly she dropped it and looked at Ivy. Had she noticed?

Robbie laughed. 'That's what makes him a perfect Bennetti.'

'What does?' whispered Ivy.

'Six toes. All the Bennettis have six toes. Me, my dad and Ricky. I was amazed when I went to Italy and found out that this goes back many many generations. We always know if

any of the women have been, shall we say, a little naughty.'
He laughed again.

Ivy went a grey colour and began to sway.

'Gran, Gran,' shrieked Pam. 'Quick, someone get her
something to sit on.'

Somebody appeared with a chair and Ivy slumped into it.

'What is it, Gran? What's wrong?'

A glass of water was put into Ivy's hand. 'It must be this
warm weather.'

The usher came out and told them court was about to
convene.

Where was Lu? Pam looked at her gran. She wanted to
go in to find out what was happening, but didn't want to
leave Ivy.

'You go on, love, I'll be all right.'

'I can't leave you.'

Robbie's wife spoke quickly to Robbie.

'Look. Maria here says she'll stay with your gran if you
want to go inside.'

'Would she?'

The beautiful Maria smiled and nodded.

'I'll come in with you,' said Robbie.

'Thanks.'

Inside, Pam asked where she might find her husband.
When she caught sight of him at the far end of a corridor,
she had Robbie at her side, but as soon as she saw Lu she
realized what a mistake that was.

His face went deathly white, then it turned to thunder. He
shook his head and Pam felt sick. She wanted to yell out
that she loved him and only him.

He turned and quickly walked away.

Chapter 30

Pam was hot and bewildered. What was going to happen to them? She was angry with herself for not thinking about how Robbie being with her would upset Lu. There were noises and voices reverberating all around her and she couldn't concentrate. It was as if her head was full of cotton wool.

Robbie was talking to someone. Suddenly he took hold of her arm and pulled her along. 'They've thrown it out. Didn't even go to a proper trial! They believe him. Lu's just gone outside, come on.' He rushed her over to her gran and his wife who were sitting outside. He was talking very fast in both English and Italian.

In turn, her gran and then Maria hugged and kissed Pam. Her gran had tears rolling down her cheeks.

'Where is he then?' asked Ivy.

'I don't know.'

'It's wonderful news,' said Ivy. 'Now you can pick up your lives again.'

Robbie was laughing in delight, his arm round Pam's shoulders. She suddenly caught sight of Lu again. He did a swift double take, then walked away from them.

'Lu,' she screamed, running after him. 'Lu, Lu! Where are you going?'

'You don't need me. Not now that he's back on the scene.'

'What are you talking about?'

'Bennetti.'

'I didn't know he was going to be—'

'Don't give me that. It's too much of a coincidence that he's here today. Was you both hoping I'd be sent down?'

'It's not like that.' Tears of frustration and worry fell from her eyes. She clenched her fists and stamped her foot. She was so angry. 'Won't you just listen?'

'What is there to say?'

She raised her fist. 'There are times when I could really hit you. You make me so angry.'

He held on to her arm. 'Well, don't worry. I won't be making you angry any more.' He let go of her arm and stormed off.

She ran after him. 'Please, Lu, just listen. He's here for his parents' wedding anniversary. He read about this in the newspaper.'

'And he came here for a good laugh?'

'No. He's here with his wife and son.' Pam stopped. What was the use?

Lu took a few more steps then he stopped too. After a few moments, he slowly turned.

Pam was standing looking at him. She didn't move. Tears were blurring her vision. 'I'll never be able to convince you you're the only one I love,' she whispered. 'What's the point, you don't believe a word I say.'

Lu hesitated. Pam turned and began, with leaden steps, to walk away.

'Pam. Pam, wait.' He was at her side with a few strides. 'I

do believe you. I suppose it was the shock of seeing him with you. The way he was looking at you. Then outside I saw you laughing together.'

'I was laughing because I was happy that you didn't have to go to trial! Are you going to spend the rest of your and my life looking round every corner, waiting for a member of the Bennetti family to pounce? I've had enough. I just want a peaceful life far away from here.'

With Lu just a step behind, she walked back to her gran. Robbie and Maria were still waiting.

'Congratulations,' said Robbie, extending a hand to Lu.

'Thanks,' he said morosely.

'I'd like you to meet my wife. Maria, this is Lu, the one who won Pam in the end.'

Pam felt herself blush. She looked at her gran who quickly looked away.

'Hello,' said Lu to Maria.

'How about us going out one night for a meal?' said Robbie.

'I'll have to think about it,' said Lu.

'Well, give us a ring sometime. I was telling Pam we're here till the end of August.'

The baby began to cry and Maria said something to Robbie.

'It's feed and nappy-change time. Hope to see you around.' Smiling, Robbie walked off with his arm round Maria's trim waist. At the corner they both turned and waved.

'What was he doing here?' asked Lu.

'I told you,' said Pam.

'Did you see that baby's foot?' asked Ivy.

'Can't say I took any notice of it. Why?'

'It's got six toes.'

Lu laughed. 'I bet that upset him. Couldn't even turn out a perfect kid.'

'According to him, he is perfect. Seems all the Bennetti boys have got six toes.'

'It's not really a toe though, is it?' said Pam. 'It's more that the little one's fat and got a dividing line down it.'

'Call it what you like, I still say it don't look right.'

'Robbie's proud of it.'

'Did he have six toes?' Lu asked Pam.

'How should I know? I ain't ever seen his feet.'

Ivy laughed. 'Come on, let's go home. My feet are killing me. And no, I ain't got six toes, only a bloody great corn that's giving me gyp.'

Ivy was singing all the while she was putting the cups and saucers out.

'You sound happy, Gran.'

'Course I am. I'm pleased because you two can start again.'

'What's going to happen to your brother then, Lu?' asked Granny Mallory.

'Don't know. He could be for the high jump if he comes back.'

'I'm surprised the police haven't found him,' said Pam.

'I've got a feeling he's left the country.'

'Why? What makes you say that?' asked Ivy.

'Dunno. Just a feeling I've got.'

'Has he got a passport?' Pam began pouring out the tea.

'Yes, he has. Got it a while back. He was going off

somewhere before when he got into a spot of bother.'

'Well, the police haven't found him.'

'So you'll be out on your own then?' said Ivy.

'Not selling ice cream, he won't,' said Pam.

'Why's that?'

'He's sold the vans.'

Ivy sat down at the table, shocked. 'Why?'

'I'd had enough.'

'So what're you going to do now?'

'Don't know.'

'You'll have to find a job somewhere,' said Pam.

'There's always plenty of driving jobs going.'

'Pity Rose didn't know, she was looking for a driver.'

'Mum couldn't afford to pay what Lu will be expecting.'

'No, I don't suppose she could. I still can't get over that baby having six toes.'

'Robbie's certainly proud of it,' said Pam.

'Look, d'you mind if we don't wait till your mum gets home?' said Lu.

'No. She might be late anyway if she's got a rush order,' Ivy said.

'I'm really pleased for her,' said Pam. 'And she seems happy enough.'

'She is. At least her future is taken care of,' said Ivy.

They said their goodbyes and set off home.

Pam suddenly found herself very apprehensive as they turned the corner. What would they find? Would more windows be broken? Even though, according to the police, they had put the fear of God into the fence's family.

She clung to Lu's arm. 'Well, it's certainly been a day to remember,' she said.

'I'd say more a day I'd rather forget.'

'What are we going to do?'

'Dunno. I think we ought to try and gee that solicitor bloke up.'

They arrived at the house and could see everything was fine.

'As soon as we can I reckon we ought to get shot of this place.'

'I'm all for that. But what about Marc?'

'The way he's turned out he ain't got a lot of say in the matter.'

They closed the front door and made their way into the kitchen.

'He must have his share of whatever there is,' Pam insisted.

'We'll have a talk with Al.'

'Pam, did you know Bennetti was going to be there today?'

'No. How many times do I have to tell you? D'you know, that man with a stick who was at your dad's funeral, well, that was his father.'

Lu plonked himself down in the chair. 'Well, I'll be buggered. We said he looked familiar. What was he doing there?'

'Something to do with business, Robbie said.'

'Did Rob know anything about them being friends or whatever?'

'No. He said his dad told him it was something to do with shares. But I don't think he knew any more than that.' Pam fidgeted with the teapot. 'Look, why don't we go out with them one night, have a meal somewhere. Then you could ask what this is all about.'

Lu stood up. 'You must be joking.'

'Please yourself. I just thought you'd like to know a bit more about it.'

'Not if it means going out with him.'

A week later, just as Pam walked into the office, the phone began ringing impatiently.

'Give me a chance to get me coat off,' she said out loud. She was taken back when she heard Marc's voice.

'Marc? *Marc!* Is that you? Where are you?'

'I won't tell you, that way you can't get into any trouble.'

'Marc, I think you've got a bloody nerve phoning me here after running away like that.'

'I'm sorry, Pam, but I had to. I couldn't stay. But I had to phone to find out what's been happening?'

'How do you know my number?'

'You wrote something down once on your office paper. Anyway, what's happened?'

'Not a lot. Didn't think you'd be interested.'

'Course I am. He is me brother.'

'Lu got arrested, that's all.'

'I'm sorry.'

'So you should be.'

'What can I say?'

'Not a lot,' Pam repeated.

'How long did he get?'

'There wasn't enough evidence to go to trial.'

'But what about his fingerprints on the paintings?'

'Because he'd been so helpful on other things they believed him when he said he'd just looked at them after he'd caught you hiding them.'

'So he's really burned my boats!' Marc groaned.

'What do you expect? The police are after you anyway.'

'I know that,' he said quietly.

'Where are you?' There was something different about his voice, it didn't sound the same as normal, was he abroad? 'Marc. Where are you?' she asked again.

'I can't tell you.'

'What are you going to do?'

'Nothing. I'm not coming back.'

'How will you manage for money?'

'I've sold my bike.'

Pam was shocked; she didn't have a snappy answer to that. She knew that bike meant everything to him.

'I ain't doing so bad. I'm working in a bar.'

'There's going to be some money here for you.'

'What? Who from?'

'Your dad. It seems he owned the house. That's going to be sold. And he had some shares. We're waiting for it all to be sorted out.'

The line went quiet. 'Marc. Marc are you there?'

He began to laugh. 'Yes. Daft, ain't it? All me life I've wanted money; now it's fallen into me lap I can't get me hands on it.'

'We don't know how much it is yet. Is there any way we can get in touch with you?'

'No. I couldn't face going to prison.'

'So you're prepared to stay away?'

'For ever if need be. I'll ring again some time. Take care, Pam. I always had a soft spot for you, you know.'

The line went dead.

Tears filled Pam's eyes. What was it about the Cappas?

They never seemed to come out of the mire smiling.

That evening when Lu came home Pam told him about Marc's phone call and that she'd told his brother how Lu had helped the police in exchange for them letting him go. Lu paused a moment then said gruffly, 'Well, what did he expect, leaving me to face the music? He's landed me in it often enough. He can't blame me for looking after myself for once.'

Pam nodded and, in silence, they got ready to go out to Al's.

'You mean to say that Marc phoned and didn't tell you where he was?' said Al when they got to his house.

'Yes. I think it was abroad. It didn't sound right somehow, as if he was underwater.'

'And he's sold his bike,' said Lu. 'That must have broke his heart.'

'That was his choice. We're just pleased you didn't get put inside,' said Al.

'Not nearly as pleased as me.'

'Now, about the money. I've seen the solicitor and he reckons we should both go and see him, apparently it's a bit complicated.'

'That don't surprise me,' said Lu. 'When does he want to see us?'

'Can you manage tomorrow?'

'No problem,' said Lu.

'You'll have to start looking for a job,' said Pam.

'Might not have to if we're worth a fortune.'

'I shouldn't count on that,' said Al. 'I don't think Dad had that many shares. I can take the morning off.'

'So can I,' said Jean. 'I want to be there.'

'What about you, Pam?' asked Al.

'No, I'll go to work as usual.'

'Are you sure?'

She nodded. 'Lu can tell me all about it when I get home.'

'Well, I reckon we should have a little drink,' said Al. 'To toast Lu being back in the fold and Dad owning his house. I wonder what it's worth?'

'It'll want a few bob spent on it.'

'We'll worry about that after we've had it valued.' Al went to the cocktail cabinet and started to get out the glasses.

'Right, what we all having?'

'It's a pity Marc ain't here to celebrate,' said Pam.

'If Marc was here,' said Jean, 'he'd be in prison now, silly sod.'

But Pam couldn't help feeling a bit sorry for him. He was abroad and alone – or was he? She gave a little smile. Knowing Marc and his looks and charm, he wouldn't be lonely for very long.

Chapter 31

The next evening Lu was waiting outside Worth's for Pam.

'I'm so tired,' she said, lightly kissing his cheek and getting on to the back of his bike.

'Why, been busy?'

'I should say. It seems Mr Worth is going to expand, going out to one of these new towns. I've been typing and going through different documents with him all day.'

The bike roared into life. 'You ain't gonner lose your job, are you?' asked Lu.

'No. I hope not. Although I am worried about it.'

When they arrived home Pam asked, 'How did you get on at the solicitor's this morning?'

Lu was grinning. 'Sit yourself down. Kettle's on, I'll make a pot of tea.'

'Well?' said Pam impatiently. 'Tell me.'

Lu put the tea things on the table. 'You ain't gonner believe what a day I've had. First of all, Dad did own shares in Bennettis. And, according to a letter, that was dated years ago, my dad saved the old boy's life.'

'I didn't see that.'

'No, it was amongst some of those official-looking documents in an envelope.'

'Why did he do that?'

'It seems it goes back a long way. When my dad took over the business from his father, my grandad, they still had horses and carts. Anyway, the old boy, Robbie's father, fell under a horse and my dad pulled him out and saved his life. I think they were only nippers at the time. The solicitor said after that Bennetti felt he should do something to help the Cappas when they fell on hard times. Mind you it's only what Dad had told us, his dad was a miserable old bugger.'

'You never told me,' said Pam, her eyes wide with all she was trying to take in.

'It seems Granddad liked a drink or two, but the old boy was too proud to take Bennetti's money. So when the present Bennetti started to expand after the war, he felt he owed his life to my dad, so he gave him a lot of shares, but swore him to secrecy as he didn't want to upset his own father or my granddad who was still alive at the time. Are you with me?'

Pam nodded. 'I think so. But why didn't your dad tell you about the shares?'

Lu shrugged. 'Christ knows. Don't make sense, does it? Mr Parsons, that's the solicitor, reckons it just became a habit and in the end he couldn't tell us. Too proud, he reckons. Bloody daft, ain't it?'

'So how much is all this worth?'

'They've been doing quite well over the years and he reckons we should hang on to the shares, that's of course unless any of us want to sell. Dad was getting a nice little income from them and the ice-cream business is expanding all the time. Mr Parsons has been on to the Bennettis and told them we don't want to sell them.'

'But . . .'

Lu put up his hand. 'I know, we need the money. Al seems to think we'll get enough from this house to put a deposit down on a house of our own. It's being valued next week.'

'That's all very well, but we'll still have to find the mortgage every month. And you haven't got a job?'

'There's about six hundred pounds in his bank account, so we'll divide that and that'll give us a couple of hundred to go on holiday with. I'm taking you to Italy.'

Pam sat bewildered. 'I can't take all this in. What about Marc's share?'

'We're banking that and, who knows, one day when he lets us know where he is, we can take it to him.'

'You've got it all worked out.'

Lu sat back with a smug expression on his face. 'Looks like it.'

Pam stood up. 'But you still ain't got a job, have you? What if I get put off, who's going to pay the bills then?'

Lu stood up and held her close. She shrugged him away. 'I have got a job.'

She looked at him suspiciously. 'Oh yes, and where?'

he laughed. 'You're never going to believe this. I'm going to work for Bennetti!'

'What?' she exploded. 'All these years you've . . .'

'That's it. All these years we thought we was working for Dad, but in a way it turns out we was really working for Bennetti as well. Anyway after talking to Mr Parsons I went to see the Bennettis. I needed to get this mess cleared up. They made me really welcome. Robbie's dad's a nice bloke. We had a very long chat about how he really liked my dad and was sorry he didn't say who he was at the funeral. He knew me and me brothers didn't know about the shares.'

'How?'

'My dad had told him. My old man reckoned we wouldn't have put so much into working if we knew. Oh, by the way, we're going over there for a meal with them tomorrow.'

Pam's head was spinning. 'A meal at their house?'

'Yer, you should see it.'

Pam wasn't going to tell him she already had. 'I can't believe all this is happening.'

'Don't you see? In a few months time we'll have our own house. It can be wherever you want. I'll have a good job; I'm going to be in charge of the new band of reps they're employing. I'm getting a good wage plus commission, but it'll be for meself as well, as I'm a shareholder.' He sat back.

'But why are they doing this for you?'

'Didn't ask. I just mentioned we'd sold the vans and was looking for a job now this court thing was behind me. That's when Robbie said they needed an experienced bloke, and with me being a shareholder they knew I'd have the business at heart. They're going to get really big, Pam. You don't have to worry about your job, you can stay at home and have that baby we've talked about. Oh Pam, can't you see, at last everything is going our way.' He swept her up and held her close again. 'I love you so much and you deserve everything I can give you.' He kissed her long and hard.

When they broke apart she collapsed into her chair again.

Tears were rolling down her cheeks.

'What're you crying for?'

'It doesn't seem possible that our lives could turn round so fast.'

'And for the first time, it's for the better. Now come on, wipe those lovely eyes. We'll have our tea then we'll go over to see your mum and grans and tell them the good news.'

With tears still glistening on her cheeks, Pam gave him a smile that said it all.

'Well, I'll be buggered,' said Ivy as they listened to Lu telling them all that had happened.

'Just think,' said Pam looking at her gran, 'so much bad feeling could have been avoided if people only told the truth.'

'That's true,' said Rose.

Tears were beginning to stain Ivy's face.

'What's wrong, Ma?' asked Rose. 'Everything is going to be fine for them now.'

'I know,' Ivy sniffed. 'Perhaps it has worked out all right in the end.'

Pam put her arms round her gran's neck. 'Don't go worrying about things now. Just you concentrate on keeping Lil entertained. With your help I reckon she'll be talking in no time. It's great news that she's coming home at last.' She turned to Lu. 'We must come over and see her when she's settled in.'

'Don't bother to bring her flowers,' said Rose. 'Unless of course you're getting them from my shop.'

They all laughed.

'I'm sorry,' said Ivy.

'What for?' asked Rose.

'I suppose I'd better tell you why I hated the Bennettis so much.'

'You don't have to, Gran,' said Pam. 'That can be your little secret.'

'No. No, I must tell you. I can't go to me grave without you knowing.'

'I'll make some tea,' said Granny Mallory.

'No, sit down, Alice. You all might as well know.' She dabbed at her eyes. 'I couldn't tell you before, I was so ashamed.'

Rose touched her hand. 'Ivy, you don't have to tell us if it's that painful.'

'But I must. I want to. You see, Harry, my husband, was in the navy. We hadn't been married very long when he was captured during the first war and interned in Holland. They were neutral that time. Well, they used to let them come home on leave just as long as they promised to go back.'

Lu laughed. 'That sounds a funny sort of war.'

'It wasn't funny,' said Granny Mallory quietly.

'No, I don't suppose it was,' Lu said sheepishly.

Ivy continued: 'I was working in the munitions factory at the time and when I knew Harry was coming home on leave I went and asked Bennetti if I could have time off to be with him.' She stopped and twisted her handkerchief into a tight ball. 'I had to go to his office as he was the manager. He started to touch me. I was very young. He said the only way he'd let me have time off was if I . . .'

'The bastard,' said Lu quickly.

'Nine months later I gave birth to my son.'

Rose took a loud breath. 'So. Was Dan a Bennetti?'

Ivy shook her head and a smile lifted her tear-stained face. 'No. I did worry about it even though Dan looked like Harry. It wasn't till I saw that baby's six toes that I knew for certain. My Dan didn't have six toes,' she said in a choked voice.

Pam burst out crying. 'All these years you've kept that secret?' she sobbed. 'Oh Gran! Why didn't you tell us?' She hugged her softly again.

'I was too ashamed and I never thought I'd have to.'

'Did Harry know?' asked Rose.

'No, he would have killed Bennetti if he had.'

'And he brought Dan up as his own?' said Rose.

'I was almost totally sure he didn't have any reason not to, but there was always that little doubt.'

'And you've carried this burden all these years alone?' Rose whispered.

Ivy nodded. 'I never thought I'd have to tell anyone. But when I found out Pam here was going to Italy with that boy, it brought it all back. I had to stop it. I was frightened, very frightened, it could have been . . .' Ivy sobbed into her handkerchief. 'Will you ever forgive me?'

'No wonder you didn't want me to go out with Robbie, you thought we might have been related.'

Ivy nodded.

Lu stood up and began to pace around the room. 'That bloke wanted hanging.'

'In those days women did as they were told.'

'But that was a form of rape.'

Rose sat open-mouthed.

'I'll make some tea,' said Granny Mallory.

'You mustn't be sorry, Gran. I'm glad I didn't go to Italy. I wouldn't have gone out with Lu if I had. And what about Jill? She wouldn't have met Billy. But I don't think Lu should be part of their firm, not now,' said Pam.'

'Yes. Yes, he must. This is a different generation and you mustn't let the past stand in the way of your happiness.'

'But, Gran—'

'There are no buts about it. This is your future and you must make the most of it. Nobody should be accountable for the sins of their fathers. I can't tell you how grateful I am for you going to court. If that young man hadn't been there with his baby, I would never have known – well, not for sure anyway.'

Rose was still sitting with a dazed look on her face. 'No wonder you kept on about his baby's six toes. I can't believe that you've kept this to yourself for so long,' she whispered.

'It wasn't easy at first. But after Dan died I thought no more about it. Then when Pam said she was going out with that boy, I didn't know what to do. I almost told her the reason, but Lil decided to set herself alight then, remember?'

Pam, who was still crying, nodded. 'Gran, I'm so sorry. I was a cow to you.'

'It's all over now. You are happy with this one, ain't you?'

Pam tried to laugh. 'He's caused me a bit of grief now and again, but yes, I love him and wouldn't change him for the world.'

'She's only saying that now I'm worth a few bob!' Lu

kissed Pam when she began to protest at that remark.

'I've brought the whisky bottle in,' said Granny Mallory, reappearing in the doorway. 'I think that'll be much better than tea, don't you?'

If you enjoyed this book here is a selection of other bestselling titles from Headline

Headline books are available at your local bookshop or newsagent. Alternatively, books can be ordered direct from the publisher. Just tick the titles you want and fill in the form below. Prices and availability subject to change without notice.

Buy four books from the selection above and get free postage and packaging and delivery within 48 hours. Just send a cheque or postal order made payable to Bookpoint Ltd to the value of the total cover price of the four books. Alternatively, if you wish to buy fewer than four books the following postage and packaging applies:

UK and BFPO £4.30 for one book; £6.30 for two books; £8.30 for three books.

Overseas and Eire: £4.80 for one book; £7.10 for 2 or 3 books (surface mail).

Please enclose a cheque or postal order made payable to *Bookpoint Limited*, and send to: Headline Publishing Ltd, 39 Milton Park, Abingdon, OXON OX14 4TD, UK.
Email Address: orders@bookpoint.co.uk

If you would prefer to pay by credit card, our call team would be delighted to take your order by telephone. Our direct line is 01235 400 414 (lines open 9.00 am–6.00 pm Monday to Saturday 24 hour message answering service). Alternatively you can send a fax on 01235 400 454.

Name ....

Address ....

....

....

If you would prefer to pay by credit card, please complete:
Please debit my Visa/Access/Diner's Card/American Express (delete as applicable) card number:

Signature .... Expiry Date ....